By The Gun

A True Testimony
Of How Choices
Intertwine With Fate
By Derrick D. Williams

United States Office of Publication Data
Williams, Derrick
    By The Gun
    1. Spiritual   2. Urban Real (based on truth)
    3. Police corruption   4. Saint Louis

USPS CMR# 7012 2210 0002 3729 9751

CONTENTS

Dedications

This is **truly** the most important part of the book for me. I would first like to thank my Father God... for giving me the vision, the persistence, and the dedication to write this book... this book is dedicated to my most precious gift, Derricka Donnella Diamond Williams and her Mom, Tasha Spencer. This book is dedicated to my Father God... I asked My Father God... that the proceeds from the written works of this book... be **so** abundant! That they will enable me to build a foundation for my Sisters and Brothers to stand on... my Sister and Brothers who have no foundation but have a vision and are ready to build something positive using that vision... this book is dedicated to you Sisters and Brothers...

This book is dedicated to all of Gods Children who hold **firm** to their faith in God and who hope for peace and do their best **every day**, to be a part of the peace they hope for... those who teach peace by being living examples of the Word. This book is dedicated to those who help others understand, that violence only breeds more violence, destruction and hopeless despair... But peace, breeds positive growth and development and more peace... Keep on teaching and being that positive example y'all...

This book is dedicated to **all** of the women who have taught me, what a woman loves in a man and what a woman expects from a man:
Grand Mom Agnes Willis rest in peace. Grand Mom LiLi Cleveland Williams rest in peace. My Mother Goldie Willis, My second Mom Gloria Jordan, My third Mom Joann Gordon, My fourth Mom Carol Washington rest in peace Momma. My favorite Aunties: Jonell Brox, Jaqualine Heard, Joyce Jones, Dana Moores, Aunt Earlene I love you. Aunt Iris I love you. My Big cousin Vadus Jordan.

Thanks To's

All of the people who kept me inspired to keep on writing my book: Bakari Tunner, with-out you, the story wouldn't have been right, good LYIN-ASS, but you a good dude and still FOLKS so PML G.

VG Deloney, Ron-Ron Turner, Lenn Chicago Dukes y'all have BECOME examples for our younger brothers to live by. Keep progressing positively and producing productively. Plenty Much Love Family. Evelyn Lewis thank you **so much**, you know how much time I was facing for-real, I owe you big time Big Sister. Ms. Robbie and the Sweetie Pies Family, Big Boom Jackson, Uncle Horace Jackson, Lenny Duncan, Uncle Lonnie Jones, Uncle Ronald Saunders, Uncle Carlos, Uncle Fredrick Lee "Tuffy" thank yall for not giving up on me. Alfonso Man of God Williams love You Big Bro.

Rashawd Davis, Najja Beno Washington & Ashlee Washington, Eddie Byrd Da-Hustler, L.J. Go Harder Cater, Alitta Barnes, the examples of real Growth & Development. Johnny Spann, Caleb Spoon Anderson HE GOT THEM BEATS!. Couzin Ursala Saunders, Tavia Garland, Simeon IceBerg King, Louis Nelson, Kamisha Nelson, Minister Devon Franklin glad I met you man thanks for the inspiration. Katrina Brox Demtrious Brox Carnell-C-Murder Willis, **'CMB! we all we got!'** I love y'all.

David 'Wavy-Dave' Bates, Lareese Lay I love you lil-sis, Talia Holden Brooks thank God for you being so smart lil-cuzin you helped **a lot**. La Rhonda Lott, Rodrick Watson right-on for them pep-talks Family, Latoya Stewert Jackson, Tony Liano with BLUE RAIN FILMS all that advice paid off thanks Tony, The Master Sergant Larry Lay think u Dad for the discipline and strength, the main two things a man needs. SaCoya Willis, Donna Hightower, especially you Momma Goldie and Tasha Spencer.

Thank you all for your support, best wishes and prayers. They want be in vain... Thanks again. Rest in peace Dad... Dennis Williams Jr.

Thanks to the Create Space Publishing Platorm Creators

Introduction

All of my teenage life, I've wondered about the things my big brother has done. He kept a photo album of, newspaper-articles and clippings of crimes that had been committed and police had no leads to. I never saw him commit any of the maleficent acts, though he spoke of such things often... robbing stores, killing the opposition, home invasions, mysterious assaults. I'd listen to the stories and ruminate on the details curiously. I truly believe, most of the things I've done... are because of the influence my brother had on me. Are we alike? In some ways... yes.

It's really easy to be influenced by someone when you have no influence at all... especially at a juvenile age. At one point in my life, I had a positive influence... but that positive influence was smothered by the negativity that pervaded my childhood. I became a cynic charged with feelings of indignation and suspicious of every ones motives and agendas. Who was for-real or who was fake... who were the good and who were the bad... who were the ones who had my best interest in heart, and who were the ones who could give a shit-less if I lived or died... the whos and the whys... the truths and the lies.

Someone once told me, "If you want a person to believe a lie then you have to mix a little bit of the truth with it." I say: If a person knows part of the truth... they'll be able to discover **all** of the truth, separating it from the lies. My point is... if you don't want anyone to know about something, leave them clueless instead of offering pieces to the puzzle. If you tell part of the truth, you may as well tell **all** of the truth... I have a story to tell. Whether it's the truth or not... I'll leave that up to you to decide... just remember... I did tell you... Ooh, and... The end of this story... is not this story's end... It's only the beginning.

July 1977 Little Soldiers

1977, on the south side of *Flint Michigan*, at a Marines Corps training facility... camouflage uniforms adorned with fresh young spirits, whose minds and bodies were being conditioned to become soldiers, killers and leaders in a world of many wars. I was at military school, ten years young going through intense training as a Junior Marine. I met with the other Junior Marines Monday, Wednesday, Friday and Saturdays at the training center. We were learning everything that the Marines learned in boot camp: weaponry, war tactics, hand-to-hand combat, marksmanship, survival in the wilderness and in rough terrain, physically training our bodies and minds.

We were becoming powerful thinkers and forces of unmovable strength. Gunny Sergeant Strong, a real Corpsman, was our drill sergeant. Standing at 5 feet 10 inches tall, with a stocky build and possessing the stamina of a worker ant and the strength of a Kodiak bear... his last name, Strong, ascribed to his character and he personified what a true Marine was supposed to be. Even though Gunny Sergeant Strong was of European descent, he had not **one** racist bone in his body. He treated all of us the same; females or males, Spanish or Asian, African or European. Gunny Sergeant Strong's mission was to shape us all into strong dedicated Junior Marines.

Our C.O. (Commanding Officer) was Mr. Webster, also of European descent. He was the one who inspired me to get in-tuned with my spirituality. My Granny kept me and my brother in church, but at that time, I was young and didn't quite understand what spirituality was. It was not until C.O. Webster told me, that there was something divinely special about my spirit and I should consider being a chaplain, did I begin to recognize and comprehend the benevolence that allowed me to shine so bright. It was the benevolence that God borne me with.

For as long as I can remember, I have never been a malicious or vicious person. I've always been an advocate for fairness and justice, even if it was in the form of street justice, either way, street justice or legal justice, if it was justice for my people... I stood for it. I hated seeing people get mistreated or not getting the true justice that they deserve in situations of adversity and misfortune. I've always wanted to do something to help those people who suffered but I was only a child, visualizing a dream.

I will never forget that Saturday morning. The bedazzling brightness of the Sun blanketed the earth with warmth. The freshness of grass being cut pervaded the air; my bedroom window was open. I could see directly out into the backyard where Major was. Major was our Doberman Pincher and the back yard was his domicile. Major was about a year and a half young, very care free and energetic and highly protective of the family. At the time, my Father was a Master Drill Sergeant in the Army so the name that we had given our dog, Major, was befitting.

I watched Major run around the yard, barking at me wanting me to come play with him, but I had to get ready for my Junior Marines meeting. My brother and I starched and pressed our uniforms with the precision of dry cleaners; sharp creases and shined boots with mirror like finishes and then we suited up... the better your appearance and uniform looked, the more praise you received for the immaculacy you displayed. I don't like being praised but I **do** like being sharp in my appearance.

I was all ready to go. I skipped my usual bowl of Frosted Mini Wheat's, one of my favorite cereals. That morning I opted for two hard-boiled eggs that were leftover from Mom's potato-salad. The hard-boiled eggs sat in the Tupperware container with just enough water in it to keep them moist. They were cold and I wanted to eat them warm with some hot sauce; I **love** hot sauce. I put the hard-boiled eggs on a saucer and placed it in the microwave for about twenty seconds... I think... When I took them out, they felt warm and not **too** hot, but just right. Now as a child, I was naive to the mechanics of microwaves which heated things from the inside out. On the outside, the eggs were the desired temperature. However, on the inside, they were five times hotter and full of steam. I doused the eggs with hot sauce and commenced to bite into the egg... bad... move.

'BOOOF!'

It sounded like a firecracker exploding inside of a cup with the lid on it, muffling the sound. The eggs explosion in my mouth caused by the build-up of hot steam; felt like boiling water being poured into my mouth. The pain was searing and constant but I let out no scream or cry to express my pain. I held the yelps in, rushed over to the water faucet at the kitchen sink, and literally began drowning my face in cold water. My Mom walked into the kitchen and for a few seconds, observed my crazed face washing.

"Wuanie! Why in the world are you washing your face in the sink? Boy you getting water all on the floor...!" she said in a curious and concerned voice but not too upset in tone.

I came up from my submergence, fanning my mouth, trying to indicate to my Mom that my mouth was on fire! Not able to talk, all I could do was gesture. I **really** couldn't talk! She asked me what was wrong, but I dipped my head back under the faucet letting the cold water run into my mouth again, trying to alleviate some of the pain. Mom stepped over to the sink and took hold of my arm seeking my attention. She pulled me away from the sink, gently turning me to face her so she could examine my injury. She held my water soaked face in her hands and she tilted my head back slightly, looking at my mouth.

"Baby how did you do this? Your mouth is all red and your lips look swollen."

I stepped over to the kitchen table where the culprit sat, still steaming on the saucer. There was a sizable hole at one end of the egg. I displayed to my Mom how I put the egg in the microwave, heated it up, took it out and bit into it. Pointing to the egg, I did my best impression of an exploding egg. Momma smiled and chuckled a little at my unintended ("jestorical") antics, but I was in pain, trying my best to explain what happened.

"Ooh Baby... does it hurt?" asked my Mom.
I nodded my head yes, as the searing pain persisted. She asked me if I wanted to skip the Junior Marines meeting and stay at home. Frowning, I shook my head no. I **loved** going to my meetings! I looked forward to attending each one. My Mom packed a small zip-lock bag of ice for me and we were ready to go. We all headed out to the car. My big brother, two years older than me, sat in the front seat of my Mom's black and gray Pontiac Trans Am. I sat in the back, in the low gray seat of the T.A. and buckled my seat belt. She backed the car out of the driveway and I unzipped the plastic bag, and fished out a piece of ice and **immediately** began nursing my mouth. Feeling instant relief, I let out a sigh, glad to be relieved of the intense pain. My brother looked back at me with a mischievous grin on his face as if he

had orchestrated the whole "exploding egg" thing.

There is this verse in the *Bible,* in the book of **Proverbs**, *chapter 17, verse 17* that say: *"A friend loveth at all times and a brother is born for adversity."*

Since the day I was born, my brother has been that adversity We're working on that though.

Pulling up at the training facility, we were about fifteen minutes early. My Mom liked being early for **everything.** She and C.O Webster liked to talk for a few minutes about the happening events for the Junior Marines and amongst other things. At precisely 0900 hours, our platoon leader would call for all the Junior Marines to fall into formation. We would then form a uniform square, opening the meeting with the 'Pledge of Allegiance', facing and saluting the American flag, followed by roll call.

It was almost time for the meeting to start. My Mom was out of her car already, talking with C.O. Webster. Pushing the driver's seat forward, I reached for the door handle and got out of the car. I loved to take in the scenery, indulging in the tranquility that the landscape provided. The Marine training facility sat at the back of a quiet south-side neighborhood in Flint Michigan, at the end of the street. A sizably, dense patch of forestry sat just in front of the facility. Two types of trees, maples and pines, hid the facility from the view of on-comers. About 40 or so yards back, once pass all the trees, the facility became visible.

The driveway was shaped like a half oval, with exits at both ends, spanning the length of the building before it extended out into the street. The training facility was a two-story building, about 280 feet long and 160 feet wide, made of beige brick. Three feet tall, manicured shrubs, spaced about a meter apart, lined the facade, with a window behind every other shrub.

At the rear perimeter of the landscape, there was a thin tree line and a small cliff that dropped down about twenty feet into a murky Flint River. Just before the tree line, a large concrete section that came all the way up to the rear of the building is where we would practice our drills, and occasionally do P.T. (physical training) there.

"FALLLL INNN!"

Everyone heard the platoon leader yell and the gymnasium quickly filled with young soldiers, eager to start drills. The formation was made even and square by extending the right arm out to the side and placing the fingertips on the Junior Marine's shoulder that was standing to the right of you. And also: by taking the right arm and extending it forward, making sure you were an arm's length away from the Junior Marine who was in front of you. Head and eyes locked straightforward, shoulders slightly pulled back, chest out and heels together at a 45-degree angle; we became statues. Our platoon leader walked by, inspecting every Junior Marine's posture as well as the sharpness of our uniforms.

"Private Carpenter, put a better shine on those boots... Private Rodriguez, straighten up that back... Lance Corporal Willis, good job on the uniform... put more shine on those boots... Corporal Williams, pull those shoulders back."

At the time, our platoon leader was Sergeant Major Webster, C.O. Webster's son. During those inspections, his way of complementing us without any criticism... was by looking us over and nodding his approval. Back standing in front of the platoon, our platoon leader gave us the command:

"LEFFF! FACE!"

The entire platoon moved in unison, pivoting on the right toe, spinning on the left foot, keeping it flat on the ground until our bodies were facing the left; bringing the right foot back together in place with the left foot. We struck the right heel of our boot against the left heel, creating a sharp snapping sound that echoed throughout the gymnasium and into the halls of the building... Now facing the American flag, the command was given to salute.

"PRESENNNT! ARMS!"

We brought our right hand sharply to the brim of our hexagon caps and immediately, in sequence, begin reciting the Pledge.

"I pledge allegiance, to the flag, of the United States of America..."

That day, I was excluded from reciting the Pledge, calling cadence, and anything else that had to do with speaking, due to the ("eggplosion").

The robust and full voices of the Junior Marines filled the gymnasium with vibrant sounds, vibrating the very floor that I stood on. I was filled with an extra sense of pride. I was **more** motivated... I wanted to do more and be the best at all I did. The Junior Marines raised the standards in my life... more than any one person could have ever done. I excelled quickly as a Junior Marine. By the time I was 13, I was already a Staff Sergeant... In drills, I was a squad leader and in PT, I was a motivator. One of the smallest in the platoon, I always pushed harder. I was the inspiration for others who would have more than likely given up if I hadn't been their motivation. In the field, I was a warrior; enduring everything that Gunny Sergeant Strong put us through. Sometimes, we would have to do P.T. in the PIT: every push-up, every mountain climber, every jumping jack and even sit-ups.

"Gunny's PIT" was an **enormous** hole in the ground, about a foot and a half deep, 30 yards wide and 40 yards in length, completely filled with mud. I powered through every exercise with ease, loving the way the mud made it harder for us... it was only making me stronger. Dedicated, determined and driven, by a force that I knew not where it came from. It was almost as if I had embodied the spirit of some great military soldier the way I was able to retain knowledge of compendious military curriculum and endure physical training.

After we finished the reciting the Pledge, we were given the command to disengage our salute.

"FOWARRRD! ARMS!"

With precision, sharpness, and all in unison, each Junior Marine dropped their arm to their side and roll call began.

"Private Blackmon!"

"HERE SIR!"

"Private Booker!"

"HERE SIR!"

"Private Carpenter!"

"HERE SIR!"

"Lance Corporal Carpenter!"

"HERE SIR!"

"Sergeant Carpenter!"

"HERE SIR!" The Carpenters were all brothers.

"Private Mills!"

"HERE SIR!"

"Staff Sergeant Mills!"

"HERE SIR!" Julie and Jonathan Mills were brother and sister.

"Private Rodriguez!"

"HERE SIR!"

The platoon leader made it down the list of names to the last few.

"Private Vanderkarr!"

"HERE SIR!"

"The other Private Vanderkarr!"

"HERE SIR!"

Sherry and Julie Vanderkarr were twins; two white girls who had a thing, for my brother and me.

"Corporal Williams!"

"HERE SIR!"

"Lance Corporal Willis!"

"HERE SIR!" and roll call was done.

Our meeting continued as usual, the pain in my mouth had started to subside and I began to feel better... that was until I went home and tried to eat something. The pain was still too un-bearable for me to chew food.

Back home on the north side of *Flint Michigan*, on Burgess Street, the house we lived in sat on the middle of the block. A **huge** pine tree about 40 feet tall stood in the front yard. The house was light green with wooden siding. One mulberry bush sat at each end of the house; one in front of the dining-room window and one in front of the living-room window. The driveway was just to the right of the house and it led all the way back to the garage and the back yard.

Next to the driveway: there was a large grass lot, large enough to put another house on, but it was empty, and still is 'til this day... My

Mom used a small part of the grass lot for her garden and the rest of the field was ours to play in; my brother, my cousins, all my neighborhood friends and me. We did **everything** in that field! We had camp-outs, played football, played military war games, had wrestling matches, boxing matches, shot off fire-works and practiced martial arts, just to name a few things. I had grown to love living on Burgess Street.

Mostly girls stayed in the neighborhood and on my block so that made it **all** the more enjoyable. There was another empty field down the street, where a **big** weeping-willow tree was struck by lightning. It formed the tree into a unique shape and we made it into a two level tree house; little cots and all. My neighborhood was truly ideal for the positive and productive growth of a child though one day... that would all change drastically for me.

November 1978 TERRIFIED

Throughout my Mom and Father's entire relationship together, I can hardly even remember them sharing any good times. My Father was very abusive to my Mom, physically. They always seemed to be fighting; about what I don't even know. That led my Mom to drink a lot and she developed a drinking problem that would later prove detrimental to her being successful.

My Father had security bars put on the doors and the windows of our house. You had to have a key to unlock the doors and even the windows from the inside. That evening, my Mom was at home with my baby sister, Lareese, just the two of them. I wasn't there at the time it happened, so I'm going off of my Mom's account of the incident. At the time, my brother and I were at my Grandma's house.

My Father had come home that evening with something on his mind. He was absent of emotion and silent in his thoughts. My Mom said she could feel the malignant mania that exuded from him. Overwhelm by the uneasy feeling that something was terribly wrong, my Mom didn't hesitate. In the kitchen, she gathered some things for my little sister, putting them into a small baby-bag. She moved quietly and swiftly to a closet just pass the living room. She grabbed a stack of pampers and stuffed them into the baby-bag. The door to her and my Father's room was about fifteen feet away. In their room, my Father had a shotgun rack with four different shotguns on it. He was an ardent hunter.

As my Mom closed the closet door; trying her best to be quiet as possible. She heard the sound of shotgun shells, being loaded. She was frightened by the rigid sound of shotgun shells being pushed into the chamber... a chilling cold came over her body. She was stuck for a short moment... She quickly shook the freeze of fear from her and moved fast, back towards the living room, picking my little sister up and covering her with a thick baby blanket.

With the baby-bag hanging from her shoulder and Lareese on her hip, she stepped through from the living room into the kitchen, calmly and quietly making her way to a small case of stairs that lead from the kitchen to a small hallway. She was at the side door of the house now. She inserted the key into the lock of the heavy steel-barred security door, turning the key slowly so that it wouldn't make the loud clicking sound that it normally made; the door was unlocked. She heard the sound of footsteps and sensing that she had not a second to spare, she opened the door and stepped out into the nipping, numbing November night, with only her pajamas on.

My Mom hurried down the street to my Auntie Gloria's house. The air was brisk and cold... As she turned back to look at the door in which she had just retreated from... she saw the dark silhouette of my Father standing in the door-way. My Mom continued to move, looking back, no more.

Doof Doof Doof Doof...! Knocking on the door of my auntie's house, my Mom wanted to turn around to see if she was being pursued but she didn't. She was too afraid that if she did, my seemingly demented Father would be standing behind her; ready to take her back to the house to do Lord only knows what to her... She waited anxiously for my aunt to open the door. The curtain that covered the small window on the door moved slightly. It was Auntie Gloria peeking out to see who was at the door. She was stunned to see that it was my Mom standing on the other side of the door holding ReeRee. Seeing the worried and panicked expression on my Mom's face, my Auntie unlocked and whisked the door open, pulling it so hard! That it made a WOOOSH sound from the force of the pull.

"Goldie! What in the **world** you doin out here without no coat on! And with ReeRee?! **Come in girl!**"

My auntie already knew what the problem was: "Larry was probably trying to fight with her again" is what she was thinking, but she still asked the question with anxiety and curiosity. Auntie Gloria knew about the abuse and would often talk to my Mom, trying to advise her to leave before things got any worse. That advice hit home that night. My Mom was in fear of her **and** my little sister's life.

She stepped inside the side door of my Auntie's house, passing the kitchen and the dinning-room, going directly to the living room to lay ReeRee down on the sofa. Mom made her way back to the dinning-room, pulled a chair out from the table and sat down, sighing in relief. The kitchen where my Auntie stood was adjoining to the dinning-room by a high, wide, arched entryway; it allowed you to see the full view of either-or. Mom and Auntie Gloria, locked gazes for a brief moment; engaging in a mental acknowledgement of what was wrong. Auntie's compassionate gaze provided some comfort to my Mom's troubled mind.

Aunt Gloria, skillfully made two cups of coffee, she **loves** coffee! Mom closed her eyes and tried to collect the thoughts that were passing through her mind. Auntie Gloria walked over to the table and quietly sat a cup of coffee in front of my Mom. She pulled out a chair, took her seat, and took a sip of Folgers; timidly tasting the coffee for it was hot... She looked at my Mom. My Mom began to talk, speaking quietly about what she felt, emphasizing her feelings at certain points.

"Gloria, I just **know** he was about to kill me... I **felt it**! He came in the house and he didn't say **anything**... he didn't **look** at us... he just walked **straight** back to the bedroom and started loading up a-damn shotgun...! All I could think was... is, he about to kill me if I stay... so I did what my mind told me to do... I got the hell-up outta there..! Why else would he just come home and start loading his gun? He ain't never-done-no shit like that before?"

My auntie gave my mom a concerning look then responded:

"Goldie, you did what yo first mind told you to do and it's good you did... Ain't no tellin what crazy mess was going through Larry's mind?"

My Auntie spoke fast when she was angry or excited, and at that moment, she was on rapid fire. She continued:

"He been **beatin** on you fah no reason for the **longest...**! giving you **black** eyes and **busted** lips... You should've **been** left his ass... Where are Carnell and Wuanie?"

"They at Momma's house... Carnell gone be glad to hear he ain't gotta go back to Larry's house... I'm not ever 'goin back there... I'm leaving fah-good...! Tonight I felt a fear that I ain't never felt before and I **refuse** to live in fear like that... in fear of losing my **life**... fearing that he might kill **all of us**! Aun aun... I won't live like that... and you **right**... I should've left his ass a long time ago..! Ma stupid ass tryina stay around, thinking things might get better, when all the while, they been getting worse!"

"Goldie, you know you welcome to stay here if you want to, for as long as you need to."

"Thank you Gloria. I appreciate the offer, but this is **too** close to Larry. I don't want him coming down here to yo house causing any problems."

"Girrrl, you know I got ma .25! I'll SHOOT-EM IN HIS BUTT! HE BET NOT COME DOWN HERE ACTIN AH-DAMN-FOOL!"

My Mom laughed at the humor my Auntie interjected in her statement. She was smiling now, and feeling a lot better in the comfort of my Auntie's support.

"Gloria... I think I'm gonna go to the women's shelter until I find me a place **far** away from here."

My Mom never did move back to that house.

The Y.W.C.A. Women's Shelter

This is where I remember Momma, Ree-Ree and myself going to stay for a while. My brother stayed at my Granny's house. He wanted to stay with my Granny anyway, and the opportunity had presented its self. Grandma would have been glad to have us all at her house, but it was crowded there already and my Mom insisted on only staying for a couple of days until she could get into the shelter. In those couple of days: she managed to retrieve some of our things from my Father's house with my Auntie Gloria's help, all while avoiding running into him. With some of our clothes, Mom, my little

Sister and my-self, were off to the shelter... a place where abused woman go to feel safe and to evaluate their lives and to figure out what move they would make next.

The Y.W.C.A. facility was about ten stories high and the shelter floors were seven and up, for the safety of the women. The ground floor where the entrance was, had an armed security guard who sat at a small command center with closed circuit TV monitors, showing visuals of the parking area. In addition, the perimeter of the building and the ground floor entrances and exits, were being monitored. There was an intercom system used by the security guard to communicate with people wanting to enter the building.

The security guard would buzz them in if they were cleared to enter. Walking into the Y, I looked around wondering what it was gonna be like to live in a women's shelter. Momma told me that we wouldn't be there for too long, so I thought on a short term basis. As we approached the small command center, the security guard stood, peering over at me as I wobbled over to the lounge area, carrying our bags of clothes and things. He looked at me then looked at Momma and ReeRee.

"Good morning, how can I help you Ma'am?"

"Good morning. My name is Goldie Willis and I spoke to Ms. Regina Rice about checking into the women's shelter, she told me to come down this morning."

"Yes Ma'am. Let me just call up to let her know you're here. I also need to see your identification please."

"Yes of course." said Mom.
She walked over to where I was and sat ReeRee's carrier down in a seat next to me. My baby Sister looked up at me with an inquisitive expression on her face showing concern. I wondered if she knew what was going on. I put my little hand in her carrier and freed her tiny arms from the thick blanket. I touched her hand and she took hold of my little finger, wrapping her tiny fingers around mines. I liked when she did that... it made me feel really close to my baby Sister.

Momma looked at us and smiled then went back to what she was focused on. She opened her purse and took out her id then walked back over to the small command center to give it to the security guard.

"Here it is."

The security guard looked it over and handed it back to Momma.

"Thank you Ms. Willis. Ms. Rice is expecting you", he said, as he hung up the phone.

"She's on the seventh floor. You have to use the far left elevator to get access to the floor."

"Thank you."

My Mom walked back over to where ReeRee and I were, collected ReeRee in her carrier and threw a small bag strap over her shoulder. I followed suit, grabbing two of our bags, throwing the straps over my shoulders, wobbling as I walked towards the last elevator on the left... From what I recall while staying at the shelter... we lived in a small room about 12 feet by 12 feet. There were two twin beds, a large dresser drawer and a small closet. We had to share the rest-rooms and the showers with the other women and children. All the women had their share of chores around the shelter.

My Mom was assigned to keeping the TV room clean. I can remember her vacuuming around the TV stand while I straightened up the bookshelf. I did what I could to help Mom as much as possible. She had worked hard to provide for my brother, ReeRee and me, all on her own. At one point in time, she had her own house, but after General Motors had one of the biggest lay-offs in the history of the automobile industry... she couldn't afford to keep it. That's when my Father convinced her to move in with him. Before my stay at the shelter, I hadn't realized that so many women were being abused and needed help getting their life in order.

The shelter opened my eyes to the reality of a domestic abuse that disseminated far beyond my Mom's life. Some of the women in the shelter became close friends with my Mom. They told her stories of their abusive relationships, and of situations that they had escaped from... the mental torment that afflicted their minds. Even though my Mom was in pretty much the same situation as the other women, her perception and position, as a battered woman seemed brighter and more favorable. I guess she felt like she had broken away from the chains that bound her for so long. She was more of a confidant and counselor to some of the women than anything. Momma was an easy person to talk to.

Sometimes, I would listen to the one-on-one conversations between the Ladies and become sadden by the dis-heartedness they displayed. I would become, **filled** with indignation by the stories of abuse they told, and think to myself, how could a man be so cruel to a woman...? And I would **never** become that type of man!

My Mom always gave seemingly good advice to the women. When the stories got too graphic, my Mom would ask me to go to the playroom, allowing the women to, candidly discuss their problems and plight, and the prostrate effects they had on them. Only they could formulate a plan to prevail against their formidable past. The words that you have just previously read... are only a small portion of the people and things that have shaped me into the man I am today. This story is only a small chapter of my life, and is based on the truth... the rest is to be told... Enjoy.

CHAPTER 1: THE STORY BEGINS

S abrina was young and beautiful, I mean **fine**! It was unfortunate but also a blessing at the same time, but Sabrina got pregnant at the age of 17 and had her daughter, Porsha, at 18. She finished school though, continuing to further her education while still staying with her mother. Her mom insisted that she did. Sabrina's boyfriend was the love of her life and very involved with her and their daughter. He was a young man, rising prominently in the music industry as a producer/promoter. His name was Porshaé.

Porshaé worked vigorously to make his business, M.I.G. Make It Good entertainment, a success... all while being a good father to his Babygirl, and an even greater companion to Sabrina. They had been together since junior high school and planned on getting married when their financial status was where they wanted it to be. Sabrina wanted a **big** extravagant wedding and Porshaé wanted her to have just that. If it meant that much to her then it meant just as much to him.

After they found out Sabrina was pregnant, they gave each other promise rings to symbolize their commitment. And to love, honor and cherish each other in the most loyal and faithful way possible, and that's just what they did. However, three years after their daughter was born... Porshae's life would take a **very** drastic turn. Some may say that it was for the worst, but in the ways in which God works, by the end of this story, most will perceive that it was for the best. Porshaé was in prison out of state in Missouri for murder. He received 20 years for killing a police officer who was posing as a robber. 20 years for killing a cop...! That's **all** he got, you ask. Well... we'll get to how that came about later on in the story, but let me continue. Porshaé had been gone now, for four years, and the yearning for physical companionship had been growing in Sabrina. She didn't just want any companionship though... She wanted her man. Sabrina wanted to be with Porshaé so bad that it hurt her stomach at times from wanting him so much. He was the one who had captivated her and won her heart with his curious charm, his genuine generosity, and his rudiment romantics. Porshaé was loving and loyal, and his personality in its entirety is what kept Sabrina so faithfully in love with him.

To her and the majority of her family and friends, Porshaé was the type of man that every woman was hoping to have some day. Sabrina knew that she had the man she wanted to spend the rest of her life with, and she was not about to let him go... even **if** he had to serve the whole 20 years in prison, she wanted to be there for him through it all.

Young Love

Sabrina began to reminisce about when they first met each other in junior high school... Porshaé Perfect, Prince... She didn't believe that, that was his real name when they were initially introduced by a mutual friend named Michelle. Porshaé was new at McKinley Junior High and Michelle was walking him to his fourth period social studies class and there and behold... Sabrina was standing about 10 feet away from the classroom door at her locker, putting books up and pulling others out.

"Who is that?" Porshaé asked Michelle quietly.
Michelle, let out a barely audible snicker and with a smirk on her face,

she answered Porshaé.

"That's Sabrina Sheree, Dukes."

"What's so funny?" he asked.

They made it to the classroom door and he stood there stuck like a deer caught in a car's headlights, just glaring at Sabrina.

Michelle responded:

"That girl ain't about to give you no **play**.... She don't talk to dudes that go to the same school she goes to. She says it's a conflict of interest... that interest being school and not boys. That's ma girl though and she cool people... here she comes."

Michelle nudged Porshaé and whispered:

"Boy, stop staring at the girl, **dang**!"

"Right." said Porshaé.

He acted like he was looking for something in his folder as Sabrina made her final approach towards them. Michelle gave Sabrina a hardy greeting.

"WHAATZZUP GIRRL! Tomorrow is the big birthday party! I know it's gone be OFF THE HOOK! Yo **Mom** doing the catering **too**! **And** you got Stormin Norman from WDZZ radio to DJ for the party!"

Michelle was a big girl... one of the biggest girls in the school... not fat big... but Amazon, thick and tall big! She was excited about Sabrina's birthday party and she expressed her enthusiasm, unable to contain it. Sabrina responded cool and nonchalantly:

"Yeaaah girl... you know I had to go all out on this one, this being the last party that I'm gone throw while I'm at this school. Then it's on to high school to do bigger and better thangs."

"You **sho** right about **that**!" said Michelle.

They both giggled at Michelle's indirect reference to her future high school sexual adventures, because that's what Michelle was thinking about and Sabrina knew it.

Sabrina looked at Porshaé, feeling a bit rude that she hadn't spoken to him yet.

"How you doin?" she asked, directing the question/greeting towards him, but Porshaé was immersed in his folder, trying diligently to pretend as if he was searching for something and he hadn't heard what she said.

"Porshaé!" snapped Michelle.

"**Aaah**! Here it is!" he exclaimed, as he pulled out his class schedule then Michelle continued:

"Sabrina asked you how you were doing", she said, glaring at Porshaé then at Sabrina.

He just stood there, gazing at Sabrina. His eyes were fixated on hers. Michelle nudged him again then said:

"Sabrina... this is a good friend of mines. He's new at school, as you've probably already noticed. His name is, Porshaé Perfect, Prince." Michelle looked at Porshaé again.

"Porshaé... this is Sabrina Sheree, Dukes and as a matter of fact... Y'all two have the same fourth period class. Sabrina, I gotta get to class before the late bell rings. One mo tardy and ma-ass is in detention! You two get acquainted. I'll see y'all later. Don't let Porshaé get lost Sabrina!" said Michelle, walking away fast and hurrying to her next class.

Sabrina took a good look at Porshaé then asked him:

"So... that's your real name huh? Porshaé Perfect, Prince?" She asked with a curious, sassy and interested tone of voice.

He shook his self out of the hypnotizing trance that Sabrina's beauty had put him in then answered:

"Yep... that's my real name" then he pulled out his student id and showed it to her to satisfy her suspicions. He continued:

"My Dad wanted me to have a name that would motivate me to be the best at whatever I do."

Sabrina was still looking at Porshaé with a suspicious scowl, as she handed him back his id then she asked him:

"So are you?"

Porshaé didn't get her question.

"Am I what?" he asked.

"The best at what you do." said Sabrina, slyly with her usual hint of sassiness in her voice, moving her head from side to side and glaring at Porshaé.

For some reason or another, Porshaé thought Sabrina's sassiness made her all the more attractive. He let out a slight laugh, smiling at her body language, though taken aback by her question. He wondered if she was implying something sexual. He responded:

"I try to be... But practice makes perfect right?"

He smiled at her and all she had to say was:

"Humm." while still looking at him suspiciously.

The class bell rung... they stood there for a few seconds longer staring at each other then came unglued from their glare of admiration and wonder; she wondered and he admired. The two stepped through the door of the classroom just before the sound of the bell ended. Mr. Monroe was the name of the teacher who taught the social-studies class, and Sabrina was one of his favorite students. She was always on time and very ardent about her schoolwork. He admired her passion for learning.

"**Aaaah**, Ms. Dukes! You brought us some fresh meat!"
Mr. Monroe always displayed good humor. He continued:

"There's no assigned seating Mr. Prince, so take an empty seat where ever there is one and lets' get this show on the roll."

There were four rows with five desks in each. Porshaé took the third seat in the last row by the windows. Sabrina sat in her usual seat, second row from the door, second seat in the row. Mr. Monroe took attendance and class had officially begun. Mr. Monroe gave the class instructions to open their textbooks to chapter 9... While everyone was doing so, Sabrina glanced over at Porshaé, watching him flip through the pages of his book. She turned away and smiled to herself before anyone could notice her looking.

From that moment, she knew already that Porshaé was someone she wanted to have in her life... as a friend if nothing more... His eyes showed her **true** honesty and no signs of deceitfulness. She had never come across someone of the male gender, her age, who showed such honesty... until Porshaé.

Sabrina's reminiscing of her junior high school years was interrupted. The phone rang in Sabrina's room and she answered it.

"Hello?"

"Bitch...! Put-yo **hottest** dress on cause we goin OUT TA-NIGHT!"

It was Sabrina's friend Michelle, and Michelle had been doing her **best** to get Sabrina to go out... but Sabrina was reluctant. Sabrina didn't feel right going out to the clubs anymore now that Porshaé was gone. Normally, Sabrina and her girls would go wherever Porshaé was promoting a show. They always got-in free and Porshaé made sure that his Lady and her girls got V.I.P. service.

When Porshaé first got locked-up, Sabrina tried to go clubbing to get out of her depression mood, but it wasn't the same for her anymore. Porshaé was the reason she went to the clubs in the first place. She liked watching her man do his thang at the different venues, and she loved how he would show her lots of affection amongst all the other girls who tried to talk to him in the clubs. He made her feel secure and special; like she was the only girl in the world for him. And she knew it in her heart, that as far as he was concerned... she **was** the only girl for him. Going out to the clubs now, only reminded her of how much she missed him, so she quit going period.

Sabrina responded to her friend's powerful instruction:
"Michelle, you **know** how the clubs make me feel... it's been **three** years since I last went out and I'm not in no mood to go to the club."
Michelle fired back but in a more sympathetic tone of voice:
"Bitch look... I **know** you miss yo man... That's ma nigga too! But I know he don't want you, moping around being miserable! I know he want you to be happy out here... so put on somethin sexy, **not fah-no other niggas**... but fah yo man... We gonna go to this new club called the *"Copa."* We gone take some **sexy-ass pictures** and send-em to Porshaé. I know he would **love** that! I'm tellin you Girl... that's gone put a **big** smile on his face."
Sabrina was contemplating then she responded to Michelle's comment:
"Chelle... I don't know Girl. It sounds good but-"
Michelle stopped her before she could say anything else.
"Bitch, but **nothin**! Get-yo-ass dressed because Tammy is already on her way to pick you up. Bye Bitch." and Michelle hung up the phone...
Sabrina held the receiver and quietly said to her-self, with a smile on her face:
"That Bitch is so **crazy**... but that's ma girl though."
Sabrina pressed the end button on the cordless receiver and just sat there on the bed for a moment, looking blankly at herself in the mirror that was attached to her dresser, which sat across from her bed. She thought about it aloud:
"Ma Baby **would** like some nice sexy pictures of me. I haven't

sent him any sexy photos since he's been in there. That **would** put a smile on his face and let him know that I'm trying to be okay out here... fuck-it!" Sabrina had made up her mind. She was going to the club.

1988 The Night Before Mothers Day

The *Club Copa* was in the downtown area of *Flint, Michigan*. The inside was classy, plush and sexy. It seemed like **everyone** was dressed to impress. As Sabrina and her entourage walked in, David a police officer moonlighting as a security guard, noticed her. That night, what man **wouldn't** have noticed her? She was beautiful! Sabrina was 5 feet 9 inches tall. She held her head high on her slender neck. Her frame was slender as well, with all of her curves slightly hidden by the silk charmeuse and lace evening dress. The dress seductively told her body's secrets. It revealed her long toned legs on both sides of the dress. Her skin-tone was flawless! It was a soft butter pecan color like the ice cream. Her hair was pecan-brown with naturally thick bouncy curls that cascaded down to the middle of her back.

Her back was bare except for the spaghetti straps that were connected to her dress. Sabrina was truly beautiful. Her face reminded me of *Africa* and *Asia...* a beautiful *Nubian Princess,* having *Asian* ancestry. Her eyes were almond shaped, light brown, and slightly slanted. She had a pretty, little nose that complimented her soft, pouty lips. She was a sensual sensation. Her stride was graceful as she strolled pass the security check with her small entourage of Lady Friends. The three and a half inch heels, of her red, *Sergio Rossi* designer shoes, struck the floor methodically, and they matched her dress flawlessly! David was captivated and eager to make her acquaintance, but he would wait until the Ladies were done with their night at the club before he approached Sabrina.

All of Sabrina's friends were settled in a nice section of the club, in a **huge** booth, seemingly, like it had been reserved, specifically for them. The night had gotten under-way and to Sabrina's surprise... she was having a really good time. The Ladies ordered their drinks, sipped some, hit the dance floor and took a few group photos. Michelle made sure Sabrina took a couple by herself so she could send them to Porshaé. They danced together and talked lively when they were seated at their booth. Everyone was happy that Sabrina had finally decided to go out with them after so long. Her girls had been missing their good friend.

David periodically made his rounds through the club, glancing at Sabrina occasionally, making sure she noticed him noticing her. He tried to be conspicuous when he was being security, and **inconspicuous** when he was being the interested admirer; however, Sabrina did take notice of him admiring her. David stood at 6 feet 2 inches. The all black security uniform covered his caramel brown frame. He wore a black tee shirt with the word SECURITY, printed in silver on the back and on the front of the tee shirt. He wore black military fatigue pants and black combat boots. The short sleeved tee revealed his muscular arms and fitted neatly around the rest of his upper body; showing the definition of his chest, shoulders and his back. At certain angles when he was moving around, Sabrina could see the imprint of his trimmed abdominal muscles. She tried not to focus on David but it was taking her some effort after she noticed that he was interested in her. She **loved** that caramel brown complexion on a man, though it was only because of her first love, Porshaé. He had a smooth, beautiful, caramel brown complexion, which she enjoyed kissing **all over**...

The club closed at 3am and it was 7 minutes to 2am. David observed the Ladies preparing to leave so he made his way pass the crowd and over to their section and as if he was their personal security... he cleared a way for Sabrina and her entourage to walk through. The Ladies were awed by his show of chivalry. They strolled passed the packed dance floor and pass the bars and another plush lounging area until they made it to the clubs exit. They were feeling special because of the treatment they were receiving. Sabrina and her entourage were out in the parking lot now; some of her friends drove by themselves and some rode together. Sabrina rode with Tammy, her good friend since elementary school.

Tammy was the party enthusiast and drink connoisseur. Her take on life was, "enjoy it as much as possible while it last" and that's

exactly what she did whenever the opportunity presented its self. Nevertheless, regardless of Tammy's party animal enthusiasm, she was an intelligent woman; fun to be around and just as beautiful as Sabrina, but with more of a conceited personality.   She wasn't conceited in a negative way though. Her concept on conceitedness was, "it only meant that a person was important to them self, and in-order to be important to anyone else, you had to be important to yourself first." Tammy's conceit didn't come from her being beautiful... it came from her being important to herself. Standing at 5 feet 7 inches with practically, **perfect** body measurements: 34B, 25, 34, she **unintentionally**, tantalized, most of the males she came into contact with, and some females too, whenever she was out and about being seen.

Tammy dressed seductive and sensual but still maintained some conservativeness while enjoying her womanhood. She loved to wear clothes that accentuated her sexuality and that satisfied her style in fashion. Tammy was a very attractive woman. She had a cocoa-brown skin tone, flawless like Naomi Campbell. Her eyes were light hazel-brown like Tyra Banks. Her look was unadulterated and she hardly **ever** wore make-up. When she did, it was very little to maintain her natural 1950's and 1960's look of pureness. Tammy's conceit came from her intelligence. She knew she was smart. She understood that knowledge was the key to many of society's economic, political and social problems.

If a person had knowledge of certain things, and that person **knew** how to use their knowledge... that person could possibly become a catalyst in alleviating or eliminating some of society's problems and more importantly... their own... She was a visionary with practical ideas that could possibly bring about a positive social revolution. Tammy wanted to help people live better lives, especially her Fellow Sisters. She had self-importance, self-motivation, and was self-determined, to be a force in stimulating a positive life influence in her "Sisters of The Struggle" lives.

Back in the parking lot of the club:

"Tammy, Girl get-cho-ass in the car!" said Sabrina.

Tammy was drunk. She had sampled all of the clubs specials and could barely keep her eyes open... she was sleepy from drinking; just one of the effects that alcohol has on the **millions** of us who drink. The other effect was that she became extremely talkative. She was talking to David in a slightly drunken slur:

"Thaank yoou for walking us outta the club... you made us feel **sooo** special... Do you do that for **allll** the girrls or just for the pretty ones? CAUSE DAT AIN'T RIGHT if you don't do it for the not so pretty girls too... They women too and we **all** should be treated like it!"

Tammy's voice fluctuated going from an extremely appreciative tone to an indignant tone... then to an apathetic one, and then... back to an indignant tone again. Sabrina laughed to herself, at her friend's drunken efforts to try to express her devotion for her Fellow Woman, to David.

"Tammy **let's go**! Get in the **car**! That man got-ah club to tend-to! He ain't got time to listen to yo drunk-**ass**..! I'm sorry about ma friend." said Sabrina to David, looking at him apologetically.

"**Ooh no**... Please, don't be... I know she's probably had one too many... that's why I wanted to make sure you all got to your cars okay."

David was charming. He looked at Sabrina and smiled modestly and they both shared a small laugh at Tammy's drunken expense. Tammy ranted on and David **tried** to respond to her question that she had asked, but his attempts were futile. Tammy's focus was gone. She was in her own drunken world, indulging blissfully in her views of women; what they represented and how they needed to be loved and respected.

"TAMMY...! TAMMY!" Sabrina's voice snapped and broke Tammy out of the world she had locked herself in.
Tammy stopped her ranting and looked in Sabrina's direction... her eyes were still half closed. Sabrina continued:

"The man is **trying** to say somethin to you!"
Tammy's head swung in David's direction abruptly. She tried her best to open her eyes so she could see David.

"Ooh...! Ma fault. Go ahead then. Say what-chu- gotta say." said Tammy, waving David on, as if he now had her permission to speak.

Tammy crossed her arms, leaned back against the passenger-side door of her black Honda Civic and locked her mental focus on David, since she wasn't able to keep her eyes open to see him. David began to answer Tammy's question, but not for Tammy's sake... that really didn't matter because she was drunk and wouldn't remember anyway... he wanted to answer the question for the sake of impressing Sabrina. David continued:

"Ms. Lady... the other security staff, and myself, see to it that **all** of the ladies get to their cars safely... pretty ones and not so pretty ones too."

Tammy's eyebrows rose in hearing David's response, but her eyes were still closed. She gave him a smile that expressed her approval and she remained silent after that. David took the opportunity to say what he wanted to say to Sabrina; so very gentlemen like, with the utmost respect, David said to Sabrina:

"Ms... I don't wanna give you the impression that I do this all the time because I don't... but I had to say something to you before you left the club. I've seen a-lot-of beautiful women, but when you walked into the club... I was like, WOW! That girl is **amazing!** I've been working at this club since it open and one of my rules is: don't approach the women for personal reasons... That was until now... Hi... my name is David Day and I would love to get to know you."

Sabrina was filled with admiration and was doing her best to conceal her esteem. She felt that David's approach was genuine and sincere. It made her feel wanted... a feeling that she hadn't felt in years. Not saying that Porshaé didn't want her, but Sabrina was feeling that physical wanting from David, something that Porshaé couldn't provide her with at the moment. David continued:

"I'm not in a relationship and I'm not dating anyone... I wrote my number down earlier hoping you would accept it."

David fished inside of his pocket for the white napkin with the *Copa Club* logo and his name and number on it.

"Here it is."

Sabrina looked at the napkin as David held it, wondering if he was having second thoughts about giving it to her because he just held it... staring at it like he was proof-reading and checking for errors. There was a brief silence and Sabrina broke it.

"My name is Sabrina."

David finally looked up from the napkin, directly into Sabrina's eyes.

"It's a pleasure to make your acquaintance Sabrina", said David, extending his hand out towards Sabrina.

She extended hers as well and they joined hands and engaged in a soft handshake. Sabrina felt something when they touched hands. It was that feeling you get when the physical aspect of a person turns you on; that good vibe of attraction, but there was a downside to this...

Her minds morals and her hearts loyalty to her man... were conflicting with her physical desires. She didn't have to but she chose to suppress her urges for physical companionship. Sabrina released her grip of David's hand and he released also. She still was gonna be nice though. She continued:

"Sooo... are you gonna give me that napkin or are you gonna use it to wipe that sweat off your forehead?" she said, smiling at David.
He smiled back, embarrassed by his show of nervousness.

"Ooh yeah... here you go. That's my house number and my pager number too", said David.

Sabrina accepted David's number and her conscience wasn't making her feel too bad about it, for one: Porshaé had told her during one of their recent phone conversations that he wanted her to move on with her life and be happy with someone else. Sabrina was pissed off at him for making a statement like that, but he told her he **knew** she was miserable and only trying to pretend she was okay. He could see it on her face every time she came to visit him. He could hear it in her voice on the phone every time they spoke. He told her he would be ok with it, as long as she stayed in-touch and brought their Daughter to see him every now and then. For two: Sabrina knew deep down in her heart that she was not ready to move on.

David seemed like a genuinely nice guy, so she accepted the number for that reason alone. Sabrina glanced into the Honda Civic and to her surprise. Tammy was in the car, with the seat laid back, apparently sleep... Sabrina hadn't even noticed that Tammy got in the car. She looked back at David then said:

"David, it was nice meeting you. Thank you for being such a gentleman, but I think I need to get my friend home to her bed."

David looked inside the car seeing that Tammy was passed-out. He hadn't noticed Tammy's disappearance into the car either. He commented:

"Yeah..... It looks like she's out-fah-the-count."

He laughed a little, remembering Tammy's ranting then nodded his head in agreement with Sabrina then continued:

"Well you drive safe Sabrina, and don't forget those seatbelts."

"I will... and I won't forget the seatbelts", said Sabrina, smiling modestly at David.

David gave Sabrina a gentle wave and said:

"Goodnight."

"Goodnight." said Sabrina also then got inside the car.

She cranked the engine, looked over at Tammy, and whispered:

"Drunk ass... That's ma Girl though."

The black Honda pulled off the lot and David walked back towards the club.

Mother's Day, May, 1988

The phone rang at Sabrina's, mom's house. It was 9:30 in the morning and Sabrina was still slumbering well, due to her night out at the club with her girls. Her mom was glad that she had gone out with her friends. She knew how much Sabrina missed Porshaé, but she still wanted her daughter to get passed that and have an active life again... Ms. Dukes, Sabrina's mom, **loved** Porshaé, and he loved her too. They had a mother and son relationship... but reality was reality... and Ms. Dukes, as well as Porshaé, wanted Sabrina to face it...

The answering-machine picked-up on the fourth ring. Ms. Dukes' voice was on the first part of the message; Sabrina's was on the second part, and Porsha's, the Babygirl was on the third.

"You have reached the Dukes residence of, Flois, Porsha and Sabrina."

"Sorry we missed your call, but if you leave a brief message."

Last was Porsha's cute little, high-pitched, girly voice.

"We will get back with you in-ah-minute, have-ah-good-**day**!"

Beeeep!

On the other end, the operator recording was already playing:

"You have a collect call from a Missouri Department of Corrections facility, from: "Porshaé."

Porshaé was a soft-spoken man but his voice was powerful in its own right. If someone heard him speak on the phone and had never met him in person... they would've thought he was much bigger than what he actually was. Porshaé was only 5 feet 7 inches tall and had a very muscular 165 pound frame.

Sabrina hadn't cared that she'd out grown Porshaé in height since junior high school... he was her first love and she was in-love with him and that's all that mattered to her. He loved the fact that Sabrina was taller than he was. For some strange reason, he enjoyed looking up to his Boo... it made him feel good and it drove him wild every time he'd kiss Sabrina. He would look up into her eyes; wrap his arms around her waist... she would rest her arms over his shoulders and then, they would smile at each other because of the thought they shared. That thought was; it's suppose to be the other way around. ☺

Society made those rules and they didn't give-a-damn about what society thought. It was fun to them... it made them smile every single time before they partook in a passionate kiss. Those kisses, always sent electrifying thrills through Sabrina's body... and Porshaé always felt it. His kisses brought her great pleasure and that's what made him love her the way he did. He knew that she was truly satisfied with him, no questioning it.

Ms. Dukes got to the phone just as Porshae's voice sounded through the answering machine. She picked up the receiver and listened to the rest of the recording: "To accept this call, press 1 now."
Ms. Dukes pressed 1 on the cordless phone and the operator recording finished: "Thank you. Your call has now been connected. You may begin your conversation."
"Hello." said Porshaé, his voice vibrated softly through the phone.
Flois responded cheerfully to the sound of her should have been son-in-law's voice.
"Hey Porshaé!"
"Hey Momma! Happy Mother's Day."
"Thank you Baby... you're the first one to tell me. I'm glad you

called this morning, because the girls and I have a **full** day planned. We gonna go shopping then we going to visit Sabrina's grandmother on her daddy's side. After that... we're taking little Porsha over to your momma's house so she can see her grandbaby then... we're **all** going out to dinner... probably to Red Lobster. It's gone be a **wonderful** day and you calling this morning to say Happy Mother's Day was a perfect way to start it off. How you doing in there Baby?"

Flois was always happy to hear from Porshaé... she never faked with him about anything. She told him **and** Sabrina, exactly how she felt when Sabrina became pregnant. She had some choice words for the both of them but primarily for Porshaé. She told him:
"If you not planning on being here for Sabrina's entire pregnancy and the baby after the baby born... then don't plan on being here at all."
She gave them both some words of wisdom and a good scolding at the same time for being irresponsible. She told Porshaé:
"You're the type of young man that I wished Sabrina's Dad could've been, but that don't mean **ah-damn-thang** if you not gonna be around to be a father to your child."

Ms. Dukes also told them, that the baby in Sabrina's stomach was a gift from God and it was their responsibility to take care of that gift to the best of their ability and God would bless them for it. Neither of them, Sabrina, Ms. Dukes or Porshaé, wanted anything to do with an abortion. Ms. Dukes was supportive in every way and she encouraged Porshaé and Sabrina to embrace the new addition to the family with love and no worries.

Porshaé responded to Flois' question:
"I'm doing ok Momma... just missing you and the girls like crazy. I'm having ma case looked at again... by a different legal team though."
"**Ooh yeah...** by who?" asked Flois.
"I don't wanna let that be known just yet, but they supposed to be really good with cases like mines."
"That's **really** good news Baby! You know we've been praying for God to help you... We miss you Porshaé and we want you home. Your Baby girl needs you too."

"I know Momma... I'm still working on getting out... Momma... I don't want you to say anything to Sabrina about my case being reviewed. I don't wanna get her hopes up and then have to let them down if nothing good comes out of it."

"I understand Baby. I'll keep it between you and me."

"They haven't promised me anything... only that they'll look at every detail of ma case to see if there's anything that can be done. I feel good about it though."

Porshaé already had **two** other lawyers look at his case, but they both claimed; that there was nothing in his case that was appealable under the appellate courts requirements. He couldn't accept that though. He **knew** there had to be **something** there. He didn't get discouraged... he just continued to pray and have faith in God that the right people would be put in his life to help him. He claimed it in **Jesus'** name... that God would have him home sooner than the 16 years he had left on the 20-year sentence. He continued:

"I'm not gone get my hopes up either but like I said, I do feel good about it this time. How's ma Baby-girl doing?"

"Porsha is fine Baby. She been wondering if she's gonna be your height or Sabrina's height. She says she likes your height but she doesn't know why. I told her she probably gone be Sabrina's height and she put a-little frown on her face. She just misses you... She been tryina do **any** and **everythang** to be close to you."

"Momma, is she up right now?"

"Yeah... since we been on the phone, I think I heard her get up. She probably fixing a bowl of cereal. She knows how to do **a-lot** on her own now... your Baby-girl growing up."

"I **know**... and ma-ass sittin in here missin it all."

Porshaé was getting upset and Ms. Dukes knew it...

"Try not to be too hard on yourself Baby. It's not your fault you in that place... We know how crooked those police can be, and that's why God is gone get you outta there. Just keep your faith Son."

"I am Momma. I am."

Ms. Dukes got back on a happier note:

"Guess what kind of cereal Porsha likes?" said Ms. Dukes.

"I don't **even** know. I remember her liking **all** the cereals with cartoon characters on the boxes." said Porshaé, smiling at the memory of his daughter and him at the grocery store. He continued:

"Cookie Crisp, Fruity Pebbles, Lucky Charms. Daddy, can we try this one? Daddy, can we try that one? I always got her whichever one she wanted to try. I can't imagine her liking **one** specific cereal."

"Porshaé, about a month ago, we went grocery shopping... and when we got to the **cereal aisle**... Sabrina made a comment about the cereal you like, you know, the Frosted Mini Wheats?"

"Yeah." said Porshaé.

Ms. Dukes continued:

"Well, Sabrina picked up a box then said: "I don't see **why** your Daddy loves this cereal so much. It's nasty." Then Porsha said, and it was **so** cute: "Mommy... that's the cereal I want. Can we get Daddy's cereal, pleeease?"

After Porshaé heard that, the tears started forming in the wells of his eyes, but he held them back, not wanting them to fall.

Ms. Dukes continued:

"Baby... Sabrina told Porsha that she wasn't gonna like it and listen... Every since then, whenever we go grocery shopping, that's the **only** cereal Porsha picks out now."

"Good morning Granma." said little Porsha, as she strolled into the living room, still stretching and yawning.

Her Care Bear pajamas were hanging loosely on her little body. She had a silk headscarf, wrapped around her head. Sabrina and her mom wore one too when they went to bed, to keep their hair from breaking. It was a beauty tip that Flois had taught Sabrina, and Sabrina taught Porsha. The three of them, all had long beautiful hair...

Ms. Dukes turned, smiling, glad to see her beautiful granddaughter. She leaned forward slightly off the beige Lazy Boy recliner chair to embrace the hug that Porsha was offering.

"**Good** morning Princess... ummmm." Their hug was tight and warm.

Flois rocked her granddaughter from side-to-side as they hugged then, after their embrace, she said to Porsha:

"Guess who's on the phone? Your **Daddy, Princess**!"

Porsha's eyes got wide and her drowsiness left instantly.

"He **is**!" said Porsha, excited, gazing at her grandmother with star struck eyes. Porshaé could hear the excitement in his daughter's voice.

"Put her on the phone Momma." he said, anxious to talk to his daughter.

Ms. Dukes gave Porsha the phone.

"Hello?" said Porsha, in an inquisitive tone.

The pure, soft, sweet, little voice of his daughter was soothing to his ears. The tears that Porshaé held back earlier had now started to fall.

"**Hey** Baby Girl!"

"**DADDY!**"

The two spoke on the phone for almost an hour. Porsha **always** had to tell her Daddy **everything** that went on since the last time they spoke. And Porshaé loved to listen. The feeling that they felt while talking to each other on the phone, was un-describable. Only a father and daughter could comprehend it... They wrapped up their conversation... Porshaé didn't like for Ms. Dukes' phone bill to get too high from him calling.

"Are you gonna call again soon Daddy?"

"I'll call next Sunday Princess. I would love to call you **everyday** but I don't want Granma's phone bill to be sky high... so once a week, ok Princess? But we can write as **many** letters as we want."

"Ok Daddy. I can live with that."

Porshaé smiled at her comment. His Baby Girl **was** growing up.

"I love you Princess... Put Granma back on the phone."

"Ok. I love you too Daddy."

Porshaé called out to his Daughter before she could get off the phone:

"PRINCESS!"

"Yeah Daddy?" There was a long pause before Porshaé finally said what he wanted to say. He continued:

"Princess... I love you **so** much and I miss you... you will **always** be ma Babygirl no matter what... and I will always, always, always, always, always--"

"**Daddy!**" Porsha exclaimed, playfully interrupting her Dad, sensing that he was playing too.

Porshaé finished:

"always love you."

Porsha smiled big, enjoying her Dads playfulness on the phone. She responded:

"I will always love you too Daddy... no matter what."

Porshaé could feel the tears in his eyes start to form again. He didn't say anything else, and Porsha went to find her Granma to give her the phone.

Sabrina was still lying down with her eyes open, wondering where Porsha was. Normally, Porsha would wake up early and go in Sabrina's room to lay down with her Mommy for a while. Sabrina had become use to it and she enjoyed waking up with her daughter next to her. It showed her that regardless of how much Porsha missed her Daddy... she **still** wanted to be close to her Mommy.

When Sabrina looked over at the clock, it was 10:40am. She hadn't been a-woke for that long. She wondered; "had Porsha come in earlier and then opted to leave to let Mommy sleep?" Just as Sabrina finished her thought, she glanced over by the nightstand on the left side of her bed. Sabrina saw Porsha's, little baby-doll, slightly hidden, between the plush comforter and the nightstand. Sabrina smiled at her daughter's little baby-doll and the anxiety she was feeling, left. She knew that Porsha was becoming more independent of herself by the day, and soon... Porsha would want to do things on her own. The thought made Sabrina feel a little uneasy and she hoped that day... wouldn't come anytime soon.

Flois walked into the room and seen Sabrina gazing at Porsha's baby-doll.

"She's on the phone with her Daddy, Baby", said Flois, seeing her daughters wonder.

Her soft, motherly voice brought Sabrina out of the trance she was in... Sabrina's whole body felt stimulated at just the **thought** of Porshaé, **especially** in the mornings. If she had been in the room by herself... she would've taken the moment to indulge in her thoughts of him; remembering how he made love to her; how he always knew just how she wanted to be made love to... She would've closed her eyes and played with herself until she reached her climax... but... Her mom was there so she had to shake off the thought until another time. Sabrina sat up, placing her back against the plush pillows that sat against the headboard of her bed.

"Momma?" said Sabrina, collecting her thoughts then continued:

"Uhmm – how long he been on the phone?"

"Since about 9:30... We talked for about 15, maybe 20 minutes and then Porsha got on the phone with him. She gets **so excited** when her Daddy calls. I prayed **hard** last-nite that God help him outta that place so he can get home soon."

Flois almost mentioned the news about Porshae's case being reviewed again, but she remembered what he said. Sabrina was a little annoyed at her Mother's comment and responded:

"Momma, you **know** he done already had **two** lawyers look at his case! They said there is nothing they can do!"

Sabrina was expressing some frustration. She wanted to face reality, and she was indeed attempting to do so when she made her statement... but deep down inside, she was still really hoping that something would happen to get her man out of prison sooner. Flois glared at Sabrina with an accusing scowl and said defensively:

"Sabrina, I know what them lawyers said... but that aint what **God said**! I've been **praying** for Porshaé and **you...** need to pray for him too if you really want yo-man home! I know what God can do, and so do you Sabrina. I don't see **why** you acting like you don't! If you ask God for something, don't let **no** doubt come into your mind about what you asked God to do for you! You hear me?"

"I hear you Momma." said Sabrina apologetically.

Ms. Dukes continued:

"I didn't raise you to have any doubt in what God can do... you **know** where God done **brought** me from, as far as me going through all that **bullshit** with yo Daddy!"

"I know Momma." said Sabrina.

Sabrina didn't want her mom to get into that story again. She knew how much it pained her mom whenever the subject of her dad came up. She tried to take the thought off her Mom's mind.

"Momma, it's not that I don't believe God can't do it... It's, it's just that..." Ms. Flois finished for her:

"It's just that you're not having faith." she said, calmly and composed once again. Ms. Flois continued speaking with force and feeling:

"Sabrina... God is gonna help Porshaé get outta that place... if that's God's will. But He's gonna do it in **His** time and I'm claiming that, in **the name of God**."

Ms. Dukes had spoken her words with such confidence and such assurance, that it served as fuel for Sabrina's dying fire of hope.

"Granmaaa!"

Porsha was calling for Flois, after not being able to find her in her usual areas of the house. Flois responded:

"I'm in here with your Mom Princess!"

The door to Sabrina's room was ajar. Porsha poked her little head inside seeing her Granma sitting at the foot of the bed. She walked in with her arm extended, handing Flois the phone.

"Daddy wants to talk to you again Granma."

As soon as Flois got on the phone, she let Porshaé know that Sabrina was up, seeing the anxious look on her daughter's face, for she was ready to talk to Porshaé. Nevertheless, the only thing he said was:

"Momma, I'll call y'all again next weekend. The guards are about to do count so I gotta get off this phone or they gone put ma-ass in the hole. Tell Sabrina I love her and I miss her **so** much."

Flois was a little uneasy about him not saying anything to Sabrina. She knew that Sabrina would wonder **all week** about why he hadn't gotten on the phone with her; not even for one minute. She made another attempt to get him to say something to Sabrina before he got off the phone.

"Porshaé! Sabrina is **right** here next to me!"

But as if he hadn't even heard the words, he said:

"Momma, I gotta go! I'll call next weekend ok. I love you." and the call ended...

Flois brought the receiver down from her ear and pressed the end button on the cordless disappointedly. She put the phone down in her lap then looked over at her daughter. Sabrina's dejection showed on her face. With an encouraging voice, Flois said:

"He had to go Sabrina. The guards were about to do count. He said he loves you and misses you **so much** and that he'll call next weekend."

Sabrina was **pissed** and she fired off:

"Momma, he couldn't even get on the phone with me for **one, damn, minute** to tell me happy **mother's day**?"

Flois tried to defend Porshaé, responding to Sabrina's comment:

"Look around you Sabrina! He has already **told** you happy mother's day. You have cards and gifts **right here** in your room that he done sent you for mother's day... You know that boy loves you and I know it too! I also know when a man is trying to distant his self from a woman. Not because he doesn't love her or because he don't wanna be with her... but it's because he **does** love her... Under y'all circumstance... he would rather **distant** his self from you because he can't be with you like you need him to be... than to allow you to hold on to him." Flois paused then continued:

"He knows you pretending to be happy, knowing **good** and well you miserable... That man cares about you **that much** Sabrina. I **know** it's hard for him not to get on the phone with you but, he doing what he thinks is best for you... Now if you wanna be a strong woman and wait on yo-man, you can... but that's the burden Porshaé doesn't wanna put on you... **that's** why he's doing what he's doing. Baby... if God's plan is for you and him to be together then y'all **will** be... God will give you what you want, if you ask Him for it... as long as it's righteous... but sometimes God won't.

Sometimes God's plans for us, don't correspond with our own. Sabrina... if you **really** wanna wait on Porshaé... then you should ask God to give you the strength to continue to do so. And you and Porshaé should get married."

Sabrina responded:

"Momma I **do** wanna wait for him and I **have** faith... but it's been **so hard** not having him here with me... I know he wants me to move on... he told me already... Momma, I just feel like... if I do, I'm gonna lose the man I **really** want and that's **him**... and I don't think he's gonna wanna get married while he's in prison."

Flois responded:

"When he calls next week, you two just need to discuss it, ok? Tell him you're willing to wait on him because he's worth waiting for and see what he has to say then, ok Baby?"

Flois patted Sabrina on her leg and continued:

"Everything will be fine Sabrina... you'll see. Now stop worrying yourself... we have a beautiful day planned."

Flois got up to leave the room.

"Come on Princess. Let your Momma have a little time to herself."

Porsha was one-step out of the room when she **ran** back and jumped into Sabrina's arms. She gave her Mom a kiss on the cheek and said:

"Happy Mother's Day Mommy... I love you."

Sabrina melted in her daughter's embrace, feeling every bit of love that came from little Porsha.

"Thank you Baby... Mommy loves you too", said Sabrina, while giving Porsha a tight hug and big kiss.

Porsha jumped down and left out of the room with her Granma and Flois closed the door behind them. Sabrina sat in her bed thinking about Porshae's actions... wondering what was **really** going through his mind. Her Mom had given her a good explanation but that didn't sit well with her. She picked up the cordless phone and was about to call Tammy then she opted not to. Sabrina was mad as hell at Porshaé for not talking to her and she wanted to vent. Just not to her Mom though because **she** was **always** on his side. Tammy lived a few houses down from Sabrina and Sabrina had made sure Tammy got in the house and in her bed safely last night. Then she walked down to her house.

She spoke her thoughts aloud:

"Tammy is probably still knocked-out... I know he wants me to be happy, but what about **his** happiness? I care about his happiness just as much as I care about mines... damn this... Let me just get ma-ass up. I'll write his ass a long letter when I get back."

CHAPTER 2: M.E.C.C.

MISSOURI EASTERN CORRECTIONAL CENTER
"PORSHAÉ PRINCE! YOU HAVE A LEGAL VISIT! GET READY!"
The corrections officer yelled over the P.A. system.
Porshaé **hated** that loud ass thing. It was so **annoying**...

It was the Wednesday morning after Mother's Day and someone from the new legal team had come to see Porshaé. He was in his cell reading a book called: *"The Destruction of A Black Civilization"*, by *Chancellor Williams.*

He got up from his bunk, gathered his hygiene bag then went to the bathroom and shower area. There were about seven sinks with mirrors above each one. He chose the one to the far right of the bathroom area. He brushed his teeth and washed his face then examined his self in the mirror, making sure his appearance was appropriate for his legal visit. He stared at his reflection in the mirror for long a moment. His eyes were honest; his face, still traced with indignation from the misfortune that befell him four years earlier.
He lowered his head towards the sink and he closed his eyes and began to pray quietly:

"Father God... I know there's a reason why you have me going through this... but it's been **four years** and I **still** don't know what that reason is... I don't feel it's to humble me. I've always been humble and I've always did my best to be a good person... Father God... what I'm asking you for today is... to **please** help this new lawyer find **somethin** that will get me in appeal court so I can get home to my family soon. Please Father God... I need you to help me... I **thank** you Father God for giving me the strength to remain strong and not give up... I **thank** you for the people you've kept by my side during my trail and tribulation. Father God... I ask this of you and I **thank** you... in your name... amen."

The room for legal visits was small. There was a metal office desk, a padded metal frame chair for the attorney and a beige, plastic reception chair for the prisoner. An old black, square, push button telephone sat on the desk, along with a large desk calendar. Porshaé opened the door to the small room and greeted his visitor that sat awaiting him.

"Good morning." he said, as he entered the room.

"Good morning Mr. Prince. My name is Evelyn Lewis," said the beautiful Ms. Lewis, extending her hand out to Porshaé. He gently shook her hand then she continued:

"Have a seat Mr. Prince... I'm an associate and friend of Mr. Cochran and basically, what I'm here to do is... ask you about **every** single detail that took place the day of the incident."

Porshaé hadn't seen a woman as beautiful as Evelyn since Sabrina last visited. Evelyn was about an inch and half shorter than him, even in her two inch heels.

At their introduction while they were standing, he took noticed of Evelyn's height. She was **very** attractive he thought. Evelyn was a petite woman with beautiful dark brown skin. Her hair cropped short and cut in a style that made every lovely feature of her face stand out even more. Her eyes were dark brown and the sclera's of her eyes were **brilliant** white. Porshaé had never seen the white of a person's eyes so bright. When he caught her gaze, Evelyn's eyes emitted glimmers of hope for him. He tried not to sound too forward but he **had** to tell her:

"Ms. Lewis. You have some **beautiful** eyes."

Evelyn tried to keep a stern look on her face, but she couldn't help it and smiled modestly then responded:

"Thank you Mr. Prince."

Evelyn's presence was a comfort to Porshaé and he was thankful that Mr. Cochran had sent her. The other two attorneys, both from different firms, had been blunt, coarse and seemingly apathetic towards his situation. Already wasted time and money on **two** lawyers who weren't willing to dig through the evidentiary dirt that buried the truth... he **hoped** that the third time would be a charm.

THE COCHRAN FIRM

The Cochran firm had officially started in 1982, in Los Angeles. Mr. Cochran opened a small office on Wilshire Boulevard. He was a **true** advocate for justice and for defending the minority against the injustices that were very prevalent at the time. The corruptions in the law enforcement agencies, as well as the legal system, were wide spread at the time. Mr. Cochran knew all **too** well, of the clandestine agendas that the "majority" had behind politics, poverty, prison and racism... and not just against Blacks... but against the less fortunate. All which were influenced by money and, a hate for the so-called, "inferior."

Over the past years, Mr. Cochran built a reputation for being one of the best civil **and** best defense attorneys in the legal system. During those years, he established strong friendships and built loyal alliances with other attorneys across the States that shared his same vision. Ms. Lewis had become a part of that alliance and vision... That vision was... to defend those whose rights had been violated. To defend those who were wrongfully accused of a crime. To be enforcers of our Constitutional Rights, ensuring that we **all**, especially the minority, receive the protection afforded by the U.S. Constitution. To defend a legal system that **guarantees** the presumption of innocence and **every** individual's right to a fair trial and equal protection under the law... **That** was the vision.

Mr. Cochran believed, the only way we could be assured of that, was if **every** citizen in this land, was assure that the legal system would treat them fairly and act accordingly under the law, without biases. He also believed that if one of our rights were violated then **all** of our rights were violated; speaking specifically of the African American race. His name would later become renowned worldwide, June 1994, when he defended O.J. Simpson and won the murder case in October 1995...

How Porshaé Came Across Cochran & Associates

While in prison, Porshaé met a guy by the name of Tony Rone. Tony was a Blood Gang member from Los Angeles California. He was trafficking cocaine from L.A. to Saint Louis. Tony Rone started a Blood Gang in Saint Louis, using the members to move his cocaine. While in the "Show-Me-State", Tony had become a certified street king. He made his mark in the city, but the Saint Louis born Hoods were vexed about the out-of-towners success in **their** streets. That hate, would ultimately lead to the demise of Tony Rone's drug empire. When he found out that it was his own Saint Louis gang that set him up... he dodged a Federal case by giving **all** of them up, along with some others and only receiving 10 years state time.

In Los Angeles, before he started traveling to Saint Louis, Tony was in an altercation that involved gunplay. Mr. Cochran had been his legal representation on the charges of, (attempted murder and unlawful use of a firearm). Mr. Cochran got the unlawful use of a firearm charge, amended to, (possession of an un-registered firearm), based on self-defense evidence that he presented during pre-trial. He convinced the court that the use of the weapon was lawful based on the evidence. The attempted murder charge was dismissed, based on the same evidence.

Porshaé heard of Mr. Cochran, but Tony enlightened him on **who** Mr. Cochran was. Tony gave Porshaé Mr. Cochran's number and advised him to call as soon as possible because Mr. Cochran was in high demand. Porshae's optimism was low but he accepted the number and promised Tony that he would call... That **one** phone call, led to Mr. Cochran calling Ms. Lewis, who had her own law office in Saint Louis. She was to obtain Porshae's case-file, and a detailed statement from him then, convey those details to Mr. Cochran to see what the expert attorney could come-up-with. He would then examine the details and advise Evelyn on what steps to take next... **if** there was something to take steps on...

Evelyn began:

"Mr. Prince... I first need to understand... why do you feel your case is appealable? What reason or reasons can we present to the appellate courts so they will grant us a review?"

Already, Porshaé liked the way Ms. Lewis was talking. She asked the questions as if she already had the appeal in her briefcase and only needed his confirmative statement to make it official. The sound of her voice and the look in her eyes said: "I'm here for you and we can do this... as long as you keep it real with me and don't bullshit me." It was as if she already knew something that he was oblivious to... **but...** that was her job... to know the unknown. He responded:

"Ms. Lewis. I'm not familiar with the law at all, but I **know** I have a right to protect myself and **that's** what I was doing... it was **self defense.**"

While Porshaé spoke, Evelyn glared at him with curious eyes and a wondering mind... She relinquished her curiosity to reason and continued her questioning:

"Mr. Prince, why don't you tell me **why** you were there at the recording studio in Saint Louis in the first place... just start from the beginning." said Evelyn, pulling out a file that she had obtained of Porshae's case from the Saint Louis circuit-court records.

She sat the file on the desk, reached back into her black, soft, leather, expandable briefcase, and pulled out a yellow legal tablet and black ink-pen. With an attentive look on her face, she postured herself to listen and take notes. She had **thoroughly** reviewed the file, and what she wanted to do now was: compare stories to see if there was anything new that Porshaé might have left out, that he hadn't thought of before. Porshaé began:

"Ms. Lewis, I'm a producer and a promoter. Someone might call me to produce a song or promote a show. I was well known in Michigan... I'm from Flint but my reputation for being a good producer, precedes where I'm from. I got a call from a guy in Saint Louis named, Clyde Pulliam. He owns *We Got Music*, it's a recording studio. He heard some of my work and asked me if I would be interested in coming to Saint Louis to produce an album for Archbishop, one of his artists. He told me he would take care of all my expenses, **just** to come down and check out his studio... I was cool with it. I told him to give me a day to get some things wrapped up... a day after that... I called to let him know I was ready; he called me back with my hotel and plane ticket, conformation numbers and an hour later... I was on my way to Saint Louis. It was a morning flight. I got to Saint Louis, Lambert airport at 9: am.

When I got to the passenger pick-up area there was a light blue Jaguar with a white poster board on the window with my name on it. The windows were tinted so I couldn't see who was in the car... I expected it to be Clyde but when I approached the car, the passenger side window let down and it was a female. She leaned over and asked me:

"You got your ID?" she said, just to make sure I was the right guy. I showed it to her and she told me to get in.

"My name is Keisha. I'm Clyde's personal assistant. He asked me to pick you up... Lets' get you to your hotel."

We drove to the Adams Mark hotel, in downtown Saint Louis. I checked into my suite with Ms. Keisha still at my side to make sure everything was cool. After that, she gave me her business card and told me:

"If you need anything, call me, but I should be back around 1pm to pick you up, to go meet with Clyde... Just relax a little and get settled into your room." Then she left."

CHAPTER 3: HOW IT ALL BEGIN MAY 1984

S.P.D. NARCOTICS DIVISION Surveillance

"S1 to S2, over?" said one of the officers through the Motorola 10 channel, two-way walkie-talkie.

"Copy S1." said the other officer.

"Subject in the blue J, has just left the Mark without the airport passenger, over."

"Copy S1."

Officer Dennis Harris had been following Keisha since she left her house. Officer James Vincent was staked out at Clyde's house. Officer James had been on Clyde since late last night and stayed on him until that following day. A few of Clyde's artist and two other artists from another label had a show in East Saint Louis, Illinois and Clyde didn't make it home until 3am. Officer Vincent was tired but doing his best to stay awake and on surveillance fearing that he might miss an opportunity to find the guy they were looking for... *We Got Music* had come under investigation for suspicion of drug trafficking, primarily because of a staff member at *We Got Music,* by the name of, Big Mo. He got busted with an eighth of a kilo of cocaine in the trunk of his car, during a traffic stop in Saint Ann Missouri...

One Week Before Porshaé Got To Saint Louis

The phone rang at the studio and Keisha answered it:

"*We Got Music* recording studio, Keisha speaking, how may I help you?"

Big Mo responded frantically on the other end on the line:

"Keisha, this is Mo! I need to talk to Uncle Clyde! I'm in jail at the Saint Ann Police station."

Keisha **instantly** got heated and responded:

"**Mo**, why in the **hell** are you in jail?"

"These muthafucka's charging me with drug possession! Keisha, I **really** need Uncle Clyde's help! Where's he at?"

"Mo, he not here right now, and he's gonna-be **pissed-off** when he hear about this shit! Uncle Clyde done gave you **chance** after **chance** and you keep on **fuckin**-up Mo! You know... right now he probably out looking for somebody to **replace** yo-ass!"

Keisha was so angry with Mo that she snatched her phone headset off and pushed herself away from her desk. She glared at the headset, disgusted with what she had just heard. Clyde had put a lot of work into making *We Got Music* a well-known and well respected recording studio, the legit way. He saw how passionate Mo was about making music so he paid for Mo's audio engineering training.

Clyde & Mo's Father

Gerald Moore and Clyde had been best friends since their childhood. They came up together in the hard dangerous streets of Saint Louis, and when I say came-up... I mean, **came up**! Back when they were younger, Gerald was a heroin dealer and Clyde was the biggest weed-man in Saint Louis. He and Gerald made **a-lot** of money back then and when Clyde felt he had made enough to do something legit... he contemplated on getting out of the drug business... However, Gerald wasn't quite ready yet.

One night... in an area on the south side of Saint Louis called the "Dark Side", over by highway 44... Gerald was murdered in his own car... Clyde always suspected that it was an associate of Gerald's, who committed the murder... but that associate was never found... Clyde stepped back from everything after that and really began evaluating his situation... He evaluated his status in the drug game, and he evaluated his life. He came to the undeniable conclusion that it was definitely time to get out of the drug business. Gerald had one son and that son had been left fatherless, and since Clyde and Gerald's son already had a close uncle and nephew relationship, Clyde decided to raise Mo. At that time, Mo's mother wasn't fit to do the job because of her addiction to heroin.

Clyde got out of the drug business and got into real estate. He did very well. He had done something positive with the money that the streets had brought him... And he vowed to do his best to keep Gerald's son away from those same streets... When Mo was old enough, Clyde bought a nice building in the Central West End area of Saint Louis and turned it into a top-of-the-line music-recording studio just for Mo. Clyde let his young niece Keisha, work at the studio wherever she wasn't in school... She would later become his assistant in helping manage the business, and Mo was the in-house engineer.

Back to Keisha & Mo's phone call:

Mo was trying to keep calm on the other end of the phone-line. He called Keisha's name a couple of times only to be answered by silence.

"Keisha... Keisha... I know you hear me **girl**!"
Mo took a deep breath, exhaled, then spoke again:

"Keisha... **please**... just find Uncle Clyde fah-me and tell him I'm in jail... I **know** I fucked-up and I **know** he gone be pissed off but I gotta explain this shit to him."
Keisha had pressed the speakerphone feature and heard everything that Mo had said. She was debating on whether or not she should respond or hang up on his ass. Her conscience wouldn't let her hang up thought. She would feel bad for Lord **knows** how long... She took a deep breath and let out a long sigh, shaking her head at the voice coming from the phone and she opted to hang it up.

Making It Happen

We Got Music had been open for only four years and was already making phenomenal headway in the music recording business. Clyde had got into the business at just the right time. A new era of music had been born, which was Hip-hop & Rap Music, and they were flourishing rather quickly in the music world. The studio schedule **stayed** booked up! The only problem that Clyde was having... was keeping his one and only engineer, away from the life style that killed his best friend. Clyde's main artist, Archbishop had been networking and heard about a producer in Michigan, by the name of Porshaé Prince.

Many people were talking about him, saying he was becoming a young master at producing tracks for Hip-hop and Rap music. Archbishop knew that Clyde was considering bringing in a second engineer/producer, not to replace Big Mo but just to handle the heavy booking schedule and to give his artist and clients a variety of sound to work with... The one thing Clyde **didn't** want to happen was: for Mo to inadvertently think that he was trying to replace him. That would **definitely** push Mo away, further into the streets. He didn't want that at all... What Clyde wanted: was for Mo to step-it-up and start handling his responsibilities at the studio... after all, the studio was really for Mo in the first place, Clyde was only backing his nephew's passion and trying to keep him out of the grimy STL Streets.

Keisha Gets Uncle Clyde On The Phone

"Hello."

"Hey Uncle Clyde." said Keisha, in a low, disappointed voice.

"**Hey** Keisha Baby." said Clyde in his soothing, southern drawl.
His parents were born and raised in Savannah, Georgia so he had inherited some of their southern traits. Keisha liked her Uncle's voice. He was always pleasant to listen to. Clyde continued:

"How thangs at the studio? Did Mo make it in yet? That artist from Tennessee, 'Memphis Ten' pose-ta-be comin at 2:o-clock... Mo needs to be there."

"I know Uncle Clyde. I remember booking the appointment... and that's what I was calling you about."
Keisha paused and after a few long seconds, she continued:

"Uncle Clyde... Mo is in Saint Ann."
Clyde frowned and responded with agitation in his voice:

"He out there, foolin-round with that white girl... I done **told** Mo bout takin his ass out there! Them white folks don't like him out there messin wit that girl. Dem racist ass police try-ta stop **every** nigga they see out there...! It's only 11: o-clock so he got ah couple of hours to make it to the studio. Make-sho you page his ass just to remind him... You know how he is."

Keisha didn't want to give her uncle the bad news but she had to. Clyde was the only one that could get Mo out of jail. She responded:

"Uncle Clyde." she paused for a brief moment before she continued:

"Mo is in **jail** in Saint Ann, Uncle Clyde."

Clyde wasn't surprised, but he didn't know what Mo was in there for yet. He stayed calm and composed like he always did when a discouraging situation presented its self. He wasn't the type to lose his calm. Clyde was well composed. He was a ("resolutionist") who would think things through, thoroughly and logically before acting on a heated impulse... There was a long silence before Clyde finally broke the muteness.

"Keisha, when you talk to him?"

"About five minutes ago. He said he wanted to explain the situation to you... why he got arrested, so I didn't bother asking him."

Keisha knew what Mo was in jail for, but it was best to let Mo do whatever explaining he was gonna do first. She didn't wanna be the one to bring Clyde to the point of anger.

"Alright... Let me call Joe so he can call out there and see what's goin on."

"Ok Uncle Clyde. Do you want me to call Memphis-Ten and re-schedule his appointment?"

"Naaw... Let me find out if we can get Mo out first."

"Ok... Uncle Clyde?"

"Yeah Baby?"

"I love you, and no matter what it is... don't get too upset ok?"

"I love you too Keisha Baby... I won't get too upset about it. That's sweet of you being concern about yo-ole uncle... thank you Baby. I'ma be cool though. I'll talk to you later Keisha."

"Ok Uncle Clyde. Talk to you later."

After Clyde hung up the phone with Keisha, he got **right** on the phone with his lawyer, Joe Hogan, to put the ball in motion to get Mo out of jail.

Clyde's phone-call to Joe:

"How are you today Clyde and what can I do for you?" said Joe.

Joe was a prominent lawyer throughout Missouri, with influential connections in the legal system. He had been Clyde's lawyer for **years.** They had more than just a client lawyer relationship... they were friends in every aspect of the word... Whenever Joe had some free time, he would call Clyde to go out for a round of drinks or a round of golf, whichever was fitting at the time. They would get together just to catch up on the latest happenings in each other's lives, and to hangout. Clyde responded:

"Joe... My nephew is in jail in Saint Ann. I need him outta there as soon as possible. I ain't called out there yet to find out what the charge is. You know how I feel about dealin with the police."

"I know Clyde, that's why you have me... to take care of all that legal shit for you. Just give me his full name and his birthday and I'll have him out-of-there by noon."

"Joe, that's cool man... I owe you big fah this."

Joe had a bit of humor in his voice when he responded:

"**Ooh**, don't worry! I'll bill you" he said, smiling on the other end of the phone line.

Clyde smiled as well, feeling relieved. He was grateful to have such a good lawyer, as well as a great friend. Clyde continued:

"Joe, his name is Moreese Mosiah Moore and his birthday is March 3, 1967."

"**Oh**, so he just turned twenty-one a-couple of months ago?"

"Yeaah... and I been doin ma **best** ta keep him away from that lifestyle I use to live... he **attracted** to it though Joe... like a magnet to metal... He's like-ah son to me... and at times... I feel like I cain't protect him."

Joe could hear Clyde's frustration through the phone. He responded:

"Clyde... in-order for a person to straighten up and fly right, they have to be afraid of the consequences for flying crooked. If they don't know what those consequences are or have never experienced them... then they're less likely to wanna fly straight, you know what I'm saying?"

"Yeah... I know what you sayin Joe." Clyde knew what Joe was implying.

"Just something to think about Clyde... incase Mo puts his self in troubles way again... but this one... I got it covered for you, whatever it is."

"Alright Joe... thanks so much man."

"No problem Clyde... just don't be too hard on yourself though. I'll pick Mo up so you don't have to worry about going out there to Saint Ann. I know **too well** how they operate out there. I'll call you when I have him."

"Alright Joe. Thanks again man."

"In-a-minute Clyde."

"In-a-minute Joe." and they both hung up their phones.

Joe got right to his task and Clyde got his self ready to head to the studio.

CHAPTER 4: BIG MO GETS OUT OF JAIL

*"*I appreciate you fah having Joe come get me Uncle Clyde." said Mo as he sat in the plush leather chair in Clyde's office.

Clyde responded:

"It ain't no thang Mo... but I'm not gone be-able to help you if you get into some serious shit... I don't even know how you gone come out on **this** charge! The Feds might pick it up... it all depends on what Joe can do about it though... but Mo, this **bullshit gotta stop man!**"

Clyde was upset and he rarely displayed his anger, but in this case, it was showing. Mo felt bad about what he had put Clyde through over the past years. He could see the care, the concern and the conflict in Clyde's expression. He could hear it in Clyde's voice as well.

Clyde was battling with his self to keep Mo apart of the business. He didn't want to let him go. Mo responded:

"Uncle Clyde, I know I messed up, but I need to tell you why I was tryin to make some extra money!"

Mo was gonna try to plead his case to Clyde. Clyde looked at Mo like he was crazy, thinking to his self: "**Nigga**... I pay yo-ass **more** than I pay ma self **and** Keisha! **Just** so you wouldn't have to get out there in them streets and do what me and yo Daddy did!"

Clyde tried not to let his anger get the best of him, but it was growing hotter as he glared at Mo. He **slammed** his hand down on top of the mahogany desk and with a repressed voice, in a cynical tone he began to speak, **flinging** his other hand towards Mo.

"Go ahead **Mo**... explain to me why you had four ounces of cocaine in the truck of yo car, out in Saint Ann? You **know** they pull nigga's over fah **nothin** out there!"

Clyde could no longer restrain his anger. His brow was at a deep scowl, expressing his dissatisfaction. He yelled:

"GO AHEAD MO! EXPLAIN THAT SHIT NIGGA!"

Mo was almost afraid to say anything but he began his explanation:

"Uncle Clyde... I went out to Saint Ann to check on Jenny... she pregnant Uncle Clyde. I was tryin not to depend on you so much, because I have been pretty much all my life... fah **everythang**! Even today, I had to depend on you. Uncle Clyde, you've always given me all that I needed... I just wanna be able to do the same fah-ma son when he gets here...."

Clyde wanted to say, "You won't be able to do **shit** fah-um if you behind bars young Nigga." but Clyde held his words.

Mo continued:

"So I went and talk to Mark about makin some money."

Clyde's scowl left abruptly and was replaced with a look of surprised and disbelief. Clyde interrupted Mo then asked:

"Hold-up... Mark **Huggins**?"

"Yeah... Mark Huggins." said Mo.

Mark Huggins had a son who recorded his music at, *We Got Music* recording studio. Mark's son was an up and coming young rapper with **tons** of potential to make it the music industry, and Clyde saw that before the studio was established. Mark use to do business with Clyde and Gerald back in the day. Mark was about ten years younger than Clyde and he seemed to be **born** to hustle. He was copping the most dope from Clyde **and** Gerald, out of any of their cliental back in the day.

When Gerald was murdered and Clyde decided to leave the drug game and try a new "legitimate" life style. He tried to persuade Mark as well, to leave the drug business, to become his partner in the real estate and the music business. Mark told Clyde:

"Man I appreciate the offer... but I gotta get this money that's out here **right now**... I aint got time to wait on no houses and records to be sold... When you get the studio goin, I'll let Junior come on over there. He loves that music shit."

Clyde told Mark: "Well... whenever you get tired of hustlin in them streets... ma offer still will be there fah you."

They've always maintained a good friendship.

Mo continued:

"Mark told me: "You should talk to yo Uncle Clyde first Mo." but I told him, "I need to do somethin on ma **own** fah once."

He asked me, "You know anythang about the business I'm in."

I told him, "**Hell yeah** I know about the cocaine business... I know alotta people in Saint Charles and in south county, who be wantin that shit **all** the time!"

He asked me, "How you know all these people?"

I told him, "From clubs, parties, hangin out... shit like that. When Jenny and me be out with her friends, they always askin me if I got any coke, so I was like fuck it. I need to make some extra money anyway so I might as well get some of that shit to sell."

Mark told me to have a seat. He left outta the living room... When he came back, he had a little black leather case. It looked like one of those shaving kit cases. He threw it to me and said, "Is that what you want?"

I unzipped the case and there was a plastic bag inside, filled with cocaine. I told Mark, "Yeah... this what I'm lookin fo."

He asked me, "You know how much cocaine you holdin?"

I looked at it again and told him, "No."

He left the living room again and came back with a scale. Mark sat the scale down on the coffee table, took the plastic bag out, and sat it on the scale. He told me,

"This is a quarter of a kilo... if you break it down into ounces, you can make 15 hundred an ounce. This is some **premium** shit right here... not none of that shit that's been stepped on and cut four and five times. You can make 13,500 dollars. Now if you break it down into grams, which is probably what you wanna do... then you can make 2,800 dollars per ounces, at 100 dollars ah gram... That's, 25,200 dollars... Mo, since you like family... all I want back is, 6,500. Take yo time with this shit Mo, you hear me? The game is to make as much money as you can, with what you got, you understand?"

"Uncle Clyde! I was **so excited! All** I could **think** about was being able to buy my son **everything** he **needs**...! And being able to help Jenny... I thought about puttin money into the studio and **everything** Uncle Clyde!"

Clyde's frown had faded and his face was now wearing a faint smile from listening to Mo... Clyde thought the same way when he was younger and started making money in the drug business.

He admired Mo's intentions but shook his head at Mo's ignorance. Mo was being sincere about what he was saying, and that sincerity alleviated a portion of the anger Clyde was feeling, not much though. He kept his gaze intense, his scowl strong and his mind open. Mo had been in trouble before, but the trouble he was in now, was far more serious than the troubles in the past. Clyde knew too well of what came next after someone was caught with that much cocaine. His smile wore thin at the thought of the Feds and dirty cops. "I hope Joe can work his magic on this one," thought Clyde.

He continued to listen to Mo.

"I was doin **good** too Uncle Clyde! I sold **half** the cocaine already, I paid Mark all of his money, and I still have about 7 thousand dollars."

Mo was clearly still excited about making that much money. The fact that he had just been busted with a large amount of cocaine hadn't fazed him yet. He knew not of the consequences that were behind the charge; the consequences that Joe spoke of earlier. Mo continued with his explanation:

"Uncle Clyde, I was on ma way out to Saint Charles to get rid of the **last** 4 ounces and ma mind was on Jenny. I had to pass by Saint Ann before I got to Saint Charles... I figured I would stop by to check on her and the baby. Her stomach is gettin **big** Uncle Clyde."

Mo was smiling wide. He tilted his head back for a moment,

trying to hold back the tear that was forming from the thought of his Lady and his son that was in her stomach. Mo brought his head down out of the cloud of thoughts that formed in his mind. His eyes fell directly into the introspective gaze of Clyde. It was as if Clyde, were examining his self through some type of peripheral imagery as he stared at Mo. Clyde was in deep thought. He knew they might have to fight the Feds on the case... It was rare that **anyone** won against the Feds.

Mo could sense Clyde's apprehension. He understood why Clyde was feeling the way he was feeling. It was because of him... The nephew he looked at like a son. Clyde's wisdom, his experience in the streets and his knowledge of the law, had kept him out of jail and prison... and possibly even the grave... Mo needed that wisdom right now. Mo continued:

"I know you upset with me Uncle Clyde... but I hope you not mad at Mark. I fucked up... I went to him... and like I said... he told me I should talk to you first. I know I might have to spend some time in prison... but I **hope** not."

Mo seemed to be at a vulnerable point and Clyde had never seen him at such a point. Clyde sensed that Mo understood the seriousness of the situation. Mo attempted to keep his composure but it was hard. The tears started to form in his eyes and a lump formed in his throat. He let his head fall back and he looked up at the ceiling. His body slumped down a little in the plush armchair. He was discouraged. Clyde began to speak:

"Mo... I'm not that upset with you son. I'm **more** upset with Mark because he **shoulda** told you **no**... He **knows** how I feel about that shit, but I'ma talk to him about that later. The first thing we need to find out, is what you up against with this charge. I'm not sure if the Feds gone pick it up... Joe will let us know what the deal is on that... in the meantime... I want you to be cool and sit back fo-ah while. I don't want you on the scene right now... but the one thang that I'm **pissed off** about, is that you didn't tell **me** about it! We **family** Mo... I should've been one of the **first** to know about Jenny being pregnant... How far along is she?"

"She's four months." said Mo.

Clyde shook his head disappointingly then continued:

"You like-ah **son** to me Mo and I thought I was like-ah father to you! **That's** what disappoints me the most! If you had asked me, I woulda **given** you some other thangs to do to make some extra money... When was you plannin on tellin me about it?"

Clyde had calmed his self down a little. Mo answered:

"Uncle Clyde, I **know** how you feel about me being with a white girl... I figured you would try to persuade me to make her get an abortion or somethin and I don't wanna do that. I want ma son and so does Jenny."

"Mo... I don't have no problem with you **datin** Jenny... I have a **problem** with you goin out to Saint Ann to **see** her... If she stayed out here then I wouldn't be trippin. I asked you to stay away from **there,** not stay away from Jenny... As-ah-matter-ah-fact... you need to call her and ask her if she'll consider movin to the city. I don't want you goin back out there cause them police **really** gone be fuckin with you now... Mo, I know you 21, you grown, and can make yo own decisions, but I'm here to help you son, not hurt you... I got-a-nice two bedroom brick house, over on Sullivan and Jefferson, I know she'll like it... You, her and the baby can stay there for as long as y'all want to."

"Uncle Clyde, that's too much. You done did enough fah-me already."

Clyde rose up out of his plush swivel, office chair and threw both his arms up in the air then responded, keeping his voice cool.

"That's what's **wrong** with you Mo! You lettin that **fools**-pride get in the way of good logic and **reason**... Don't be ah fool son. You need help and I'm right in front of you, and you turning it down. What you want me to do Mo...? put ah kilo of cocaine in yo hands so you can get caught-up out there in them **streets**...! That's the wrong kinda help Mo... I'm offering you the **right** kinda help... That's what I'm here fo son... I don't **want** you fuckin-up yo life, messin around in that street shit... It ain't worth it Mo!"

Clyde was becoming angry again and his tone of voice started to reflect it. He continued:

"**I'm not gone put no dope in yo hands fah you to go out there and become ah target fah police... and fah them shady muthafucka's who'll do whatever they can to stop you from comin-up...!**" Clyde cooled down a-bit then continued:

"Me and yo Dad done **been** through that shit already but I'm still here Mo, he **aint**! Yo Dad is **dead** because of them streets! Now here you is, tryina jump out there with them **same** type-of muthafucka's! **Nigga,** is you **crazy**...?" Clyde paused and calmed his self before he continued:

"Mo... if you wanna be in them streets... then you take that 7,000 dollars and go talk to Mark... but don't call ma muthafuckin number if you get into some shit, you hear me?!"

Mo had never seen his uncle so emotional and angry, but he was witnessing it right now; things were really starting to hit home with Mo. He saw tears in Clyde's eyes and knew the tears were there **only** because of his Dad Gerald... Clyde's best friend was gone. Mo was the unadulterated version of Gerald and Clyde wanted to keep that part of his best friend, safe.

Clyde took a deep breath, trying to stay calm then he continued:

"Listen to me Mo... If you wanna be a man to yo family, you do what's **best** to keep yo family together... not some **irrational** shit that might break yo family up... because that's what's gone happen if you go to jail... That **same** family you was tryina do some good fo, is gone be in an even **worse** situation because you locked up and cain't do **shit** fo-em."

Clyde paused, taking a moment to read Mo's face. Mo was paying attention. Clyde continued:

"Mo, I'm here to guide you in life so it'll be easier for you to **live** life... Them niggas who don't have no guidance are the ones who have-ah-hard time gettin they shit together. When yo son is old enough, are **you** gone let him just run off and do whatever? **Naaw,** you not... you gone do yo **best** to guide help him so his life turns out good... with as less trouble as possible, right?"

Mo Nodded his head yes then Clyde continued:

"Like I said son, I'm here to help you... but if you don't want ma help... all you have to do is let me know right now."

Clyde glared at Mo with serious sympathetic eyes and Mo glared back with a similar, if not the same look, projecting empathy. Mo postured himself up-right in the plush leather armchair then responded sincerely:

"Uncle Clyde... I don't know where I would be without you... and at this point in ma life, I'm not tryina find out... I do want yo help and guidance Uncle Clyde... it's obvious I need it, right... I'ma call Jenny as

soon as we done talkin... to see if she wanna move to the city."
Clyde responded abruptly:

"We done Mo... I think you know where I stand as far as the bullshit goes... and you know what the bullshit is... From here on out, I expect you to handled yo responsibilities like ah man. Men don't go through life fuckin-up... boys do... You-ah man now, it's time to get yo act together... I didn't invest in this studio fah ma-self, I invested in it fah **you**... to keep **you** away from the shit that get young Black Men, killed and locked up in prison fah 10, 20, and 30 muthafuckin years. This record label is **yo** responsibility. This is somethin you can bring **yo** son into, somethin **legit** that cain't **nobody** take away from you. **This** is what you need-to-be devotin yo time and effort to..."
Clyde paused for a moment then continued:

"But fah right now... I want you to devote yo time to takin care of that pregnant woman of yours. Go ahead and call Jenny.
Don't tell her about this shit you done got yo-self into. You don't wanna put no unnecessary stress on her and the baby. Just let her know, with the baby on the way, you feel y'all need to have y'alls own place."

Clyde leaned to the right, reaching towards the bottom draw of his desk. He pulled the drawer open and took out a little black, metal box. Clyde sat the little box on the desk then took an ink-pen from the apple shaped pen and pencil holder that sat on his desk. On one of those "sticky notes", he wrote down the address to the Sullivan house then slid it across the desk to Mo. Clyde flipped opened the lid on the little box and fished out the keys to the Sullivan house. He had about ten sets of keys in the box with numbers taped around them, all for different houses. He slid the keys over to Mo then closed the little box and put it back in the bottom drawer. Clyde began to speak:

"like I said Mo... I don't want you on the scene right now... Have Jenny meet you at the Sullivan house a.s.a.p. and y'all go from there... but don't go back out to Saint Ann. I don't want them police knowin where you at. I'm gone have Joe get one of his people to get-yo car out. We gone put-it-up though and get you somethin different to ride in, alright?"

"Alright Uncle Clyde... But what about the studio?"

"The studio too Mo... I know how them muthafucka's get down and I know they gone be around here tryina keep eyes on you. I cain't

stand them muthafucka's! Just chill fo-ah-while with yo Lady. You should be spendin as much time with her as possible while she pregnant. It helps that bond between y'all get stronger, you dig?"

"Yeah, I dig Uncle Clyde."

Mo sat there holding the keys to the Sullivan house, wondering what the future held for him. He braced his self on the arms of the chair, took a deep breath and stood up strong. He held his head high and straight, trying to muster a strong image. Clyde, seeing the plain display of bravado said:

"Just chill with yo Lady and don't worry about nothin... we gone get through this, alright?"

Mo looked up, let out a long breath then looked at Clyde, incredulously:

"I hope so Uncle Clyde."

Mo started towards the office door and was gone... Clyde sat there for a long moment, meditating on the situation before he called Joe.

The Traffic Stop May 1984 When Mo Got Arrested

Detectives Schlesta and Rosimono both lived in the Saint Ann area. There was a local sports bar in Saint Ann they liked frequenting. The officer from the Saint Ann police department, who pulled Mo over, was at the sports bar when Schlesta and Rosimono arrived. Officer Bradshaw was indulging in a pitcher of Budweiser, him and a few fellow officers. Most of the officers from the Saint Ann police department frequented the bar. They all were comrades who often got together to brag about their arrest and bust, or to complain about policies or procedures with-in the departments that impeded them from doing their job "effectively".

There would be grumbles concerning the pay, but for some officers, those things didn't even matter. They simply enjoyed having the authority that the badge gave them. It was their token to a special membership in society; a society with **relentless** ambitions to preserve their self-felt superiority; to protect their world from the adulterations, threatening to contaminate their white society...

Officer Bradshaw was conversing openly and making derogatory comments about the recent traffic stop he made, which led to the small drug bust and Mo's arrest:

"So this fuckin **nigger** is **always** out here right... and I'm curious, thinking to myself: "**What the fuck...** is this spook doin out here? He don't know better?" So I pull behind his car and hit the cherries and siren before he turns into the neighborhood. He stops. I walk to his car:

"What's the problem officer?" he says.
I wanted to tell him flat-out, "You're ah **nigger** and you're out-of-bounds you **muthafucka**!"
The other officers erupted into laughs as they sipped their beers, anticipating the rest of Bradshaw's story. He continued:

"So I come up with this bogus explanation as to why I stopped him:

"Sir, there's been a robbery and this vehicle matches the description of the vehicle in the robbery."
This **moron** looks at me with this **shit** face expression and beads of sweat started poppin up on his forehead. First thing I think is, "Why in the **fuck** is this moron sweatin so **hard**? Something is up."

"So he's sweatin bullets right!"

"Sir, do you have your license and registration?"
He says yes and starts reaching towards the glove compartment, I **grab** my side arm! "**Sir!** Nice and **slow**!" I says.
You should've **seen** this muthafucka's face! The **spook** was **spooked**! The other officers erupted into laughter again, Bradshaw continued:

"I'm just gettin my paperwork you asked for." he says.
I'm playing this moron like a **fine** tuned piano right. I says:

"I **understand** Sir, but you're an armed robbery suspect right now and I have to take precaution. Slow movements for me Sir."

"I run a check on-um and everything comes back clean. I go back to his car to fuck with-um some more:

"Sir... everything seems to check-out, but I have to do a routine search of the car and of your person for weapons."

"Officer, I don't **have** any weapons. I didn't **rob anybody**! My girlfriend lives out here. I'm just goin to see her. Her name is Jennifer Zalensky."

Now... my spidy senses are **really** kickin-in! I **know** he's worried about something."

Officer Bradshaw was amusing, almost comical like, with his slightly Italian like accent. His voice sounded a little like Joe Pesci. He continued:

"So I tells this fucker:

"Sir, once I conduct my search and if I find no weapons or anything from the robbery, I can let you go your way. I'm gonna need you to step out of the car Sir."

I pat-um down, no weapons. I tell-um I have to put-um in the squad car while I searched his vehicle. He just looks down at the fucking ground and shakes his head. The muthafucker **never** says another word after that. So I checks the inside of the car, still no weapons, it's clean. I goes to the trunk, **just** to make him sweat a little longer. I'm lookin and I'm lookin right? **Nothin**! but my spidy **wouldn't** let up... I un-do's the spare and **BAM! What-da-ya-know**! A small, black bag hiding under the spare. I opens this bag right?

My eyes got **wide** as the fucking **moon**! I **knew** it was coke but I never seen **that much** fucking coke before. I've busted fuckers with ah couple of grams of the shit, but **this**! This was a bag **full** of the shit! I leave the trunk open, walk to the squad car, and asked him:

"Is this yours?"

Nothin... his mouth was shut tight-as-a-clams ass. I get him back to the station right? Still, not-a-peep from-um. I book the fucker on possession of a controlled substance and gave-um a chance to make his one phone call."

All the while Officer Bradshaw had been speaking... Detectives Rosimono and Schlesta were seated close, listening with attentive ears. Bradshaw's demeanor went from being highly humorous, to extremely indignant. He began to rave-on about the situation:

"**This** muthafucker makes **one** phone call, **one phone call**! And in less than **two hours**! Some **big-wig** lawyer **strolls**-in, signs some papers... and the nigger? He's outta there **just** like that... Can you fucking **believe** that shit? Twenty-one fucking years old with a lawyer like that... I never seen nothing like it, especially with ah nigger.

From working in the narcotics division, Detectives Rosimono and Schlesta knew from experience that dealers with that type of legal pull, were major players in the drug business... not just small street level dealers. Rosimono and Schlesta were curious of **who** this twenty-one year old nigger with the "Big-wig" lawyer was.

Detective Schlesta was **especially** eager to find out so he could begin one of his secret, vigilantly missions on the so-called, "war on drugs."

The members of Schlesta's vigilante team, felt they were doing society a great service with their, self-righteous, self-approved vigilant activities. A non-bias society wouldn't be so approving though... If justice wasn't delivered in the courts the way Schlesta and his team felt in should be... then they would become the justice. The "anti-democratic" justice that said: "if the majority got it wrong... then the minority would get it right." Their small team being the minority in this case. Detective Schlesta was the senior officer in the narcotics division and the eldest of the comrades at the sports bar. He got up, took a few steps over towards Bradshaw and greeted him and the other officers:

"Hey, what's up Fellas."

The other officers cheerfully greeted Schlesta, and Schlesta with a hint of indignation in his voice to show Bradshaw that he empathized with him about the situation... he began his inquiry:

"Bradshaw, I couldn't help but hearing you talk about this guy. Is he from the city? If this fucker is doing **anything** out my way, I wanna know about... I've dealt with fuckers like that before."

Schlesta really began to show his indignation, not in the sense of being angry, but in the choice of words he used. He continued in a smooth and even tone:

"Fuckers that have these, "razzle-dazzle" lawyers, who just **walk** into the courtroom and get their scum-bag-asses off on some technicality or some complex, legal, bullshit... A lot of that shit only confuses the hell outta me. I loathe the system for its lack of lucidity and leniency to punishment... regardless of financial or political status."

Detective Schlesta was able to articulate his words so well, that even the most **liberal** of men would've followed him in his anti-Semitic, conservative agendas. Schlesta continued:

"Bradshaw... I wanna know **who** this guy is so I can keep a look out for him... just-in-case his name comes across me, I'll know who it is."

Officer Bradshaw realized the graveness in Schlesta's voice and he read it on his facial expression. Bradshaw straightened his self and became just as serious as Schlesta, then responded:

"Sure Jerry... I'm with you on that... The guys name is, Moreese Mosiah, Moore... I won't ever forget it."

Officer Bradshaw pronounced the name such repulsion, that it made him sit-up even straighter and reach for the pitcher of Budweiser to refresh his mug. He took a large gulp of the tasty suds as if he were rinsing his mouth out after tasting something foul. Schlesta responded:

"I'll keep an ear open and an eye out for the guy. Fellas... Rosi and me are gonna get outta here. I'll see you guys later alright."

The officers bided Schlesta and Rosimono adieu and Schlesta stepped back over to his table, sat a couple of dollars on the table for the server then said:

"Moreese Mosiah, Moore," as if he were speaking the numbers of a winning lottery ticket... Rosimono glared at Schlesta for a few seconds, got up then the two detectives left. The black Smokey & the Bandit Trans-Am, pulled off the lot, headed north towards I-70, carrying both detectives.

CHAPTER 5: THE INVESTIGATION

The team conducting the un-official investigation consisted of four officers: two regulars from the Saint Louis Metro Police Department, Dennis Harris and James Vincent. And two detectives from the Saint Louis Metro Narcotics Division, Jerry Schlesta and Brian Rosimono. Detective Schlesta had a good friend who worked in the county court's records office... That's where the charges on Mo had been filed. Jerry called in a favor from his long time friend, to get a copy of that file. The file included Mo's identification info, his occupation and arrest history, address and phone numbers. Everything the courts and police needed in-order to contact Mo or find him if necessary.

When Jerry received the file, he examined it carefully. Mo had no

serious arrest, only some minor infractions that weren't even court worthy. Jerry noticed that the address on Mo's driver license was the same as the address of his place of employment. A little unusual he thought. Detective Schlesta gave Rosimono the address and phone number to, *We Got Music* recording studio. Jerry asked Brian:

"Rosi, can you swing by there tomorrow and check it out... see if it looks like a legit business or if it's just a front."

Jerry also seen on the file, that Mo was scheduled to be in court that following day... Mo had been arrested, Thursday morning; the charges were filed Friday morning; Jerry and Brian found out about Mo, Saturday evening; Jerry got the file Monday afternoon and Mo was to be in court, Tuesday morning... Jerry wanted to be there. He wanted to see just **who** this "Big-wig" lawyer was; the file for some reason didn't contain his name. He wanted to see who else would come to court with Mo, to try to get an ideal of who Mo was affiliated with.

Tuesday Morning Surprise

Detective Schlesta got to the courthouse twenty minutes early just to be safe. It was 8:40 and Mo was due there at 9am. Jerry sat in the back row of the courtroom. His briefcase was open sitting on his lap and he was patiently going over the file on Mo, for the second time, studying Mo's photo studiously...

"ALL RISE!" said the bailiff.

His voice boomed through the courtroom catching Jerry off guard, startling him just a bit. He sat his briefcase to the side and stood. The bailiff continued:

"The Honorable Judge Maurah Mcshane presiding."

Jugde Mcshane was tall and slender, in her mid thirties, the youngest of the judges in the county circuit-court house. The judge took the bench and the bailiff finished:

"You all may be seated, court is now in session."

Nine o-clock had come around quick and while standing, it had just dawned on Jerry that Mo hadn't come into the courtroom yet... He sat down wondering then, Judge Mcshane began her announcement:

"Good morning ladies and gentlemen... This is the 10th day of

May 1984 and you all are in division 36, arraignment court... Please check your paperwork to make sure you are in the right court and at the right time... I would hate for you to miss your actual court-date and get a warrant for your arrest because you were in the wrong court-room."

Judge Mcshane spoke with a commading voice and she pierced the court audience with her dark green eyes as she spoke. She drew everyone to be attentive to the priority; checking their paperwork. After the formalities were over and court had officially begun, Jerry excused his self. He went to check the main court docket, just to make sure he wasn't mistaken about the date that Mo was supposed to be in court. He got to the clerk's office and stood at the counter. A short, plump, African American woman emerged from her desk and strolled over to the counter:

"How can I help you Sir?"

The woman had a nametag on, which Jerry noticed. He responded:

"Good morning Ms. Thomas. I'm Detective Schlesta." said Jerry while extracting his badge from his blazer pocket to show Ms.Thomas. He continued:

"Can you check your main docket for me to see if there's a, Moreese Moore, scheduled to appear in court today, in division 36. I think I might have the wrong date."

Ms. Thomas glanced at Jerry's badge for a quick second but it was not necessary for him to show it. The docket was a public record; **anyone** could have asked to check a name on the docket. Ms. Thomas responded:

"Sure Detective. Give me ah-minute and I'll be right back."

The little plump, woman smiled then walked around a corner of the office into another room. Jerry glanced at his watch, it read 9:07. He wondered if Mo had showed up yet. Ms. Thomas returned with a list of "case-causes" to be heard in court. She sat it down on the counter for Jerry to have a look as well.

"Detective... it looks like the person you're inquiring about, **was** scheduled for court today, but this is the old docket... here's the new one ... and it seems... Mr. Moore has been taken off."

The two looked at the dockets together wondering what was the reason for Moreese Moore's name being taken off the docket.

Jerry's facial expression showed confusion and a tiny hint of frustration. Ms. Thomas caught his eyes and saw they were searching for an answer, she commented:

"Detective, I can check our database to see if there's been another court-date scheduled for Mr. Moore."

Jerry looked up from the dockets appreciatively then said:

"Thank you Ms. Thomas. That would be great."

Ms. Thomas was off again. This time, back to her desk. She clicked away at her keyboard, entering Mo's case number into the computer: 2041-84052. After she hit the enter key, a message popped up on her screen in red letters that read:

[Effective: 5-9-1984. This case has been, WITHDRAWN.]

There was no reason or explanation attached with the message, just WITHDRAWN.

Ms. Thomas was a little surprised but it wasn't unusual. She was familiar with the message, but it was rare for it to show up. Ms. Thomas wanted to help Jerry, but there was nothing more she could do. She looked up from her computer disappointedly and called Jerry's name:

"Detective Schlesta?"

Jerry was standing next to a bulletin board. It had postings of wanted criminals, hotline numbers and leaflets to programs for addicts; numbers for troubled teens and abused women... but the one that stood out the most... the number that captured his attention so much to where he hadn't heard the clerk call his name... was the one that read:

[PLEASE CALL THE INTERNAL AFFAIRS HOT LINE TO REPORT ANY SUSPICIONS OR PROOFS OF POLICE CORRUPTION...]

Ms. Thomas called his name again, this time with her voice slightly elevated:

"Detective!"

Jerry turned around abruptly, looking at Ms. Thomas then responded:

"Ooh... I'm sorry Ms. Thomas. I got caught-up looking at the wanted postings. Did you find anything?"

Ms. Thomas smiled at Jerry's dedication to his job, but his dedication to uphold the law righteously, was feigned... Jerry was dedicated to his **own** cause and **his** cause only... Ms. Thomas would never know that... no one would, at least not now anyway. She responded:

"Unfortunately not Detective... The case has been withdrawn

from our court."

Jerry's face contorted and he responded:

"**Withdrawn!**"

"Yes Detective... withdrawn. There could be several reasons behind that... The two that I know of are: the Feds could have picked up the case or his lawyer got the judge to grant them a continuance with an open date. That's all I can give you. My computer won't let me access that information. It's very unusual, but like I said... it could be other things."

Jerry was stupefied. He didn't know whether to leave or go back into the courtroom. He shook the confused look from his face and responded:

"Well thank you for your time Ms. Thomas."

"Sorry I couldn't help you." said Ms. Thomas.

"Oh, no need to be sorry. You were plenty of help. You have a good day Ms. Thomas." Then Jerry left the Clerk's office.

Rosimono's Surveillance

Detective Rosimono drove by the studio and decided he would park so he could scope things out for a-bit. From the outside of the place, it looked really nice thought Rosimono. Clyde had done an impeccable job of renovating the place, doing most of the work his self; the outside was beautiful! Clyde had seen to it that the studio was equipped with top-of-the line recording equipment... He made sure that the studio provided **any** artist, beginner or professional, with the comfortableness they needed while working at his studio. There was a sound room for live bands to perform; a custom engineering station, a plush lounge area for on-lookers to watch artist record and view bands recording live. The mics, the soundboard, the synthesizers, the reel-to-reels, the D.A.T. machine; **everything** was of high quality, professional grade.

Rosimono was a little surprised to see actual bands, hop out of their vehicles with instruments and go inside. He really thought the place might be a front for drug deals but the longer he sat, the more that assumption proved to be wrong. He continued to take down license plate numbers of those who parked and entered the studio. A van pulled up and a group of white guys wearing tie-dye shirts and weird hats got out. They passed around a joint, each took a couple of hits then, the last toker put it out. There was no smoking allowed in the studio, one of Clyde's **strict** rules. After that, they entered the building to begin one of their recording sessions...

The place seemed to be legitimate, but Rosimono wanted to get inside to see what was really happening. He cranked the engine of his black, 1977, Pontiac Trans Am and pulled off, heading towards Delmar Boulevard. Rosimono stopped at a Shell gas station to use the pay phone. He dialed the number that Schlesta had given him; the phone rang at the studio. It was a little before 12 and the day time receptionist was on duty. She answered the phone:

"Good afternoon. You've reached *We Got Music* recording studio, this is Rene speaking. How can I help?"
The voice on the line was soft, cheerful and subtly inviting. It caught Detective Rosimono completely off guard. He was stuck; bewitched by the enchanting tone of Rene's smooth pleasant voice, and her Spanish accent. Rene occupied the desk from 9am to 1pm then Keisha showed up to take over. Both girls were enrolled in school part-time, taking up business and marketing, morning classes for Keisha and afternoon classes for Rene.

Rene was Spanish and European, very attractive. She met Keisha at school when she was attending the morning classes and they became good friends. One day, Rene mentioned her financial situation to Keisha, telling her that 'it wasn't looking too good and she really needed a job.' Keisha told Rene about her Uncle Clyde's recording studio and the need for another receptionist/secretary for part-time. The opportunity couldn't have come at a more needed time. The only thing Rene had to do was switch her morning classes to afternoon and she was good to go.

Rene **loved** music, and she was excited to be able to work in a recording studio. Her enthusiasm always showed, each day she came to work. On the days when they had no classes, Keisha and Rene would work at the studio together. They brought a brightness and lots of positive energy to the studio; the kind of brightness and energy that only good women could bring...

Detective Rosimono shook his head a little, trying to snap out of the trance he was in then he responded:

"Aah, yes! Good afternoon. I mean, good morning."

Rosimono was still searching for the words to say. He thought it would be a piece of cake but realized that he didn't know **anything** about the music business and neither did he speak the lingo. He wished he had spoken to Van first. Van was a guitar player/ police officer. He was part of a band that practiced in Van's garage... **DING!** The light bulb went off in Rosimono's head and he had an ideal:

"Yeah umm... I have a band and I wanted to know, how would we go about recording at your studio and what the cost would be? We've been practicing in the garage."

Rene responded:

"Hey, there's nothing wrong with that. Some of the best music is made in the garage."

Rene's words would've been encouraging to the person really practicing in the garage, however. They were almost as inspirational in motivating Rosimono to really become part of the band. The thought stroked his mind passively but he bumped it out and got back to reality. Rene continued:

"Right now, our schedule is booked up for this week. But if you would like to, you can come by and check out our studio first... Just to see if we're equipped to accommodate your band. And if so, we can discuss a booking schedule and cost."

Rosimono couldn't understand it... The allure of Rene's voice! He was fascinated with it! Was it her accent? Whatever it was, Rosi couldn't shake it. He responded:

"Uum yeah... that'll be great."

Rene responded cheerfully:

"Ok then! Just make sure you call first so someone will be expecting you and be available to show you around the studio... Sir, I didn't get your name or the name of your band?"

Without hesitation, Rosimono blurted out his first name and the name of the band:

"Brian... my mane is Brian. The name of the band is, *Vans Band.*"

Rene responded:

"Well Mr. Brian. I hope to meet you and your band soon.
You have a good day."

"You too Ms. Rene" and the two hung up their phones.

Speaking with Rene had assured Brian that the place was indeed legit. From the sound of things, everything seemed business like, with no hints of shadiness. He wanted to leave his objective right there at the pay phone. The premise he felt after his chat with Rene, was filled with honesty. For whatever reason, Detective Rosimono was becoming more in-tuned with his internal sensory. Detective work was based on, lots of "search and find" tactics... But what to look for and where to look... It all started with the good senses of the detective doing the looking. In this renegade mission, Brian's senses were telling him, they were looking in the wrong place.

As he walked back to his Smokey & the Bandit TA, he thought about what he would report to Schlesta... unofficially of course, because it wasn't an assigned case. He leaned against the car with his arms resting on the T-tops, staring blankly at the passing traffic on Delmar Boulevard. Just as Detective Rosimono was about to get in his car, a passing vehicle caught his attention... well, not so much the vehicle but the license plate on it. The plate read: [WE GOT] and in the place of music, there was a clef symbol ♪, symbolizing the word music... He couldn't see who was driving the Jaguar because of the tinted windows. Brian thought, "It might just be this Moreese guy we're looking for." He wondered who it was and decided to trail the car. He got in his T.A. and pulled into traffic. He followed the Jaguar in the same direction that he had just came from.

Keisha was on her way to the studio, enjoying the music that was on the radio. Curtis Mayfield's, *"Diamond In The Back"*, was playing. She **loved** to listen to old-school music. It made her feel good. If she was in a bad mood, all she had to do was turn on some Al Green, Curtis Mayfield or Marvin Gaye, and she would be cool after that; those were three of her favorite artist.

Keisha pulled up in front of the building, opting to park in the front, instead of in the back, on their private lot. Detective Rosimono drove pass, observing her and continued down the street, making a left at the stop sign. He immediately came back around and parked in an inconspicuous spot. Keisha reached in the back seat, grabbed her book bag then exited the Jaguar. She pressed the button on the remote device, arming the alarm, locking the car then entered the studio.

"**Hey** Keisha!" said Rene cheerfully, always glad to see her friend. Rene continued:

"How was class today?"

"Hey Rene... class was business as usual girl. You in for a treat this afternoon... We have to pick a field of business, make a mock company, and put together a marketing plan for it... I already know what you gonna pick..."

Both girls simultaneously threw their hands in the air and said:

"**Music!**" Keisha continued:

"It's a, week and a-half long project, and it counts as 30% of our semester grade."

Rene let Keisha know what was going on at the studio:

"*Fools Crush* is in session right now and there's a guy name Brian, who's suppose to call back and schedule a tour of the studio. *Vans Band* is the name of his group."

Rene had left off with that, gazing at Keisha dubiously, showing that she had no answer for the questioning expression on Keisha's face. Keisha erased her questioning expression and came to a thought of clarity then said:

"Hey... maybe it's a band for a Van Club. You know how popular those things are right now."

Rene nodded in agreement and responded:

"Yeah... you're probably right. I gotta go girl... call me when you get home so we can share some ideals on this project."

"I will... talk to you later girl." said Keisha.

It was time for Rene to leave so she could start the second part of her day. Rene's car was parked in the back of the studio, on the private lot. She left through a side door of the studio that led to a hallway, which led to the rear door of the building. You could also gain access to the second and third floor of the building from the hallway. Rene opened the heavy metal door and stepped out into the brilliance of the afternoon Sun.

Brian had chosen a different surveillance viewpoint from the previous one. He could now see the front entrance of the studio and the rear access alleyway of the building that was adjacent to the street. He scribbled on his note pad, writing down the plate number of the Jaguar and the description of who was driving it. As Rosimono looked up from his notes, he noticed a light brown Chevette coming from the access alleyway. The girl driving appeared to be in her late teens or early twenties with Spanish features. He wrote down a brief description of the girl driving and the plate number so he could run an owner's registration check on it. His stomach began to turn and twist... an anxious feeling came over him. Brian was wondering if the girl driving was the girl, he had spoken to on the phone. "Is that Rene?" he thought. He would find out soon enough... Suddenly! Another thought overtook Brian's previous one. All the while he had been there... he hadn't noticed **any** black guys... not one. He opted to end his surveillance and head back to HQ to do some follow-up work on the plate numbers... plus he had to talk to Van about going to check out the studio.

The registration information came back on the plates. The light blue Jaguar belonged to a: Sidney Clyde, Pulliam. The light brown Chevette belonged to a: Maria Rene, Vasquez. The other vehicles that carried the bands, Brian wasn't really concerned with. Detective Schlesta and Rosimono were conversing about the informal investigation... trying to map out a plan to find out just who-in-the-hell was behind this eighth of kilo of cocaine. It wasn't a **huge** amount, but Schlesta was looking to score big with the "little fish big fish" method... He anticipated it. Detective Rosimono on the other hand... was just going along with the flow of things. Schlesta commented on Brian's idea:

"Good thinking on bringing Van's band in so we can get inside. You gotta put the spin on Van though... He can't know anything about why we want in there", said Jerry, calling his self, schooling Brian.

Van Smith was a rookie officer who was oblivious to the special renegade squad that Schlesta ran. Using Van was the best way to infiltrate the studio but Brian was almost sorry that he had come up with the idea. Jerry continued:

"You've heard his band play before, right?"
Brian nodded yes, Jerry continued:

"Let Van know, you think his band is great, and they should really consider recording an album... Tell-um... you found the perfect place for them to record. I'll put Harris and Vincent on surveillance and keep trying to locate our mystery guy, Moreese. Try to get that band booked-in a.s.a.p. We need to make this thing happen quick, and remember... once you get inside, don't even ask about Moreese. If someone asks you, how do you know him... it'll be hard to explain it... let them volunteer any info. You know what he looks like so when you meet-um, stay interested in the music, not the mission... this guy is young so he might open up to you."

Brian was young as well. He came into the force from the academy at age twenty-one and was now five years in. After a few years in, he felt as if he had made a mistake joining the narcotics division and Jerry's "special-squad." He wanted to clean up the streets but not in the way Jerry wanted to. The "code of the cop" had been driven into Brian, by other officers who were apart of the "special-squads" and who had the same mind-set as Detective Schlesta. Brian never really accepted it... He only dealt with it... never fully adapting to the "code of the cop."

Secretly, Detective Rosimono harbored a small resentment towards the renegade team that he was a-part of... he probably wouldn't have felt that way if they went after **all** ethnic groups, instead of just the African Americans. Rosimono knew from watching criminal and drug war documentaries that, Black Americans were not the high man on the totem pole... They were near the bottom. Jerry felt contrary to that though. Brian's views were his own views... views that **none** of the other officers, except for Van, would ever know about. Brian, using some of Detective Schlesta's ideology... tried to convince his self... that they were still cleaning up the streets no matter **how** it was being done. Deep down though, his conscience was slowly eating away at him. Jerry had finished "schooling" Brian, though Brian needed none. Brian responded:

"I'll talk to Van this evening... I'm going over to the Loop to listen to some live bands play and he's gonna be there. I know he'll be cool with it though. He's always talking about it... I'll keep you posted Jerry."

Rosimono got up to leave for the day and Jerry called him back:

"Hey Rosi!"

Brian turned around to face Jerry then responded:

"Yeah Jerry?"

Brian had been unusually distant during their conversation, as if his thoughts where somewhere else and not present. Schlesta picked up on it. Schlesta continued:

"You ok Son? You look a little spaced-out there... something on your mind?"

Brian thought about confiding in Jerry... letting Jerry know how he really felt would've taken a lot of weight off his shoulders... But who knows. "It might just add more weight" thought Brian. He didn't wanna risk it so he decided against it. If he said any such thing, that was contrary to Jerry's views... Jerry would have look at him as a threat and no longer trustworthy. Brian's presumptions, reasoned that time would alleviate the weight he was bearing... he would just have to bear it for now... He opted to tell Jerry something else:

"I'm ok Jerry... women troubles... you know how it is." said Brian, mustering a half smile, trying to convince Jerry that he was having woman problems.

Brian could see that Jerry had accepted it as the truth so Brian turned to leave. In the light of the matter, Brian **was** having woman problems. He could not get Rene off his mind! The image of her was **engraved** in his brain and he had only caught a brief glimpse of her... that voice... her words.

"Well Mr. Brian. I hope to meet you and your band soon."

He felt Rene's words were an invitation and they played repeatedly in his mind. He tried to shake her voice from his mind but his efforts were ineffective... The truth of the matter was that Detective Rosimono was lonely.

Brian was divorced from his high school sweetheart. He married her fresh out of high school. When they went off to college, she grew apart from him, even though they attended the same college. Their communication with each other dwindled like the flame of a burning candle when its wick was at its end. Brian's young wife, Rachel... had become more involved with her sorority sister and less involved with him. He developed a deep resentment towards the cult like sorority that she had become a-part of... However, his resentment was probably **more** than resentment... it may have been flat out hatred. Whatever it was, it led to Brian's verbally violent venting, and

Rachel's, raging rebellious rebuttals.

Rachel became intimately involved with one of the sorority sisters and the two made it **vividly** clear, that they were lovers. They ostentatiously flaunted their abominable adultery at a gay pride march. Brian was **devastated** by the discovery of their licentiousness when he turned on the news and seen the gay pride march being televised live. He witnessed **his wife...** involved in a lewd act and was embarrassed, hurt, and humiliated by the whole ordeal. They were never able to reconcile and he filed for divorce... After the divorce was final, he never heard from Rachel again.

Trust and loyalty issues became the main reasons why Brian found it difficult to become too emotionally involved with a woman. He had been a single man since his divorce. It was hard for him to see honesty in **any** woman anymore... even if she was wearing a nun's uniform. He had felt that way for **years;** until today when he spoke to Rene. It was **truly** amazing to Brian! Because he could actually **hear** the honesty in Rene's voice, and he didn't even know who she **was!** He just knew he had to meet her.

CHAPTER 6: THE DELMAR LOOP

Brian got off work at five and went straight home to take a nap. The day had worn him down for some reason. No physical activity had taken place... his mind was just fatigued. He felt mentally drained. Today, he thought of his past, his present, his future... however dubious it might have seem.

When Brian awakened, it was 7:15 in the evening. He laid there in bed, not wanting to get up at all, but he told Van that he would be there to hear the band play, and he didn't wanna disappoint his closes and probably only **true** friend. Brian got to his feet, stretching hard and yawning big. He was running about fifteen minutes behind schedule. The bands started playing at seven, but it was cool... he could be fashionably late. He took a quick wash-up, gargled with some mouthwash, splashed on a little of his favorite cologne, *Santa*

*Fe, a*nd threw on a fresh set of clothes then he was ready to go.

The Delmar Loop was made-up of shops. Music shops, music lounges, coffee shops, bake shops, smoke shops, small bars, restaurants and boutiques. All **kinds** of festive things were going on in the Loop. It was a place for people to get away from the hustle-and-bustle and just chill out. It mainly attracted college students and tourist but the locals enjoyed the Loop just as well.

Calicos, was the name of the place where Brian was meeting with Van. It was at the end of the Delmar strip. *Calicos,* a nice spot, bar/restaurant/lounge... it had it all. There were three electronic dart games against the wall, just before the back entrance. Three pool tables sat on the sunken floor, almost in the center of the place. In the same area, in the corner, there was a raised staged to accommodate the performers for whatever night it happened to be: open mic night; karaoke night... but tonight... it was live band night. Brian arrived at *Calicos* at about 7:40 that evening. He parked on the lot at the rear of the building. It was the main parking lot for several other businesses as well.

He walked down the long, narrow hallway from the rear entrance that led right to the sunken floor... From where he stood, he could see the stage and the bar was to his right. Van and another member from the band were seated at the bar on bar stools. Van spotted Brian right away and called out to him:

"**Hey Brian**!" said Van, putting his arm up, signaling to Brian. Brian strolled over and Van continued:

"Hey man! You made it! The first band just finished its set. I'm glad you could make it man. I thought you were gonna be M. I. A. for a-minute there."

Van was smiling at the other band member and at Brian.

Brian responded:

"I almost **was** M.I.A. My short nap turned into **two** hours! As bad as I wanted to stay in bed sleep, I told myself, I had to get up to come see you guys play. I wouldn't miss a chance to listen to you guys play for nothin... You guys are great!" said Brian with genuine sincerity and excitement. The place was loud but they were still able to hear one another just fine. Van looked at Brian with astonishment... It was Vans first time hearing Brian speak so admirably about the band. Van responded:

"Wow Man! That means a-lot coming from you! Most people think this is just a hobby for me but it's not... this is what I **really** wanna do, you know man? I know we're no *Arrow Smith* or *Black Sabbath*... but even those guys were where we're at, as far as getting started."

Van paused for a moment then continued:

"Man... I feel we can really make it in this music business and so do the other guys... All we need to do is play at the right place at the right time and in front of the right people... You never know who's connected to who you know... Somebody could really open up a doors for us."

Van called the bartender over:

"Cindy!" and a beautiful young brunet, delightful to look at, appeared.

Cindy's was Egyptian and her complexion accentuated her dark hair and her beautiful dark brown eyes. She stood at 5'8", the perfect height in which to greet her customers. She responded to Van's call:

"What can I do for you Van?"

Van reached for Brian, putting his hand a-top Brian's shoulder then said:

"Get my good friend, Brian here, whatever he wants to drink, and I'll have another Bud Light."

Brian glanced at Van then looked to the beautiful bartender and said:

"Make it **two** Bud Lights please."

"Two Bud Lights, coming up." said Cindy and whisked over to the beer cooler.

Van and Brian were both checking Cindy out as she walked away. She had a **flawless** figure and could have easily put one of those belly dancers to shame. Cindy could have had a long lucrative career in the modeling business if she wanted to. She had several offers but chose not to. Even though she was very attractive and had a beautiful figure, she didn't like to flaunt it. She was a very down to earth girl who loved the laid-back social life... not the fake-ass Hollywood people and overrated glitz and glimmer of the modeling world. She was majoring in psychology and her minor was sociology, so her bartending job was befitting of her academic interest... She had the opportunity to mingle with all sorts of people. Cindy was back with the two Bud Lights.

"Here you go fellas, two Bud Lights."

She sat the two bottles down on the counter and pulled a bottle opener from the pouch on her bartender's apron then opened the bottles in front on the fellas. She had a thing about bringing people open bottles, something she just didn't do... it was part of her bartender's etiquette. She collected the four dollars that were on the counter, two dollars for the beers and two dollars for her tip. She held the two dollars up, looked at Van and Brian then said:

"Thanks fellas." then Brian said jokingly while smiling:

"For your extra hard work..."

Cindy smiled and shook the dollars at Brian then walked over to her tip jar that sat on the glass shelves. The glass shelves were lined with all types of liquors! When Cindy was out of their sight, Van swiveled his bar stool in Brian's direction and said:

"**Man**! She's **so** hot!"

Brian took a sip of his Bud Light then nodded in agreement with Van. Trying not to show **too** much interest in the Egyptian Enchantress, Brian swallowed his sip then said:

"Yeah, she is Van... you thinking about trying your luck with her?"

With a puzzled expression on his face, Van looked at Brian then said:

"Naah... she's probably got some strict ethnics on who she dates and I probably don't fit that profile."

Van actually did wanna try his luck with Cindy but his confidence wasn't quite there. Brian responded:

"You'll never know if you don't ask her Man... how long has she been here?"

"About two or three month's now." said Van.

"And how long have you been coming down here?"

"For about a year now."

"A **whole** year?" Brian exclaimed.

"Yep... A whole year." said Van.

"So everybody who works here, knows who you are right?"

"Yep." said Van.

Van didn't know where Brian was going with this, but he continued to follow and answer the questions.

"Van, what I'm trying to tell you is... that **anybody** here can tell her what a great guy you are. You just have to let her know you're interested in her... and trust me... she's gonna ask one of her co-workers about you if she's interested too... just go for it Man... Like I said... you'll never know until you try."

Van let Brian's words digest in his mind then he responded:

"Yeah... I guess you're right man... I might say something to her later on when she goes on break... what can it hurt, right?"

Brian responded:

"Right..."

Brian took hold of Vans shoulder and gave it a little shake then continued:

"Come on... let's get down there with the rest of the guys."

Brian and Van grabbed their beers and headed towards the lounge area. Brian put his arm across the top of Van's shoulders and said:

"I got something I wanna run by you after you guys finish with your set... just an idea I have for the band."

The wheels in Van's mind were already spinning. He wondered what Brian wanted to run by him. Van knew if he didn't find out what this "idea" was right away... his mind would be preoccupied the entire set. Van didn't like performing if his mind was focused on something else. He commented:

"Brian, man, you know I'm not gonna be able to focus on my music if you don't tell me what's on your mind before I go on stage. We still have about ten minutes before we hit the stage... will it take long?"

"Naah... it won't take long at all Van... let's go over to the booth." Brian presented his idea to Van about the studio and of course... Van loved it! He was all for it. To record professionally was what he had wanted to do for a long time now. Van knew his band was ready. His only concern was the cost, but Brian told him:

"Don't worry about any of that... just get in there and record the best music you possibly can."

Brian told Van, it was like an investment. He could see the excitement in Vans eyes and all the images of success in the music industry starting to formulate. Van was about to go tell the rest of the band but Brian stopped him:

"**Hold-on** Van... We still have to go by the studio to talk with the people about a few things first. Their schedule is booked solid right now. I'm supposed to call back to schedule a view of the studio but I wanted to talk to you first. So... whenever you're ready, just let me know man, and we can get this thing rollin!"

Van was eager to get things started. He responded:

"How about tomorrow after work?"

Brian nodded his head in agreement then responded:

"Sounds cool man... I'll make the call to the studio tomorrow morning and let them know we'll be there around 5:30."

All of the bands equipment had been set-up and it was time for *Vans Band* to hit the stage. A grill-cook at *Calicos,* who was doubling as an announcer for the night, stepped onto the stage, still wearing his cook's hat... The short plump grill-cook, took hold of the mic as if it were **him** that was about to perform his latest hit:

"*Don't Burn Me In The Kitchen*" ☺ With his best nightclub host voice, he began smoothly:

"**Once again**... Good evening Ladies and Gentlemen... I hope you enjoyed our first band for tonight... but without further adieu... please give a **hearty welcome**... to our next band performing tonight... *Vans Band*!"

The small crowd erupted into whistles, cheers and applause. A lot of the audience knew who *Vans Band* was already and they loved hearing the band play... The electric guitar that Van was holding sounded the first note, opening the chords of their latest song. The serene melody from the guitar captivated the audience's attention instantly... The name of the song was called "New Star." Cindy was Van's inspiration behind the song. He had written it for her but never told her or anyone where the inspiration for the song came from. Van had only hoped that Cindy would recognize, that he was singing about her when they played. The crowd grew quiet, letting the velvety smooth melody of music soothe them. That's the feeling Van wanted people to get from the song... the feeling of soothing love.

Wednesday Evening At The Studio:

Van was **so** eager to get to the studio that evening, he was gonna wear his police uniform, but Brian told him:

"Van... the studio isn't going anywhere man... you have time to change."

The bell-chime sounded in the receptionist area of the studio... it indicating that someone entered the lobby. It was after 5:30 pm and Keisha was expecting her potential client's arrival. There were four chairs in the small lobby, two on each side. The walls were lined with promotional posters, of some of the hottest artist and bands in the music world... as well as local artist. There was a small security camera in the top right corner, covering the lobby area. A soft pleasant voice, sounded through an intercom system mounted next to another door, inside the lobby.

"How can I help you Gentlemen?"

Brian was looking at a promo posters then turned towards the voice. Van was already at the intercom responding:

"Ummh, yes... we're here to view the studio... we're *Vans Band*."

"Come right in Gentlemen." said Keisha, pressing the button to unlock the door.

The buzzer sounded on the heavy wooden door. Van opened it then he and Brian stepped through into the reception area of the studio. The two didn't know what to expect going in, but from the expression on their faces... Keisha could discern with ease that they were impressed with what they saw... Her uncle Clyde was a music connoisseur/collector, and what better place to display his collection and connoisseurship then his own show-case... the studio.

The reception area was comfortable... the walls were love-red with beige crown moldings and bottom borders. A different instrument hung picturesquely on the middle of each wall, just above each wall's middle point. Clyde's music collection was decoratively and strategically assembled around the instruments. Some of the greatest trumpet players' albums were situated around the trumpet; the greatest guitar players' albums were on the wall with the replica of B.B. King's guitar, "Lucille." And on the wall behind where Keisha's desk sat, there was a variety of albums... Albums of some of the world's greatest vocalist were situated neatly around five gold microphones.

The fourth wall... well actually, it was the archway, that led to a hallway. And from that hallway, you could access the recording areas, and the restrooms were just across the hall. If you continued down the hallway, you would run into a T. To the left was a small kitchenette and to the right, was another door that led to the access hallway for the rear exit and the rest of the building. At the end of the T, directly in the middle, was Clyde's office door... At the top of that archway in the reception area, there was a snare drum with a pair of drumsticks on it. On the sides of it, were albums that contained some of the best drum solos ever recorded.

The floor was carpeted with a beige durable office carpet, the same color as the crown molding and borders. The room created an optical contrast that brought forth palatable agreement to the eyes and mind. Keisha let Brian and Van take in all of the décor then with a light hint of enthusiasm, she greeted them:

"Good evening Gentlemen. My name is Keisha Pulliam. I'm one of the managers here at the studio. Welcome to *We Got Music* recording studio."

Brian and Van both returned the greeting and introduced themselves, Van going first:

"Thank you Ms. Pulliam. Glad to meet you. I'm Van Smith."

Van extended his hand to shake Keisha's. Brian followed suit:

"Brian Rosimono. It's a pleasure to meet you Ms. Pulliam."

Then, the tour of the studio began.

There was a session going on and Keisha allowed Brian and Van to sit-in just to observe things. She explained to them, that in-order for things to run smoothly, the audio engineer had to know what he was doing. Keisha spoke:

"We have an in-house engineer available if you guys need one... but if you guys have someone who knows the equipment and how to operate it, you're welcome to use your own engineer... We **do** have a liability contract that has to be signed if you guys use your own engineer... it covers the equipment."

Keisha continued to go over the studio policies and rules, answering Van's question whenever he had one. Brian really didn't have any.

It was 7: pm, almost an hour and a half into their meeting and not even seeming like it. There was a question burning in Brian's mind... he wanted to ask about Moreese but he remembered what Jerry told him, "Don't ask about Moreese."

Brian doused the burning of trying to figure out if Moreese was an actual component in this music mix or not. He asked clandestinely:

"Ms. Pulliam, who would we be working with if we were to need an engineer?" Keisha answered:

"Moreese is our in-house engineer. He has a bachelor's degree in audio engineering and a bachelor's degree in music production... He does a great job at mixing and master recordings. He's not here right now, but if you guys decide to record here and use him... you'll meet him soon enough."

Keisha hadn't known of the conversation, Clyde and Mo had last Thursday, about staying away for awhile. She spoke as though everything was still as it was, before Mo's arrest. Even still, regardless of how irresponsible Mo could be at times, Keisha spoke highly of him when it came to his skills in the studio. Mo really knew what he was doing... probably more-so than the so-called pros did. Brian and Van had seen the entire studio and they **loved it**! Especially Van... Keisha spoke:

"Well Gentlemen... this concludes our tour of the studio. All there is to do now, that's if you guys decide to record with us... is get you guys booked into a schedule."
Brian responded:

"Ms. Pulliam... we'd like to record here... we'll need an engineer as well."
Van glared at Brian confusingly because Brian knew the band had a sound-guy already. Van spoke:

"Brian... we have a sound guy already... you know, Tom, our keyboard player?"

"Yeah, I know Van... but we need an engineer who knows his way around the studio... and what better person than Moreese, the in-house guy. We want the best quality sound we can get, Van." said Brian, grabbing Van's shoulder and giving it a little squeeze.

"Yeah... I guess you're right man. The in-house guy can probably show Tom a-thing-or-two."
Keisha watched gleefully as the two came to an agreement then she commented:

"Gentlemen... tomorrow is Thursday and our formalities are not handled on Thursdays or Fridays, however. Saturday we'll have both managers here and we can go over everything else then, with either me or Rene."
Bells started ringing softly in Brian's head at the mention of Rene's

name. Keisha continued:

"So all you guys have to do is... show up here Saturday, anywhere from 10am to 4pm; bring a five hundred dollar money order made out to the studio; that secures, 4, four hour recording sessions, for your band... and you don't have to use all of the hours in one session. Whatever hours or minutes you have left will just go towards the next session. The five hundred dollars also assures us, that you guys will keep the schedule you book. The schedule is flexible though, so if something comes up and you guys can't make it... we can work with you."

Keisha was now standing by her desk, indicating to Van and Brian that their meeting had come to an end. She took two of her business cards from the crystal cardholder and an ink-pen from the matching ink-pen holder. She wrote on the back of one of the cards: Saturday, 10am to 4pm and five hundred dollar money order. She gave that one to Van and the other to Brian. Van extended his hand to shake Keisha's once again then said:

"Ms. Pulliam... this has been a **true** delight. The place is amazing. We'll be seeing you Saturday."

"Thank you Mr. Smith. I'm glad you like it."

Brian extended his hand as well, shaking Keisha's hand, biding her, the rest of a good evening:

"Thank you for showing us around Ms. Pulliam. You have a good evening."

"You two have a good evening as well Gentlemen", said Keisha then the two men turned, exiting the reception area, into the lobby and out of the door to outside.

The Trans Am's engine cranked and Brian pulled away from the building.

"So Van... what-do-you-think?"

Van responded with excitement still in his voice:

"The place is fucking **amazing!** The guys are gonna **love it!** How did you find the place?"

Brian drove down Lindell Boulevard, towards Grand Avenue with his mind blank of any answer for Van's question. The light turned yellow and Brian began slowing the car down to a full stop... The light turned red. It gave Brian a moment to come up with something to satisfy Van's question:

"I uuh... I was over in the area and saw these guys taking their equipment in the building... it made me think about you guys... So I took down the number on the place, call-um, asked them a-few questions and **here we are**... Cool right?"

"**Damn right**, it's cool! From the looks of the place, it looks like they might have some major connections in the industry. **Man,** I'm so excited..."

The light changed and they were on the move again. Van lived on the south side of Saint Louis... that's where they were headed. Van did most of the talking... Brian listened with his attention blinking in-and-out on Van's words, and staring distantly at the road as if it were a long stretch of desert highway... He passed up Van's street and Van had to call Brian's name to get his attention:

"Hey Brian!" Brian snapped back to focus. Van continued:

"Hey man, you passed up my street... you were zoned-out man."
Brian responded:

"My mind is just on so many things right now... I'm wondering about the possibilities for you guys... this could be big you know?"

Brian wasn't being one hundred percent truthful with Van. At the time when Brian was zoning-out... he'd been totally void of any thoughts. He pulled the car over and when the traffic was clear, he made a u-turn, heading back towards Meramac, the street he passed up. The T.A. made a right at the light on Meramac and went down about a block, stopping in front of Van's house. Van looked at his house then at Brian and said:

"Hey man... I really appreciate you for this... you know with the kids and all... and me being a single dad... it's hard to save any real money, you know."

Brian looked out the window of the T.A. at the little toys in the front yard and responded:

"Hey Man, don't even sweat it... like I said before... this is like an investment for me. I'm hoping you guys make it. When you guys start selling all those records and making **millions**, you can give me ten percent."

Both of them shared a short friendly laugh then Van opened the door and exited the T.A.... Before he closed it though, he leaned into the car then said:

"You got it man... ten percent is yours... I'll see you tomorrow.

You're a good dude Brian... we won't let you down Bro."

Van closed the door and stepped back from the car. Brian felt his conscience kicking in, but all he could say was:

"Thanks Van... I know you guys are gonna make one hell-of-a album."

Van nodded and casually saluted Brian then Brian drove off... Van stood there for a moment, watching the black T.A. as it disappeared into the darkening evening.

Police Head-Quarters

"Vincent! Harris! In my office..."

It was Thursday morning and Detective Schlesta called the Officers into his office to debrief them on their surveillance. Schlesta had Officers Harris and Officer Vincent on surveillance the same day he obtained Mo's file. Brian hadn't known about it though.

"Have ah seat fellas." said Jerry, waving towards the two chairs in front of his desk. He continued:

"Any sign of our guy Moreese?"

Vincent responded:

"Not-a-trace... he hasn't showed up at his so-called place of employment/residences yet... we've been on the place since Monday."

Harris offered his opinion:

"Maybe his lying-low because he owes somebody money for the dope he got busted with... he could be trying to stay clear of a bullet or something."

Jerry bounced the notion around in his mind for an instant moment then dropped it. He had his own suspicions of why they hadn't seen Mo or been able locate him.

"That's a good theory Harris... but this guy has money... an eighth of a kilo, at the most is five thousand dollars... with the type of lawyer this guy has... five grand is nothing."

Vincent tossed in his suggestion:

"Maybe we could show his photo to some of our C.I.'s and see if they know who this guy is."

Jerry's look of wondering-thought, turned into a scolding frown, as the words of Vincent's suggestion pierced his precepts. Jerry responded:

"Vincent... this isn't a formal investigation... we can't just **go** around inquiring about someone we don't want people to know we're interested in... we have to be tactful in everyway... Rosimono is gonna get inside to see what's what. He should have something on our guy soon."

Just as Detective Schlesta finished his sentence, there was a knock on the door... it was Brian.

"Come in Rosi." said Jerry and Brian entered.

"You got ah-minute Jerry?"

"Yeah, sure Rosi... the fellas are just briefing me on the surveillance, which is turning up **diddlysquat** right now. It looks like our guy is still a mystery because **none** us! Seem to be able to locate this fucker!"

Jerry's tone of voice lowered a-few notches. He continued:

"How did it go on your end?"

Brian was a little hesitant before he spoke. He looked at Vincent and Harris then to Jerry and began speaking:

"We got inside just find. From the looks of everything, the place is legit... As for Moreese... one of the managers speaks highly of him... Ms. Keisha Pulliam. Van and I have to go back Saturday to fill out some paperwork, pay our session fees and we'll officially be clients."

Harris was a peculiar fellow. His demeanor always seemed to imply that he was searching for the worst in things no matter what it was. Officer Harris stared at Brian then at Jerry... His head turned to Brian again... then, back to Jerry... With a confound look on his face, Harris asked Jerry:

"What does he mean... becoming clients and session fees? What's going on Jerry?"

Detective Schlesta smiled villainously at Officer Harris then began explaining the plan that Brian had come up with, to infiltrate Moreese's place of employment and supposed residence. Jerry's fire was burning now and he felt like spitting a flame:

"If this Moreese guy is doing any dealing, we'll know about it soon... we'll find out his routine... we'll find his source... and then... we'll take his ass down... **our** way... Remember fellas... we're still taking scum off the streets, but for **good**! We're not gonna give those sons-of-bitches the chance to get-outta-jail and go back to dirtying up the streets we risk our fucking lives cleaning up... Its combat out there fellas... and in combat you don't take prisoners... you kill the sons-of-bitches...! Unless their valuable... Vincent and Harris... I want you guys to continue surveillance... Rosi, you keep me posted on how things are unfolding at the studio. I'm gonna do a little research on this Clyde Pulliam guy."

Jerry wasn't going to find **anything** on Clyde... During Clyde's drug dealing days in the streets, he managed to steer clear of the police, staying under the radar and never getting so much as a **traffic** ticket... He was one of the fortunate few.

CHAPTER 7: THE DAY PORSHAÉ GOT TO SAINT LOUIS

The Sullivan House

The house is great Mo! I **love** it!" said Jenny. She was excited, finally being in, **their** own house, instead of her sister's, out in Saint Ann.

It was 9am, Saturday morning and the sky was clear of any clouds. The temperature was seventy-two degrees, with a nice breeze blowing in from the south, and the Sun was shining bright. Jenny's sisters husband, Todd... had a truck and agreed to move Jenny's things over to the Sullivan house... Jenny's brother, her sister's husband, and Mo, were at the Sullivan house unloading the truck.

After Jenny found out, she was pregnant... she wanted Mo and her to have a house of their own. Now, that it had happened... she was happier now than she had ever been in her whole life... so far... She had her man, she had a house with her man... and she had their baby in her stomach.

"Baby, why don't you sit down and relax yo-self... us fellas can handle this," said Mo, taking hold of Jenny's hand, rubbing her stomach with the other one. Mo continued:

"Baby, you need to relax... these are the most important months of the baby's development. You shouldn't overwork yo-self..."

Jenny looked into Mo's eyes, surprised by what he said. She put her arms around his waist then responded:

"So.... You've been doing your homework huh?"

Mo smiled at his Lady then answered her:

"Yeah... I've been doing ma homework."

He kissed her lips softly then continued:

"I wanna know **everything** I need to know so I can help this pregnancy go as smooth as possible for you... for us." He rubbed her belly again, showing her that his reference to 'us', meant the baby too...

"Awww, Baby that's so **sweet**.... That's why I love you so much."

Jenny adjusted her arms, moving them up to Mo's shoulders and neck, letting them rest there. Mo lowered his hands from Jenny's waist, to her ass, taking a firm grip with both hands and pulling her closer into him then said:

"Why you love me so much?"

Gazing into his eyes, Jenny answered him:

"Because.... You're always thinking of me." she said then gave him a soft peck on his lips. She continued:

"You always know what I want..." giving him another soft peck on his lips then continued:

"And you really care about us being together..." she said, giving him one last soft peck on his lips. Mo licked his upper-lip then said:

"Ummm... those lips, making me **hot**..."

Jenny's hand slid from Mo's shoulders, down to his chest then she gave him a little playfully push and said:

"**Boy**... you **stay** hot! That's why we got this one on the way now."

Mo grabbed Jenny by her ass and pulled her back to him, gently pressing his body against hers. He bent his knees slightly, grinding his dick against her pussy then said playfully:

"Don't be acting like you ain't hot fah-this... I know you is...."

Grinning wide, he held Jenny and continued to grind on her slow.

Jenny, spoke in a barley audit voice, hardly putting up any fight.

"Mo, you better stop boy, before you get somethin started."

"That's what I'm tryina do." said Mo.

"Moreese-Baby... Todd and Justin are still here... Y'all got some more stuff to unload, so go help them Baby... then they can leave... and we can have the house to ourselves."

Jenny rubbed the sides of Mo's face, as if to calm and soothe the freaky beast.

"We gone get freaky after they leave?" asked Mo while kissing Jenny on her neck.

She put on her voice of authority:

"**Boy...** Go help them unload the truck with-yo freaky-**ass...!**"

She was smiling on the inside but doing her best to maintain her serious exterior... if she hadn't... Mo would've gotten what he wanted regardless of who was in the house. Mo left, giving Jenny a look that said, "When I get back... I'm gone rip them panties off yo-ass and fuck that pussy reaaal good... so get ready."

It was hard for Jenny to resist Mo's sexual advances, but today she had to... She could feel the wetness of her pussy without even touching it. Jenny was ready for Mo's piece to penetrate her pussy, but she had to wait... This was their first day in their new home together, and she wanted to bring the house warming in with a good bang... **literally!** The pregnancy had her hormones raging, making her highly sensitive. The blood surged to her clitoris and vulva, swelling both areas, increasing her urge for sexual pleasure. She wanted the fellas to hurry up and finish, so her and Mo could go wild with each other. Jenny had some things she wanted to do to Mo and she was **sure,** that Mo had some things he wanted to do to her as well.

Jenny was anxious now. She stepped around some boxes that were on the living room floor to peek out-of the window, just to see how much the fellas had left to unload. The truck was still half-full. She let out a small sigh of frustration and decided to take Mo's advice. Jenny walked to the hallway then to the right towards the back bedroom. Mo's bed was already setup.

Several days before Jenny moved her things in, Mo had done the cleaning, moved his things in and situated them accordingly. Jenny was starting to feel tired from the activities of the morning. She had been up since 5:30am, making sure all of her things were packed and ready to go. She laid down on Mo's bed, now hers too... then buried her face into one of the soft goose-down pillows. Almost in an instant, she was dozing off... squeezing Mo's pillow... smelling it... taking in his scent through her nostrils... thinking of him as she dozed off, saying quietly in a sleepy voice:

"My Baby's bed... my bed..." Another thought swept through her mind and Jenny whispered it softly to herself:

"Thank you God for these blessings", then drifted off into a deep sleep. The other thought that swept her mind was; the baby she was carrying.

"Jenny!"

Jenny's brother, Justin was calling for her. He walked through the house, not seeing her anywhere then called out to her again:

"Jenny! We're done unloading the truck. Todd and me are about to take off!"

Justin continued walking towards the kitchen and still no sign of Jenny. He went back to the dining room from the kitchen then stepped into the hallway, calling his sister:

"Jenny...!"

Justin made it to the back bedroom door and it was half-ajar. He tried to push it open a little further but there was something behind it preventing it from opening all the way. He didn't wanna force the door open, so he poked his head inside and saw his big sister curled up on the bed, holding a pillow as if it were her significant other. Justin took-a-look behind the door and saw the objects that were blocking the door... it was two crates of Mo's vinyl albums. Justin pushed the door open gently, just enough for him to get his body through and Justin he was a **BIG GUY.**

"Big Sister?" said Justin softly, but Jenny didn't answer.

He walked over to a basket of folded linens and took a thin blanket from the top. Justin put the blanket over his big sister, letting it fall over her gently. He leaned down and gave her a kiss on the cheek then said:

"I love you Big Sis."

Jenny nestled around under the blanket for a few seconds then settled again. Justin went back to the front room, seeing Todd and Mo bringing in the last piece of Jenny's things from the truck... Jenny's dresser-chest, which her Grandmother had given her, was the last item.

"Be **really** careful guys... that thing is about sixty year's old", said Justin.

He quickly cleared the way, making sure the area was clear for them to walk through. Todd followed Mo's lead, taking the dresser-chest to a second room of the house at the opposite end of the hallway.

"Alright Moreese... that's all of it man." said Todd, looking at Mo with a modest sign of relief on his face.

The two walked back to the front room where Justin was.

"**Man**... I really appreciate you guys for helping get Jenny's stuff over here", said Mo, looking around for Jenny.

Justin knew what Mo was looking for, or **who** he was looking for. He held his hand up, slightly signaling to Mo then said:

"Moreese, she's asleep in the bedroom Bro... She's out like a light."

"Ok, good... I told her she needed to relax... you guys want somethin to drink? We got, papaya juice, ginger-ale, O.J." said Mo.

He loved keeping plenty of fruit juice in the refrigerator. He could go through a half-a-gallon of papaya juice in a day. That was his favorite juice. He told Jenny, "that if they ever had a daughter, he was gonna name her Papaya." She just looked at him and didn't comment...

Todd responded to Mo's offer:

"Moreese, its cool man... Justin and me, have to get back to the house. The girls are cooking breakfast and we told them we'd be back by ten... but thanks for offering man."

Todd extended his hand and Mo reached out to shake it.

"Thanks again man." said Mo.

"No problem, glad I could help." said Todd.

Mo reached out for Justin's hand but Justin didn't reach back. He felt him and Mo were family already so he gave Mo a quick 'man-hug' then after, said:

"Tell my Big Sis, I love her."

"I will." said Mo.

Justin and Todd started towards the door... Justin was really glad that his sister was with Mo. He could see that she was truly happy with him... Justin turned around then said:

"Moreese... I'm glad you're part of our family man... I can't wait to see my little nephew when he gets here."

Justin was smiling big at the thought of having a little nephew. Mo commented:

"Thanks Jus-Blaze... I'm glad I'm part of the family too Man."

Jus-Blaze was the nickname Mo had given Justin, because Justin **loved** smoking lots of marijuana. Todd and Justin headed out, got in the truck then left... Mo stood at the door for a moment... It really just dawned on him that he was about to have a family of his very own.

He closed the door and locked it. Mo thought about the three little kisses Jenny had given him earlier. The thought roused his nature and he went **straight** to the bedroom. He took his shoes off, pulled the thin blanket back and got in the bed with Jenny. He scooted next to her, spooning his body with hers. Mo put his arm around her, holding her tight. Mo snuggled up against his Lady and he too... drifted off into a deep slumber.

The clock read 10:30am at the *We Got Music* studio. The phone rang and Rene was at the desk to answer it:

"Good morning. You've reached *We Got Music* recording studio. This is Rene speaking, how can I help you?"

It was Brian calling... Hearing Rene's voice again, had Brian stuck and at a loss for words.

"Hello?" said Rene.

Brian snapped out of it then responded:

"Uuh yes... hello Ms. Rene. This is Brian... with *Vans Band*."

"Ooh, hello Mr. Brian! Keisha told me you guys would be coming by today."

"Yeah... we'll be there around 11:30. I'm just calling so you guys will be expecting us."

"We're already expecting you, so just **come** on in" said Rene cheerfully.

Rene made Brian smile on the other end of the phone. He was **so** anxious to meet her in person, but felt uneasy about the situation and the circumstances in which he was meeting her under... He responded:

"Ok Ms. Rene... we'll see you when we get there."

"Alright Mr. Brian... see you then." and Rene hung up the phone.

Rene got back to her work, and Brian's mind began to wonder:

"Is she **always** so cheerful? Is she like that with everybody?"

Brian finally put the receiver down in its cradle and wondered for a few seconds longer... He picked the phone up again to call Van. Van answered on the second ring:

"Hello?"

"Hey man! You ready for today?"

"**Damn right**! We all set to go?"

"Yeah, we're all set man. I just got off the phone with the studio. I told them we'll be there around 11:30. Is that cool?"

"Yeah, that's cool man. I'm about-to-get ready and I'll meet you there."

"Alright... see you then Van." Brian hung up phone.

Brian and Van made it to the studio at precisely 11: 30. They handled all of the paperwork-formalities and Brian finally got the chance to meet the woman who had been occupying his mind since Tuesday. In addition, they setup their first recording session.

It was close to noon, and Keisha still hadn't made it to the studio. The phone rang at the studio and Rene answered it in her normal, cheery voice...

"Good afternoon. You've reached *We Got Music* recording studio. This is Rene speaking, how can I help you?"

It was Keisha on the other end. Brian observed Rene and got the answer to the question he wondered about earlier.

"**Hey** Keisha!" said Rene then excused herself from the room to take the call in back, where the kitchenette was. She wanted to speak with Keisha in private.

"Girrrl, where **are** you? The guys from *Vans Band* are here and I was hoping you would be here too, to make sure I went over every-thing."

"Rene, I know you covered everything, but I'll be there in a-little-bit. My uncle needed me to go pick somebody up from the airport this morning and take him to the Adams Marks. I **still** have to go **back** to the hotel and bring him over to the studio to meet with Uncle Clyde... So like I said, I'll be there in a little-bit."

Rene could sense that Keisha was a little irritated from the tone of her voice. With Keisha being Clyde's "Personal Assistant", Rene knew, that at times, Clyde could get a little besides himself with giving Keisha errands to run... Still though, Rene was curious so she asked:

"Keisha, what's going on? Who's meeting here with Uncle Clyde, and what for?"

Anything that had to do with the studio, Rene wanted to be **well** aware of it. She didn't like being unprepared for a situation and right now, she felt unprepared. Keisha responded:

"Rene, I wasn't even aware of it until Uncle Clyde told me about it last night when he called me... He had some producer from Michigan, fly down here to have a meeting... something about bringing him on as a producer and engineer... **Girrrl**, I'm **so** irritated right now because he **knows** he could've told us about it sooner..." said Keisha.

Rene agreed with Keisha:

"I know right... He knows we don't like to be unprepared for things." said Rene.

Keisha responded:

"Uncle Clyde should be there in-a-minute, if he's not already there. You know how he likes to come in without anybody noticing."

"Yeah, I know Girl... He's probably in his office right now." said Rene.

"I'll be there in a-bit Rene."

"Okay Chica. See you in a-bit." said Rene then pressed the call end button on the kitchenette phone.

She went back to the front where Brian, Van and Tom, had been waiting. Tom and Van had 'dipped-off' into the pre-recording studio to check out the music recording equipment. Brian chose to wait for Rene to return. He was standing over by the wall with the replica of "Lucille" hanging on it, looking at Lucille in awe.

Rene made it to the archway to see Brian gazing at the guitar. She stepped over quietly and stood at his side then said:

"It looks like the real one doesn't it?"

Brian was startled just a little, but happy that Rene had chose to stand next to him. He responded:

"Yeah, it does. I **love** B.B. King's music... Is everything alright?" he asked, noticing that Rene had to take the call in the back.

"Oh. Yeah, everything is fine. We just have an unexpected guess coming in today. Keisha didn't find out about it until last night and I didn't find out about it until just **two** minutes ago."

Rene smiled at Brian. She wasn't really upset... Brian was curious of **who** this unexpected guess was.

"So who's the guess?" he asked casually.

Rene answered without any hesitation:

"The owner flew some producer/engineer down from Michigan, to talk to him about joining our studio."

"Did something happen to the other engineer, Moreese?"

"Oh-no... Nothing happened to Moreese that I know of. I think the owner just wants to bring-in some new sound for our music production... and some help for Moreese."

"So that's good right." said Brian.

"Well **yeah**. It's **great**! But that all depends on whether or not this guy is-as-good-as Moreese."

"Moreese must be really good?" said Brian.

"Yeah... he is... it's the reason why artist and bands try so hard to get here... even though they may have their own engineer... Mo, can **always** make their music sound better after he is done with it. He just loves making music sound its best."

"So when will we meet him?" asked Brian.

Rene was stumped for an answer because she really didn't have one. She had no idea where Mo was. Normally, he would have been there to assist, but he hadn't been there all week. Rene responded:

"You know Mr. Brian... come to think about it... he hasn't been in this week... but I'm sure nothing has happened to him. Keisha would've told me about it if something happened. She can probably answer that for you when she gets here. She'll be here shortly."

Brian didn't wanna seem **too** interested in Mo, so he stopped with the questions. Rene continued:

"I assure you though Mr. Brian... There's no need to worry... we'll take care of you guys."

Brian liked Rene... there was no doubt about that. He could listen to her voice all day. He was captured in their conversation... but from Rene's actions, she seemed to wanna escape from it. She turned to her desk, picking up the scheduling book, thumbed through it, to the present date.

"Mr. Brian, if you'll excuse me. I have to make a call to a client... They're supposed to be here at 12:30 and it's important for me to make a reminder call."

"Ok. I'll just go back there and check on the fellas."

Brian began to walk off then Rene stopped him:

"Ooh, no Mr. Brian. I'm not asking you to leave. This will only take me a-minute then we can continue to talk."

Brian was taken aback by her comment. In his mind, what she had just said was, "No! Stay **right** there! I **wanna** talk to you."

He suppressed the urge to smile and said:

"Alright..."

Brian turned, continuing to look at the albums on the wall. His back was to her now. He smiled, listening to the sound of her voice while she made her "reminder call."

The Adams Mark

Porshae's head, relaxed on the plush pillow. He stretched out on the bed, with his hands beneath the pillow, looking up at the ceiling. His thoughts were on his daughter Porsha and his girlfriend Sabrina. There was a soft knocking at the door... doof doof doof doof... He got up to open it without asking who it was... it was Keisha.

"Good afternoon Mr. Prince."

Keisha was no longer irritated... or just not with Porshaé. It wasn't his fault that her uncle had been so inconsiderate of her plans for that day. Her uncle had his reason behind it though but Keisha didn't know what that reason was... However, she left her attitude at home and decided to bring her normal cordial self. Porshaé responded:

"Good afternoon Ms. Pulliam, but please... call me Porshaé. I still get a little embarrassed when people call me Mr. Prince."

"You have a cool name and you shouldn't be embarrassed about it. I would **love** it if people called me, 'Ms. Princess' because that was my real name... That would be **so** cool."

Keisha was still in the corridor and Porshaé found his manners:

"I'm sorry Ms. Pulliam. Please, come in."

He moved to the side and let Keisha step-through.

"Please... call me Keisha."

Keisha felt a good vibe coming from Porshaé, so it made it, all-the-more-easier, for her to be cordial. As Keisha stepped through pass Porshaé, he had a mental flash of Sabrina... He shook his head and as he did... Keisha turned to see him doing so.

"You ok Porshaé? I've been known to have that effect on a man."

Keisha was only joking, but Porshaé wanted to say, "**Yeah**... I can see why." He responded:

"Yeah, I'm ok. I'm just shaking the drowsiness outta ma head. Have a seat if you'd like to."

Keisha walked over to the table and chairs that were by the window in the suite.

"So Mr. Prince... I mean, Porshaé... you're from Detroit?"

"No, actually, I'm from Flint."

"**Flint**?" Keisha exclaimed questioningly then continued:

"I've never heard of it... where is it?"

"It's about thirty minutes away from Detroit... and just as bad, if not worst."

Keisha relaxed her purse on the table. She was casually dressed but still presented herself with an elegance that pulled at Porshae's attention.

"We can leave whenever you're ready. My uncle is probably at the studio by now, waiting on us."

"So Clyde is your uncle?"

"Yep. Clyde is my uncle... and I'm his niece/personal assistant/ manager of his studio. He had a show to run late last night, so that's why I picked you up instead of him."

"It's cool... I didn't mind you picking me up." 'Tone it down Porshaé.' he told his self.

He found himself struggling to pull away from Keisha's allure. She was very attractive and seemingly pleasant to be around. It was something about being in a nice hotel suite, with a beautiful woman all alone... that made his temperature rise. He was just a little uncomfortable and Keisha took notice of it. She didn't want him to feel any more uncomfortable than he already did, so she stated again:

"Like I said Porshaé... we can leave as soon as you're ready."

Her reiteration of the statement helped him to break loose of her allure. He responded:

"Ooh... Ok. Just let me get my things and I'll be right back."

He dashed off to the other room to retrieve his small bag with his audio and video materials, which he wanted Clyde to listen to and view. He went back into the suites sitting area and stepped over to the door.

"Ok... I'm all set."

"Alright then... let's get you to the studio... did you have lunch?"

"Not yet. I figured I could get something after the meeting with your uncle", said Porshaé, watching Keisha as she walked over towards him.

They were both standing near the door now. Keisha put her dark sunglasses on. They made her look like every-bit-of-a big-movie-actress. She looked at Porshaé then responded:

"Good, because I know **just** the place to take you... you like soul food?" and the two, left out of the hotel suite, walking towards the elevator.

He instantly thought about his Grandma's cooking at the mention of soul food. Porshaé responded with a small bit of exhilaration in his voice:

"That's what I was **raised** on! My Mom told me when I was a baby... I didn't eat baby food... She said the only way that I would eat, was if she smashed up regular table food and fed it to me. But **yeah**... I **love** soul food!"

Keisha noticed his change of demeanor. He was more relaxed now than when they were inside of the hotel suite. She responded with a friendly, welcoming voice:

"I wanna take you to *Sweetie Pies...* It's the best soul food restaurant in the Midwest. They serve lunch and dinner so we can head right over there after the meeting with my uncle... and **trust** me... you **won't** be disappointed."

He was thankful for her invitation... It made him feel welcomed. He responded:

"Good... I'm looking forward to it. I can get a chance to see how y'all throw-down in the Show-Me state." he said, smiling at Keisha.

The two stepped into the waiting elevator and Keisha pressed the button for the lobby. The doors closed and the ride down began.

"So... what's it like working with your uncle?" asked Porshaé.

The ride down was short but Keisha's answer to his question wasn't. She responded:

"It doesn't feel like I **work** for him... It feels more as if... I work **with** him. I've been there since he opened the place, so I really consider myself his partner. I make a-lot-of decisions concerning the studio... I came up with the décor-scheme too, so I hope you like what you see when we get there."

He could tell from looking at Keisha that she had classy and exquisite taste. He wanted to comment on what she just said. That comment would've been: "from looking at you... I'm **sure** I'll like what I see." However... he chose to keep those words to his self.

Porshaé loved to compliment a woman... especially when something pertaining to that woman was compliment worthy. It was just his nature... it was something Sabrina found very appealing and so did other women. Keeping his response respectful of Sabrina, even though she was not there... he responded:

"I'm sure I'll like what I see... it seems like you have nice taste." Keisha loved the modesty in his compliment... but she could tell that he wanted to say something else...

Ding! The elevator bell sounded and the doors opened. They stepped off and Keisha responded with a surprised tone in her voice:

"Well **thank** you **Porshaé**... that's very nice of you to **say**." Keisha continued explaining her status at the studio:

"I'm taking business and marketing classes right now. I wanna use that knowledge to build the recording studio into a major recording company. My uncle is basically, the foundation and I'm the building. He's good at putting money behind the right business, at the right time. And I'm good at managing whatever it is that's in-front of the money."

"The two of you sound like a good team."

"We are... now if only Mo could get his shit together."

"Who's Mo?" asked Porshaé.

"Mo... he's like my uncle's nephew/son, and he's like a little brother to me. He's also the in-house engineer... in due time, you'll meet him."

Outside now, Keisha pressed the button on the remote to unlock the car then they got inside. She started the engine then the light blue Jaguar pulled away from the *Adams Mark* hotel.

The drive from the hotel to the studio was around ten minute's tops and that was with heavy traffic... but it was the weekend and there was hardly any.

"Porshaé... I'm gonna stop at the gas station to fill the tank up before we go to the studio."

"Ok... that's cool with me", he said.

While taking in the new scenery, Porshaé thought about Keisha. He was truly impressed at her desire to pursue a career in the music business. He too wanted the same thing and that commonality between the two of them, helped him to feel even more comfortable in Keisha's presence. He glanced over at her for a few seconds as she drove. He felt a strong admiration for her already... The Jaguar pulled onto the lot of the Shell's gas station. As it did... a brown Chevy Caprice continued down the street, passing them slowly. Porshaé took notice, though thought nothing of it. Keisha opened her door then said:

"My uncle is probably gonna wanna to show you around... you know... take you to the clubs... spots where we have shows."
She reached in the back seat where her purse was... It also was where Porshaé's bag was. She felt around in her purse for her money pouch and thinking nothing of it, she left her purse unfastened.

"I'll be right-back", she said then he nodded his head and said, "ok."
Before Keisha got out of the car, Porshaé asked her:

"You want me to pump the gas?"
Keisha responded, smiling at Porshaé:

"You're **such** a gentleman... but it's cool... I got it. Thanks for asking though."
She got out of the car and walked into the service station. He resumed what he was doing, which was, looking out of the window, still taking in the scenery of Saint Louis. Porshaé admired what he saw. Saint Louis was actually a beautiful city... it was the **gateway** to the west.

He reached in the back to get his camera from his bag, and as he did... he caught a glimpse of Keisha's opened purse. He didn't probe or touch it... he only looked. His mind was not playing tricks on him. His eyes saw what he thought they had saw. Keisha's purse contained a small caliber .380 automatic-pistol. Porshaé turned around and put his focus back on the scene he was admiring. With the window down, he pointed the camera at some old and probably historical building then snapped his shot, capturing the image on his camera. Keisha was on her way back to the car. He turned, watching her as she approached the car. He didn't want to admit it to himself, but the truth was indisputably undeniable... he was attracted to Keisha. He put his camera in his lap and just held it. Porshaé had never cheated on Sabrina, and he **didn't** want to... There was just something about Keisha's entire being, that gave him a **strong** sense of tempting interest. Now, he was anxious to get to the studio so he wouldn't say anything out of character... the character that had always been faithful to Sabrina...

"What-the-fuck is wrong with me...? I've been around **hundreds** of women and **never** felt like this before?" said Porshaé, quietly to his self.

Keisha finished pumping the gas and Porshaé put himself in check, before Keisha got back inside of the car. She got in.

"I don't know if this is weird or not... but for some strange reason... I **like** the smell of gas." said Keisha, looking awkwardly at Porshaé.

He responded:

"Naah, it's not weird. I like the smell of new tires and mothballs."

"**Mothballs**", Keisha exclaimed, while letting a short laugh escape her then she continued:

"Now **that's** weird... **mothballs?**"

Keisha turned nonchalantly to the back seat to put her money pouch away, still humored by Porshae's unusual like of smells. She felt the ice had officially been broken.

"I like your city... It really looks nice out here."

Keisha glared at Porshaé because he had **no** clue then she responded:

"Oh yeah... you think it's nice out here huh?"

"Yeah... I already took a picture", he said, lifting up his camera.

"Well... it is not all what it seems, I can tell you that," said Keisha with a critical tone of voice. She continued:

"It's like the **wild-wild-west** out here! You gotta be careful and be on your P's and Q's."

"So is that why you keep your little sidekick back there." said Porshaé, motioning his head towards the back seat then he continued:

"I didn't mess with your purse... I noticed it when I reached back there to get my camera."

Keisha was taken a little off guard and felt she had to defend her purpose for carrying a gun:

"You **damn-right** that's why I have it! This city **looks** nice but it **hardly** is... I like to ride in nice cars, and I like having nice things... but these drug-addicts, jackers and robbers, are **always** out to get little helpless girls like me... so yes... I packs the heat, in these streets."

The Lady **gangsta** had come out-of Keisha, and Porshaé kinda liked it. She was sweet, sophisticated and gangtsa if she needed to be.

"As a-matter-of-fact..." said Keisha, reaching in the back seat to grab her purse then she continued:

"I need to put my '**sidekick**', as you call it... up here with me. That won't bother you will it?"

"**No**... Not-at-all. I'm a firm believer in packin the heat in dangerous streets... **definitely** nothing wrong with that. I'm from Flint Michigan... one of the most **dangerous** cities in the country, so I understand... You know how to use that thing?"

Keisha started the car then responded:

"**Ooh I know** how to use it alright! My uncle takes me to the gun range and sometimes I go by myself."

"So I'm sitting here next to a **real live Calamity Jane**, huh?" said Porshaé while smiling at Keisha.

Keisha felt comfortable around Porshaé... he was easy to talk to.

She responded:

"I don't know if you can say **all** that. But like I said... I **do** know how to use it", she said, smiling back at Porshaé.

Keisha pulled off the lot and headed to the studio.

"Porshaé, you seem like a **pretty** cool guy... At first I was a little irritated about having to pick you up, you being a total stranger and all... But I have to say... so far, it hasn't been unpleasant at all."

Porshaé responded:

"I **was** a little nervous at first when I saw you. I wasn't expecting for a woman to pick me up and take me to the hotel."

Keisha gave him a quick glance then said:

"**Nervous**? Why would you be nervous?"

"I don't know? I'm still trying to figure that one out... I've been around **plenty** of beautiful women before... it just felt kinda awkward... but I'm cool now."

Keisha took that as a compliment. She knew that Porshaé was nervous inside of the hotel room... but she never expected for him to admit it. She had never known of a man to be so honest and candid about his feelings so soon, if at all... Keisha asked Porshaé:

"So, do you have a girlfriend?"

"Yeah I do... her name is Sabrina." he said then paused for a moment before he continued:

"We have a daughter together... her name is Porsha."

"Awww, how cute.... Porshaé and Porsha, Daddy's little girl. How old is she?" asked Keisha.

"She's three years old... What about you Keisha, do you have someone in your life you're exclusive with?"

"Naah... no significant other in my life right now... I'm staying focused on my career in music. I don't want **anything** taking my focus off of that... besides... I'm only in my twenties so I have **plenty** of time to indulge in romance after I accomplish these first set of goals."

"Well that's good you have your priorities in-order", said Porshaé.

The Jaguar pulled up in front of the two story red-brick building.

"This is it", said Keisha, putting the car in park.

Porshaé surveyed the area... It was nice he thought. Several blocks of residential houses and small businesses, all intermingled to make up the 'lovely neighborhood'... It was **far** much nicer than his neighbor in Flint. The Saint Louis neighborhood had clean cut lawns and business fronts with huge sidewalks; yards clear of debris and beautifully trimmed trees and clean streets. Keisha was out of the car, standing over by the door already. Porshaé was still indulging in the scenery when Keisha yelled out to him:

"Well... let's go **Man!** My uncle is probably waiting on us."

"My mind was just taking in the scenery", he said, turning to Keisha.

He liked the way she looked in front of the building. The name of the studio was directly above her, and he wanted to capture a picture of both, her and the studio name, together.

"Hold-up...! Let me take a picture of you right there." he said, raising his camera. Keisha made a joke:

"**Man...** you're worse than a Chinese person on vacation."

Still though, she smiled beautifully for his camera then raised her hand upward towards the *We Got Music* company banner. He snapped his shot of Keisha then said:

"That was perfect... Alright, let me grab my bag."

He went back to the car to retrieve his bag from the back seat. Through the rear window, Porshaé noticed the **same** car that passed them earlier at the gas station. He caught a glimpse of the brown Chevy Caprice driving down the street slow. Porshaé grabbed his bag and exited the car; still not thinking much of it... but it sat on his mind this time.

"**Come-on,** Mr. Photographer! I haven't had breakfast **or** lunch and I'm **starving**! The sooner we get this meeting over with, the sooner we can go to *Sweetie Pies*!"

Keisha's mouth was already watering for some of the famous soul food from *Sweetie Pies*. Porshaé smiled at Keisha's antics then walked over to the door, which she had already opened. The bell chime sounded in the reception area. Rene looked at the monitor then said:

"Good... Keisha is here."

Rene pressed the button, the buzzer sounded, unlocking the heavy wooden door then Keisha and Porshaé walked in, finally at the studio. Porshaé took in the décor, and he liked what he saw.

Back To The Surveillance:

Officer Harris parked just down the street from the studio after Keisha and Porshaé entered the building.

"S2 to S1 over..." Officer Harris was trying to contact Officer Vincent.

"S2 to S1 over..."

Vincent pressed the button down on the two-way walkie-talkie radio then responded:

"S1 here, over"

"Vincent, can you get to Schlesta? The two from the Adams Mark just walked into the studio. The guy she picked up from the airport carried in a nice size bag but still no sign of our guy Moreese. See what Schlesta wants me to do. I think something might be goin down in there and I wanna move on it, over."

Officer Harris was somewhat of a hot head. At times, he'd do things that were irrational and without logical reason. It made Schlesta wonder, "how in the **hell** did Harris become an officer?" Harris was the type of cop that would provoke someone into a situation... Often those situations would result in someone being shot, or taken into custody, most times, using **excessive** force... Detective Schlesta liked Harris though, because Harris was loyal to his cause... Detective Schlesta's cause, that is... Officer Vincent replied:

"I copy you Harris, but let's give Rosi a chance to see what's going on first before we jump the gun. He's inside so I'm sure if he suspects something, he'll let us know, over."
Officer Harris got a-bit annoyed at Officers Vincent's remark about 'jumping the gun'. Officer Harris felt that Detective Rosimono was too soft for the work they were doing. He responded:
"Roger that S1... I'll hold surveillance. Radio back after you talk to Schlesta. Over and out."
Feeling frustrated and like they were wasting time, Harris slammed the radio down on the front seat of the Caprice... It hit hard and bounced up, landing on the passenger side floor. Harris reached down to pick it up. When he rose up from the floor of the car, he caught the intense gaze of an elder man, passing by on the sidewalk.

Dressed 'business like', the elder man wore a charcoal gray suit, black soft leather shoes and a black fedora. The man broke his gaze and continued down the street towards a coffee shop that was at the end of the block. It was hard for Officer Harris to shake the image of the man from his mind. The strangers face was stone and stoic, with a cold expression. Harris shudder from the cold feeling the man's gaze had given him.

Whenever Officer Harris felt any sign of fear, it made him become that much more erratic and irrational. Harris wondered who the man was... and why had his look been so cold? Officer Harris had the audaciousness to walk down to the coffee shop and begin interrogating the man... but that audaciousness only came when the subject appeared to be weaker... **this** man, seemed just the opposite. Officer Harris was feeling inferior in this case. The act would be inept if he chose to carry it out. He thought for a long moment then the erratic side of Harris, took over. Officer Harris, got out of the car, checked his sidearm and began walking towards the coffee shop.

Mr. FitzPatrick was one of the **first** to open a business in the neighborhood. His small coffee shop was like the cornerstone for other small businesses to build on. Everyone in the neighborhood knew Mr. FitzPatrick, and most of them paid his shop a visit on a regular basis, including Clyde... Joe entered the cozy little coffee shop and saw Mr. Fitz behind the counter. Mr. Fitz saw Joe and gave him a hearty greeting:

"**Joe**! Good afternoon my good friend!" then came from behind the counter, embracing his longtime friend with a hug.

Joe Hogan was also Mr. Fitz's tax lawyer. The first law office that Joe ever had, was located in the Central West End area. When Mr. Fitz ran into some tax troubles... he walked into Joe's office. Ever since then... the two have been good friends.

"Hello Fitz!"

Joe's, tall husky, 6 foot 3 inch, 276 pound frame, engulfed the smaller Mr. Fitz's, 5 foot 8 inch, 214 pound chunky frame as they embraced in their hug. In his seventies now, Mr. Fitz was elderly and the body of his youth was gone. However... his Spirit was still just as fiery now as it was fifty years ago... With his raspy Irish accent, Fitz responded:

"**Joe**! **Joe**! How are you this fine afternoon?"

"Just fine Fitz... just fine. I'd be better though if I could get one of those fresh croissant sandwiches of yours." said Joe, as he took off his fedora. He sat it down on one of the chairs at a nearby table.

Fitz responded:

"So what brings you by today my friend?"

Mr. FitzPatrick pulled out a chair from the table to take a seat in. Fitz gestured for Joe to take a seat as well and both men sat down.

Joe responded:

"Fitz... I have this incredible **urge** for a fresh cup of that special blend."

Fitz Mix was a special blend of coffee that Mr. FitzPatrick created his self. No one knew the blend except for Fitz... Mr. FitzPatrick called for his granddaughter, Sarah who worked at the shop on the weekends and when school was out:

"Sarah darling... can you get Mr. Hogan here, a fresh croissant sandwich and a fresh cup of grandpa's special blend?"

"Coming right up Grandpa." said the sweet youthful Sarah.

Joe was actually in the neighborhood on the account of Clyde and Moreese... but Fitz didn't need to know that. Joe wanted Fitz to feel, as though he made the visit on his account. It was more of a... respect for his elder type of thing and the old man admired Joe's respectfulness.

"Here you are Mr. Hogan." said young Sarah, sitting the cup of specially blended coffee and croissant sandwich down on the table.

"Thank you Sarah."

"You're welcome Mr. Hogan."

Sarah was very polite just like her grandpa. She walked back behind the counter and continued with her coffee shop duties while her grandpa and Joe conversed causally about trivial things. Joe was enjoying the coffee, the croissant sandwich, and the conversation, then... the sound of the tiny bells on the coffee shop door, jingled. Fitz was facing the door and gave the man coming in, a welcoming nod as he entered the shop. Joe's back was to the door and he continued to sip his coffee. He felt the ominous presents and **instinctively**, knew whom it was.

Officer Harris strolled passed the gentlemen and nodded a hello gesture. He tried to be inconspicuous as he walked up to the counter. Sarah came right over:

"What can I get for you today Sir?"

It was Harris' first time in the shop and he felt the girl knew it and so did the two men... or maybe it was Harris' self accusing conscience that was bothering him. Harris looked around, trying to become familiar with something. Sarah noticed his unawareness of things and said politely:

"Sir, this is our coffee menu and here is our food item menu. Take your time and just let me know when you're ready."

She slid the two-in-one menu across the counter to Harris. He looked over the menu and wondered: "Why the **hell**, am I feeling so nervous?" Not wanting to spend too much time in the shop, he found an item and was ready to order.

"Yes, I'm ready."

Sarah strolled back over to the counter.

"What can I get you?"

"I'll just have a cup of the special blend coffee to go please."

"Alright Sir... coming right up."

Sarah dashed off to make one cup of special blend Fitz Mix to go. Officer Harris turned around and pretended to take in the décor of the place... but he was really trying to get a good look at Mr. "Stone Face".

"Good choice." said Joe, raising his cup to Officer Harris.

Harris was stuck with no response... Sarah saved him:

"Here's your coffee Sir, and that'll be fifty cents."

Harris reached inside of his jacket for his wallet and accidently pulled out his badge. Trying to hurry and put it back inside his jacket pocket, he fumbled... missing the pocket, causing the badge to fall to the floor, unfolding on impact...

The silver S.P.D. officer's badge, caught Joe's eye and Fitz turned to see what was going on at the sound of something hitting the floor. Officer Harris picked up his badge, secured it in his pocket then, found his wallet in his back pocket. He took a crisp one-dollar bill from it then gave it to Sarah:

"Thank you... Keep the change."

"Thank you Sir. Have a good day." said Sarah, but before she was done with her sentence, Officer Harris was headed for the door already.

"Good day gentlemen." he said, passing Fitz and Joe then exited the coffee shop.

Joe knew it was the man from the brown Chevy. He also knew that the man was a police officer... possibly on some kind of stakeout. The question Joe was asking himself was... "**who** was the officer staking out?" Joe's comprehension of things, seen, and not said, was preternatural. He hardly ever was wrong when it came to his intuition.

"He seemed pretty nervous didn't he?" said Joe, looking at Fitz and taking another sip of the delicious coffee.

Fitz shrugged his shoulders, not to doubt Joe's perception, but to show his own wonder about the man. The two continued their conversation and Joe took the last bite of his croissant sandwich.

"So how's business been?" asked Joe.

"**Swell**! The bands that record music at Clyde's studio are **all** regulars now... it's nice you know."

Joe wondered if Fitz meant, that it was nice to have more customers, or just nice to have a different type of people in the shop. Joe asked

Fitz:

"What's nice Fitz?" and Fitz responded:

"It's nice to have such a **mixture** of people it the shop... the young, the old... the black, the white... even Spanish..."

Fitz nodded his head at his own statement, loving the racial unity that his little shop was promoting. Fitz pointed over to a wall and Joe looked in the direction that Fitz was pointing. Fitz had put up a large corkboard, just so the bands and artist could hang their promotional flyers and advertise their next showcase performance. Thinking of Rene, Fitz smiled pleasantly then continued:

"The little Spanish girl comes down here **every** morning and gets something different, **every** time... she the sweetest thing I know besides my little Sarah."

Sarah looked up, not able to avoid hearing the conversation. Joe seen her smiling at the comment her grandpa made. Fitz enjoyed listening to Rene's voice... he loved her accent.

Joe responded:

"That's great Fitz. I'm glad business is doing well."

The old man reached across the table and took hold of Joe's hand, giving it a firm squeeze then said:

"I couldn't have done it without you my friend." then he let go of Joe's hand.

"Well Fitz... it was you who took care of all the hard work... I only handle some small technicalities for you."

"Yes Joe... but those small technicalities could have become **big** troubles for me. My little shop would not **be** here today if it were not for you my friend. Your expertise in dealing with those... **blood suckers** saved me..."

Joe laughed a little at Fitz's show of contemptuousness then finished his cup of 'special blend'.

"Well Fitz... it's been a pleasure as usual, but I have to get going."

Joe reached into the inside of his suit's breast pocket and pulled out his money clip. Fitz frowned then said:

"**Joe**... you know you don't have to do that."

Joe responded, looking in Sarah's direction:

"College is getting **very** expensive Fitz... every little bit is gonna help when she gets ready to go."

Fitz didn't argue with that. Joe took a five-dollar bill from his money clip and placed it under the white coffee cup.

"Joe, you're a true gentleman my friend." said Fitz. "Thank you Fitz... so are you", said Joe.

The two got up from the table, shook hands, embraced in another hug then Joe picked up his fedora and headed out.

"Take care Fitz." said Joe, standing near the door about to exit.

"I will Joe. Take care my friend." and then, Joe was gone.

"S1 to S2 over..."

This time, it was Officer Vincent trying to reach Officer Harris.

"S1 to S2 over." still no response...

Detective Schlesta was now with Officer Vincent, and since Harris wasn't responding... Schlesta automatically thought Harris had resorted to one of his erratic acts again. Schlesta took hold of the walkie-talkie from Vincent:

"Harris! This is Schlesta... pick up!"

Schlesta and Vincent were on their way to see what the situation was.

"Why isn't he picking up?" said Schlesta, asking the question to himself.

Officer Harris made it back to his car. He was upset for blundering in the coffee shop... he had no plan to begin with though. He had acted on pure irrational impulse and had accomplished nothing. He opened the door, got inside of the Chevy, sat the coffee in the cup holder then closed the door. Feeling as though he compromised his position, he wanted to move to a different vantage point. Harris started the engine and pulled off.

The gray Crown Victorian cruised down the street slowly.

"Do you see his car any where?" Vincent asked Schlesta.

"No, but he should be somewhere in this area here, to be able to do any surveillance. Go to the other side of the street."

Officer Vincent continued down the block, coming to a stop at the corner. Jerry was pissed. He wanted to shout at Harris for not answering his radio... Schlesta radioed Harris again:

"Harris! This is Schlesta. Where are you? Over..."

Jerry held the radio, waiting for a response from Officer Harris... just then, Joe walked pass the car, observing the two men and their peculiar behavior. Joe had been involved with law for twenty years and had seen his share of police... in uniform and plain clothes. It was **way** pass obvious to Joe, that the men in the Crown Victorian... were plain-clothes officers... Keeping his stride, Joe tipped his hat to the two gentlemen and continued across the crosswalk.

"Do we know him?" Jerry asked ("concerningly").

"No... I don't think so", said Officer Vincent.

Detective Schlesta put the radio down, watching Joe as he passed by.

"He looks **really** familiar", said Jerry trying to pinpoint where he seen Joe before.

The savory aroma of the coffee was alluring. Officer Harris grabbed the coffee from the cup holder, took the lid off then took a sip... The taste of the special blend was like no other coffee he'd tasted before... It was soothing as it went down his throat into his belly. It brought his frustrated mind to an almost tranquil state. And his body relaxed from the tension he was feeling.

"**Damn**... what-the-fuck is in this coffee?" said Harris, indulging in the savory flavors. He grabbed his radio.

"S2 to S1 over..."

Startled by the unexpected radio transmission, Schlesta's voice snapped back a response:

"**Harris**! Where the **hell** are you?"

Harris had moved the Chevy over to the next block, parked in the direction of the studio, between two cars, in the middle of the block. With his binoculars, he could see the studio just fine. He could also see with his binoculars... Schlesta's frowning face. Vincent and Schlesta sit in the Crown-Vic at the stop sign, awaiting Harris' response.

"I'm about half-a-block in front of you."

Through his binoculars, Harris observed Schlesta and Vincent search down the street for his brown Chevy. Harris saw they were still unable to see him, so he stuck his arm out of the window to make it apparent. Then they spotted him and proceeded down the street. Joe's back was to the Crown Victorian and he was about ten feet from the studio. He turned around indistinctively and saw the Crown Victorian stopped onside of what appeared to be, the brown Chevy Caprice. Joe knew they were up to something... but what.... That, he didn't know... His wonder subsided and his intuition took over... It told him that they were doing surveillance on the studio... and the only reason for that... would be Mo's arrest.

Joe knew about corrupt officers shaking down drug dealers for money... robbing and even killing them... He thought about Mo's booking sheet and remembered... Mo listed the studio as his place of residence. There was a one-bedroom apartment above the studio that **use** to be Mo's... until his arrest. Joe recollected the Officers faces from the Saint Ann police station, but none of their faces matched those of Schlesta, Harris or Vincent. He thought as he walked towards the studio, thinking of what he would say to Clyde in-regard to what he suspected.

Clyde had come in quietly through the rear entrance as he typically did. He went into his office unnoticed by anyone, secured his weapon in the top draw of his desk and began making his calls. It was almost 12:30pm and Keisha and Porshaé should be arriving soon, thought Clyde. He knew Joe was stopping by too. Clyde looked around for his briefcase and realized he had left it in the car. He left his office and walked to the rear door. Just as he opened the heavy metal door to the parking lot, Joe was standing there, in the process of pressing the button on the intercom system. The rear intercom buzzer was wired only to Clyde's office. Keisha, Mo, and Rene all had a key for the rear door.

"**Clyde!** I was just about to buzz you man!" said Joe.

"**Hey Joe**, Glad you could make it today... I got some things I need your opinion on... let-me get ma briefcase from the trunk then we can head on in... How you doin today man?" said Clyde, smiling and patting his ole friend on the shoulder.

He walked over to his black 1981, Jaguar *XJ6* and unlocked the trunk. Clyde grabbed his black leather briefcase then closed the trunk. Joe was standing at the door of the building, and Clyde caught Joe's stare as soon as he shut the trunk, but Joe wasn't staring at Clyde... Joe was glaring **intensely** at the two cars riding through the access alleyway. Clyde stepped over to his friend and put his hand on Joe's shoulder, but Joe's stare didn't break away from what his eyes were focused on. Clyde turned to look at the passing vehicles. The brown Caprice was in front and the gray Crown Victorian followed behind. Detective

Schlesta peered slyly out of the passenger side window at Clyde and Joe. Clyde's eyes seized Schlesta's, and in an **instant...** the distant memory that Clyde had almost forgotten about... the memory that he **thought** he buried... was now at the front of his minds eyes, literally.

CHAPTER 8: CLYDE FLASHES BACK 1970

I t was a cold, late evening in February. The two men sat in the white 1967, Buick Skylark GS 400. They were engaged in a serious conversation as the snow began to fall...

"Gerald my man... it's nothing like that... I'm not telling you, you have to **pay** us for protection! We're not the **Mob**... all I'm saying is... in-order to keep your business safe... you **have** to work with the right cops!"

"Ma business **is** safe Jerry! We had an arrangement... you bring me the shit you seize from muthafuckas and I move it... we both get a cut! Now you saying I need to pay **yo boys** to be **safe...**! I got people out here making deals **fah you Jerry! Not me! I'm** taking chances moving **yo** shit! not **mine...**! You came to **me** with this remember...? I was doin fine and dandy on ma own."

Gerald was upset at what Jerry was trying do. Jerry basically, was trying to squeeze Gerald... Gerald was getting big in the dope-game and Jerry didn't want that... If Gerald got too big, he wouldn't need Jerry anymore. Jerry responded:

"Gerald... you're forgetting one thing my man."

"And what's that?" asked Gerald.

"This **is** your shit" said Jerry, patting the bag of drugs, looking slyly at Gerald as if he had the upper hand... and he did.
Jerry continued:

"Once you chose to leave that small time pot business and start selling heroin, you stepped into the major league my man... Look how much **money** you're making now."
Jerry smiled at Gerald, as if the statement was supposed to make him feel better.

"Your old partner is probably still selling quarter bags to street punks... wasn't he supposed to meet us here?"

Gerald was glad Clyde hadn't showed up. Jerry wanted to meet Clyde, and Clyde told Gerald that he would come listen to what Jerry had to offer... but what Clyde wasn't aware of... was that Jerry was a cop. Gerald knew Clyde wouldn't be cool with that at **all**... moving heroin for a cop...

Gerald responded:

"Yeah, but I don't know if he'll be cool with moving heroin supplied by a cop."

Jerry responded:

"Gerald, he doesn't have to know that I'm a cop... I'm a dealer **just** like you my man... trying to make as much money as I can, as **quick** as I can and get outta this shit before some poor shit bastard kills me."

Gerald knew that was some bullshit, and he didn't like Jerry's remark, "Poor shit bastard." It meant: poverty stricken colored boy, without a father.

Gerald was mulatto. He had a colored mother and a white father that he never knew. He was the product of a pregnancy resulting from a honky-trick. Gerald's mother, Tabatha, didn't wanna abort the pregnancy. She understood that the high-yellow coloreds had more favor in the white society in which they lived in, than darker colored folks. Tabatha wanted her child to have that favor and Gerald **did** have favor... especially with Officer Schlesta. Once Jerry saw that Gerald was mulatto and not full nigger... he decided to keep Gerald around and use him as a stooge in his web of corruption.

How Gerald Came to Know Jerry
Still In The Flash Back:

If you're wondering... yes... this is the same Gerald who was killed. Mo's father and Clyde's best friend... Detective Schlesta was just a street beat cop back then. He had informants telling him who the small-time crooks were, and occasionally those small-time crooks would lead to big time crooks. Anyhow. One of the informants told Jerry about a guy that sold marijuana... that guy was Gerald.

Jerry told the informant to set up a buy for a nice size amount of marijuana. When Gerald told Clyde about it, Clyde was suspicious of the deal and didn't want anything to do with it... Gerald went ahead with it anyway... and Jerry busted him... **never** booked him on any charges though... that's when Jerry offered Gerald a deal that he really could not refuse. Jerry, with the help of other corrupt cops, would seize large amounts of drugs from up raising immigrant mobs. He persuaded Gerald to sell the drugs for a nice cut... The immigrant mobs would grow frustrated with the shakedowns and high-jackings of their shipments and retaliation was inevitable. Gerald knew this and was opting to step away from Jerry's seize and sell scheme. Gerald responded:

"Jerry... we've been doing this shit for a **long** time now... I've made money, you've money... but this shit is getting more dangerous by the **day**...! How long you think them immigrants gone let you take from them? They **know** where my shit is comin from...! They caught up with me the other day but they spared me because they think I have no choice...! They not gonna move on you because you're a cop and the heat from your squad would come down on them like a-fuckin **ton-of-bricks**...! But who's to say how long they remain afraid... They told me I had **one** chance to step away and that was it... My **life** is on the line Jerry and I have a nine-year-old son to take care of... I'm not leavin-him fatherless... so this is it for me Jerry... I'm stepping away man."

Gerald was sincere because of his son. He had grown up fatherless and didn't want his son to experience that same thing.

Jerry went silent for a long moment after Gerald finished his say. Considering what he'd just heard, Jerry was thinking of how he should respond. Calm and with no sign of irritation, Jerry began:

"It sounds like you had yourself a little **meeting** with those fuckers", said Jerry, and it wasn't a statement, it was a question.

"Yeah... the Bosnians **and** the Russians approached me."

"What-did-they say?" asked Jerry.

"Basically... if I choose to keep moving shit fah you... then I'm choosing death... But if I get away from this shit **now**... then I won't have to worry about somebody putting a fucking bullet in ma head."

"What did you tell them?" asked Jerry.

Hearing the suspicious tone in Jerry's voice, Gerald snapped:

"What-the-fuck do you mean, **what** did I tell-em...! I didn't **have** to tell-em **shit**! They already **knew** about you and they made that clear! They know about the shakedowns, the shipments of shit coming up missing... Jerry, **do not** underestimate them immigrant muthafuckas...! They people been integrating the system since the fucking borders opened...! They got people in places, **just** like you got people in places... That's why I'm steppin away from this shit... it's gettin too dangerous for me man."

Jerry responded:

"So that's it... you're **scared** of these fuckers... You gonna, **tuck** your tail and let them force you to walk away?"

Gerald let out a sigh then responded:

"You don't **understand man**..... I'm **not** a fucking **cop**! What type of protection do **I** have against them muthafuckas? **None** Jerry...!"

There was a brief silence... then Jerry responded:

"Gerald, my man... your probably right... maybe it is time for you to step away from this shit", said Jerry, looking at Gerald ("concerningly") as if he really gave-a-shit about Gerald's well being. Jerry continued:

"I'm glad you talked to the Bosnians and Russians though... it gives me a heads-up on things, you know."

Jerry turned around, looking out of the rear window, checking the area then said:

"It doesn't look like your old partner is coming anyway... probably for the best, right?"

Gerald nodded humbly then Jerry turned around to face him again then said:

"Well, it's getting late my man... I guess this concludes our business with each other."

Gerald nodded again humbly and Jerry opened the car door. The snow had come down thick. It made a crushing sound under Jerry's feet as he stepped on the ground.

"Take care of yourself Gerald."

Jerry extended his arm and the two men shook hands. Jerry stood up straight, getting ready to close the car door to leave then he pulled it back open...

"Oh... and Gerald?" said Jerry.

"Yeah Jerry." said Gerald.

"Don't worry about those Bosnians and those Russian fuckers putting a bullet in your head."

Gerald hadn't noticed, but Jerry had his sidearm out, hidden from view... and within a split second... Jerry pulled his snub-nose .38 and emptied two hot rounds into Gerald's chest... **POW! POW!** leaving him slumped against the driver's side door. The sound was muffled by the falling snow.

Jerry headed for his car, an orange 1968 Dodge Charger 500. As he did, a car turned down the street headed in his direction. Jerry hurried, quickly opening the door, trying not to be noticed. He got inside his car but didn't start the engine... he sat there waiting for the on-coming car to pass. The light yellow 1965 Chrysler 300 L, drove slowly down the street, being cautious of the fresh snow. Clyde was the driver and he noticed someone hurrying to the Charger but wasn't sure of who it was. He noticed Gerald's car too as he approached. Clyde had a passenger with him. She was a young Lady by the name of, Queena Robinson. Nine years younger than him, Queena was the Bonnie to Clyde... She was his, "right hand dame" so-to-speak...

Queena knew just as much about the streets as Clyde did, if not more. Clyde kept Queena with him as much as possible, especially when he went to take care of any business. She watched his back the way he needed it to be watched... She wouldn't hesitate to shoot a muthafucka if they were in a threatening situation. Clyde's theory was: it looked good in the eyes of the law for a man to be out-and-about with his Lady and not just out by himself or with another male. Eliminate suspicions is what Clyde always told Queena and Gerald...

As they got closer, Clyde asked Queena:

"Baby... Look inside Gerald's car when we roll-pass... tell me what you see... reaaal cool like though Baby... don't be obvious alright."

"Okay." said Queena.

Clyde kept his eyes on the snow-covered street. As he passed Gerald's car, Queena, trying not to be too apparent, peered over at the driver's side of the white Skylark. She could see Gerald's head lying against the window as if he were sleeping. Quietly, in the proper English that she spoke... Queena told Clyde what she saw:

"Baby... it looks like Gerald is resting in the car."

Clyde knew better than that... Gerald would **never** fall asleep in his car! Gerald had asked Clyde to meet him over on Abigail's street and he would've been waiting for Clyde to show up. Gerald didn't like sitting in cars... It was too easy for someone to get up on you and kill you. Gerald would rather stand out in the cold and wait so he could watch his surroundings. "Why would he be **resting** in his car?" thought Clyde, asking his self the question in his mind. The only reasonable answer Clyde could come up with... was one he didn't wanna accept... Gerald was dead.

The Dodge Charger was about three car links down, on the opposite side of the street from Gerald's car and Clyde's Chrysler was about to pass by it. Clyde wanted to keep his eyes locked forward on the road in front of him but the **urge**, the force of his curiosity, his wanting to know just **who** was occupying the Charger, caused him to disengage his dead-bolt lock look on the road. Clyde turned his head slightly to the left and his eyes zeroed in on Jerry's face. The moment felt eternal... The eyes of each man were searching for something. Clyde's were searching for the possible killer of his best friend, and Jerry's were searching for anyone who may have suspected him of committing the murder. They both were searching to find some type of recognition in the other, but Clyde broke his gaze and Jerry saw nothing...

Clyde on-the-other-hand... saw the poisonous look in Jerry's eyes and knew that he **had** to be the snake behind why Gerald was slumped against the door of the car... It was as if the moment happened in super slow motion... like a lightweight snowflake falling from the heavens on a windless night... but in real time, it was only a matter of seconds. Jerry's face was etched in Clyde's mind forever.
Clyde continued down the street about ten houses away from where the Charger was parked. He pulled into the driveway of Abigail's mother's house. Clyde shut the engine off then turned to Queena. With a grave look of importance on his face and the same importance in his voice, he began speaking:

"Queena Baby... somethin bad done happen to Gerald... this here is Abigail's house, his Lady... we both gone get outta the car and go up to the door like everythang is cool, okay Baby?" Queena nodded yes then Clyde continued:

"Gerald told me to meet him over here tonight so we could meet with somebody. I think that somebody done killed Gerald."

Queena kept cool. She saw that Clyde was genuinely upset but trying his best to remain cool... probably for her sake. Queena knew how close Clyde and Gerald were... They were like brothers and she sensed his concern and worry. While Clyde was looking down the street to see if the Charger would move, Queena reached over and took his hand then said:

"Come on Baby... there's still a light on inside."

Clyde gazed at Queena for a brief second then got out of the car quickly. He didn't want her to see the tears of hurt and anger that were building-up in his eyes. He walked around to her side of the car, squeezing his eyes with his hand to clear his tear ducts then he opened Queena's door. He helped her out of the car, still being a total gentleman regardless of how he felt. Clyde shut the door and put his arm around Queena's small waist and they walked up the walkway to the porch then up the stairs, now out of view...

Jerry never knew of Gerald's girlfriend, Abigail... so as far as he could tell... Queena and Clyde were just a couple coming home from a night out. The Charger's engine cranked and the car pulled away from the curb, heading towards the end of the block. Clyde was now for sure that the man in the charger was responsible for whatever happened to Gerald. Clyde stepped out from the porch that hid him and Queena from view and saw nothing but the fading tail-lights of the Dodge Charger...

"Baby, you alright?" he asked Queena... she nodded yes.

Clyde seemed hesitant, still wondering what he was gonna do. He wanted Queena to be safe before he did anything. He knocked on the door, hoping that Abigail would be the one to answer. A little light-skinned face peeked through the curtain that was in the small window of the door then the sound of locks unlocking commenced. The door opened and it was Abigail.

"Clyde..." she said, surprisingly in a low voice then continued:

"What in the world are you doing here so late...? Gerald isn't here."

"I'm sorry Abby, but somethin done happened... can we come in."

Abigail waved Queena and Clyde inside, turned off the foyer light and they all went into the living room where the light was still on. The expression on Abigail's face showed curiosity and worry. Clyde didn't know what to tell her just yet.

"You two want something to drink?" asked Abigail.

Clyde glanced at Queena, communicating with her through his eyes. They said, "Baby its cool... go-on and get somethin if you want to."

Queena read Clyde's eyes perfectly and responded to Abigail:

"A cup of tea would be nice if you don't mind."

"Nothin fah me Abby." said Clyde.

Abby made-off to the kitchen. Queena and Clyde had never been in a situation like this before... something had happen to one of their own and it was something tragic. Even though Clyde's thoughts were a little erratic and uncertain, he still managed to act as though he were calmly mapping things out to execute them with precision. Clyde took hold of Queena's hands then said:

"Queena Baby... you know Abby and she knows you, so you cool right?" Queena nodded and Clyde continued:

"I'm about to go back outside to check on Gerald and see what done happen... If Abby asks you what's goin on, you go ahead and tell her, okay Baby?" Queena nodded yes again.

Clyde & Queena

Clyde met Queena when she was 18 and he was 27. She had become his hairdresser by-way-of her cousin, Delon Morgan. Delon was a good friend of Clyde's, who bought weed from him on a regular. Up until that night of Gerald's murder, Clyde and Queena had known each other for seven years. They would fuck, they would make love... and they would even argue a little. They went to the movies together, out to dinner to social gatherings with friends. They did **everything** that a regular couple did together and probably more... but that was just the thing... They had never become an actual couple. She was free to do as she pleased and so was he. Although Clyde, never had sex with any other woman while he was sexually involved with Queena... he didn't believe in that 'multiple partner' shit...

That night... the night of Gerald's murder... Clyde felt as if his life might end as well. As he stood there holding Queena's hands.

Facing her, he took the time to admire her beautiful dark brown skin. Clyde wished he had asked Queena to marry him. Even though she was a street chic, she was a **good** street chic... she was **his** street chic. At that very moment, Clyde realized that he was really in-love with Queena... he had been denying it for all these years. Clyde was in a daze... He had a firm hold of Queena's hands, not wanting to let go. He gazed into her eyes for what seemed like forever... looking in at her soul and recognizing that her soul was the reflection of his own. They spoke to each other's Spirit and they both were saying the same thing: "I hope I never lose you... because I would be lost without you." Queena's gaze was just as passionate, for her feelings ran even deeper than Clyde's.

Without thought or any apprehensions of what was to come after... Clyde leaned in to embrace Queena then kissed her tenderly... For the first time ever... he told her with genuine sincerity and true feeling:

"Queena... I love you **so** much Baby."

Queena's gaze did not break. She could now see Clyde's true feelings for her... his want for her... his care for her and his **real** love for her. It was all genuine and bona-fided. A tear escaped from Queena's eye and ran down her cheek. Both her eyes started to fill with tears then began falling on both sides. Clyde loosened his embrace and moved his hands up to her face to wipe her tears. He kissed her gently on her forehead and on her lips then said:

"I'ma be right back Baby... I promise."

Queena nodded and Clyde turned to leave out of the house. Their relationship would now be changed forever for the better.

The snow was falling pretty heavy and sticking to the ground. After Clyde surveyed the area to make sure there was no one lurking around... he dashed across and down the street. He was now standing next to the Buick Skylark. Being cautious, Clyde pulled out his handkerchief, placed it over the door handle then pressed the button to release the door latch. He checked the area again and it was all clear. Clyde pulled the door opened smoothly then ducked inside. He carefully examined his best-friend's body... it was lifeless and void of the vigor it once possessed.

"Damn man...!" said Clyde in a low dejected tone of voice.

It hurt him to see his friend in such a state. Clyde checked Gerald's pulse and there was nothing... the body was even starting to get cold... it was chilly to Clyde's touch. He continued:

"What the fuck **happen man**." he said, half-expecting Gerald to answer back.

Clyde looked directly at the two bullet holes in Gerald's coat, near his chest area. The holes were clearly visible. Clyde's mind was racing. His emotions were twirling, feelings of rage and sadness, feelings of guilt for not being there sooner... He continued in a low, sadden voice.

"**Man**... I should've been here sooner... you still would be here."

He was almost at the point of crying but trying hard not to. You could hear the resistance in his voice as he spoke to his departed best friend:

"Shiddd, who knows... we **both** might been gone." said Clyde, trying to muster a laugh to lessen his hurt.

His heart was heavy with grief and the result of the laugh was a barely audible snicker.

He continued:

"I promise Man...I'm gone look after Mo fah-you... you ain't gotta worry about that."

Clyde's tears started to fall as Clyde thought of Gerald's young son Moreese.

"**Man**... I don't even know what-the-fuck to **do** right now?"

CHAPTER 9: FLASH FORWARD BACK TO 1984

"Clyde! Clyde! Snap-out-of-it Man!" said Joe, grabbing Clyde by the shoulder, giving him a little shake, trying to bring him out of the hypnotic state he was in.

"**Clyde!**" said Joe, one loud final time.

Clyde came back from the journey through his minds dark, distant memory. Clyde was a little dizzy and trying to get his mind to focus on the present... it seemed like an arduous task. Joe's keen perception was aware of the fact that something Clyde saw, triggered him into the memory lapse... whether it was the vehicles passing by or the persons occupying the vehicles, it caused Clyde to freeze in his spot... Joe put his arm around his friend's shoulders then said:

"Let's go inside man... I think we have a **lot** to talk about." then the two entered the building...

Clyde flopped down on the big brown comfortable leather couch in his office. Joe went over to the copper and bronze liquor cart to make a couple of drinks. The cart had a shiny polished copper top made in tray form and a shiny polished copper bottom that served as a shelf. The frame of the cart was bronze, and it matched well with the mahogany desk, the brown leather sofa and the plush leather arm chairs with their bronze buttons. Keisha was quite a decorator... Clyde had become absent-minded of his meeting with Porshaé and had his focus on the drinks Joe was making... he needed one.

There were several liquors to choose from on the cart, but the one in particular that the two gentleman favored... was 'Old Grand Daddy'. It was a non-expensive brand of whiskey but amusingly coincidental... it was Clyde's Mothers favorite, and Joe's Mothers favorite as well. Clyde kept it in a crystal decanter. Joe walked the drinks over to the couch, handing one of the short crystal glasses to his distraught friend. Clyde took a generous sip, letting the liquor relax his mind... Joe brought over one of the armchairs from in front of Clyde's desk and sat it by the sofa. He sipped some of the whiskey from his glass, sat down and waited on Clyde to say something... Seeing that Clyde was still a-bit discombobulated, Joe spoke up:

"Clyde... I don't know **what** it was that you were so zoned-out about back there... but whatever it was, whatever it is... I'm here if you wanna talk about it."

Clyde was looking at his glass, watching the whiskey swirl around inside as he rotated his wrist slowly. Clyde had only discussed what happened the night of Gerald's murder with **one** person... and that person was Queena...

The night after Clyde left Gerald's car... he hurried back to Abigail and Queena. He told Abby that: "it would be best if you didn't call the police... let one of the neighbors discover Gerald's body... stay away from the car and when the police arrived... don't go outside. They gone ask you too many questions if you do... like, whether you knew the victim, and if you say yes... they gone ask you **more** questions... I don't want you breakin down Abby..."

Clyde told her she didn't need to go through that and that he would do all he could to find out who killed Gerald. He had an image of the suspect in his mind, but he knew nothing of who the suspect was. Clyde and his "right-hand-dame" tried to obtain info on a 'white-male, driving an orange Dodge Charger', but their efforts produced no useful results... So after a while, Clyde and Queena put it to rest.

Clyde took another sip of the 'Old Grand Daddy' finally fully focused now... he spoke up:

"Tell me somethin Joe... why was you so focused on them cars ridin by back there?"

Joe sensed the suspicion and uncertainty in Clyde's question... he wanted to **assure** Clyde, that he had no reason to distrust him. Joe spoke in a forceful, reassuring tone:

"**Clyde**... I have **never** seen those guys, until today... I parked my car down the street from the studio... you know how I like to walk the neighborhood and go see Fitz when I'm over here... I passed the brown Chevy on the way to Fitz's and that's when I noticed the guy. I get to Fitz's and the **same** guy comes in and orders a cup of coffee... when he goes to pay for it... he drops a **badge** on the floor... S.P.D. I think he was trying to see who I was or something, but he leaves... I finish up with Fitz and when I get outside... I noticed the gray Crown Vic and the **other** two guys. One of the guys was on a walkie-talkie and automatically, I knew they were up to something... some type of surveillance or looking for someone... The only thing that came to mind... was Moreese's drug arrest and some crooked ass cops looking to score on him... I've talked with the District Attorney and got something worked out on Moreese's charges, so they have **no** reason to be bothering with him."

Joe paused, looking at Clyde curiously then said:

"I can see that **you're** not too fond of those guys either for some reason or another... what's that about?"

Joe lifted his glass and took another sip, waiting for Clyde to answer.

"It's been **fourteen** years Joe," said Clyde, really stressing the fourteen. He swirled the liquor in his glass again, looking at it as if it were images from his minds past... Clyde continued:

"I won't ever fah-get that face... that man's eyes were **cold**... like he ain't have no soul inside his body... **just** like the man I seen parked across from Gerald's car the night he was murdered... I tried ma **best** to find out who killed Gerald... But none of my people in the streets could lead me in the right direction... **nobody!**"

Clyde's tone of voice went from angry to discouraged as he relived the emotions he felt the night of his friend's murder, and the discouragement he felt when he and Queena could get no leads. Joe continued:

"Clyde... Who is Gerald?"

"Gerald, is Mo's father... He was ma best friend... since we was **kids man....**"

Clyde had a tiny smile on his face at the thought of when he and Gerald were younger. Clyde looked up and now Joe could see the anger and hurt in Clyde's eyes. Clyde was in his thoughts. Back then, Clyde's intuition told him... the man in the Charger was Gerald's killer. He told his self that if he **ever** saw that man again... he would not hesitate to put two hot forty-five rounds in his fuckin head... Clyde stood up from the sofa with urgency then walked over to his desk. He opened the top drawer and took out his weapon. Clyde put his shoulder-holster back on that carried his *Blue Steel Commando .45.* He spoke calmly as he straightened his gun.

"Joe... if this muthafucka **is** a cop... you better let me know how much I need to hire you as ma defense attorney... cause I'm about-ta kill this muthafucka."

Joe **knew** Clyde was serious, but he couldn't let his friend threw his life away like that.

"**Clyde...! Slow down man...**! You've got **too** much to live for...! You don't wanna go out like that... life in prison... the death penalty... I **know** you want some justice for your friend, but let's get it some other way that doesn't involve **you** risking **your** life for it... that's the smart way to do it...."

Clyde responded:

"Yeaah... but it won't **feel** as good..."

Joe tried to calm Clyde down, not wanting his friend to make any rash decisions. Joe continued:

"I know this guy **looks** like the man you remember but let's not be too hasty about things... let's not get paranoid... let me do some research on this guy and see what I come up with first."

Clyde put both of his hands down on the mahogany desk calmly then said:

"Joe... do I look like I'm paranoid? I'm **mad as hell man...**! That sorry **muthafucka murdered ma best friend...**! That's probably why I couldn't find out anythang on-um in the streets... because he's ah fuckin cop..."

Joe saw the sureness in Clyde's eyes, and Joe being Clyde's friend for years, was well aware of: if Clyde wasn't sure about something then he wouldn't even speak on it until he **was**... Joe asked Clyde:

"So you **really** think it's the same guy?"

Clyde glared at Joe like, **come-on-man...**! then answered:

"Joe... I **know** it's the same cat."

Doof Doof Doof Doof.

"Uncle Clyde, it's **me**.... Are you in there?"

Keisha's voice sounded through the door. Joe was still seated so Clyde walked over to answer the door. Keisha knew her uncle carried a gun, so when Clyde opened the door... it was no surprise to her to see it on him. Porshaé on the other hand... who was standing just behind Keisha... was a little spooked by Clyde's open display of artillery... Seeing that Joe was there, Keisha asked:

"Uncle Clyde, were you busy?"

Clyde responded:

"**No** Baby... come in, come on in." he said, waving his niece and Porshaé inside the office. He continued:

"So this here must be Mr. **Porshaé** Prince!"

Porshaé responded:

"Yes Sir. I'm Porshaé. Glad to meet you Sir."

Porshaé extended his arm to shake Clyde's hand.

"Glad to meet you too Son." said Clyde.

Joe got up from the armchair and brought it back over to the desk. Clyde's demeanor had changed **instantly**. There was a smile on his face. He was cheerful and his tone of voice was pleasant. A person would've never known that he was just involved in an emotionally-charged conversation and ready to go kill a cop...

Porshaé was impressed with the studio already and Clyde's office only added to the studio's impressiveness. Clyde introduced Joe:

"This here is ma good friend, Joe Hogan... **best** lawyer in the mid-west." Joe extended his arm to shake hands with Porshaé then with a hearty smile said:

"How are you young man?"

"I'm fine Sir. Good to meet you Mr. Hogan." said Porshaé.
Joe replied the same and they released their handshake.

"Y'all have a seat," said Clyde, returning to his chair then Keisha and Porshaé sat down.
Despite that fact that Clyde was wearing a shoulder holster with a **big-ass** .45 in it... Porshaé felt fairly comfortable... he was cool.

"So Porshaé... how do you like the studio?" asked Clyde.

"I **love** it! It's all state of the art... the atmosphere is comfortable... you got **plenty** of security."
Porshaé gestured to Clyde's **big-ass** .45 **and** to Keisha... she smiled at his comment and Clyde smiled back genuinely as well.

"Alright then... let's get down to business" said Clyde then continued:

"Porshaé, what I wanna do is... **branch** out... expand into a wider range of business. I want *We Got Music* to be presentin and promotin shows and concerts **all** over the country, but we gone start with the Mid-West first... I wanna have some of the **best** producers and engineers in music, working out of our studios... that's why I contacted you... hoping you would come aboard. I want you to represent us... I know you got yo-own thang goin-on, but I'm **sure**... if you decide to come aboard with us... we can build somethin bigger and better... together in this entertainment business."
Clyde paused to give Porshaé time to digest what he just said. Porshae's mind was somewhat mystified. He wondered: "why did Clyde want me? Out of **all** the producers and engineers in the mid-west, why me...?"
Clyde saw Porshae's uncertainty and wanted to assure him of his self.

"Porshaé, I know what you thinkin Son... there's **hundreds** of cats out there who might be better than you... but the truth of the matter is... when I did ma research... it turns out, that you **are** one of the best... and you just so happened to be available to come out here to meet with me... Your reputation precedes you young man and it's a pleasure to have you here in our studio."

Keisha would every now and then, glance at Porshaé while her uncle spoke to him. She found herself attracted to him... the aura that surrounded him made him almost irresistible. Porshaé was charming, nice looking, he had something going for his self... and he knew how to conduct his self... Keisha kept it cool though. She knew how to keep her personal feelings in check... beside... she knew he had a girlfriend and a daughter with the woman.

Porshaé responded to Clyde's last statement:

"It's a pleasure to be here Mr. Pulliam."

"Call me Clyde. I'm not good with too much of that formal shit."

Porshaé smiled a little at Clyde's remark then responded:

"Will do Clyde... I feel the same way."

Porshaé grabbed his bag that he had sat on the floor next to the chair.

"Mr. Clyde, I brought some audio and video materials, so you can check-out some of my work."

Clyde responded:

"Son... I've already **done** that... that's why you **here**..."

Clyde was smiling because of what Porshaé had just said... it sounded to Clyde, as if Porshaé was considering joining his team. Clyde continued:

"I'll check it out though... there's plenty of time for that... you had somethin to eat yet?"

Keisha responded before Porshaé could get a word out:

"Uncle Clyde... I was gonna take him to *Sweetie Pies* for lunch."

"Aaaah, good choice... Ms. Robbie's place is the **best** for some good-ole-fashion soul-food." Clyde stood up cheerfully, in a good mood then continued:

"Well... y'all gone and get somethin to eat and I'll see y'all when you get back. Keisha baby, tell Ms. Robbie I said hello if she there."

Keisha and Porshaé stood then Keisha responded:

"Okay Uncle Clyde. I will."

Keisha and Porshaé turned to leave the office, both waving and saying, "See you later," to Joe.

The two left then Joe looked at Clyde. The smile on Clyde's face was authentic and Joe could discern that. Clyde's mood was better because of the new face in the place, Mr. Porshaé Prince, the Prefect Producer.

The two cars were parked on the next block over. Harris had gotten out of the Chevy and into the Crown Victorian.

"What the fuck is goin on Harris...! We've been trying to radio you and you don't answer us! We thought something was wrong...!" said Detective Schlesta in a scolding tone of voice. Harris responded:

"No Jerry... everything is cool. I went to the coffee shop down the street and I left the radio in the car, that's all. The coffee is fucking **amazing!**"

"**Well... fill us in** since we're here already," said Jerry.

Harris was eager to do so. He began:

"You saw the white guy that was standing next to Pulliam when we drove by, right?" Jerry nodded yes then Harris continued:

"Well, he showed up, not too long after the two from the *Adams Mark* got there... And you two saw, just like I saw, him and Pulliam back there in the trunk of the car, grabbing a briefcase."

Harris made the whole thing seem **so** dramatic and **so** suspicious. He paused for effect... then continued:

"I can feel it and it's obvious that **something's** going on in there... First, she picks this guy up from the airport, takes him to the hotel then to the studio where he takes in a black bag of **who knows** what...! The Pulliam guy shows up not too long after that. **Then...** the white guy gets there after Pulliam, and the two go get a briefcase from the trunk of Pulliam's car... and you guys don't think nothing is going on?"

"Harris, we didn't **say** we didn't think anything was going on. I only said... that we should wait to hear from Rosi. Him and Van are **still in there**," said Officer Vincent with slight agitation.

Harris responded:

"Who **knows** what Brian is doing in there? He might not even be **around** those guys...! Jerry, we need to make-a-move or we might miss our chance..."

Schlesta responded:

"Hold your horses Harris. I gotta an idea."

The Interruption

"That is so cool Ms. Rene!" said Brian with fascinated interest. He

continued:

"I would love to be able to speak another language. You sound so good speaking English. And speaking Spanish... you sound **great**!"

Rene smiled, blushing a-bit then responded:

"Thank you Mr. Brian... that's so nice of you to say. I don't think anyone has ever complimented me on my voice, but yeah... I'd be glad to teach you some Spanish."

Brian's eyes widened when he heard her statement, and with a truly shocked expression on his face, he responded:

"Wow! Are you serious?"

"Sure I'm serious." she said.

Brian was enjoying his time with Rene... He figured he might as well because there was no sign of Moreese. His objective for being there was no longer his objective... getting to know Rene was. He basked in the thought of spending time with Rene. He wanted to get caught up in the thought, but his thoughts changed, almost instantly as he realized the mission he had put himself on. Brian had to figure out away to get Jerry to back-off of the studio. There was nothing illegal going on and Brian's good commonsense told him that... right along with his detective senses.

Dolefully, Brian responded to Rene's comment:

"Ms. Rene... that would be really nice, but I uuh... I don't know how long me and the band are gonna be around."

Rene gave him an awkward look then said:

"Mr. Brian... you sound as if you and the band are gonna **fade** away sometime soon. You guys **just** got here. Only bad bands fade away, but you guys... you'll be around for awhile... you're really good."

Brian was surprised to hear Rene say that. The band had never played at the studio and he was curious of how she knew that... so he asked her:

"Oh yeah... how do you know we're good?"

Without hesitation, Rene responded:

"I've heard you guys play down at *Calicos*... but come to think of it... this is my first time seeing you."

Brian didn't know how to respond after that. He came up with something and ironically, it was the truth. He responded:

"Yeah, uum... I'm actually not a band member, but I'm the money behind the band."

"Ooh, I see. **That's** why I haven't seen you until now... So you're the man with the plans are you?" said Rene jokingly, showing her humorous side.

Brian laughed and smiled big. He looked at Rene, gazing in her eyes, still smiling half way then said:

"Are you always this cheerful and optimistic?"

Rene responded:

"Yeah... when there's a reason to-be... and most of my life, God has provided me with good reasons **to** be happy."

Her answer was very straightforward, but Brian wanted to know more. He tried reading between the lines, wondering if she considered him, one of 'God's good reasons.' He lacked not the gumption to ask her, (was she referring to him as one of God's good reasons?) He only lacked the moment. Just as he was about to ask her, the phone rang. The first word came out his mouth and Rene stopped him before he could get the second word out. The phone rang again.

"Hold that thought Mr. Brian." said Rene then she reached for the phone to answer it:

"Good afternoon. You've reached *We Got Music* recording studio. This is Rene speaking, how can I help you?"

The person spoke on the other end of the phone line and Rene responded:

"Yes, he's right here Mr. Harris, just a moment."

Rene handed the phone to Brian. He peered curiously at the phone, wondering who it was.

"It's Dennis Harris... one of the band members. He says he needs to speak with you", said Rene.

Brian cringed at the mention of Dennis' name... not from fear but from pure disdain. The call was totally unexpected and caught Brian off guard. He took hold of the receiver then spoke enthusiastically into the receiver, **laboring** mentally to stay cordial:

"Dennis! **Hey** man! What's going on?"

Brian was actually acting at first. But when he saw Rene smiling at him as he spoke... it made his enthusiasm real. The irritation he felt, dissolved. Brian continued:

"**Yeah man!** The place is **great!** No flaws as far as I can see."

Brian looked at Rene, referring his comment to her more so than the studio. Officer Harris told Brian, that Schlesta wanted to see him A.S.A.P. and to meet him at Forest Park, on the 'Barnes Jewish Hospital' side. Brian responded:

"Okay, I'll be there in-a-minute."

Brian was about to hang-up and Dennis said:

"**Hey** Brian!"

Brian was listening and Dennis continued:

"You sound pretty **good** in there... what is she doing? Giving you a Spanish **blow-job**?"

Dennis laughed then hung-up the phone. The remark got under Brian's skin but he kept cool, not letting it show. He gave the phone back to Rene. She saw the slight hint of irritation on his face and asked him:

"Is everything okay Mr. Brian?"

Hesitantly, he responded, trying to sound just as enthused:

"Yeah! Everything is cool... I just have to go meet with some of the guys and handle some things... yeah, but everything's cool. I'm gonna let Van and Tom know I have to go. Their probably gonna stay though."

Rene and Brian were standing facing each other. There was a silent moment. The two were feeling an attraction towards one another but neither wanted to move prematurely on what they were feeling. Brian didn't wanna press the issue because there was no telling how the situation would play out... especially dealing with Jerry Schlesta. Brian stepped away from Rene, unsure of if he wanted to go or not. Then, said again:

"I'm gonna go let the guys know."

Rene responded:

"Okay. I'll be right here." then she turn to sit down at her desk.

Brian walked towards the prerecording studio where Van and Tom were listening to *Fools Crush* play. *Fools Crush* had their own engineer and he was giving Tom some pointers on how to operate the equipment. The door opened and Van noticed Brian first.

"What's up Brian? I think I'm getting the hang of this audio engineering thing", said Van with a huge smile on his face.

Van and Tom were happy. They were in their element and learning new things to become better in that element... but for Mr. Brian... it was a complicated situation. His best friend and the potential love of his life were at stake. With a slight indication of disappointment, Brian responded:

"Fellas... I gotta get going. I have something I need to take care of this afternoon, so I'll see you guys later on. I told Ms. Rene you two are probably gonna stay."

Van and Tom nodded in agreement and Brian continued:

"Alright fellas... have fun." then he turned to leave.

Van called out to his friend:

"Hey Brian..." Brian turned towards Van and Van continued:

"Thanks once again man... This is a big deal for the band."

Tom nodded, agreeing with Van's statement then said:

"Yeah man. This is awesome. This is the best."

Brian put his head down for a brief moment and nodded... Was it a gesture of humility, or ignominy? Probably the latter... Brian gathered his guilt wretched thoughts and responded modestly:

"It's nothing fellas, really. You guys just have fun and do what you do best... **make great music! Ok...?** later fellas." Brain gave has friends one last modest smile and turned to leave. As he closed the door to the prerecording studio, Keisha and Porshaé were passing by, coming from Clyde's office, headed up to the reception area. Keisha spoke:

"Hey Mr. Brian... Is everything going okay?"

"**Yeah, yeah**... I just have something to take care of this afternoon, so I gotta get going. The other guys are gonna stay though."

"Okay, that's cool." said Keisha as the three of them made their way to the front.

She walked over to the desk and took her purse from the bottom drawer then told Rene:

"Rene... me and Porshaé are going to *Sweetie Pies.* Do you want something back?"

Rene responded hungrily:

"Ooooo, **yes girl!** You know how much I **love** me some black people food."

Keisha, Porshaé and Brian, all smiled and snickered at Rene's comment.

"What's so funny?" Rene demanded. She continued:

"Can't a Latina girl love black people food?"

"Rene... girl, how many times do I have to **tell you**... It's, **soul food**! **Soul food** Rene..."

Keisha smiled at her friend, loving her innocence then said:

"What-do-you want girl?" and Rene fired off her order.

"I want the baked chicken and gravy, the baked mac and cheese, some of those greens and a piece of Ms. Robbie's **famous pie!**"

Brian was still smiling at Rene and taking a mental note of how much she loves soul food. He anticipated the opportunity of taking her to lunch one day.

"Well you guys. I have to get going. It was nice meeting you Porshaé. You have some impressive work there man" said Brian, gesturing towards Porshaé's black shoulder bag.

When Porshaé and Keisha first got to the studio... Porshaé was introduced to everyone and had shared the contents of his bag with the others in a preview room. Porshaé responded:

"Thanks man. It was nice meeting you too Brian." and the two men shook hands for a second time.

"Ms. Keisha. Ms. Rene." said Brian, gazing at Rene for a few seconds longer than, Keisha. Then he turned to leave.

After the door closed to the outer lobby, teasingly, Keisha commented:

"Oooo... it looks like Mr. Brian is sweet on you Rene."

Rene blushed, remained composed then responded defensively:

"He's just being a **nice guy Keisha**. The guy **just** met me."

"All it takes is that first time... that's what tells it all... well most of the time anyway... right Porshaé?"

Keisha caught Porshaé off guard with the question, but remembering how he felt when he first met Sabrina, he responded:

"Yep, that's all it takes... that first impression. Most women know if they would be with a man or not during the first few moments of that initial meeting, and vice-versa."

Keisha gazed over at Porshaé and wondered: "if he wasn't involved with Sabrina... would he be interested in me?" The look on his face as he caught her gaze... gave her the answer... it was yes. Keisha continued:

"**Thank** you Porshaé... you ready to go?"

"Yeah, I just need to put my bag up."

Keisha stepped over to Porshaé and took hold of his bag then said:

"I'll put it in here for you."

She walked over to a closet that served as a coat/supply closet, and put his bag on the top shelf. Then the two of them headed out, on their way to *Sweetie Pies*.

"DON'T FORGET MY FOOD!" shouted Rene.

The Forest Park Enlightening

The black Trans-Am pulled-over and parked on Kingshighway, across from Barnes Jewish Hospital. Brain got out of the car and immediately saw Jerry sitting on a park bench and the other two officers standing near him, talking amongst themselves. Brian approached and they all watched as he did... he wondered what they were talking about... he felt as if he was an informant, bringing information to the cops. Brian had **never** felt that way before. He continued to walk towards the officers, feeling their blazing glare. Brain was glad to have nothing to tell Jerry... other than that the place was legit and there was nothing illegal going on from his observation. Brian greeted the men:

"Vincent, Jerry... Harris... Afternoon fellas."

Harris and Vincent nodded and Jerry began speaking:

"Afternoon Rosi... Harris here seems to think, there's a drug deal going down **right** under your nose Rosi... guys coming in from the airport with bags... guys going to the trunks for briefcases... what's going on Rosi?"

Brian could hardly wait to tell Jerry who Porshaé was and what was in the bag so their suspicions could be put to rest. He responded:

"The guy from the airport is an audio engineer and a producer from Michigan. The owner is trying to build up his studio staff to handle the clients. And the guy's bag... all he had in it, was some audio and video materials of the work he's done. I've seen it... no drugs, no money."

Brian paused for a moment then he continued:

"Jerry... I don't think we're ever gonna find this Moreese guy at the studio. One of the managers told me he hasn't been there all week... I think he's gone and this other guy from Michigan is here to replace him."

Jerry glared at Brian... Jerry's mind was examining what he just heard. Brian had told Jerry the absolute truth about what was going on... and he was hoping for Jerry to say, "Okay fellas... let's not waste any more time on this. Let's pull off of this thing."

Jerry stood up from the bench, took a-couple of steps over to Brian and took hold of Brian's shoulder then said:

"You sure there's nothing going on Rosi?" looking Brian square in his eyes.

Brian answered:

"I'm sure Jerry."

Jerry nodded then said:

"Alright then Son... I trust your evaluation of the situation... We'll back off of this one... especially since there's no sign of our key guy anywhere near the place."

Brian was relieved that he had gotten what he'd hoped for, but the look on Jerry's face was saying something else and Brian wasn't sure what that something was. Jerry continued:

"So Rosi... what are you gonna do about Van and his Band?"

"I'm gonna let those guys go ahead and record. I think they're gonna record a great album... and who knows? Those guys **might** make it **big**... Van really feels they can, and his heart is all set on recording... I can't let him down."

"Yeah... I hear you Rosi." said Jerry, though he wondered where Brian's mind really was... so he asked, indirectly:

"You don't seem too upset about this not being a big score."

Brian needed no thought in his response... it was quick and honest.

"Why should I be upset Jerry? Something good came out of this for Van... later on, something good might come out-of-it for me too?"

Brian had a grin on his face that he **could not** get rid of... and you all know why he was grinning...☺ It was his thoughts of Rene... Jerry thought it was suspicious and wondered: "why in the fuck is he grinning so damn hard." He asked another indirect question:

"You think you're **really** gonna cash-in on those guys huh?"

Brian responded:

"I wouldn't say **cash**-in on-em... but like I said... who knows Jerry."

Brian was still thinking about Rene and how he could now move forward in building a relationship with the Beautiful Spanish-Euro, Senorita... Jerry stepped back and sat down on the bench again, exhaling loudly as he sat down then said:

"Brian, my boy... it's good you're looking out for a friend's interest. I admire that about you Son... Just don't forget **our** interest... what **we** have established... don't forget we're a family Rosi... I know a person can get exhausted from what we do out here and I sense you're growing a little tired... you just let me know if you need a break from this shit. God knows we all need a break sometimes."

Jerry's words sounded concerning and sincere, but Brian had grown to know Jerry all **too** well... Jerry was implying something. The underlining words that stuck out to Brian were: "tired and exhausted."

A long time ago... Jerry told Brian: "that once a cop was tired and exhausted... he was no longer good to serve the purpose... he would be a liability more than an asset. Once you were exhausted and tired... you were **done** being a cop." That's what Jerry told Brian. Since Brian had been on the force, there were a few officers who had been killed... no suspects, no witnesses, no evidence, no **nothing**. Coincidentally... those **same** officers were officers who had some kind of beef with Jerry... Officers who opposed Jerry...

Brian was not stupid. He hadn't had to before, but he knew how to play the game with Jerry... Brain, showing some of the guilt that he felt in the studio while talking to Van and Tom, responded to Jerry:

"No... I'm cool Jerry... I just feel like a piece-of-shit for using my best friend like I did."

Jerry seen the disgust in Brian's face and it was real. Jerry responded:

"Don't be too hard on yourself Son... you were only doing what you felt you needed to do, to get the job done... look... we're off this thing so relax... support Van however you want to but don't beat yourself up about the shit, you hear me?"

Brian glared at Jerry, keeping a stern look of guilt on his face then said:

"Yeah Jerry... I hear you."

Jerry looked at Vincent and Harris, stood up then said:

"Well fellas... I think we're done here... Rosi, I'll see you Monday morning."

Schlesta and Vincent walked over to the Crown Victorian and Harris followed, on his way to his Chevy... Brian stood there by the park bench. His mind drafted as he watched the two cars drive off. He sat down on the bench, blankly staring at the passing traffic on Kingshighway. The cars in front of him halted at the red light and as they did... his thoughts, also halted on the streets of his mind. Once the light turned green, the cars started moving again and so did the thoughts in his mind:

"It feels like I'm at a crossroad and my life is on pause right now... where do I go from here? Maybe I **should** take a break from work, or from being a fucking crooked cop. I'm a **police** officer... someone who is supposed to be **up-right** and **up-hold** the law... Someone people are supposed to respect and trust... I can't **believe** that I've been out here sacrificing my honor and my integrity for this **bullshit** cause of Jerry's...! The only thing we've been doing is, setting-up black guys, taking drug dealers money, putting it in our **own** pockets. And if **that** isn't dishonorable enough already... we've murdered several for our **own gain**! I need some peace-of-mind... some forgiveness and relief from this guilt I'm feeling."

Brian's thoughts were deep and his guilt was even deeper. He stretched his arms out across the top backrest of the bench. He allowed his head to fall back slowly until it rested on his shoulders. He exhaled quietly and directed his eyes to the brilliance of the sky. The day was still temperedly pleasant and no clouds had presented themselves the entire day thus far. As he gazed up into the heavens, a massive group of cumulus clouds began to roll in, culminating over the hospital and the park area, blocking out Brain's view of the sun. The celestial area around him was now dark.

Brian was about to get up to leave then his grip on the park bench tightened, but not under his own control. He couldn't let go of it. His arms were still stretched out across the top of the bench. And as he held it, a portion of the massive cumulus clouds separated, releasing a beam of sunlight directly down on Brian. The light was warm and soothing, and after a short moment, he embraced the light and he was able to release his grip from the bench. He let his position remain the same except for the loosening of his hands. Brian's entire body was relaxed. He closed his eyes, letting his head fall back again, just satting there... letting the warm beam of sunlight radiate over him. Brian was having a revelation. He wasn't a religious person but for the first time in his life... something was stirring inside of him.

Like a spiritual being of divine good and truth, had filled his body and opened his heart and mind... **reproving** him of the maleficent acts he'd been a-part of, and also... forewarning him at the same time...

Brian's eyes were still closed and by-the-time he opened them... He seen the brigade of clouds moving on silently... like a troop of highly trained soldiers, on their way to their next mission... carrying out the orders of their Commander in Chief... and in this case... that Commander, is God.

CHAPTER 10: PLAN

Clyde and Joe were in the office still talking after Keisha and Porshaé left:

"I can do a little background work on this guy. It's only been 14 years... things won't be that hard to pull up."

Clyde was curious of what Joe wanted to pull up, and how he planned on doing it. Clyde commented:

"We don't even know this cat's **name**... how you plan on pullin somethin up on him?"

With an air of arrogance, Joe answered:

"Clyde... I'm **Joe Hogan**, remember... one of the **best** in the business."

Joe was one of the **few** lawyers who could be arrogant without actually being extravagant... if he said he could do something or get something done... then best believe Joe was capable of getting it done. He never let his mouth over-load his ability.

Joe continued:

"I'm gonna check the DMV registrations of 1970, for a 1968, orange Dodge Charger... then cross-reference those names with the names of old police officers from the same year. I can get a list from an old friend of mines... Daniel Isom. He's the Chief of Police for the Saint Louis Metropolitan Department."

Clyde wanted Joe to be cautious. He commented:

"You don't think yo-ole friend is gonna be suspicious of why you need a list of officers names from the 70's?"

Joe answered:

"I **know** he's gonna be suspicious... and I'll ease his suspicions with good reason."

"What reason is that?" asked Clyde.

Joe stood up from the big brown leather sofa, hopping into his 'courtroom grandeur' then said:

"**Well**... if you most know my friend... I'll tell him the truth."

"The **truth!**" Clyde exclaimed. Joe responded, keeping his 'court room grandeur':

"**Yes!** The **truth** my friend! That is... there's an old case I'm looking into... it involves a murder. My client, who I can not disclose, told me that a 1968 Dodge charger was involved, and that the driver **may** have been a police officer. My client saw his face plain as day and I wanna show them a book of officers. Whichever face my client picks out... that's the one I'll run through the DMV, checking to see if that officer ever registered an orange Dodge Charger."

Clyde looked at Joe sideways then said:

"Just like that Joe?"

Dropping the grandeur, Joe responded:

"Yes Clyde... just like that. Trust me man... Daniel is a good guy... if there's some foul shit going on, **he'll** be the one to do something about it... Look, try not to worry about none of that. Let me take care of it alright?"

Clyde knew well enough that Joe Hogan could get done what he said he could get done. Clyde responded:

"Alright Joe... just be careful man... If word gets out you lookin fo-ah bad cop... them cats might get agitated **real** quick, you know."

"Yeah, I know man... but like I said... I got this covered, you'll see... we'll figure this thing out."

Sweetie Pies

The line at *Sweetie Pies* was trailing out of the door as always. However, once you were in, you were good to go. The restaurant had a cafeteria style serving system, so you didn't have to wait on your food... but you **did** have to wait in that line. The food was placed on a 'hotline-table' and the servers would give you what you asked for... to go or to dine in. At the end of the serving line was the cash-register where you paid for your food then moved on to the dining area to enjoy the ever-so-delicious, taste of **Sweetie Pies Soul Food**...

The afternoon was passing rather quickly and Keisha had lost track of time. She was enjoying her lunchtime with Porshaé... good food, good conversation, and good company. Keisha just happened to glance up at the wall clock in front of her:

"**Damn**...   it's almost 3: o-clock... we gotta get back to the studio."

"What's the rush?" asked Porshaé.

He was enjoying the experience. The atmosphere at *Sweetie Pies* was nice. It was Porshae's first time ever, being in a classy, black owned restaurant, where you could sit down and dine in. Keisha responded:

"We've been gone for almost **two** hours... I'm still at work you know. And poor Rene is probably **starving**."

Keisha got Ms. Linda's attention. Ms. Linda was one of the head staff members at *Sweetie Pies,* also Ms. Robbie's sister. Ms. Linda signaled that she would be over in just a moment. She made it over to their table and greeted Keisha:

"Hello Keisha. Was everything okay?"

"Hello Ms. Linda, and yes, everything was fantastic as usual. I just need a to-go order if it's not too much trouble."

Ms. Linda was a high yellow woman with straight black hair. A look that said she could be Creole. She responded in her pleasant soft-spoken voice:

"**Trouble**... Child**,** trouble is when people **not** taken nothing home. Thank God we don't have that problem though", said Ms. Linda smiling. She took Keisha's to-go-order and finally acknowledged Porshaé.

"How are you young man?"

"I'm fine Ma'am." said Porshaé then Keisha spoke up:

"I'm sorry. Where are my manners? Ms. Linda... this is, Porshaé Prince. He's visiting from *Flint, Michigan*."

Ms. Linda smiled at him then said:

"Oooh, okay! It's nice to have you here Mr. Prince. You make sure you tell **all** your family and friends up there in Michigan about how good the food is down here at *Sweetie Pies*."

"Yes Ma'am, I will. I don't even wanna leave right now!" said Porshaé, smiling big at Ms. Linda. She smiled back then said:

"Let me get that to-go-order for you and I'll be right back. Nice meeting you young man."

"It was nice meeting you too Ms. Linda." said Porshaé and then Ms. Linda dashed off.

Keisha pulled out her money pouch from her purse and as she did, Porshaé, jokingly, put his hands up and ducked towards the side of the table... as if he were afraid of her pulling out her "sidekick." Keisha felt a flush of embarrassment come over her. She whispered at Porshaé in a scolding motherly voice:

"Quit playin boy before you have these people thinking somethin is wrong with us... **get up!**"

Porshaé got up slow, saying:

"Is it safe?" He was smiling at Keisha.

She couldn't help but smile back and snicker a little at his humor.

"Boy you **silly**." she said, still smiling a-bit and shaking her head.

Keisha didn't even know Porshae's girlfriend, Sabrina... but she envied her still. Porshaé was different from any other guy she'd met or considered dating... different in all the right ways she liked. Keisha continued to fetch for the money in her money pouch and hadn't even noticed the ten-dollar bill sitting on the table. Keisha had paid for both their meals, which came to twelve dollars and some change. At some point during his little act of humor, Porshaé managed to place a ten-dollar bill on the table... As Keisha pulled the crisp five and two one-dollar bills from her money pouch, she finally took notice of the money on the table... Surprised, she commented:

"Porshaé... you're a guest... You don't have to do that."

He responded:

"I know, I know... but I don't feel right letting a woman that I **just** met, pull her money out to pay for something I ate, so please... just use that to pay for Rene's food and for the tip."

He slid the ten-dollar bill over to Keisha... She looked at him with admiration and humbly picked up the ten-dollar bill then said:

"Alright... I can only respect that."

Ms. Linda made it back quickly with the to-go-order.

"Here you go Keisha... baked chicken and gravy, baked mac and cheese, mixed greens and cornbread, and a slice of pie."

"Ooh, Ms. Linda. I didn't ask for the corn bread."

"I know. I threw it in there... Child you **gotta** have some cornbread with them **greens**... it wouldn't be right", said Ms. Linda, smiling at Keisha.

Keisha responded:

"Thank you Ms. Linda" then handed her the ten-dollar bill.

"I'll be right back with your change."

Ms. Linda was about to turn and walk away but Keisha stopped her:

"Ms. Linda... you can keep the change for the tip or the bus person. Porshaé wanted to show his gratuity."

Ms. Linda leaned back and took a good look at Porshaé, acting overly grateful then said:

"Well **thank** you young man! George will **appreciate** this."

Sweetie Pies was a family run business and George was another one of Ms. Robbie's relatives. Ms. Linda continued:

"You enjoy your stay here in our city. And come back to see us alright?"

"Yes Ma'am, I will."

"Keisha, tell your uncle I said hello."

"Okay, I will." said Keisha then Ms. Linda disappeared into the back of the restaurant.

Keisha and Porshaé got up to leave, to head back to the studio.

The city was beautiful thought Porshaé, as the car rode down West Florissant Avenue, making a right on Lucas and Hunt...

"I could see myself living here", said Porshaé as he gazed out of the car window.

"Oh you could huh." said Keisha.

Porshaé responded:

"Yeah... I mean, it's gotta be better than Flint! Don't get me wrong though, I'm not ashamed of where I'm from... but if I could move somewhere better, I would."

Keisha glared at him a-few seconds, contemplating on a thought that popped into her head... then she put her focus back on the road.

Porshaé continued:

"It looks like this city has a lot to offer. Flint only has a few automotive plants and that shit is falling apart as we speak. I already know... when the car plants shut down, the **whole city** is gonna shut down... People are gonna be trying to find any type of work they can just to maintain... Saint Louis on the other hand... seems like it has lots of other options."

Keisha couldn't shake her thought so she spoke her minds question:

"So... would you move here by yourself or bring the family with you? I'm only asking because, I'm wondering what your girlfriend has going on... I mean... would she be willing to just, up and leave what she's doing?"

Porshaé thought about it for a-few seconds then responded:

"You know... I think she would want me to move down here first, just to get things situated for her and my daughter then, she would probably come down after that."

Porshaé paused. He was in thought... then he continued:

"As far as reasons why she wouldn't move... the only ones I can think of... are her mom and a few close friends... but other than that... she doesn't have anything going on."

Porshaé paused again... That's what Keisha was looking to find out... what did Sabrina have going on. She accomplished her goal with her indirect line of questioning. Porshaé continued:

"She hasn't started a career or anything like that yet, but she spends a-lot-of time teaching our daughter at home. She wants Porsha to be just as smart as she is, and she's **really** smart."

After Porshaé said that, Keisha could feel herself slumping in her seat because of the train of thought she was having. She straightened herself up and tried to dismiss **everything** she just thought of... then she responded:

"That's **great...!** Whenever I **do** have children... I'm hoping I can be at home with them as much as possible while their young."

The Jaguar crossed I-70 and continued down Lucas and Hunt, headed towards Natural Bridge. Porshaé continued to take in the scenes of different neighbor hoods and small thriving business stripes, liking what he saw. The Jaguar made it to Saint Charles Rock road and made a left at the light. Keisha thought about it and Porshaé was right. Her city did have a lot to offer, and she could see why he admired it so much... probably for the same reasons she admired it. A person only had to steer-clear-of the many traps that destroyed ones admiration for the Show-Me State's "Gateway to the West" city... That seemed to be the one thing that proved difficult for **many** young black boys and men.

Beep, beeep, beep, beeep, beep, beeep.

Keisha grabbed her pager and quickly checked the number. It was Clyde, paging because he had finished talking with Joe and Clyde was ready to go meet with Mr. Galloway, at one of Mr. Galloway's clubs. They had to discuss some details about the show tonight and Clyde wanted Porshaé to come along.

"It's my uncle... we're almost there." said Keisha.

"What's on the agenda for tonight?" asked Porshaé.

"There's a show tonight at this club called '*The Spot.*' Some of our artists are gonna be there performing... my uncle is definitely gonna want you there."

"Are you going?" Porshaé asked Keisha.

"Probably not." said Keisha.

She peered over at him for a couple of seconds after she had given her answer then she continued:

"Why you looking like that?"

"Like what?" said Porshaé.

"Like you just lost your dog or something", said Keisha.

Porshaé laughed then said:

"**Damn!** Do I look like **that?**"

"Yeah, you do." said Keisha, smiling.

She felt good knowing he wanted her to be there, even if he hadn't said it. Porshaé responded:

"It's that obvious huh?"

"That all depends on what **it** is?" said Keisha, but she knew what **it** was... she wanted to hear Porshaé say it, just to satisfy her ego. Porshaé answered:

"Right now I'm in an unfamiliar place... and being in unfamiliar places can make a person feel uncomfortable... I know we just met and all... but I feel **more** comfortable having you around than not... When I sat down to talk with your uncle, I was uncomfortable. Then, when you sat in the chair next to me, I was cool... not trying come on to you or nothing like that. I'm just sayin... I don't like being uncomfortable, so yes... I was hoping you would be where ever I am while I'm here in Saint Louis."

Keisha glared at Porshaé and she wanted to say: "even in your hotel room." but she didn't... it was a thought that she would keep to herself. She only smiled mischievously, keeping her eyes on the street then said:

"That's good. I'm glad I'm able to make you feel comfortable, but Porshaé... I don't go to the 'club shows', even if our artists **are** performing. I leave that to my uncle, Rene, and Moreese... I'll go to a **big** venue though, but small clubs... umm um, not for me."
Keisha turned into the access alleyway, drove down a-bit then turned into the private parking lot.

"Alright... here we are." said Keisha, pulling the light blue 1979, Jaguar *XJS,* onto the lot, parking next to Clyde's black 1981, Jaguar *XJ6.*

"**Damn...!** Y'all rollin **real** good down here in Saint Louis...!" said Porshaé, admiring the cars.

Each Jaguar by itself looked good... but together, they looked even better... Both were clean, in mint condition, and still practically new. Porshaé smiled, feeling the prominent aura of the studio which diffused success. The two got out of the car and headed towards the door. Keisha responded to Porshae's comment:

"Yeah.... we do pretty well with the studio, but my uncle had money before he opened the studio. He's been into real-estate for awhile."

"An all around business-man huh?" said Porshaé.

"Yeah. I guess so." said Keisha as she put the key in the door then turned the knob to open it...

Keisha had opened the door to their business **hundreds** of times... to walk into a relaxing work place, free from worry. She pulled the door open, letting Porshaé go inside first then she followed, pulling the door shut behind her. The door was just about shut, maybe a few inches away from the frame's latch... just as it was about to shut... **suddenly...!** The doorknob **yanked** from Keisha's hand... A masked man, armed with a gun, **rushed** in, pointing the gun at Keisha and Porshaé, shouting:
"GET DOWN ON THE FUCKING FLOOR! GET DOWN!"
The armed man ordered them. Keisha was in disbelief of the man's presence and she froze. The man shouted at her again:

"GET DOWN ON THE FLOOR! NOW!"

Porshaé was calm. He sat Rene's food from *Sweetie Pies* on the floor then he grabbed Keisha's arm gently, pulling her closer to his side.

"Okay man... ok... we gettin on the floor... just be cool man... we gettin down." said Porshaé with one hand up and the other around Keisha.

Porshaé put both his arms around Keisha, turning her away from the aim of the gun. He bent one knee and began motioning his body down towards the floor in the kneeling position. His arms were still around Keisha, holding and covering her, and coaching her to the floor along with him. They were kneeling now.

"Keisha, you alright?" he asked her.

She only looked at him without any verbal response and barely a nod. The door was still open and feeling no threat, the gunman turned to close it. He checked the area outside, signaled to someone then began pulling the door close. While he was in the process of doing all of that, Porshaé, quickly reached into Keisha's purse which was out of the gunman's view. He took hold of the small .380 automatic... The heavy metal door shut, and just as the gunman was turning around to face Porshaé and Keisha... Porshaé, as if it were his natural proclivity... instinctively, pushed Keisha to the right side of the hallway and open-fired on the gunman:

POW! POW! POW!

The shots rung-out, echoing loud through the hallway. The rest of the building was very well insulated for sound to be kept out, so the gunshots were muffled by the insulation. The music from the band playing, also played a factor in masking the sound of the shots.

The three shots hit the man square in the chest, throwing him into the door. Everything went still for a moment. Keisha was against the hall wall with her head tucked into her arms. Porshaé was still in the kneeling position with the .380 aimed cautiously at the falling body of their attacker. The man hit the floor with a thud, slumping against the corner of the wall and part of the door. The sound broke Keisha free from her frightened frozen state. She uncovered her head a-bit, peeking straight towards the door and saw the motionless body. She looked to her left and saw Porshaé was now in his own frozen state. Keisha lifted her body off the floor and was on her bottom. She scooted over to Porshaé slowly and leaned her body against his, trying to find some comfort. Porshaé lowered the .380 and placed it on the floor. He kept his eyes on the body and put his arms around Keisha.

"You alright Keisha?"

He could feel her head nod yes against his body. He looked down at her and she looked up at him... there were tears in her eyes. Keisha was trembling.

"I think he's dead... go call the police and I'll check the body."

Porshaé went to get up and Keisha grabbed him. She held on to him and he realized how afraid she was. In a soothing voice, he said:

"Keisha, its' okay... you're alright... Go get your uncle and call the police, alright."

He continued to get up but this time pulling her up along with him.

"Go ahead Keisha... I'm gonna be right here."

He held her hands trying to calm her trembling then he let them go and Keisha turned to go get Clyde and call the police. She opened the door that led to the studio from the hallway and her uncle was standing on the other-side, holding his 'Big Ass 45'. Rene was about five feet away from him. They were the only two who heard the shots... barely though.

"**Uncle Clyde!**" said Keisha.

Clyde lowered his 'Big Ass 45' as Keisha jumped into his arms, sobbing a-bit. Clyde, in a panic-stricken voice, asked her:

"**Keisha**! You **alright Baby**? What happened?"

She gained her calm and her composure then responded, telling Clyde as best she could, of what just happened to her and Porshaé. Clyde stepped inside of the hallway and saw Porshaé at the end, by the door, looking down at the body.

"He's dead Mr. Clyde... did y'all call the police?"

Clyde answered:

"Rene and Keisha just went up front to call-em... they should be here in-a-minute."

Clyde continued to walk towards the body.

"Come on Porshaé... leave him just like he is."

The Dirty Clean Up

"Available units, please respond to a, 'shots fired' call, in the 4656 block of Maryland, called in by a, Rene Vasquez."

The dispatcher's voice was smooth and tranquil as she communicated the call through the radio.

"JERRY! DID YOU HEAR THAT?" Officer Vincent asked.

Angered by what he just heard on the radio, Schlesta responded:

"Yeah I fuckin heard it Vincent! I'm just wondering what-in-the **HELL** went wrong...! All Harris had to do... was go-in there, demand some **fuckin info** on the Moreese guy...! Drive around there... we'll pick-up the call before the street unit gets there."

Vincent was a little hesitant about going around to the studio. He thought it would be a bad idea for them to be there. Jerry glared at Vincent then said:

"**Well**! What-are-you waiting for? Let's **move Son!**"

Vincent drove the Crown Victorian around to the studio, immediately seeing the two women standing out in front of the building. Vincent stopped the car right in front of Keisha and Rene. Rene was holding Keisha. She was still traumatized from being attacked and seeing a man get shot.

"Jerry, I got a bad feeling about this. Van is still in there... we don't know what's going on with Dennis... things could really get crazy for us, you know?"

"I know that Vincent. That's why I wanted to get here first, so things **don't** get crazy... just let me handle this."

Vincent put the Crown-Vic in park and they both got out of the car and approached Keisha and Rene.

"Good afternoon ladies. I'm Detective Schlesta and this is Officer Vincent."

Jerry and Vincent were in plain clothes and an unmarked car. Schlesta could see the light trace of suspicion on Keisha and Rene's face. They both pulled out their badges to show Keisha and Rene then Jerry continued:

"The regular unit will be here in a moment. Ms. Vasquez.?"

Jerry looked to Rene, **acting** as if he didn't know who she was only assuming that she was Ms. Vasquez. Rene answered:

"Yes, that's me."

"You made the 911 call correct?"

"Yes, that's correct. But she's the one who was actually

attacked." said Rene while rubbing on Keisha's back.

Jerry knew well, who everyone at the studio was... he was playing the role. He continued:

"Miss..?"

"Pulliam." said Keisha seeing that the detective was wondering what her name was. Keisha continued:

"Keisha Pulliam."

"Ms. Pulliam, can you tell me what happened here."

Keisha nodded yes then Rene released her motherly like hold of Keisha so she could talk to the detective. Keisha gave Jerry a descriptive statement of what happened. The regular unit was in route and would be there soon, Jerry had to move fast.

"Ms. Pulliam, can you take me to the area where the incident took place? I also need to talk to the other person involved."

"Yes, of course." said Keisha, leading the way into the studio.

Rene asked Detective Schlesta:

"Do you want everyone to come out of the sound rooms?"

"No Ma'am. It's best if everyone stay where they are."

Porshaé came out of the restroom just as the four entered the reception area. His face still a little wet from splashing water on it.

"Porshaé" said Keisha, in a concerning tone of voice then continued:

"This is Detective Schlesta and Officer Vincent. They need to speak with you about what happened."

"Oh... okay." said Porshaé.

He was **so** nervous... He wanted to leave but couldn't. He thought to himself, "What I did was justifiable... I was only defending myself and Keisha. I'm okay... everything is cool."

Porshae's mind switched to his little family... Sabrina and Porsha were now heavy on his mind.

"Sir... Sir..." Jerry called out to Porshaé and Porshaé snapped out of his thoughts then responded:

"Yes Sir... I'm sorry... my mind is still a little off from what happened here."

Porshaé composed his self. Jerry continued:

"Officer Vincent here is gonna take your statement. Ms. Pulliam, if you could show me to the body please."

Keisha led Jerry to the hallway and Officer Vincent stood in the reception area, taking Porshae's statement, with Rene looking on. Keisha and Detective Schlesta were at the door of the hallway.

"This is the door to the hallway Detective", said Keisha, but she didn't dare wanna go back in there... so what Jerry asked her next, she welcomed it.

"Thank you Ms. Pulliam. Now if you could... please wait up front with the others."

This is what Jerry wanted to see and he still wondered, "Just **how** in the **world** did Harris screw this up?" The words Brian had spoken to the three of them, earlier in the park, were now resonating through Jerry's mind. Jerry opened the door and stepped through. The sight of Officers Harris' body lying lifeless on the floor angered him. Although Officers Harris was an annoying son-of-a-bitch at times, Jerry loved that fact that Harris was loyal and dedicated to 'the cause'. Harris was one of his guys... apart of **his** team...! and now... one of his loyal subjects was dead... Jerry walked over to the body, knelt down and in a low voice, began talking to Harris' corpus:

"Damn you, you poor son-of-a-bitch... you still have me cleaning up behind your mess... we gotta make this look good."

Jerry pulled the mask off-of Harris' head and stuffed it in his own jacket. He pried the gun from Harris' hand and put it back in Harris' side holster. Jerry patted Harris' pockets, looking for the badge-fold. He pulled it from the inside of Harris' jacket pocket and placed it in Harris' gun hand to make it look like, it was the badge-fold Harris was holding and not the gun. Jerry did one last thing before he got up. He smoothed Harris' ruffled hair.

"There you go Dennis... you're all set... May God have mercy on your soul Son." then Jerry kissed him on the forehead.

The door in the hallway opened and the regular uniformed officers walked in. Officer Vincent hadn't told them any details yet. He only told them to head-on-back where Jerry was and that's what they did.

"What-do-we-got Detective?" asked one of the uniformed officers.

Jerry stood up and Officer Grazo could **clearly** see... that it was his comrade. Officer Grazo was about to reach down towards Harris' body and Jerry stopped him.

"Just stay cool Grazo!"

"BUT DENNIS IS FUCKING DEAD!"

Jerry pulled Officer Grazo away from the body to talk to him. The other uniformed officer was still standing at the doorway. He was a rookie cop, fresh on the job, and what a hell-of-a-way to start it off.

"Look ... I need you to stay composed, alright...? It's very important that you do. I've got things under control here and I need them to stay that way", said Jerry.

Officer Grazo glared at Detective Schlesta. Jerry could see the anger and curiosity in Officer Grazo eyes. Grazo was also one of Jerry's subjects, so Officer Grazo **knew** that something was going on and he should let Jerry handle it. Jerry attempted to appease the Officer's curiosity.

"Dennis was on an **unofficial** assignment and things went totally wrong... me and Vincent, are already on it so just stay cool... we're gonna bring the shooter in."

Officer Grazo knew what Jerry meant by "unofficial assignment."

Jerry started walking Officer Grazo up to the door. He continued:

"Go ahead and radio dispatch... tell-em to get a CV over here a-sap. When they get here, have-em come around back... after that, you guys can head-out... and like I said... I'll handle this, alright fellas."

The three of them went back up front. The uniformed officers went outside and Schlesta stopped in the reception area.

"So Ms. Pulliam... the weapon is yours correct?"

"Yes. it is", said Keisha.

"Where is the weapon at this time?" asked Schlesta, but Keisha had no idea.

She looked to Porshaé and he responded:

"I put it in the desk drawer."

"This desk?" said Jerry, pointing at the desk in the reception area.

"Yeah, that one." said Porshaé.

"Vincent, can you get two evidence bags out of the car for me."

Officer Vincent went to retrieve the bags. He wondered what Jerry had done back there in the hallway and what had he told the two uniform officers.

"Ms. Pulliam, I'm gonna have to confiscate your weapon for the time being to run it through ballistics... its standard procedure."

"Yes... I understand Detective", said Keisha.

She looked to Porshaé again and he appeared a little ill looking.

He felt woozy and sat down on the couch in the reception area. He didn't understand where the sickening feeling had come from, but he knew something was wrong. An ominous presence was looming near him... circling like voracious vultures, ready to devour their prey one piece at a time... or maybe it was one **giant** vulture ready to devour him whole. Porshaé understood not what the omen pertained to... only that whatever it was... it was not good.

Keisha saw the anguish and uncertainty on his face. She went over and sat next to him. She put her hand on his back then asked:

"Porshaé, are you alright?"

He looked directly into her eyes, unable to conceal the despairing spirit he tried to hide inside of his body. He answered her:

"Keisha... I don't know what's about to happen to me", he said quietly.

Keisha gave him a tight squeeze around his shoulders then said:

"Everything is gonna be fine."

She tried to reassure him, but his facial expression didn't present the appearance of assurance... it still indicated despair. The omens grip on Porshaé was tighter than Keisha's squeeze. With pounds of guilt on his mind and deep regret, Porshaé responded:

"Keisha, I didn't wanna kill anybody... a man's life is gone because of me... I shouldn't have reacted so quickly... it was like... like I wasn't myself... like something just **took** over me."

Keisha glared at Porshaé, questioningly and she thought to herself, "I told him about the robbers, addicts and jackers who are out to get whoever they can..." then she responded:

"Porshaé... if you hadn't done what you did, **we** might-have been dead right now and not him... That man who attacked us was the one doing wrong... **not you**, and **not me**..."

Keisha's eyes were strong now. Strong with passion and grateful appreciation for what Porshaé had done. In her mind, when the gunman came in, she thought she was gonna die. Porshaé had saved her from sure death and she was forever in his debt.

Detective Schlesta stood nearby, listening. He was tired already of the self-righteous bullshit that Keisha and Porshaé were talking about... he was apathetic to **any** of Porshae's or Keisha's concerns and worries. Jerry didn't give-a-shit... "I'm getting sick of this shit.

Where in-the-**hell** is Vincent with that evidence bag? And where is the CV so I can get the **fuck** outta here." thought Jerry... but for him... it was about to get worse. Porshaé began to pray:

"Father God." he said quietly with his eyes closed and Keisha took hold of his hand, holding it tight. Porshaé continued:

"Please forgive me for breaking one of your commandments... I ask you Father God... to **please** forgive me... Whatever is to be done of me, let it be your will Father God... and I ask you, to please... keep me faithful in you and strong through-out your will being done... I love you Father God. In your name I pray Father God... amen."

Porshaé lifted his head and now felt... that whatever it was that was causing him to feel dispirited, he could now handle. In Porshae's prayer, Keisha heard the voice of a man who was truly upset with what he had done and **truly** wanting God to forgive him... When she looked into his eyes after he lifted his head from prayer... she could see the confidence and strength back in him like it had never left. He appeared to be stronger than he was before, and in some unseen faith-filled reality, she knew that he was...

Hearing the door-chime sound off, Rene got up to open the door. She put the door-stop down so the officers could go in and out as they needed to. Vincent came back with the evidence bags... He'd been speaking to the other officers about what was going on. Detective Schlesta took the evidence bag and stepped over to the desk.

"Which drawer is the gun in Sir?"

"The bottom drawer." said Porshaé.

Schlesta reached down and pulled the drawer open. He peered in at the 380 automatic. Jerry looked at Porshaé and for a few long seconds, he felt something... Jerry's brow frowned and he disconnected his eye contact with Porshaé. The prayer that Porshaé prayed... penetrated the armor of Jerry's heart. Jerry felt a convicting guilt and Porshae's eyes were the ("convictors"). It was as if Porshaé know exactly what Jerry was up to, but keeping silent, only to leave the situation in the hands of a higher authority...

The guilt in Detective Schlesta rose and the feeling made him angrier. The feeling was strong and he tried to kill it... he succeeded. His malicious mentality was stronger and "Convicting Guilt", fell victim to, "Vicious Maliciousness."Detective Schlesta lifted the 380 from the drawer and put it in the evidence bag then handed it to Officer Vincent.

"Secure that in the car. I'm gonna go collect the round casings from the hallway. I'll be right back."

Vincent headed out and Schlesta headed back to the hallway.

When Schlesta got back up front from collecting the round-casings, Officer Grazo was stepping through the doorway of the lobby.

"Detective, the CV is here. I sent them around back already."

"Good. We can start wrapping this thing up", said Jerry, handing the second evidence bag to Vincent.

One-half of the coroner's team came in with an examining kit and camera. Schlesta took her to the back while the other half of the coroner's team drove around to the back of the building.

The bright flash lit-up the dim hallway as the examiner took pictures of the scene and body. She got closer then snapped a shot: **CHAUURRMM...** the sound from the camera's flash was loud in the hallway. She didn't know who Officer Harris was but she noticed the badge-fold in his hand... it wasn't open. Jonelle asked Jerry:

"Is this one of your guys?"

Jerry was non-responsive to her question, but only in words. He motioned to the badge-fold indicating, "yes. It is." Jonelle got even closer... so close that she could see the grain of leather in the badge-fold. She snapped her shot of Harris' hand holding the badge-fold. Jerry was a little curious of why she did so. His indicative gesture is what prompted Jonelle to take the photo.

Jonelle was a 32 year old Beautiful Black Woman. She had her graduate's degree in business, but the dead interested her more... so she took-up Forensic Pathology and became a coroner. She was becoming an expert in the "body-after-life" arena.

Doof Doof Doof... the knock on the backdoor could only be the other half of the coroner's team, Ted. She secured her camera and with the off-white latex gloved hand, she opened the door for her partner in cadaver examination & extracting. Ted stepped to the side as the door opened outwardly. He looked inside at Jonelle then said:

"What do we got Nelle?"

She responded:

"Multiple gunshots to the chest; small caliber weapon it looks like." Jonelle paused and glanced at Detective Schlesta and he finished the comment for her:

".380... I have the gun and the casing already in the evidence bags." Jonelle asked Jerry:

"Detective, do you wanna collect his personal items?"

"Yes." said Jerry in a drained tone of voice.

While Jerry collected Officer Harris' things, Jonelle and Ted went to the coroner's van to fetch the gurney and a body-bag.

"So what's up with this one?" asked Ted.

Jonelle responded:

"I don't know... the Detective is being pretty quiet about it. The dead guy is a cop though."

Ted was curious about what happened in the hallway. He had a profound interest in detective work; wanting to find out just what happened to the unfortunate people, prior to Jonelle and him coming to pick them up. Ted said nothing else. He and Jonelle rolled the gurney to the back door and Ted handed Jerry a bag to put Harris' property in. The body was now in the cadaver-case and on the gurney.

"Detective, if you could sign here, we can be on our way."

Jonelle handed Jerry a clipboard with a paper saying, that the body was clear to be taken from the scene and to the morgue. And another paper saying that he received Dennis' personal items. Jerry scanned the papers and signed the bottom of both.

"Alright Detective Schlesta... we're gonna be on our way... an autopsy report will be ready in three days. Should we do a 'toxi' examination as well?"

Jerry shook his head no then handed the clipboard back to Jonelle.

The gurney rolled out the back door and Jerry watched the two coroners load Harris' body into the coroner's van. He still couldn't believe this shit. He thought to his self, "Brian said there was nothing here. I should have pulled off of this thing like I told him I would." Jerry pounded his hand against the frame of the door, upset with his self for being so persistent and unrelenting. The van drove off and Jerry continued to stand there, staring blankly out at the parking-lot. He wondered what he was going to tell Harris' family. The Detective closed the door and headed back to the front of the studio.

Porshaé and Keisha were still sitting next to each other and Rene was standing, talking to Officer Vincent, who wasn't saying much at all. Jerry didn't want to arrest Porshaé... He knew that at **least** three people saw Harris with the mask on and the gun, posing as a robber... He had a plan.

"Ms. Pulliam, Mr. Prince... I have to ask you two, to come downtown to the station to give formal statements. You can drive yourselves down... The body has been picked-up so we're all done here."

Jerry walked towards the small lobby with Vincent leading then turned around.

"Ms. Pulliam... is there anyone else who may have gotten a look at the scene?"

Keisha thought about what the Detective said, and about her uncle. Clyde had gotten a look at the scene, but Keisha knew Clyde, wanted **nothing** to do with the cops; no questions; no statements; no contact what-**so-ever**... Keisha responded:

"Just us three, Detective... everyone else was and still are in the sound rooms."

Jerry wondered where Clyde was... He saw that Clyde's car was still in the back: "maybe he left with the white gentleman that we seen him with earlier... or maybe he **was** in a sound room like she said he was." thought Jerry... Either way, Jerry didn't press the issue.

"Thank you Ms. Pulliam... you and Mr. Prince try to make it down to the station with-in the next hour. That will give you sometime to gather yourselves. I'll see you folk's then." said Jerry. Then he turned to leave.

CHAPTER 11: THE STATEMENT

"Uncle Clyde, they want us to go the police-station and give a statement." said Keisha.

Keisha and Porshaé were in Clyde's office. Clyde responded:

"That's normal Keisha. You and Porshaé just go down there and tell-em the same thang y'all told-em here," said Clyde, looking at his niece and Porshaé.

Clyde felt **terrible** about the ordeal Keisha and Porshaé just gone through. He wanted to do whatever he could to show Porshaé that he was grateful for him protecting Keisha the way he did. He continued:

"Porshaé... I'm sorry this shit happened man... but I'm thankful to God that you was here... aint no tellin what might-have happened to Keisha if you wasn't, you know?"

Porshaé nodded yes and Clyde continued:

"Thank you Son."

Porshaé nodded humbly and Keisha touched his arm and said:

"Thank you Porshaé."

She looked him in his eyes, letting him see the true gratitude she was feeling him. Clyde stood from his desk.

"Y'all go-on down there and get this shit over with as soon as possible. Tell Rene, not to let **anybody** know about what happened in here. I don't want it effecting business."

They all got up to exit Clyde's office. Keisha and Porshaé went to the front to get Keisha's purse and to speak to Rene. Clyde went to the hallway to see if there was any blood on the floor that he might-have to clean up... but to his surprise, there was none.

Keisha and Porshaé headed back to the hallway after talking with Rene. They saw that it was just as it were before the incident took place; no blood, no visible bullet holes... the only thing there was... was the mental image in their minds of the dead man lying on the floor. Clyde opened the door for them and they exited the building.

"We'll be back as soon as we get done uncle Clyde" said Keisha, as her and Porshaé walked over to the light blue Jaguar.

"Alright Baby." said Clyde, watching the two of them get in the car and drive off...

The phone rang at the desk in the downtown Saint Louis Police Station's Homicide Division.

"Homicide Division, Detective Spinoza here."

"Spinoza... this is Schlesta."

"**Jerry**! What can I do for you?"

"Sam... I had an officer trying to gather some Intel on a suspected cocaine dealer... he was shot in the process."

"Damn Jerry, I'm sorry to hear that... is he alright?"

"He's dead Sam."

There was a short silence on the phone then Jerry continued:

"It was Dennis Harris."

"**Damn**... Dennis the menace huh... He was a good kid underneath that badboy image he tried to portray. What happened, Jerry?" asked Sam. Jerry responded:

"Apparently, the shooter thought Dennis was trying to rob him and the girl he was with... I have the gun already. Crime scene photos will be ready in a few days... I'm basically turning this thing over to you Sam... This is your field. I still need to find my guy."

"Who, the shooter?" asked Sam.

"No, the cocaine dealer... I was able to talk to the shooter and he's bringing his self in sometime today... He's gonna ask for me but like I said... this is your field... handle it however you need to. The guys name is, Porshaé Prince."

"Jerry, how-in-the-**world** did you get him to do that?"

"I just made him feel like everything would be fine and not to worry."

"Does this guy know that Dennis was a cop?" asked Sam.

"Now **that**... I don't know. If you have to hold him until the report is ready then hold him... but like I said, handle it however you need to. A girl is coming with him too... Keisha Pulliam. I'm gonna send these evidence bags and info about the incident, over to you."

"No Jerry. I'll have one of my guys come over to pick them up right now."

"Okay, I'll be waiting on-um. Keep me posted on what's going on okay Sam?"

"Alright, will do Jerry." and both men hung up their phone.

Detective Spinoza gave the front counter officer instructions for when Keisha and Porshaé arrived, to call him instead of Detective Schlesta, and to have them escorted to separate interviewing-rooms...

Keisha and Porshaé showed up at the police station. She was placed in one room and he was placed in another.

"The detective will be with you in a moment", said the uniformed officer while placing them in separate interviewing rooms.

"Why are we being separated?" asked Keisha, her being the last to go into one of the small interviewing rooms.

"Its standard procedure when taking statements Ma'am." said the officer as politely as he could, then shut the door.

The words Porshaé had spoken to Keisha were now playing repeatedly in her head: "I don't know whats gonna happen to me... I don't know what's gonna happen to me." The words echoed in her mind and she tried to clear them from her head. She told herself things would be fine, just as she had told Porshaé earlier. She didn't wanna be in the room by herself though. She wanted to be around Porshaé... she wanted to know how he was feeling and if he was ok.

Porshaé was resting his head on his arms, which were folded on the table. He felt empty and persecuted... the door opened.

"Mr. Prince." Porshaé lifted his head and Sam continued:

"I'm Detective Sam Spinoza." Sam stepped inside.

"I'm taking over for Detective Schlesta. I'm gonna take Ms. Pulliam's statement first and then I'll be back to take yours... sound good?"

Porshaé nodded his head yes then said:

"Ladies first right."

Sam nodded then said:

"Exactly... Can I get you anything?"

"No Sir. I'm cool thank you."

"Okay then... Sit tight and I'll be back shortly."

Porshaé nodded and Sam left the room, closing the door behind him...

Sam Spinoza was a great Detective. He served with honor and purpose to up-hold the law... and not only the law, but the truth as well. Sam was a God loving man and one could say... that God showed appreciation for Sam's love by allowing Sam, to become one of the most prosperous Officers the Metro District has ever seen thus far. The Detective Lieutenant holds the record for most cases solved, but he wasn't the one counting. He only wanted to do his job the best he could. Justice was his passion and seeing families find closure from his work, is what motivated him to continue to do the best he could at his job, which was bringing murderers of homicide victims to justice. God, gifted Sam with a **keen** sense of discernment. He could tell whether a person was being truthful or not... and he always seemed to know just where to look for evidence and suspects... it was preternatural.

Doof Doof... the knock on the door was welcoming for Keisha. She was ready to give her statement and get this thing over with so she could get back to her life. The door opened and Sam walked in.

"Good afternoon Ms. Pulliam. I'm Detective Sam Spinoza. I'm taking over for Detective Schlesta. Are you ready to give your statement?" Keisha was more than ready.

"Yes, I'm ready." said Keisha.

Detective Spinoza pulled out a mini-recorder, sat it on the table then pressed the record button. Sam began:

"This is Detective Sam Spinoza. Today is Saturday, the fourteenth day of May, 1984. I'm here with, Ms. Keisha Pulliam, and she is about to give a statement concerning the shooting that took place at 4656 Maryland, the same day as mentioned, at approximately 3: o-clock pm... You can begin whenever you're ready Ms. Pulliam, and please state your name."

Keisha began recounting the unfortunate event of the afternoon, giving Detective Spinoza a full account of what happened. About ten minutes had passed and Detective Spinoza finished taking Keisha's statement. He wrote down her contact information and concluded the interview.

"Thank you Ms. Pulliam, you can have a seat out in the lobby if you'd like."

Keisha stood up happy to retreat from the small claustrophobic room... it seemed to suffocate her. The detective stood as well then opened the door for Keisha to leave. She was concerned for Porshaé and wanted to go to the room where he was, but she knew it wouldn't be allowed. She walked quietly to the door of the lobby, looking towards the room where Porshaé was. Sam was a caring man. He felt Keisha had told him the truth about what happened, and he noticed the troubled look on her face.

"Ms. Pulliam, he'll be out in a moment... Try not worry okay?" Keisha nodded and made her way back to the stations lobby. The door to the lobby latched, making a loud click that startled her. She sat down trying to shake her jitters... "Everything is fine" she told herself... "Everything is fine..."

Sam was now in the interviewing room with Porsshae. He hadn't asked Keisha the question, but he wanted to ask Porshaé since he was the actual shooter. Sam wanted to judge Porshae's reaction and his response to the question then have him give his statement. Sam wanted to see if Porshae's statement would be consistent with Keisha's, after he was told he shoot a police officer. He began:

"Mr. Prince, before you give your statement... I wanna ask you a question."

"Alright." said Porshaé, sitting up straight in his chair.
Sam continued:

"Mr. Prince... did you know that the man you shot, was a police officer?"
Porshae's arms **flung** out across the table and his face went flush of its caramel brown color.

"**POLICE OFFICER**" he exclaimed in an outraged tone and shook his head in disbelief.
Porshaé was shocked by the news and Sam could discern that Porshae's reaction was authentic and honest. Sam continued:

"Yes Mr. Prince."
Porshae's facial expression remained in a state of disbelief and his next comment would further let Sam know, that Porshaé apparently had **no** idea that Harris was a cop:

"THEN WHY-IN-THE-HELL...!" Porshaé paused and calmed himself down then continued:

"Then why was he wearing a **ski-mask** and pointing a **gun** at us like he was about to **rob** and **kill us**?"
Porshaé had a-bit of outrage still in his voice. Sam continued to examine Porshae's demeanor. Porshaé continued:

"Why would a police officer do that?"
Porshae's expression now showed the questioning curiosity that his mind was concerned with... 'cops playing robbers'... He was clearly upset about the situation he had been put in. Sam put his hands on

the table and laced his fingers together then said:

"Mr. Prince... that I don't know... so I take it your answer is no."

Porshaé tried to keep his calm as he responded:

"That's correct Sir. I **didn't** know the man was a police officer. Keisha told me when I arrived here today, a person had to be careful and watch their back here in Saint Louis because it's pretty bad here... I thought the man was **really about** to **rob us** and **kill us...!** So without hesitation, I reacted as soon as I had the chance to... I didn't feel like myself though... it was like I was somebody else... I've **never** done anything like this before... shit, I've never **been** in a situation like this either."

Sam analyzed while he listened then he responded:

"Mr. Prince, you say "here in Saint Louis." Are you not from here?"

"No Sir. I'm from Flint, Michigan... This is my first day in Saint Louis."

Sam managed a small laugh, not in humor but only in the unfortunate irony of the situation. Sam responded:

"Hell-of-a first day huh?" then with every bit of disappointment in his voice, Porshaé responded:

"Tell me about."

Seeing Porshae's discontent, Sam felt a little embarrassed at the comment he just made. He cleared his throat and began taking Porshae's statement.

"Okay Mr. Prince... let's begin."

Sam did just as he had done with Keisha. He sat the mini-recorder on the table, pressed record and began:

"This is Detective Sam Spinoza. Today is Saturday, the fourteenth day of May, 1984. Here with me is, Mr. Porshaé Prince. He is about to give his statement concerning the shooting that took place at 4656 Maryland, the same day as mentioned, at approximately 3:o-clock pm. You can begin when you're ready Mr. Prince and please state your name."

Porshaé gave his recount of the incident. His statement was precise. It explained to Sam just how Porshaé ended up with Keisha's gun. Things had happened so fast that Keisha wasn't quite sure of how Porshaé got possession of it. Sam had asked her the question but she couldn't explain it... Porshaé finished giving his statement. Sam pressed stop on the mini-recorder.

"Thank you Mr. Prince." said Sam.

He stood up from the table, put his hand on his chin then peered down at the young colored man. The Detective took a few steps back then said:

"Mr. Prince... in all my years of experience in police work... I've come across **all types** of people... people who have done **all types** of things... but no matter **how clever** or **how sly** the person may have been... I've **always** taken honor in the gifts God blessed me with... being able to distinguish a person's rights from wrongs and the truth from a lie... The thing I'm at conflict with Mr. Prince is not that you're lying to me because I believe you're telling the truth... it's Detective's Schlesta's advisement... He said that I should hold you until the crime scene photos come back, but I'm wondering... if he felt this was an unjustifiable shooting... why didn't he just arrest you himself? You **were** at the studio when Detective Schlesta arrived correct?"

Sam asked the question because he was curious. When he asked Schlesta: "how did you manage to get the shooter to come in?" Jerry hadn't made it clear of whether he talked to the shooter in person or on the phone. From the answer Schlesta gave, it sounded as though he spoke to the shooter over the phone. Porshaé responded:

"Yes Sir. I was there when he arrived... The officer that came with him took my statement there at the studio... Officer Vincent."

Sam nodded, deep in his thoughts, still holding his chin then he asked:

"So why do you think he would suggest I hold you until those photos come back?"

"I have **no** idea Detective... All they would show is that I'm **telling** you the **truth**", said Porshaé with a hint of frustration and worry in his voice. The worry started to show on his face.

Sam was in an awkward position. Part of him wanted to let Porshaé go and part of him wanted to keep Porshaé until the crime scene photos came back. That uncomfortable feeling had arisen in Porshaé and he wanted Keisha next to him... She was the only one in Saint Louis who could alleviate that feeling of uneasiness. Sam continued:

"Mr. Prince... as of right now I see no reason to hold you... Detective Schlesta would've brought you in his self if there were a reason to."

Porshaé felt relieved by Detective Spinoza's comment. Sam continued:

"This is what I'm gonna do Mr. Prince... I'm gonna let you go but **do not** leave town. Monday or Tuesday when those photos and report come back, I'll go over them... seeing that things are consistent with yours and Ms. Pulliam's statement... you won't ever hear from me again concerning this matter. **But...!** Let those photos and report tell other wise... and there will be a cruiser on its way to pick you up **immediately**! Do you understand Mr. Prince?"

Sam wasn't trying to sound bullish, but his voice projected his authority still. Porshaé nodded then said:

"Yes Sir. I understand."

Porshaé was relieved for now... For a moment, he thought he was about to be placed in some small, stinky jail cell, for Lord only **knows** how long. Sam continued:

"I need you to write down where you're staying here in Saint Louis and I need to make a copy of your Michigan id."

Porshaé gave the Detective his id then Sam excused his self to go make a copy of it. Porshaé did as the Detective asked him to do, writing down where he was staying for the time being... Sam returned and said:

"Mr. Prince, here is your id back, and... you're free to go."

Porshaé stood up from the table.

"Thank you Detective." he said, then exited the small room and headed towards the lobby.

Sam stood at the doorway of the interviewing room, watching Porshaé as he left. "He seems like a nice young man... I hope I don't have to bring him in", thought Sam.

While They Waited

The weekend moved-on slowly and Porshaé was feeling an enormous weight bearing down on him as the new week grew closer. The events of the weekend took place as scheduled. Keisha made an exception and joined Porshaé at the club for the show. She actually enjoyed herself. Plus she wanted to be around Porshaé as much as possible. From what Porshaé told her, Rene and Clyde... He could be in jail come Monday or Tuesday... but they all were being optimistic. Rene, Keisha, Porshaé and Clyde did what they could do to keep their minds off the situation. They could hardly wait for Monday to arrive so Porshaé could be, "officially" cleared of any suspicions, and so their worries could be put to rest. Clyde was also eager to get started on the background work Joe suggested they do, pertaining to Gerald's murderer.

It was now Sunday night and Keisha was dropping Porshaé off at the *Adams Mark*. She parked in front of the hotel and shut the engine off. Keisha turned in her seat to face him.

"Today was pretty fun right?" she said, smiling at Porshaé and reaching over tapping him on his thigh.

"Yeah, yeah... it **was** pretty fun. I didn't know you and Rene were two parts of the *Labelles*."

Porshaé smiled big chuckling a little. The image in his head of Keisha and Rene in the sound room, singing one of Patty Labelle's group, 'The *Labelles,* hit song, *Lady Marmalade.*

"I had **no idea** y'all could sing like that!" he said, still amazed by the vocals the two women possessed.

Keisha laughed too then said:

"That girl Rene **loves** her some R&B music! And she **loves** when we sing together... Today was the **first** time we ever sung in front of anybody though. We don't like singing in front of people."

Porshaé responded:

"Why not? Y'all sound **good** together. I would've thought y'all **were** the *Labelles* if I hadn't seen y'all!"

"You **really** think we're that good?" asked Keisha.

"**Yeah**! No lie! You got this... Areatha Franklin thing goin-on and Rene... she has that... Tina Marie, swag... I'm tellin you Keisha... y'all have a hot sound together. It's my business to recognize things like that. Y'all should consider doin something with those beautiful voices y'all have instead of hidin-em."

"You're just being nice Porshaé."

"No, I'm not... I'm just being honest about the singing I heard... You and Rene **really** have talent!"

Keisha smiled modestly, taking in the compliment she just received.

"Thank you Porshaé." said Keisha, gazing over at him adoringly.

"You don't have to thank me... I'm just callin it like I see it, you know."

Keisha laughed subtly then said softly:

"No.... I don't mean, **thank** you for the compliment... I mean... thank you for what you did.... Porshaé, I feel like you saved my life... and I will **always** be grateful for that."

Keisha spoke with deep sentiment. Her voice was sensual and delicate... The words off her tongue seemed to invite Porshaé... like an alluring spell pulling him closer to her, calling him to a place that he'd never been before. Keisha took hold of his hand and at that moment... Porshaé felt something sensational surge through his body. Keisha continued:

"I cannot thank you enough... there **are** no words that can express my gratitude... I do want you to know this though... no matter where you are, or where I am... I will **always** be there for you, if and when you need me."

He tightened his hold of Keisha's hand then said:

"Thank you Keisha... but you don't owe me anything. I just did what **any** man would've done to make sure his lady was safe."

Keisha gave Porshaé a peculiar look after his comment. Then, after realizing what he just said, Porshaé corrected himself:

"I mean... lady-**friend,** in our case."

They both smiled at each other. She wiggled his hand then said:

"Come-on... let's get you to your room."

She got out of the car swiftly and began walking towards the doors of the hotel, giving Porshaé **no** chance to say, "No, that's okay. You don't have to do that." By the time he exited the car, she was almost by the doors of the hotel. She was eager to get to his room. Keisha felt Porshaé needed her right now and in away, she needed him too.

Keisha was young but still a young woman, not a girl. She's always been so focused on her education and business, that she never really experienced the love from a man, intimately. The only love she ever received from a man... was the Fatherly love from her Uncle Clyde. Clyde loved Keisha like a good father loved his daughter. Keisha's biological father had been in prison since she was two years old and their communication with each other, was minimum if that. Clyde had been more than willing to take on the role as Keisha's father figure...

Porshaé exited the car, shut the door, and hurried to catch up with Keisha. She pressed the button on the remote car-alarm... Porshaé reached her side and the two stood there for a moment, admiring the night. The almost full moon, shined brilliantly as the nights breeze moved the clouds pass it slowly...

"It's nice out here tonight, isn't it?" said Keisha.

"Yeah, it is." said Porshaé.

The two entered the hotel building, walked past the lavish lobby to the lifts, and headed up to the eighth floor... **Ding!** The elevator bell sounded, the doors opened and they stepped off. They were silent during the walk through the corridor, but when they made it to the suite's door, Keisha broke the silence.

"Well Mr. Prince... here we are." she said timidly with coyness, not knowing what her next words or actions would be.

"Yeah... here we are Ms. Pulliam", said Porshaé playfully while putting the key in the door to open it.

After the door was open, Porshaé turned around to bid Keisha a goodnight, and without **any** hesitation... Keisha stepped in close to Porshaé, minimizing the space between them, put her hands gently on his face then kissed him softly on his lips... "Her plump, moist lips feel **sooo** good", thought Porshaé.

Keisha's kiss sent sensational feelings through Porshae's body, and he didn't withdraw from her advance... so from her perspective, he seemed to have welcomed it. When Keisha pulled back from the kiss, she saw that his eyes were closed... it was a good sign for her. He enjoyed what she had done... But what now... what was next', thought Keisha. Porshaé opened his eyes, looking dazed from her kiss. They gazed at each other for a few seconds then Keisha advanced further... She put her arms around his neck, stepped in closer, but this time... pressing her body against his. She was hot for him. He could actually **feel** the heat radiating from her tight, soft, beautiful little body.

Out of his daze, Porshaé took Keisha in his arms and kissed her lips passionately. When she felt his kiss, it was her confirmation that her advances had not been in vain. He wanted her too, just as she wanted him... The way he held her in his arms... the way his mouth pressed firmly against hers... Keisha could **feel** his want... The way his tongue moved wildly inside of her mouth, circling frantically... he wanted her **bad**...

To Keisha, everything about Porshaé felt right. She never felt so **stimulated**, so **stirred** up on the inside... so **aroused** by a man... not until this night. Her sexuality was wide-awake now and she was horny as ever. Keisha could feel muscles contracting in her body, nerves in areas becoming more sensitive, and sensations that she had never felt before... Her nipples were tingling and blood rushed to her clitoris making it **so** sensitive... that she had to step back from Porshaé.

The hard swollen bulge in his pants was rubbing against her "love below" and it was driving her wild. As Keisha stepped back, breathing rhythmically, trying to regain her composure and posture. She wanted to tell Porshaé that she never had sex before. She wanted to tell him that she was a virgin, but the words wouldn't come out... All she could do... was look at him with authentic willingness in her eyes that said, "I'm yours, so take me."

Porshaé took Keisha by the hand and led her into his suite then closed the door... The room was dark... the only lights that illuminated the suite, were the lights shining in from the city, through the windows. Porshaé still had a hold of Keisha's hand. He led her to the couch in the sitting area.

"Sit down Keisha." he said, in a pleasant concerning tone of voice, however. The tone was displeasing to Keisha. She knew from his tone of voice, what direction the night was headed in, and it **wasn't** in the direction she wanted it to go. He sat down next to her and lifted her hands to his face, kissing them affectionately, tenderly. He continued:

"Keisha... I promise to God.... That kiss... was the **best** kiss I think I've ever had... It made me wanna make love to you **so bad**... that it's taking all my **strength** to keep me from picking you up and taking you into that bedroom to make love to you."

"That's what I **want** you to do." thought Keisha.

Porshaé continued:

"Keisha... I could really see myself with you... we have a lot in common... we get-a-long good together, and we have fun... you're intelligent, you're beautiful."

Porshaé smiled and touched Keisha's face softly. She tried to assemble a smile but her fire had died. He continued:

"I've never been so impressed with a woman. **Truthfully**... not even Sabrina... but I'm with Sabrina... I made a commitment to her and if I go any further with you... I'm never gonna feel right when I go back to her... that's not how I wanna do someone I love."

Keisha was sunken and Porshaé could see that she was. No words could lift her out-of the pit of humiliation that she had fallen in. She was dejected. Keisha spoke up:

"Porshaé, look... you don't need to explain anything to me. I understand... I shouldn't have kissed you in the first place... I mean... what was I thinking, right?"

Keisha managed to let out a muffled laugh, but only at the thought of her own, now seemingly, vain advances. She continued:

"I know you have a girlfriend and I shouldn't have disrespected her **or** you like that."

Keisha was almost in tears and choked-up with humiliation. Porshaé could hear it. He tried to assure her.

"Keisha, stop... You didn't disrespect me or Sabrina... If anyone did any disrespecting, **I'm** the one to blame. The only thing you did... was recognize that I'm going through a bad situation right now, and try to **be** there for me... I appreciate you for that... You don't know how **glad** I am to have you here. I honestly feel, that you can feel everything I'm feeling right now, and you felt I needed some support... and that's why you're here... I **do** need you Keisha."

She felt a little better now that she had heard Porshaé explain to her, he understood why she did what she did... but she was tired of the talking. She stopped him.

"Porshaé, can we not talk about this anymore...? Can we just, go into the room and lay down together, as friends... I want you to hold me Porshaé... hold me until tomorrow gets here. I don't want us to think about **anything** else, except... how good it is and how good it feels to have a special friend by your side when you need them the most."

Keisha had spoken her words with more passion and love than Porshaé had ever heard or seen. It was as if she were the Beautiful Starlet in a love story, putting **all** of her love, into her role...

Porshaé gazed into Keisha's eyes, which were shining bright in the dark because of the lights from city, gleaming in through the hotel room's windows. He didn't need time to think about what she said. It did **indeed** feel good to have her by his side... If not for her being there that night... he might have worried himself half crazy waiting on tomorrow to come. He stood up slow and gazed down lovingly at Keisha, adoring everything about her... especially her boldness in showing him she was willing to give herself to him intimately. He put his hand out and she took hold of it. She stood up then, he embraced her and she embraced him. Porshaé rested his head just atop hers and she rested her head on his shoulder. They held each other for a long moment. Keisha was enjoying the long loving embrace and she could have relaxed in Porshae's arms forever. He lifted Keisha's head then gazed at her again. He kissed her affectionately on the forehead and tenderly on her lips then said:

"Thank you for wanting to be here with me" then he led her into the bedroom.

She was happy that he accepted her proposal. They took off their shoes and Keisha took off her thin windbreaker jacket. Porshaé pulled the comforter back and they got in bed. He held her close and tight in his arms, taking pleasure in having her there and she laid comfortably in his embrace, taking pleasure in being held by him. After about five minutes into their snuggling session, Keisha mumbled:

"Porshaé... you're a really good man."

He didn't respond verbally. He responded with his body, nestling himself closer into her. Keisha let out a sigh of pleasure, smiling with her eyes closed. The two of them, pacified by each other's presence, drifted off to sleep, thinking about nothing else except... how good it felt to have someone who was genuine... someone who honestly cared about you... by your side when you needed them the most.

It was now Monday morning and Keisha had made up her mind last night, that she would not be attending class today. She wanted to stay with her new, close friend until she knew **exactly** what was gonna happen to him. It was after nine and Keisha called Rene at the studio:

"Good morning. You've reached *We Got Music* recording studio. This is Rene speaking, how can I help you."

Keisha smiled at her good friend's cheerful voice. This seemed to be one of Keisha's darkest moments and Rene was still able to put a smile on her face.

"Good morning Rene." said Keisha, trying to be as cheerful as possible, though Rene could hear the feign efforts of her friend.

"**Hey girl**.... What's wrong Chica?" asked Rene.

"I'm alright Rene. I'm here with Porshaé so I'm not going to class today. I'm gonna stay here with him until we hear something, or hopefully **not** hear anything at all... No news is good news in this case."

Rene could hear Keisha's worry. She knew Keisha really liked Porshaé, and she knew Keisha felt that it was her fault he was in this mess. Rene told her friend:

"Keisha, I can hear it in your voice Chica... stop being so hard on yourself... this thing that happened was probably **meant** to happen. That cop was more than likely a bad cop in the first place and God probably planned this **whole thing**.... Chica... if I don't know **anything** else, I know this... **nobody** can stop Gods plan once He puts it in motion... **nobody** Chica... and I **know** God isn't gonna punish Porshaé for this. Things will be fine so stop that worrying okay?"

Keisha felt better already after hearing Rene's words of encouragement...

"Okay Rene... I'll try to stop worrying... you always know what to say... thank you girl. I'll talk to you later."

Rene responded:

"Tell Porshaé I said hello okay."

"Porshaé.... Rene says hello."

He was close by and he responded:

"Tell Ms. Tina Marie, I said hello too."

Keisha smiled, hearing that he was in good spirit.

"Did you hear him Rene?"

"Yeah.... I heard him girl", said Rene with a smile on her face. She continued:

"Alright girl... I'll tell Uncle Clyde that he's gotta handle things until you get here."

"Okay. Thank you Rene."

"You two be gooood", said Rene mischievously then hung up the phone.

Keisha smiled amused by Rene's remark then she too hung up the phone.

The morning moved on rapidly. The two spent the time talking about everything... their childhood, their aspirations, their goals and passions. 11:30 am came and Keisha decided to order room service. She picked up the hotel room phone.

"Porshaé, I'm gonna order something to eat for lunch... do you want anything?"

"What they got on the menu?" he asked.

Already knowing what she wanted, she handed him the hotel menu. He scanned over it while Keisha gave her order to the room service kitchen clerk.

"You ready?" asked Keisha.

"Yeah... let me get the mushroom-Swiss-burger, fries and a, A&W Root Beer."

Keisha nodded and gave the clerk Porshaé's order.

"Alright, thank you", said Keisha to the room service clerk then hung up the phone.

"Fifteen minutes tops." she said, turning in Porshae's direction. '11:35... 11:40... 11:45 Doof Doof Doof Doof... the knock on the door was welcomed by Keisha and Porshaé. They both were hungry and ready to eat.

"ROOMSERVICE!" the foreign voice announced through the door. Porshaé answered the door and greeted the hotel worker. The older woman pushed the cart inside of the suite, over to the table area, acknowledging Keisha as she entered the area:

"Hello."

"Hello Ma'am" said Keisha.

"You folks enjoy your meal", said the older Spanish Lady.

"Thank you." said Keisha, extending her arm out to pass the hotel worker a tip.

"Thank you Ma'am" said the older Spanish Lady, humbly accepting the tip then exited the suite.

Porshaé smiled at her as she left. He was admiring the Spanish woman's humble eyes and beautiful smile. He closed the door and walked over to the table area where the food was.

"This smells **really** good." he said, uncovering the plates.

Keisha got up from the couch to go sit at the table. Porshaé sat both plates on the table then sat down to join Keisha for their lunch. He took one bite of the mushroom-Swiss-burger, chewed it thoroughly and was about to take another bite then... Doof Doof Doof... there was another knock on the door but this knock wasn't welcoming.

Porshaé frown his brow a little then he asked Keisha:

"Didn't you give her a tip?"

Keisha nodded yes, as she chewed a bite of her shrimp pasta with white sauce.

"They probably forgot to give us something", said Porshaé.

He looked at the cart and snapped his fingers, seeing that something was missing:

"My **Root-Beer**!" he exclaimed.

He excused his self to answer the door. As he opened the door, he spoke at the same time:

"I just noticed, my Root-Beer is..." and in mid sentence, because of what he saw, he came to a dead stop.

"**Porshaé**.... Did they bring your Root Beer...?" asked Keisha with her voice slightly elevated.

When he didn't answer her, she got up and went to the door. She paused in her stride then picked it back up as she realized her fears were right in front of her. The two plain-clothes Officers stood at the doorway of the suite. The eldest of the two spoke:

"Mr. Porshaé Prince?" he said, questioningly.

"Yes. I'm Porshaé Prince."

"Detective Spinoza has asked us to bring you down to the station."

Porshae's heart sunk to his stomach and his appetite vanished instantly.

"You're gonna need to come with us Sir." said the eldest Officer.

"Let me get my shoes on." said Porshaé.

Keisha started getting herself ready to go as well. She put her jacket and shoes on and stayed close to Porshaé. He was about to exit the suite with Keisha right behind him then the younger officer put up a polite hand and stopped her:

"I'm sorry Ma'am... he has to come alone."

Keisha's heart sunk. Her face showed agitation, aggravation, and anger, all at the same time. She responded:

"Well... can I at least drive down to see what's going on?"

The two officers look at one other and the eldest responded:

"I don't see why not... I'll let the Detective know you're on the way down when we get there."

"Thank you." said Keisha graciously.

The two officers walked off with Porshaé in tow then Keisha dashed back into the sitting area, grabbed Porshae's burger, wrapped it in some napkins and then rushed it to him. She reached him and her heart was racing. Her face expressed an almost, panicked look. She moved a strand of hair from her face then said:

"Here Porshaé... take your burger... I know you might not be hungry any more, but take it anyway."

Porshaé could hardly conceal his hearts aching-admiration. He looked at Keisha and took hold of the burger. The youngest officer touched Porshae's shoulder indicating they had to go. Porshaé and Keisha held each other's gaze for a brief moment, and then the two officers turned him away, escorting him down the corridor.

The three men entered the elevator and before they disappeared behind the doors, Keisha yelled:

"I'LL BE RIGHT DOWN THERE PORSHAÉ!"

She saw his hand come up, waving his mushroom-Swiss-burger then the elevator doors closed. Keisha wanted to smile but she couldn't. The situation was too serious. She watched the doors close then said, quietly to herself, "I'll be there..."

False Report

At the police-station, Porshaé was once again inside the small interviewing-room. More chilling now than it had been the first time, thought Porshaé. He sat in the seat, at the table once again. Sam walked inside and closed the door behind him.

"Good afternoon Mr. Prince."

"Good afternoon Detective."

"Mr. Prince, I'm not gonna dilly-dally around. I'm gonna get right to the point... which is this."

Sam held up a large manila envelope then dropped it down on the table.

"Mr. Prince... why don't you open that up and have a look at what I received today from the crime scene examiner."

Porshaé picked-up the manila envelope, opened the flap and pulled the contents out. When he saw the 8" by 10" photos of the scene, his face **immediately** expressed deep confusion... His mind was trying to understand it, but it couldn't calculate the two realities.

One being: the actual truth of what took place that past Saturday. And two: the present reality of what he was now facing... **pictures** of what **didn't** happen, plainly right in front of him... Porshae's confusion was unshakable. He looked at Detective Spinoza with bewilderment in his eyes then said:

"Detective Spinoza... I... I don't understand this... I mean... these photos... they don't show what really happened... There **has** to be some type of mistake!"

Porshae's voice elevated and became shaky:

"The man had a SKI-MASK ON! And he had A GUN in his hand! He attacked us and that's the truth!"

He was clearly upset and disturbed by the photos he saw. Sam took a mental note of Porshae's pure, pronounced protest then continued:

"Mr. Prince... Based on what's in front of you... I should be charging you with murder... I **believed** you were telling me the truth when I took your statement... but these photos..."

Sam put his hand down on top of the photos then continued:

"These photos Mr. Prince, show otherwise." then he stepped away.

Porshaé couldn't accept what he was seeing and hearing. He tried to pull his self out of the paralyzed state of disbelief. He shook his head, slowly bringing his mind back to its mobility then said calmly:

"Detective Spinoza... If that man had **never** attacked me and Ms. Pulliam... then I would've **never** had a reason to protect myself and her, **from him**! Why-in-the-world would I come **all** the way to Saint Louis, and shoot a cop...?"

Porshaé tried to keep himself calm.

Sam responded:

"Mr. Prince... that's the question I've been asking myself every since I received these photos... and unfortunately... until I can figure this thing out... I'm gonna have to take you into custody."

Porshaé let out a loud distorted laugh then said hysterically:

"You gotta be joking right? This has to be some-type-of joke right?"

"Mr. Prince... A police officer is dead...! This is **hardly** a joke!" Sam fired back.

Porshaé continued pleading with Sam, knowing his freedom... his family... and his future were all about to be, **snatched** away from him...

"Detective... I promise **to God,** that I'm not lying about this..! **You have to believe me!** The man had a **ski-mask** on his **face** and a **gun**... in his hand...!"

Porshae's glare into Sam's eyes was intense. Sam felt Porshae's eyes blazing into him, trying earnestly to reach pass the superficial part of Sam and touch his spirit. Porshaé wanted Sam's spirit to **see,** the God-honest-truth of his story... A good spirit can always discern another good spirit, and the truth... However, Sam's spirit was at conflict with Porshae's truth... **and,** the indisputable photos that sat on the table... Sam was also at conflict with the way Detective Schlesta handled the initial process of the incident. Sam continued:

"Mr. Prince, I'm a very compassionate man... but I can't let my compassion get in the way of me doing my job... I understand Ms. Pulliam is down here waiting for you... I'll go talk to her and explain why I have to keep you into custody."

Porshaé put his head in his hands and said wearily:

"**Man**.... this **can't** be real... this **can't** be happening."

Detective Spinoza picked-up the photos then excused himself from the room. He entered the lobby where Keisha was waiting then began explained the situation to her:

"Ms. Pulliam, **please** try to calm down."

Just as Porshaé had reacted, Keisha's disbelief and outrage at the photos, was just the same, and her behavior showed it. Frantically, she insisted to Detective Spinoza, **just** as Porshaé had done, that there **had** to be a mistake. She even went as far to say:

"That Detective and those other officers who showed up, **had** to have tampered with the scene! That's the **only** explanation!"

"Ms. Pulliam, the investigation hasn't even begun. Let me do my job and figure this thing out... trust me... I'll get to the bottom of this" said Sam, trying to calm Keisha down.

Keisha still expressed her displeasure.

"**Yeah**, while Porshaé sits in jail being accused of something he **didn't do. Murder Detective**? Are you **serious?** Why don't you **do** your, 'investigation' first **then** make an arrest, **if** it's necessary!"

Sam could see the tears forming in Keisha's eyes and the anger burning behind the tears. Her emotions were getting the best of her.

With less anger and more passion, Keisha continued:

"Detective... Porshaé is a good person and he was only protecting me... He has a little girl in Michigan that he loves **very** much... I feel like this is my fault."

Keisha was somber with emotion and trying to push her words passed the lump in her throat. She continued:

"Can I see him Detective?" she asked, tilting her head back to keep the tears from falling.

Sam was not supposed to let her go back there. He had just told Porshaé, he was about to be charged with murder... it was against policy after that. The charged person might become erratic and do something stupid to harm someone... Sam didn't feel it would a problem in this case though. He was kind enough to let Keisha get a moment with Porshaé. He placed an officer by the door while he went to make arrangements for Porshaé to be transported to booking and processing. Keisha and Porshaé spoke for about ten minutes then:

Doof, Doof.... Detective Spinoza knocked on the door then entered.

"Ms. Pulliam... Mr. Prince has to be transported to processing so..." Sam didn't finish his sentence. He let Keisha comprehend what he was trying to say.

Dispirited, Keisha responded:

"Okay Detective."

Keisha and Porshaé wrapped up their conversation. They stood up to embrace each other. Their embrace was affectionate and a little lengthy... Sam interrupted:

"Ms. Pulliam."

Keisha disengaged herself from the embrace, stepped back a little then gazed at Porshaé. Her eyes said: "I am **so** sorry this happened to you Porshaé." He knew what her eyes were saying, but he didn't want her to feel she was to blame for his situation. Porshaé gathered his inner strength, took hold of Keisha's hand then said to her:

"Gods plans can't be stopped... Just pray that it's in God's plan for me to get outta this."

The words Rene had spoken earlier that morning were now replaying in Keisha's mind. Porshaé kissed her hand then let go. The officer that was standing at the door came in to escort Porshaé out of the room and over to transport. The officer was about to put handcuffs on

Porshaé and Sam said:

"Officer Banks... that won't be necessary."

The officer nodded and escorted Porshaé out of the room.

"Porshaé!" Keisha called out to him.

He and the officer stopped. She continued:

"Remember what I said... no matter where you are or where I am. I will always be there for you..."

Porshaé smiled feebly and his eyes began to glisten from the tears building up. He turned away from Keisha before she could see his emotions. Then his escort took him away...

"This isn't fair... this isn't how the law is supposed to work." thought Keisha. Her heart was aching and she had to leave before her emotions grew beyond her control.

"Detective, thank you... I have to go", she said, on the verge of sobbing... That would be her last time seeing Detective Spinoza.

Keisha drove back to the studio feeling an assortment of emotions. She parked in front of the building and dashed inside. Rene heard the door chime, looked at the monitor and buzzed Keisha in.

"Hey Rene." said Keisha, heading straight to the closet to put her jacket and purse up.

"Hey Keisha... where's Porshaé?"

Keisha opened the closet door and the first thing she saw... was Porshae's black shoulder bag. She was stuck for a moment. Then she pulled herself away from the closet, shut it, turned around... then answered Rene's question, dejectedly, with her frustration still very evident.

"Things didn't go so good Rene... they're gonna charge him with murder."

"**Murder..!** Oh-my-God...! **How can they do that**!? It was **self defense.**"

Rene felt a great indignation she had never felt before... all from the injustice of yet, another young Black Man. She was loss for words. Keisha looked at the disbelief on Rene's face then voiced her suspicions vehemently:

"Rene... I **KNOW them dirty-ass-police officers TOOK the gun outta that bastard's hand, AND TOOK the ski-mask OFF his face!**"

Keisha calmed herself a-little, although **still** clearly upset then

continued:

"They made it look like he was holding **his badge,** not the **gun**! And they took **pictures** of **that shit... instead of the fucking truth**!"

It was Rene's first time seeing Keisha so riled-up about something. She never heard Keisha use the F-word before, until now. Keisha continued:

"I have to get Porshae's things from the hotel room... is Uncle Clyde here?"

Rene answered:

"Yeah, he's here... but Keisha, girl, you need to slow **down**... you're **all** over the place! Uncle Clyde is in his office talking to Mr. Hogan, so just slow down... get your thoughts together and **then** go back there and talk to him... maybe y'all can figure something out to help Porshaé outta jail. Just try to **breathe** first Girl... I've never seen you like this before."

Rene was concerned for her friend. Her voice and facial expression showed it. Keisha peered at Rene then flopped herself down on the couch in the reception are, letting out a long breathe. Rene continued:

"You really like him huh?"

Keisha was looking at the ceiling... The moment Rene asked the question Keisha lowered her head and her eyes made contact with Rene's. The answer didn't have to be verbal... Rene could see it in Keisha's eyes... the answer was yes. Keisha was calm now and she tried to relax her frizzled nerves. She spoke softly:

"Porshaé is a really good guy Rene... I just feel **so bad** about all of this... It was my gun and I feel responsible for what he's going through.... **Damn-it** why did he have to see ma gun...!"

Keisha paused then continued:

"Rene, they're charging him with **murder**... murder of a **police officer...**! Them white folks gone try to give him the death penalty if they find him guilty...! I don't know what to do...?"

Rene got up and went over to sit by her best-friend's side. She put her arm around Keisha's shoulders... Keisha's head was down.

"Keisha, look at me" said Rene, lifting Keisha's head up then she continued:

"We're sitting in the **same** place you and Porshaé were sitting Saturday... You remember the prayer he prayed?"

Keisha nodded yes, remembering the prayer. Rene continued:

"I watched him while he was praying and Keisha... when he finished... I saw a **glow** around him... I mean, it was **amazing...!** I could not even **speak**... Keisha, God has put His Grace around Porshaé, and I feel that he'll come outta this thing okay... It might take a little time, but I know God has everything under control. All of us know that man had a gun and a ski-mask on... we didn't know he was a cop though... but you know what? That only **confirms** that he was a bad cop... Maybe in some unexplainable work of fate, this is how God planned things to go... Maybe this cop was **supposed** to be killed by Porshaé... Maybe there's a bigger picture waiting to be revealed and this is what it took to start the unveiling of it... but **who** knows except for God, right? All we can do is have faith that God will bring the truth to light and play our part... look... you go talk to Uncle Clyde... I'll stay with you today and we can both go pick-up Porshae's things from the hotel, alright?"

Keisha was teary-eyed. Rene's words were the truth and very heart-felt. Keisha didn't seem as distressed and frantic as she did just a moment ago. Without saying a word, Keisha gave Rene a tight hug and held her for a long moment. Rene returned the hug, glad she was able to help Keisha feel better.

"I love you Rene." said Keisha with genuine sincerity.

"Awww.... I love you too Keisha." said Rene and the two squeezed each other tighter and gave one another an affectionate kiss on the cheek.

When they released from their hug, the two were smiling.

"Rene... I've never had to deal with something like this before. I'm glad you're here Girl... I felt like I was about to **lose-it** up in here!"

Rene responded, gesturing comically in her Spanish accent:

"Yeaaah Chica... cause you was like, **"I gotta do dis! I gotta dat! Where's Uncle Clyde? Fuck-da-police...!"**

Keisha erupted into laughter, smiling big, humored by Rene's imitation of her, when she first arrived at the studio. Keisha responded:

"Rene, I was **not** acting like that."

"Girl, **yes** you **was!**" said Rene, smiling at Keisha...

Keisha was glad to have her best friend there... She was composed, her thoughts were together and she was ready to talk to her Uncle about the photos the Detective had shown her... After Keisha finished telling Clyde and Joe about the photos and what Detective Spinoza told her... the two men couldn't believe what they had just heard... Clyde kept his cool despite his minds outrage and Joe asked Keisha:

"Keisha. Can you describe the officer that was shot and the clothes he was wearing in the photo?"

Keisha gave Joe a vivid description of Officer Harris... all the way down to the badge-fold that he was **supposedly** holding at the time of the shooting. Joe had a glimmer of surprise in his eyes.

"**Clyde!**" Joe exclaimed then continued:

"That's the **same** guy from the coffee-shop! The **guy** from the **brown Chevy**..."

Keisha peered at Joe and then at her uncle. She was the only one in the dark about what Joe and Clyde already suspected. Joe began to fill her in, on their suspicions.

"Keisha. The man you just described... your uncle and I saw that same man hanging around here Saturday... along with some other officers as well."

She didn't understand what was going on so she asked:

"Why would they be hanging around here? Nothing ever happens around here."

"That's the **same** thang me and Joe was wondering Baby." said Clyde.

Joe had an idea.

"Keisha, you guys keep a VHS tape on record of the front lobby, right?"

"Yeah." said Keisha.

"Do you still have the one from Saturday?"

"Yeah will still have it, I'll go get it."

Keisha dashed up front to retrieve the VHS tape. Joe looked at Clyde mischievously, as if he had some amazing trick up his sleeve.

"What-are-you thinking Joe?"

Joe smiled then answered:

"Let's just wait until Keisha gets back."

Keisha returned a couple of minutes later with the VHS tape.

"Here it is." she said, handing the VHS tape to Joe.

"Alright... let's pop this bad-boy in, and see what we got."

Joe stepped over to the mahogany TV/ VCR stand, turned the power on, put the VHS tape in the VCR then pressed play. He fast-forwarded and the images popped up on the screen, showing the officers entering the building.

"Keisha, do you remember the names of the officers?" asked Joe.

"Yeah... only the two who got here first." said Keisha.

Joe pressed the pause button then pointed to one of the images on the screen:

"Okay Keisha. Who is this?"

Keisha answered:

"That's Detective Schlesta... He was the one I showed to the hallway... After I did, he asked me to wait up front... the other officer, Officer Vincent... He never went to the back hallway."

"Clyde, hand me that printout from the DMV." said Joe.

Joe had already obtained the information from the DMV that morning. If he could put a face with a name on the print out... he wouldn't need to speak with Chief Isom about the matter. Clyde handed Joe the printout and Joe let his fingers scroll down the list of alphabetically ordered names, anxious to see if there was a, Schlesta on it. The screen was still paused on Schlesta's image.

"Clyde, you're not gonna believe this man." said Joe with revelation.

Joe stepped over to Clyde's desk, took a pen from the apple shaped ink-pen and pencil holder... He laid the list on the desk, circled a name and stepped back over to the TV. Joe pointed at the image on the screen then said:

"That's your driver of the 1968 Dodge Charger... You were right Clyde."

Clyde looked at the circled name on the list.

"Jerry Schlesta." he said quietly then got up slowly from his desk, keeping his eyes on the TV screen.

Clyde stepped over to the TV. He studied the face that had haunted him for fourteen years. Keisha stood there, watching her uncle's unfamiliar behavior, and **still** unaware of what was going on.

"Uncle Clyde... Can you fill-me-in a little more... What's going on?"

Clyde directed his eyes to Keisha. She was now a-part of this... She had experienced a sobering injustice and was now **fully** aware of the corruption living inside the law enforcement agency. He could now explain to her, his suspicions of what he felt happened to Mo's father, without her having any bias opinions. Clyde began explaining everything to Keisha... from the beginning.

A lot was revealed that day... Keisha found out about Mo's arrest and Mo's father, something she had never known about. Clyde's suspicions had been confirmed and substantiated by actual video footage from **his** own place of business **and**... Official documentation from the DMV...

Tuesday morning; Police Headquarters

Detective Spinoza wanted to do a thorough investigation of the case, but when he informed the Chief of it... the Chief shut him down before he could even get started. Sam wanted to interview the Officers, the coroners, Ms. Vasquez **and** Detective Schlesta, but the Chief told Sam:

"I don't want you stirring-things-up inside the department Sam. One of my Officers is dead, so as far as I'm concerned... we have our man. This case is closed Sam... Let the lawyers and prosecutor sort it out, **if** there's anything to be sorted. But don't start a battle in here with our own guys... for your sake **and** the Departments sake."

Sam was despondent by the Chiefs stand on the case. Whether it was a crook or a cop, he wanted to know the truth behind a matter... especially in this case... because Keisha and Porshae's statements were just **too** convincing... And Detective Schlesta's actions... were **too** unusual... It didn't sit well with Sam closing the case... but he followed the Chiefs orders and closed it... The following day, Wednesday, May 16th Porshaé was arraigned for murder.

Detective Schlesta told Brian, that he wanted him to cancel the recording sessions at the studio, although... Brian was reluctant to do so and he continued going to the studio with Van. Brian felt bad for what Porshaé was going through... "Porshaé and Keisha were really good people" thought Brian, though there was nothing he could do about the situation with-out putting his self in harms way... Jerry.

Keisha went to see Porshaé everyday that visits were allowed at the jail, doing her best to keep his spirit up... Sabrina came down from Michigan to support her man, although she took the reality of the situation, **really** hard... Seeing and talking to Porshaé behind a glass, was almost **too** much for her to bear. She couldn't believe her man was in jail for murder and facing life in prison. For Sabrina, it felt like a nightmare and she was hoping to wake-up from it soon. Keisha and Sabrina bonded quickly and the two became good friends... Whenever Sabrina came to Saint Louis to visit Porshaé, she always stayed with Keisha.

CHAPTER 12: THE STRATEGY

Joe wanted to get involved in Porshae's case, but after viewing the photos in the file, it was clear to Joe, the officers had corrupted the scene. Porshaé was totally defenseless against the corrupted evidence... If he were to go to trial; Rene's, Clyde's, nor Keisha's testimonies would hold-up against the photos and sworn testimonies of police officers... The courts would convict Porshaé of murder and Joe didn't want that to happen. The photos were the nail-in-the-coffin for Porshaé. However, Joe **did** have powerful ties in the legal system... He told Keisha:

"The next time you go see Porshaé... tell him **not** to make any plea agreements and tell the judge, he's gonna try to obtain private representation. It's basically a still tactic. Let him know I'm gonna talk to someone about the case first, and then I'll let him know soon, on what to do next."

Keisha did just that on her next visit with Porshaé. He followed the advice and the judge gave him two weeks to acquire counsel before his next court date... That gave Joe plenty of time to work his magic. In the beginning margin of those two weeks, Joe made a phone call to a longtime friend of his...

"Hello?"

The voice of Judge Luiet Valley sounded smoothly through the receiver. Joe responded cheerfully:

"Hello, Judge Valley."

Luiet was delighted to hear from Joe. They had a long reputable friendship with each other.

"Joe, we're not in court Dear... You don't have to call me judge."

"I know Luiet... but I just **love** to remind myself of the authority a woman I'm so **fond** of, possesses... It makes me feel all warm inside."

Luiet could sense Joe smiling at the other end of the phone-line. She responded:

"**Ooh** Joe, stop it... I know what makes you feel all warm inside, and it's **not** my authority."

Joe was **really** smiling now. He responded:

"Yes you do know my Dear... **yes** you do."

"You're so bad Joe", said Luiet.

"Only when I'm with you my Dear", said Joe.

The two of them were smiling pleasurably on each end of the phone line, enjoying the manner and feel that the phone conversation had taken. Luiet continued:

"Speaking of being with me... when am I gonna see you again?"

Joe responded:

"Well... that's **just** what I was calling to find out... when can I see you?"

Luiet knew Joe all too well. She answered him:

"That all depends... If it's a business call then I can see you tomorrow, after my morning session... but if it's a **pleasure** call... how about this weekend...? It's been a little while since you've been inside my chambers", said Luiet, grinning mischievously.

Joe's mind began to reminisce of how Luiet felt and how beautiful her face and body looked... She was a mature woman who took very good care of herself... and Joe admired and took pleasure in **all** of her good care. He indulged in a thought of their previous ("sexcapade")...

Luiet and Joe's friendship, stemmed back more than twenty years. They met in law school... not the best of friends at first. Luiet felt Joe was too cocky and over confident in his self, and Joe felt Luiet was conceited and too conservative, to **truly** be a good lawyer. When their professor took noticed of their aversion for one another, he thought it would be a good idea and paired them together as partners on a project. That idea... turned out two of the **best** advocates of law he had ever taught... In the process of that project, the two became really good associates then soon after, good friends.

In school, they never officially dated, but during their school years, they practically were inseparable, though never becoming intimately or romantically involved. They only develop their relationship as two loving friends, who had a passion to pursue their career in law, to the fullest of their ability. Neither of them ever married, but they both had a few serious courtships.

However, those courtships proved to be unsuccessful because of Luiet's and Joe's dedication to their career. It became a conflict of interest with their significant others and eventually, brought them to parting their separate ways, however. The two bossom buddies, saw each other often in the courthouses of Saint Louis. Their friendship never grew distant.

It was not until eight or nine years earlier when Luiet was elected to sit on the bench... that the two got together to celebrate. After dinner and small private party's worth of drinks, the celebration turned into a long night of pleasurable lovemaking. They both welcomed it with open hearts that had been longing for one another, for years... Luiet and Joe have been exclusive every since... opting to keep their love life, out-of the eyes-of-the-public, as well as their associates and constituents. They seemed to enjoy having it that way.

Luiet continued:

"So, Counselor... What will it be... business or pleasure?"
Joe was grinning wide like a Cheshire cat, loving the sound of Luiet's smooth sensual voice. He responded just as alluring:

"Well Your-Honor... I was hoping you would grant me a two in one meeting."
Joe's answer roused the sexually filthy part of Luiet's mind. She responded:

"Uumm, two in one... that sounds exciting... but I don't think my chamber is big enough for that... why don't we focus on the business first and then we can give our undivided attention to the pleasure afterwards."

"Sounds good to me, Beautiful" said Joe.

The sexual innuendos faded and the conversation was back to a casual conservative one. Luiet continued:

"So after my morning session, we can have lunch and discuss what's on your mind."

"Thank you Luiet. This thing I need to speak to you about is serious."

"It **must** be if you need to talk to **me** about it... Joe, I know you're a **very** tactful man... You've always been able to handle difficult situations so **effortlessly**... you make things seem **so easy...** I'm **still** somewhat envious... however. That's just **one** of the many reasons why I'm grateful to have you like I do... so it's my pleasure to be able to assist you however you need me to, my Dear."

Joe smiled wide again. Hearing Luiet's loyalty to their friendship was heart warming... His body was getting all warm inside. He responded:

"There it **goes**."

"What is Joe? There what goes?" asked Luiet curiously.

Joe answered:

"You're making me feel all warm inside."

Luiet let out a coy laugh and responded with laughter still in her voice:

"I'll see you tomorrow Joe. I love you."

"I love you too Luiet... See you then."

The two met for lunch and Joe gave Luiet the entire run-down of what happened... from Gerald and Clyde, Keisha and Porshaé, Detective Jerry Schlesta and Officer Dennis Harris... even his own involvement in the matter. Joe knew Porshae's case could be put in front of Luiet's bench. He only had to put together a strategy for it to be so. The strategy wouldn't clear Porshaé of the murder charge, but it would get him the best sentence possible and allow him a chance for an appeal, in the case some new evidence materialized...

Keisha had written down all of Joe's advisement's for the strategy. On her visits with Porshaé, they would go over them thoroughly. Making sure they had everything right so Porshaé would be ready...

His court date arrived and he was back in front of the

arraignment judge. Keisha was in the audience that morning as usual for Porshae's court appearance. The judge for division 25, Judge Ferguson, began:

"Good morning Mr. Prince."

Porshaé was standing at the podium in front of Judge Ferguson's bench. He responded:

"Good morning Your Honor."

"Mr.Prince, you were given time to acquire private representation. Have you done so yet?"

He responded humbly:

"Your Honor... unfortunately, I was not able to come up with the finances to obtain private counsel. I'd like to ask the court if it could provide me with public counsel."

Judge Ferguson was an African American woman with deep roots in her African heritage. The reason she had taken a career in law, was to establish some balance in the legal system for the African American race. The report and statements that she read from Porshae's case file, confused her. The photos were compelling but she felt something was strongly amiss. Judge Ferguson wondered: "Why would a young man who has never been in **any** trouble before, **all** the way from Michigan... shoot an unarmed plain clothes officer."

She knew if he went to trial, he would lose and spend the rest of his life in prison... or worst, receive the death penalty.

Judge Ferguson peered down at Porshaé and responded solemnly:

"Yes Mr. Prince... this degree of a charge **is** expensive to represent. This is a **very serious** charge... Are you sure you've exhausted your efforts at trying to obtain counsel?"

Porshaé glanced back at Keisha who was sitting in the audience, alone this time... Rene had been with her the first time. Keisha smiled at Porshaé with her eyes. He turned back to Judge Ferguson and answered:

"Yes Your Honor. I have no other options at this time."

She looked at Porshaé curiously then asked the question in her mind:

"Young Man... **how** did you get yourself **into** such a situation?"

She continued:

"Alright then Mr. Prince... The court will assign you a public counselor. Your next court date will be..."

Judge Ferguson turned to the court clerk and the clerk checked a date book then said:

"June 13th Your Honor."

Judge Ferguson repeated the clerk:

"June 13th Mr. Prince, in division 21, preliminary hearings... A public counselor will be to see you before that court date, **hopefully**."

"Thank you Your Honor." said Porshaé.

Judge Ferguson nodded and with an expression of solemn concern on her face, said:

"You're welcome Mr. Prince... Stay positive young man."

Porshaé nodded and the sheriff escorted him out of the courtroom and back to the holding tank. There he would sit, waiting to be transported back to the jail.

Friday, June 1st:

Sabrina came down from Michigan to see Porshaé. The jail allowed her to stay for, four hours since she was from out-of-state. Their visit was pleasant regardless of having to see each other behind a glass... They talked the whole duration of the visit. Porshaé could feel the love emitting from Sabrina and she could feel his love just the same. They wanted to hold each other **so** desperately. Their hearts beat hard for one another and their longing to touch grew stronger as they sat on opposite sides of the glass... They spoke mostly about their daughter, Porsha, and about what they wanted to do when Porshaé got home.

At certain times during the visit, Sabrina couldn't help but let her tears fall. One particular time was when Sabrina was speaking about her Mother, Ms. Dukes:

"Baby, Momma's been praying for you... She's been keeping me encouraged and everything... Baby, I **hate** it that we're in this mess! It's **hard** not having you at home and wondering what's gonna happen."

Sabrina touched the glass and Porshaé touched the other side, matching her hand. Sabrina continued:

"I miss you **so, so much** Baby!"

Her words came up hard from her heart, passed her throat and out of her mouth. She tried to hold-up her emotions, but they were too heavy. The tears started to form in her eyes then began cascading down her cheeks.

"Baby, please don't cry." said Porshaé sympathetically.

Almost at a sob, Sabrina responded:

"**Baby**, I can't **help** it. I **miss** you so much... Porsha is always asking, "When is my Daddy coming home?" I don't know what to tell her."

Porshaé was worried that Sabrina might breakdown. He responded to her comment:

"Baby... I need you to stay strong for our Babygirl, okay? Stop cryin Baby... everything is gonna be fine. I'ma get out-of-this-mess... it's just gonna take a little time, that's all... okay Baby?"

Sabrina nodded and more tears fell as she nodded her head yes. The jailer knocked on the door of the small booth then opened it:

"Mr. Prince, that's your time Sir. I'll give you a few more minutes to wrap-it-up."

"Alright... thanks man." said Porshaé to the dark skinned brother who worked as a city jailer. Then he turned back to face Sabrina.

"Sabrina... I love you **so much** Baby. Give our Babygirl a big hug and kiss for me... Tell her that I'm gonna call her Sunday so we can talk... Tell her that's our special day okay."

Sabrina smiled at her man... Making a special day for their Daughter was sweet, she thought.

"I'll tell her Baby... just make sure you don't forget to call okay?"

"I won't forget Baby", he said.

Sabrina made a suggestion before she left:

"Baby... maybe I should just move down here... you know, temporarily, so you can see me and Porsha more."

Porshae's face crinkled into a disagreeing frown then he responded:

"Baby, I would **love** to see you and ma Babygirl more, but... you moving down **here**... that's not what I want... I wouldn't feel comfortable at all knowing you down here by yourself... Stay up there with Momma and your family... I know you have support up there with them and that helps me not worry about you and our Babygirl so much. If y'all moved down here, I would probably go **crazy** from worrying."

He laughed a little and tried to smile at his own comment... it was a small smile but it was enough to put a little smile on Sabrina's face. Sabrina responded:

"Okay Baby... I'll stay in Flint... you're right... me and Porsha need our little support team close by."

Sabrina snickered a little then said:

"I see you have your **own** little support team down here too."

Sabrina was referring to Clyde, Rene and Keisha, but mainly Keisha... Porshaé responded:

"Yeah... they all good people... Clyde's lawyer friend, been trying to do what he can to help me out."

Sabrina responded:

"I know Baby. Keisha filled me in on the "strategy" when I got here... she's really nice."

The door to the visiting booth opened again:

"Alright Mr. Prince... That's your time man."

Porshaé stood up and put his hand on the glass then said:

"Okay Baby... I love you."

Sabrina placed her hand on the glass too then responded:

"I love you too Baby." Then they both hung-up the phone like receivers.

He put his hand on his lips then placed it on the glass. Sabrina did the same... putting her hand to her lips, kissing it ever so softly as if she were kissing his lips... then she placed her hand on the glass... As she touched the glass, she felt a small sensational jolt of electrifying love, spark from her and Porshae's hands touching the glass. Porshaé smiled and so did she. They knew their love was strong... that little spark was a small reminder and enough to keep both of them confident in their love... Porshaé closed his eyes and Sabrina closed hers... They turned around simultaneously and opened their eyes... Sabrina walked away, and Porshaé exited the small booth like room.

Never Can Say Goodbye

When he was a little boy... Porshaé stayed with his Grandmother a lot. When it was time for him to go, he hated leaving and saying goodbye. His Grandmother came up with an idea to ease his discomfort of goodbyes. She told him:

"Porshaé, look at me Son... now close your eyes... Grandma is gonna turn you around and when I do... I want you to open your eyes and walk away with your Momma... when you **do**... I don't want you to look back... you just **keep-on** going forward, but **remember** what you saw when you open your eyes... Grandma will always be right in front of you, waiting on you to come see me again. okay?"

"Okay Grandma." he said.

His Grandmother would turn him around and his Mom would take hold of his little hand...

"Okay Son. I love you... Grandma will be right here Baby."

When Porshaé opened his eyes, he could actually **see** his Grandma's face, just as he had when she was right in front of him. Once his minds eyes were set on her image, Porshaé would go feeling at-ease about leaving his Grandma... Til this day, Porshaé **still** does that with Sabrina, because he hates saying goodbye.

Back To The Strategy:

June 5th, eight days before Porshae's next court date.

"Mr. Prince. You have a legal visit", said the jailor. His voice sounded through the intercom system that was inside of the cell.

The jailor pressed a button on the control panel to release the lock on the cell door. Porshaé stepped out of the cell, walked down the steel flight of stairs passed the day room then to the sally-port. The jailor pressed another button on the control panel and a loud click sounded. Porshaé pushed the sally-port door open and stepped through. When he made it to the small room designated for attorney visits, his public representation, Ms. Kelly Moyich was there waiting for him. There was a thick wire glass between them, though they were still able to communicate through a touch-less intercom system.

"Mr. Porshaé Prince?" asked the young public attorney, looking like she was fresh-out-of law school.

"Yes, that's me." he said.

"Mr. Prince. I'm Kelly Moyich. I will be your representation on this case."

It was now the second phase of 'the strategy'. Porshaé pulled the details to the front of his mind.

"Mr. Prince. I need to know, how would you like to handle this case... are you pleading not guilty or guilty? And if you **are** pleading not guilty, we have to start preparing our defense."

He responded:

"Ms. Moyich, I have a friend who's been advising me and says that I shouldn't plead guilty but I should ask for something called an "Alfred Plea" and for a bench sentence... She said I might come outta this thing a lot better that way."

Kelly was surprised at Porshae's luculent request in the matter. Since she been a lawyer... she had never encountered a client until him, that knew how to **tactfully** handle their own case to receive the best results.

"Mr. Prince, I'm impressed... Your friend sounds like she knows what she's talking about... she gave you some good advice, however... I must warn you... if you ask for a bench sentence... there's a **very** strong chance the Judge could go with the prosecutors sentencing recommendation... and it looks like..." Ms. Moyich looked at the case file again just to be sure then she continued:

"He's asking for life, without the possible chance of parole."

Porshaé went silent for a long moment... He didn't know if he was ready to gamble with his life like that... but Keisha had told him:

"You have to trust Joe's strategy."

Porshaé was only trusting in God though, and by that... trusting Joe's strategy was God sent... Porshaé glared into Kelly's light green eyes then, with the utmost confidence said:

"Ms. Moyich... that's what I wanna do."

Kelly peered at Porshaé, **knowing** he was taking a big chance and gambling on fate... but in a case **this** serious, it was a **damn good** gamble.

"Alright then Mr. Prince... It looks like we're done here."

Kelly put her file back into her briefcase and before she got ready to leave, she asked Porshaé:

"Mr. Price. Is there anything else you would like me to do, that's pertinent to the case?"

He thought for a moment, trying to think of anything he may have left out. He responded:

"Yes Ms. Moyich... there **is** one more thing."

Kelly was ready to take a mental note. Porshaé continued:

"I want my case to be expedited for sentencing."

Kelly frowned at his request then responded:

"Mr. Prince... Are you in a hurry to go to prison? You don't have to rush this case you know?"

"I'm just following my friend's advisements Ms. Moyich."

Kelly was curious about Porshae's friend, so she asked:

"Mr. Prince. If you don't mind me asking... is your friend a lawyer?"

It was critical that no one knew about Joe and Luiet's involvement in the case... it could cripple the results. Although... Keisha and Porshaé had no knowledge of Luiet's role in the matter anyway.

Porshaé responded:

"No, she's not... She just knows people who are knowledgeable of the legal system."

Porshaé was referring to Keisha as well as Joe. Kelly nodded then responded:

"I see... **well**.... I'll present everything to the prelim's judge on the 13th." Kelly stood and Porshaé stood also.

"Mr. Prince, it was nice meeting you. I'll see you again on the13th."

"It was nice meeting you too Ms. Moyich." said Porshaé.

Kelly turned and walked away from the glass and Porshaé opened the door and exited the small room.

The strategy had officially been put into play. It was important for the case to get expedited for sentencing... it would go to the judge's court that had the lightest case-load, and Luiet's division was almost clear of its cases.

It was the 13th, of June and Kelly presented the case to the prelim judge, just as Porshaé had wanted her to. From there, the case was moved to division 19, pretrial court... one of many divisions where a case went, before trial. And if both sides were not able to come up with a plea agreement, the case would be set for trial... it was also Luiet's division. Everything seemed to be moving according to plan... it was Luiet's call now.

Thursday, June 21st:

Porshaé was now in Luiet's court. It was Luiet's first time seeing Porshaé and she felt she already knew him, and in a sense, she did. Joe had never asked Luiet to interpose in any of his cases, but this was not his case. This was a matter of Joe's compassion for an innocent man. Joe felt that a good young man had been falsely accused and he made that known to Luiet. The two of them knew they had to do whatever they could to help Porshaé...
Luiet began:

"Mr. Prince, you stand before the court, charged with first degree murder. Your counsel has already entered an "Alfred Plea" on your behalf, as well as a "Blind Plea or Bench Sentencing". Mr. Prince, are fully aware of what both plea's mean?"

"Yes Your Honor."
Luiet continued:

"Well, just to be sure it's **clear**... I'll go over them for you... Mr. Prince, an "Alfred Plea", is a plea saying that you're not admitting guilt however, based on the evidence against you, you fear you may be found guilty... The "Blind Plea", is a plea that throws you on the mercy of the courts, which in this case, is me... Mr. Prince, I'm obligated to ask you... did you knowingly make these decisions on your own free will, with a clear and sound mind?"

"Yes Your Honor. I did."

"And in making these decisions Mr. Prince, were you promised anything in return, from the prosecutor, your counsel, or anyone else?"

"No, Your Honor. I was not."

"Mr. Prince, your blind plea is telling me that you feel I'll be more lenient in sentencing you. Is that what you believe?"
Porshaé put his head down, feeling as though following Joe's advice had done him no good.
He gathered his thoughts, lifted his head then responded humbly:

"Your Honor... I'm still having a hard time believing I'm in your court with a murder charge against me... I don't know whether you'll be lenient or not... I'm only following the advice of a friend in making these pleas', but yes Your Honor. I'm hoping you will show some leniency."

Luiet glared at Porshaé with sympathetic eyes, though they were still stern and judging. She got right to business:

"Mr. Prince, because this case did not have to go through a jury trial or bench arbitration... I'm disregarding the prosecutor's recommendation, which is life in prison without the chance of parole... I'm sentencing you to 20 years in the Missouri Department of Corrections, with the chance of parole, **after** the minimum amount of time has been served... Mr. Prince, that's **five years** beyond the **minimum** sentence allowed on this charge, so consider yourself **blessed** today... Also Mr.Prince. The Alfred Plea allows you the opportunity for an appeal... though there has to be **new** and **circumstantial** evidence that is **contrary** to the existing evidence, so try to work on that. Do you understand Mr. Prince?"

"Yes Your Honor."

Porshae's thoughts were all over the place: "twenty years isn't so bad... my Babygirl will be 23 and that's **if** I don't get parole... what's the minimum amount of time I have to do? How in the **world** am I gonna get new evidence? I know Sabrina is gonna be upset... I hope she doesn't break-down." His mind flickered back and forth to different thoughts like a couch potato, flicking through the channels on TV. He was grateful though... 20 years sounded **a lot** better than life.

"So it is ordered. Good luck Mr. Prince." said Luiet then excused herself from the bench.

Porshae's thoughts had muted Luiet's last eight words. Kelly had to touch his shoulder in-order for him to snap-out-of-the 'thought flickering, frenzy' his mind was in... When the flickering stopped on Court TV... he realized Judge Valley was gone. He looked at Kelly then she began speaking:

"Mr. Prince, you were very fortunate today... Judge Valley **is not** a lenient judge... God **had**-to-of-been looking out for you", said Kelly, still in disbelief at the outcome of the case.

They were sitting at the table now, going over some papers that needed signing. Kelly was also explaining to Porshaé, what each of the papers said. As she turned the pages, she got to the one Judge Valley had signed already. Porshae's eyes were immediately drawn to the bottom of the page where it read: [So ordered: 6-21-84] with

Judge Valley's signature just to the right of those words and her number underneath her signature. On the next page, there were three spaces, only one still needing a signature: [Attorney for Defendant, Defendant, and Attorney for State.] Kelly instructed Porshaé to sign in the defendant's space. He signed the page, and it was official... the case was done. As the sheriff took hold of Porshae's arm to escort him back to the holding cell, Porshaé turned to Kelly then said:

"Ms. Moyich."

Kelly lifted her head from the papers, her eyes making contact with his... His eyes showed gratitude and pain at the same time.

"Yes Mr. Prince?" said Kelly.

Porshaé continued:

"Can you tell the Judge I said, thank you?"

Kelly felt a small lump in her throat. She swallowed then responded:

"Yes. I'll tell her... take care of yourself Mr. Prince."

Porshaé nodded and the sheriff took him away. Kelly kept her focus on Porshaé as he and the sheriff exited the courtroom. She pondered on his claim of innocence.

Some may wonder: 'why didn't Luiet and Joe, get more involved in the case, **knowing** that there were corrupt police officers entangled in the matter?' The truth of the matter is... they had no **real** evidence of police corruption. They had done all they could do for Porshaé, under the circumstances, without jeopardizing their careers. They didn't know how else to help him. Porshaé wasn't depending on them though. He remained determined and kept his faith that God would send someone who would really advocate for him... someone who would uncover the truth... that someone... would be,

Ms. Evelyn Lewis, Attorney at law.

CHAPTER 13: THE COCHRAN THEORY

Back to Wednesday, May 1988:

In the small room of the prison where Evelyn was visiting with Porshaé. He had finished telling her the story of his first day in Saint Louis. Ms. Lewis was done taking notes. She put her ink-pen down on the tablet then said:

"Mr. Prince. Now I understand **why** the other two attorneys were not able to help you... you don't have anything they can use... There was no investigation done so they don't have anything at all to work with... You basically need someone to investigate this case for you and that's **not** what common attorneys do."

Porshaé felt the discouragement descending upon him.

Evelyn continued:

"But I am not those common attorneys, Mr. Prince... we're gonna start fresh."

A light lit-up in Porshae's eyes and he responded gleefully:

"So what are you saying, Ms. Lewis... is **you'll** investigate?"

Evelyn put on a spruce smile, looked Porshaé directly in his eyes then said:

"Yes Mr. Prince... I will conduct my **own** investigation as much as I'm able to."

Porshaé felt some relief and the discouraging feeling passed on. Evelyn continued:

"Mr. Prince, I'm gonna handle your case. Mr. Cochran and myself feel there's something suspicious about it... we'll discuss my fees later. He and I both read the statements from you and Ms. Pulliam... we studied the photos from the crime-scene, **thoroughly,** and both wondered: 'why wasn't there an investigation done?' Mr. Cochran has worked on **lots** of cases where there's been police corruption and tampering of evidence, so his perception in that area is very keen... Mr. Cochran brought something to my attention in one of the photos, and I never would've noticed it if he hadn't."

Evelyn pulled out the four-year-old photos from the shooting then sat the one of Officer Harris' hand holding the badge-fold, down in front of Porshaé.

"Mr. Prince, I want you to take a **good** look at this photo and tell me what you can see."

Porshaé studied the photo studiously for a moment, trying to find **something** out of the ordinary... but he couldn't find anything. He grew frustrated then said:

"Ms. Lewis... I don't understand what it is you want me to see?"

Evelyn pulled out another photo that served as an example photo of what she wanted him to look for. It was a photo of a dead man, holding an actual gun; finger on the trigger and in the ready-to-fire position. She slid the photo over to him, placing it next to the other one. He studied the two photos and could now see the similarities. Even though one was holding a gun and the other was holding a badge-fold... the hand formations were saying the same thing.

"Ms. Lewis... I can see the hands are somewhat in the same position... but how does this help me...? The officers **took** the gun."

He pushed the photos back over to Evelyn. She looked at Porshaé pitifully, knowing he couldn't have **possibly** seen what Mr. Cochran's keen mind and trained eyes had seen... her **own** eyes hadn't saw it... and even if they had, she still would not have understood what she was looking at. Evelyn explained it to Porshaé, as Johnny had explained it to her.

"Mr. Prince, if you noticed in the example photo. The trigger finger is relaxed, extended **just** a little passed the other fingers... Now in the crime-scene photo", she said, pushing the photo **back** over to Porshaé, again. Then she continued:

"The pinky, ring, **and** index fingers, are in the same position as the trigger finger... clutching."

Porshaé was confused but listening. Evelyn continued:

"Physical science has shown us... that if a person is holding something as light as a badge-fold... and that person was shot... The badge-fold would fall, **out-of** the person's hand because of how light it is. The person's grip wouldn't be that firm... Now on-the-other-hand... physical science **also** shows us... that when a person is holding something a little more **heavier** such as a gun... Then their grip tends to be much firmer... and if **fired**, even firmer."

Evelyn glanced at Porshaé to make sure he was still following her. He was, so she continued:

"And the third thing physical science tells us... is that when a

person **fires** a gun... the trigger finger pulls **back** towards the thumb, practically in the same position as the other fingers, only tighter... If a person were shot while firing their gun, their grip would remain firm because of the shock from the gunshot to the body. It would look like this", said Evelyn, pointing at the crime-scene photo...
She pulled out another photo and sat it on the desk.

"You see how the fingers are positioned around the gun...? They're almost **identical** to the hand in the crime-scene photo."

Porshae's mind took-in the information, though still trying to process it. He was a-bit confused. Evelyn saw his bewilderment and cut from the physical science lessons.

"Mr. Prince... whoever took the gun out-of your attacker's hand, had to **pry** it loose... but the one thing they **couldn't** take... is the bullet that was fired from your attacker's gun. It's probably still somewhere in the hallway waiting to be found."
Evelyn had spoken her words with **drama**... as if she were in the courtroom, delivering her case in front of a jury. Porshaé was amazed at what he had just heard, and speechless. He starting getting excited but quickly doused that excitement with doubt then asked Evelyn:

"So what you're telling me is... by looking at **these** photos... you and Mr. Cochran came to the conclusion the man **did** have a gun... and he **fired it...**? Ms. Lewis. I don't remember any other shots being fired except for mine."

"Mr. Prince... if there were-not anything for me to go off of, I wouldn't be here... I would be telling you the **same** thing those other attorneys told you... "I can't help you... you don't have anything for me to bring to the appeal courts.", but that's **not** what I'm telling you Mr. Prince... I'm telling you, we have to start somewhere."
Porshaé realized a huge reality they had to face and brought it to Evelyn's attention:

"Ms. Lewis, I hate to sound like a skeptic... but proving the bullet, **if there is one**... came from that cop's gun, is gonna be impossible! They've already made the gun disappear once, and it's been **four years** Ms. Lewis... we don't even know where it is... How are you gonna find it?"
The excitement Porshaé was feeling earlier started fading fast under the realization of the hard truth. However, Evelyn was quite the optimist and she believed, **just** as well as her mentor did... that there

was something more to uncover in Porshae's case.

Evelyn responded:

"Mr. Prince, we'll cross that bridge when we get to it, but for now... our main focus is to find that bullet."

Porshaé had to check his self. He had **just** prayed to God before he left the housing unit to visit with Evelyn, for God to help the new attorney find something that would help him out... **Now!** Here she was, **telling** him they may have found something... and he's being doubtful... it's not the mindset anyone should have when trusting in God... Porshaé put his hands on his head, exhaled then responded:

"You're right Ms. Lewis... it's a start... one that I didn't have four years ago."

Evelyn smiled then said, encouragingly:

"That's the spirit Mr. Prince... This is a door that could lead to you becoming a free man, so please... just have a little faith in us... but more importantly... in God."

"Evelyn **had**-to-have-been Heaven sent." thought Porshaé.

Writer's thought: God places certain people in our lives to help us get through it; to make it easier for us and to help us live it to the best of our ability. God wants all of His God loving children to have the best in life...He will provide us with the direction to get there... we only need to recognize that direction and put forth the efforts to walk on the path to prosperity... Live in Gods ways and live well...

Porshaé came to the conclusion that, this was Gods divine plan for him, and God had sent him an advocate. He would no longer question his faith in God. He understood that Clyde, Keisha, Joe, Judge Valley, Tony Rone the man who pointed him in Mr. Cochran's direction which led to Ms. Lewis coming to meet with him, giving him a fresh sense of hope... they all were people who had contributed to him still having a chance at being a free man. They **all** were part of Gods plan.

Evelyn concluded the visit with Porshaé. She went her way, back to Saint Louis, and he went his way, back to the prison's housing unit. Evelyn was thankful the prison wasn't too far from Saint Louis... only about forty minutes tops. M.E.C.C. was located in Pacific Missouri. Porshaé was thankful too. It was truly a convenience for Sabrina and

Porsha, and Porshae's Mom and Keisha when they wanted to come visit him.

The drive back to Saint Louis was meditative for Evelyn. She recollected the details of her conversation with Porshaé, weighing the question he had asked her, because it was now heavy on her mind: "How are we gonna find the gun?" Evelyn tried to formulate a plan that she could later put into action, but everything she thought of... succumbed to her primary focus... finding the bullet.

"Let's focus on one thing at a time Evelyn", she told herself quietly, gripping the steering wheel tighter.

Back in Saint Louis, Evelyn parked near the Shell building, in which her office was located. Her assistant, Yolanda was up front in the reception area, talking to their receptionist.

"Good morning Ladies." said Evelyn, stepping out of the elevator that opened up directly into her law office.

"Good morning Evelyn." said Yolanda.

"Good morning Ms. Lewis." said Tina, their receptionist.

Evelyn strolled to the back, to her private office and got **straight** down to business. Porshaé had given Evelyn, contact info on Keisha. She pulled it from her briefcase and called the studio first. Rene answered the phone, still cheerful after four plus years at the studio.

"Good afternoon. You've reached *We Got Music* recording studio. This is Rene speaking. How can I help you?"

"Good afternoon Rene. My name is Evelyn Lewis, and I'm calling on behalf of Porshaé Prince. I'm trying to reach a Ms. Keisha Pulliam."

Rene's face lit-up with excitement then she responded:

"**Ooh**, I've heard of you! You're that lawyer who's always on the radio...! 'Fighting to keep, **your** man, out-of-jail',"

Rene was quoting one of Evelyn's radio commercials. She was smiling big because she knew what a great reputation Evelyn had for representing Black Men in the legal system. Now... here Evelyn was, calling on **Porshae's** behalf... Rene knew Keisha would be glad to know Evelyn was on the phone.

"Ms. Lewis. Can you hold and I'll let her know you're on-the-line."

"Okay. Thank you" said Evelyn.

Rene pressed the hold button then went to let Keisha know she had a phone call. Even though Rene was still answering the phone at the studio... her status had elevated. Rene and Keisha had graduated from their business and marketing classes and Clyde felt it only appropriate, to make them partners in the business... since they were running the place anyway. Their status not only elevated but their business did as well.

We Got Music recording studio had branched into M.I.G.
'Make It Good entertainment' with Porshae's consent, and him as the head of M.I.G.... Make It Good entertainment became one of the best and most well known entertainment companies in the mid-west. We Got Music had been in the business for seven years now and made tremendous headway in the music industry. Vans Band recorded one of the greatest albums the 'Soft-Rock' category of music, had ever received. With Clyde's local connections, he managed to get a few songs from Vans Band, and Fools Crush, on the radio. The two bands created a buzz **so strong,** from people requesting to hear their music and from the rotation of their music on the radio... that major recording labels were calling We Got Music to inquire about the two bands.

Brian was acting as the band's manager. He left the police force shortly after finding out what happened to Porshaé. He had enough money to sustain his modest life style for at least four or five years. Brian had met with a few record labels, but their deals were not befitting to the needs of the band he was now managing. He ended up meeting with Columbia Records and with the help and advisement of Clyde and Joe... Brian, representing Vans Band, inked them a two-album deal, with Columbia, worth seven figures. Soon after that, Van left the police force.

Brian had asked Van and the other members, to never mention to anyone that he was a police officers. He told them it would be best because of what happened at the studio. They all understood and were glad to uphold his request. In the process of all of that, Clyde was able to meet with RCA records in regards of Fools Crush. Acting as their manager, Clyde inked them a deal just as sweet. We Got Music was an **official** record label, and they **had** music.

Brian was glad that he heeded the warning of God, at Forest Park... His life had changed for the better and he was happier than he had ever been in his entire life... He was with Rene, the love of his life, and they were great together... Things could only get better... or so one would think.

Back to the phone call from Evelyn:

Keisha was sitting at the small table in the kitchenette and she took the phone call there. She lifted the receiver and pressed the flashing hold button:

"Hello. This is Keisha."

"Hello, Ms. Pulliam. This is Evelyn Lewis, the attorney... I'm calling on the behalf of, Porshaé Prince. I'd like to meet with you as soon as possible... there at the studio if that's okay with you?"

Keisha responded with eagerness in her voice:

"**Yeah**, yes, that's fine Ms. Lewis."

Keisha was surprised to hear from the attorney... as far as she knew... Porshaé had given up on trying to get back in court and was just hoping for an early parole date. He hadn't mentioned to her anything about a third lawyer... but she was glad that Evelyn was calling.

Ms. Lewis continued:

"Ms. Pulliam. Right now its 1: 0-clock. I'm gonna grab some lunch then head straight-over afterwards, so let's say... 2:30?"

"That's fine Ms. Lewis. I'll be expecting you."

"Alright... see you then Ms. Pulliam."

"See you then", said Keisha. They both hung up their phones.

Rene stood there listening the whole time and she asked:

"What was that all about?"

Keisha shrugged her shoulders, put up a hand then answered:

"I'll guess we'll find out at 2:30."

Evelyn made one more phone call before she left out for lunch.

"Gregory Isom here, how can I help you?"

"**Hey** Uncle Greg!" said Evelyn, happy that she was able to reach her uncle at his office.

Gregory responded just as enthused:

"Evelyn! How's my favorite niece doing?"

"I'm good Uncle Greg... I just got back from the prison in Pacific... I had to interview a new client."

"Oh yeah... what happen, more charges pop-up on him?"

"Actually, no... I'm sort-of investigating his old case... and it's kinda why I'm calling you Uncle Greg... I need your help... It's nothing major though. And it shouldn't take long... so are you busy today?"

"Not really Evy... I'm just compiling some information for a client, but I could use a little break from it... what-do-you need?"
Evelyn answered:

"Let me take you to lunch and I'll fill-you-in then."
Her Uncle Greg agreed and she picked him up for lunch.

Gregory Isom, was Chief Daniel Isom's, younger brother. Both men were inspired by their father to get involved in law enforcement. Gregory, being the second youngest of six siblings, chose the private sector... 'Private Investigation'. He was a valuable and vital component in Evelyn's cache of resources, and likewise, she to him. Evelyn obtained her uncle's help whenever she needed to, though not without compensating him for his time and work. Gregory enjoyed working with his niece... They were family. And in Greg's book, family was supposed to-stick-together and help each other whenever one needed the other... just don't abuse the privilege...

Evelyn took him to the 'Saint Louis Steak House' on Grand Blvd, across from the Fox Theater... the Steak House was one of Greg's favorite spots... they have **great steaks**... There at the Steak House, Evelyn explained to her uncle, what was going on and the predicament Porshaé had been put in. She also explained to Greg, what it was they would be looking for. He wasn't surprised at the unfortunate news... Once again, more police corruption and another young Black Man falling victim to it... They finished their lunch and headed back over to his office to pick up some tools he might need. Then they headed on over to the Central West End area to meet with Keisha... Everyone was with-in a five-mile-radius of each other.

Keisha was waiting up-front in the studio so when Evelyn arrived, she would be there to greet her. Evelyn arrived.

"Hello Ms. Lewis. It's a pleasure to finally meet you in person. I've heard **so** much about you", said Keisha.

"Thank you Ms. Pulliam. It's a pleasure to meet you too."
Rene greeted the prominent black lawyer as well then they got right to the issue at hand:

"Ms. Pulliam. This is Gregory Isom... He's a private investigator who helps me investigate cases."

"How-do-you-do Ms. Pulliam." said Greg, extending his hand to shake Keisha's.

"I'm fine, thank you. Nice to meet you." said Keisha, shaking Greg's hand.

"We can talk in our viewing-room", said Keisha, motioning to the door of their viewing room.

They went inside, had a seat at the conference-room size office table then Evelyn began speaking about why she was there.

"Ms. Pulliam. The reason for my visit, is to try to find a bullet from your attacker's gun... An associate of mine, as well as myself... believe the man who attacked you, simultaneously fired a shot when Mr. Prince shot him... it's just an intuitive-notion, but based on our analysis of the photos, it's a very **strong** notion that I'm hoping will prove true... Mr. Isom is here to help me look for it."

Keisha was baffled... She couldn't understand **how**... this little dark-skinned colored woman, came up with such a notion and **no one** else did... Keisha just didn't know who Evelyn's mentor was...

Evelyn continued:

"I noticed from the files, no investigation was done on this case and it's a good thing there wasn't... The police might have found the only evidence that can clear Mr. Prince and made it disappear, just like the ski-mask and gun."

Keisha was even **more** astounded! It was the first time someone, outside of the original group of people who **knew** the truth about what took place, concurred with their truth. She was stunned with astonishment.

"Ms. Pulliam. Are you okay?" asked Evelyn.

Keisha looked towards Evelyn with a smile on her face. In Keisha's mind, she was thanking God that someone finally saw the truth... The other lawyers had never come to see her neither did they call to even **ask** her about the case...! But Evelyn was there, **searching** for the truth.

Keisha responded:

"Yes... I'm fine Ms. Lewis... I'm just thankful someone is finally here to do something... Thank you for believing in Porshaé... But let me not waste anymore time. I'll show you to the hallway."

Keisha stood and Evelyn and Greg followed suit. She led them to the hallway. As they entered the hallway, Greg asked Keisha:

"Ms. Pulliam. Has anything been done to the hall since the incident?"

"No. Everything is still the same", said Keisha.

"Good. Now if you Ladies would like to help... you can each take a wall and I'll take the ceiling... we can start at the end of the hall where the door is and work our way forward."

The three of them examined the hall closely. Moving slowly to assure they didn't miss anything...They worked their eyes up and down, over and across the hallway, making it to the end, though to no avail... their efforts produced nothing. Out of the three, Evelyn expressed the most disappointment. She felt bad for getting Keisha's hopes up, and even more so, Porshae's... Evelyn thought to herself with dejection written all over her face: "What-am-I supposed to do now? Could Johnny have been wrong about this, "bullet theory"?" Evelyn could feel the fury building-up inside of her from their lack of discovery. Greg could see that his niece was frustrated, so he intervened before the frustration set in too deep.

"Evelyn... why don't you Ladies go inside... let me take another look, alright... Let me and my Private-**eyes**, do what they're trained to do." said Greg, circling his eyes around in their sockets and raising his brows up and down, comically gesturing.
The women let out a wisp of a laugh and brandished frail smiles. Keisha and Evelyn were about to head-back into the studio.

"Evy." said Greg, calling his niece by her nickname.
Evelyn turned back to face her uncle. Greg continued:

"Can you bring me the photos of the scene please?"
Evelyn nodded then she headed-up front and out to the car to retrieve her briefcase. She brought the photos to Greg.

"Thank you Evy." said Greg.
Evelyn nodded, not saying anything, still upset.

"Evy."

"Yeah Uncle Greg?"

"Don't be too upset about it yet... yo-ole uncle is still on the case." Greg smiled confidently at Evelyn. She felt a reassurance in her uncle's statement and responded:

"I know you are Uncle Greg... thank you."
She tried to express as much optimism as possible. She turned to go,

leaving her uncle and his "private **eyes**" to do their thing. She went back up front where Keisha was and began apologizing:

"Ms. Pulliam. I'm **so** sorry for getting your hopes up without having anything solid to go off of... it's just that-"
Keisha stopped Evelyn.

"Ms. Lewis, there is no need to apologize... You are the **only** one, who has ever come to see if there **was** some type of evidence to confirm our story... that alone shows me, you at least **care** and believe in us... and I'm grateful for just that."
Keisha's face showed the gratitude she was feeling. They continued conversing candidly while waiting on Greg to, hopefully... find the bullet.

Back inside the hallway, Gregory stood in the middle, putting his strategy together to find the bullet. He examined the photos thoroughly, looking at how the body was positioned on the floor; trying to figure out, which-way the gun might have been pointing when it was fired. Greg went over the details again and from what Evelyn had told him... Porshaé was kneeling when he fired his shots, so therefore... the cop, might have aimed down into the floor, trying to shoot Porshaé.

"Why didn't I think of that shit before?" said Greg, whispering to his self. Greg began speaking quietly to the bullet:

"Where **arrre** you little bullet?"

The lighting in the hallway was dim and the floor was old. The large planked, dark wood floor had lots of knots in it and would make the work very tedious for one person examining the entire floor. But that was part of Greg's profession and he was ready to do the work. Greg opened the rear door of the hallway letting more light shine inside. He got down on the floor in the prone position and began scanning the surface of the floor. He continued to talk to the bullet, trying to generate some type of 'synergetic-energy' that would persuade the bullet to cooperate and reveal itself.

Greg moved lethargically, inspecting every scratch, every knot and every cranny that had been put in the floor over time, by wear and tear. He was about midway of the floor when he noticed a shallow scratch. It appeared to get deeper as he inched forward. It wasn't like the other scratches... they were rough and splintery. This scratch was smooth. Gregory though, "this could be a graze mark and if it is... that means... the man fired the gun as his body hit the floor."

He continued inspecting the scratch. It ended at one of the knots in the floor plank... "Knots", are part of a piece of wood's natural characteristics that resemble an eye. The eye of the knot was missing so there appeared to be a small hole in the plank. From the position Greg was in and the angle he was looking, it was hard to see inside of the small hole. He turned on his side to think for a moment then got up and went into the studio area where the women were... When Greg appeared, Evelyn stood up, literally holding her breath in anticipation.

"Uncle Greg... **please** tell me you found something..." she said exasperatingly.

"Patience Evy... I think we're almost there. But I need Ms. Pulliam's permission to remove a wooden plank from the floor."

"Mr. Isom. Do what you need to do... we can replace the wooden plank."

Greg nodded and responded:

"Evy, do you have a jack handle in the car?"

"There should be one in there. Here are the keys."

Greg took hold of the keys then dashed out to the car to check the trunk for a jack-handle. He popped the trunk and moved some things around, trying to find the jack-handle.

"Ahh... here we go." he said, after finding what he was looking for. Greg needed the flat end of the handle.

He entered the building once again... Keisha was holding the door when he whisked pass her then pass Evelyn without saying a word. Only singing the tune of some old-school song:

"It was just my imaginaaaation, runninnng awaaay with me....."

He was eager to get back to his investigative objective. Evelyn and Keisha looked at each other. Rene smiled at Greg as he strolled pass them. She loved his cheeriness. He was so **jovial** and serious at the same time. After he was out of sight, Evelyn shook her head and smiled at the small bit of comic-relief her uncle just provided. The anxiety and emotional tension was gone and the women were able to relax a-bit. Because of his jolly attitude, Evelyn and Keisha felt confident that Greg would find the bullet. Then they could proceed on to the next step.

The flat end of the jack-handle touched the floor. He positioned it so the flat end would fit into one of the creases that separated each plank from the other. Greg carefully pushed the flat end of the handle down into the crease, trying not to damage the wood then lifted gently as he pushed. He repeated the process several times down the long side of the plank until it was well loosened and able-to-be lifted from the floor. Greg sat the jack-handle down then got down on the floor. He wanted to have a close view of the plank and the subfloor...

The moment of truth had arrived and the anxiety was paining. Greg slowly lifted the plank from its setting, and cautiously flipped the plank over to view the underside. He examined the plank carefully and closely and **lo and behold...** no bullet **anywhere** in the wood...! He was dumfounded... Greg sat on his bottom to contemplate... While he was contemplating, a small dull shine in the bare exposed concrete, jumped out at him.

Over the years, areas on the surface of the subfloor had broken down, becoming soft due to erosion, leaving a sandy like substance in the area. Greg swept the sand away with a brush of his hand and there it was... partially embedded in the soft concrete, like a fossil in a stone. The elation Greg felt was tremendous! A cool chill came over his body and it gave him goose bumps. He didn't know what to think of it. Maybe it was the excitement of finding a piece of evidence that could prove a man's innocence... or maybe it was the satisfaction he felt from knowing how grateful his niece would be... she would be proud of her ole uncle for a job well done, thought Greg... or maybe it was something more than his trivial presumptions... Maybe it was Gods Divine Angels, passing over Greg, letting him know, that the Almighty God was with them on their mission to reveal the truth.

Writers thought: As long as we are pursuing good and righteous endeavors...God's Spirit will always be with us... guiding us in our missions... helping us to not become discouraged when encountering challenges. Pursuing the will of God, which is true righteousness, can only result in one thing... and that's good. Remember... never be discouraged when challenging times arise, because the way passed those challenging times is right in front of you if you are letting God be your guide. Proverbs chapter 3 verses 5 & 6.

Greg unzipped his waist-pouch and pulled out his micro camera. He snapped a few shots; one of the bullet, one of the floor and one of the wooden planks... Then, he pulled out a pair of needle-nose-pliers from his pouch and extracted the bullet from its soft concrete bed. It was like a veteran-dentist, pulling a bad tooth. After four long years, the bullets hiatus was now over. Greg held the slug up-close to his "private-eyes", checking to determine what type of 'round' it was. From his examination, he determined it was probably a .38 caliber round. Gregory secured the bullet in his pouch, got to his feet then dusted himself off. He closed the rear door then headed up front to give the Ladies the good news...

Delivering the good news:

The phone rang at the Wilshire Boulevard law office in Los Angeles, California.

"Cochran here." said the smooth tenor voice of Johnny. He took his glasses off.

"Johnny... we found the bullet." said Evelyn.
Evelyn was still elated about their finding. It was evident in her voice. Johnny responded:

"That's **great** Evelyn... but that was the easy part, so listen up... In cases like these, its absolutely **crucial,** that your information stay with-in the circle of your team... If it gets out to the opposition, it could jeopardize your case, and it more than likely will, so be discreet as possible. Police officers get **really** nasty when they feel threatened."
Evelyn felt a small wave of trepidation come over her... Some of the police in Saint Louis were known for being vicious, and in most incidents, it was impossible to prove. They would get rid of anyone who posed a threat of exposing the corruption they were apart of... even a fellow officer.
Johnny continued:

"Keep your investigation quiet as possible Evelyn."

"I will. But I have a bullet and no gun... how do I find out about the gun without raising any flags? I'm stuck."

"Okay, first thing is", said Johnny, revving-up to give Evelyn the second part of the game plan...

They conversed a little while longer about the case and concluded their phone call. After Evelyn got off the phone with Johnny, she called her Uncle Greg to let him know what was said.

Greg then called his big brother Daniel, down at the Metro Police headquarters... Daniel answered the phone:

"This is Chief Isom."

"Whats-up big-bro!" Greg's robust voice sounded through the receiver.

"Greg...! whats-going-on lil-brother... how you doing man?"

"I'm cool... ready for that Memorial Day barbeque at yo house." Daniel's famous barbeque ribs, made Greg's mouth water just thinking about them. He continued:

"**Man,** I don't know how you do it, but them **ribs**... are the **best!**" Daniel smiled and responded:

"Yeah... I've been thinking about gettin in the contest this year."

"Man you **should**...! You'd win fa-sho... them ribs would **really** be famous then... I can see it now, "Isom's Famous **Saint Louis Ribs.**" You know I know my barbque, Bro! People in Saint Louis take pride in they barbque, and Saint Louis need-to-taste them **ribs Bro!**"

Greg was excited about his brother's interest in the annual barbque contest.

"Like I said, I'm **thinking** about it... But I know you didn't call down here to talk about my ribs. What's up lil-brother?"

"I'm glad you asked... I've been doing some investigating for Evy."

"**All** shit... what she got you doing now?"

"Big bro, I really need talk to you in person about it."

"It's that serious huh?" asked Daniel.

"Yeah man, it is... And I know it's gonna be of some interest to you, once I'm done explaining."

"Interest to **me**?"

"Yeah... listen... why don't I come by after you get off work... I'll bring a six pack."

"Alright... make sure it's Budweiser and not that weak-ass Miller-Lite you be drinking."

Daniel smiled and Greg responded:

"Yeaah, Yeaah... Budweiser... I'll see you later big bro."

"Later lil-brother."

Daniel hung up the phone. He wondered what it was Greg felt would be of such an interest to him...

CHAPTER 14: Part 2 Real Hood Shit

Still Wednesday, 9pm, May 1988:

On the West-side of Saint Louis. The crew of burglars sat in their stash-house, on the 5500 block of Maffitt Avenue, waiting on the crew's leader to show up. Bakarri Tanner, nicknamed, 'Gambino'... a mendacious-ass-nigga with a scandalous reputation. Always lying and trying to be more than what he really was. He was once part of the GDN, which stood for, Gangsta Disciple Nation and Growth & Development Nation, one of the largest street organizations in the country.

After Gambino's deceitfulness and lying ways were uncovered, along with his disloyalty... the GDN coordinator of Saint Louis ousted Gambino from the GD Nation. One of the enforcers wanted to kill Gambino, but the only reason it didn't go down like that, was because the Regional Coordinator of Saint Louis, stopped him. He said, Gambino would owe the GD Nation and he would be useful one day. He was no longer a brother of the Growth & Development Nation... He was now just a goon on call for the GD Nation.

However, despite his mendacious characteristics, Gambino had a knack for making friends with the Caucasian race. He was one of the few niggas who knew the in's and out's of the white neighborhoods around Saint Louis County. For some mysterious reason, they took to this nigga like moths to a flame... never even suspecting they could get burned at anytime. The funny thing was that... he never fucked over any of his white friends... **It seemed** as if he was more loyal to them than he was to the brothers of the GD Nation. And even his **own family** for that matter. There are bad-apples in every bunch I suppose. He had his white friends in the palm of his; mostly white girls.

Gambino was their drug dealer and standing at 6'4", weighing

250 pounds. He was their protection when they needed it. Their lover when they wanted to fuck... (the females that is). And most importantly to them... he was their friend, a Gangsta... He would always brag about that... being a Gangster. His white friends thought he was the **coolest** muthafucka they knew. He still claimed his Discipleship, and even made some of his white homeboys and lil-hommies, Gangsta Disciples. Gambino had started his own small crew and they were **his** disciples. He had a tattoo of a master sergeants chevron on his chest, with a six-point-star in the middle of it. It was a high rank to carry, but no one knew who gave it to him... Had he given it to himself?

Gambino finally showed up at the Maffitt street stash-house. He stepped through the door and one of his newly 'blessed-in' Gangsta Disciples, greeted him:

"Whatz good Big G." a form of greeting in the hood amongst G's and lil-G's.
Gambino greeted everyone at once:
"Whatz crackin Gangstas."
He shook hands with all of his little G's, shaking hands in the traditional way that Gangsta Disciples did. They crossed the pointing finger over the index finger before touching hands and then connected hands to make a wing like symbol. At that point of the handshake, they locked the pitchforks in the upright position then made a G like symbol. And at the end, they formed a heart then disconnected. They use to drop the hand down with all five fingers spread, but they stopped. It was a form of disrespect, and to be respected one had to show respect... that's what Larry Hoover practiced. Every true Growth & Development member practices this.

"Whatz on the agenda for tonight G.?" asked Flame, a crazy ass white boy who had become part of Gambino's circle, in its beginning. Gambino responded:

"We got some top-notch shit out in Ladue and another spot out in south-county. Both families on vacation... At the Ladue spot, we lookin-fah-the normal shit... but at the south county spot... this old dude is supposed to be a gun collector and have **all kinds** of heat. That's what we after."

"Damn, G... How you be **knowin** all this shit like you do?" said Crime, the youngest in the crew.

With the slickness of an old-school-pimp, and sounding like, Tommy Strong from the Martin Lawrence show, Gambino smiled and responded humorously:

"That's what ma **white hoes** is **fo daawg**!"

The crew laughed and slapped hands all at the name of gullible white girls. Gambino not only had white girls informing him. But he also had his white home-boys providing him with info. So far that year, the crew was responsible for thirty five burglaries throughout the Saint Louis County area. Averaging two burglaries per week, the crew netted about sixty thousand dollars in stolen goods.

William Sheeks, aka, 'Crayzo', and another member of the crew named KG, handled most of the fencing. They both were GDN members before they met Gambino. They knew each other because of their GDN affiliation and became cool friends after they had met. Crayzo and KG were the top two guys in the crew of burglars, and probably the best B&E guys in the city. The money they got from the stolen merchandise was used to buy drugs. Not for their personal use, but for them to sell...

Gambino had this, so-called strategy, to keep the crew safe from becoming suspects and from becoming too hot. They would do burglaries from January to May and they all, **had** to have some type of job during those months... that was very important. After that, they would focus on their drug business. Using the money to buy as much cocaine, ecstasy and marijuana as possible. Then, they would sell dope from June to October. In November and December, they would relax from everything except for their regular jobs.

Gambino was truly upset about being ousted from the GD Nation and he had something to prove... not only to himself, but to the GD Nation's coordinator and all those who stood in agreement to have him ousted... So far, he was doing a solid job at being a leader, putting together a solid crew **and** generating revenues. Gambino made sure that each member of his crew **knew** and **kept** the number one concept/law, of the GD Nation: Silence and Secrecy... No member was allowed to discuss their involvement with the GD Nation or **anything** pertaining to the GD Nation, with anyone outside of the Nation... For the time being, Gambino was especially trying to keep his crew a secret. If the GDN Regional Coordinator of Saint Louis got wind of it... Gambino's punishment could be more severe than just being ousted... but he wanted to officially become part of the GD Nation again, and he would.

Ron-Ron, the Regional Coordinator for Saint Louis, was a devoted member of the GD Nation. When it came to Disciple business, Ron-Ron was by the book about it. No nonsense, no bullshit and no exceptions for violators of the laws and policies set forth to govern the Growth & Development Nation. Even though some sanctions for violations were harsher than others... Ron-Ron was fair as far as handing out those sanctions to members who violated. He gave his GD brothers the benefit of the doubt when they deserved it and they had to **really** deserve it... he was far from a pushover.

It was 9:35pm and Gambino was going over the routine for the night with his crew:
"Flame, you drivin... Crayzo and KG, y'all ride with Flame. Me and Ghost will lead the way to the Ladue house. After y'all done hittin the house, y'all know what to do."
Their routine was smooth. Gambino and Ghost would be close by inside of a friend's house with the car the parked on the street with the trunk unlocked. After Crayzo and KG were done with the burglary, Flame would drive them to the car that Gambino and Ghost drove, pull up on the side of it then Crayzo and KG would hop out, quickly load the stolen goods into the trunk of the other car, lock it, and drive back to the stash-house on Maffitt Street. Then it was on to the next hit.
Crayzo and KG were the pros and taught the rest of the crew how to "leave the scene clean." The average burglar would probably breakout a window, bust in a door, or cut lines tied to an alarm... but not them... They knew about alarms... systems that ran off phone-lines, electrical panels and battery packs. Just by looking at part of the system, they could determine which were which... They had methods of getting around all of them. They would disconnect the alarm source without damaging or tripping the alarm then enter the dwelling using look-pick tools. After they were done and out of the house. They would reconnect any wiring. No alarm would trip, no

window would be broken and the house would appear to be as it were before the burglary took place... But when the owner got home and inside of their house... that's when they would probably notice their things missing, depending on what was taken. Houses without alarm systems were like sitting ducks... but if they didn't have the scoop on a house, they wouldn't touch it.

The crew was ready to roll-out to the first house. Gambino drove by the house and slowed down in front of it. That indicated to Flame where to stop. Crayzo and KG entered the house smoothly. They held their L.E.D. flashlights low. The light from the flashlights was blue and not too bright, emitting hardly any light-flare. They hit each room quickly, like soldiers running an obstacle course. No room was left un-searched by their gloved hands and roving eyes. They never spoke in or outside of a house. Not until they were back inside the car, would they speak. Quick and quiet was how they operated.

11pm:
Flame, Crayzo, and KG made it back to the stash-house and Gambino and Ghost got there about ten minutes after them. It was a good hit.
    "Everything go alright?" Gambino asked Crayzo.
    "Yeah... You see what's in the trunk?" said Crayzo boastfully, as they stood at the trunk of the car, getting ready to unload the goods.
    "Cool... let's get this shit down to the basement and head to the next house. Then we done fo-the-night... as-a-matter-of-fact... we gone be done fah- the rest of the year!" said Gambino, happy with the crews four-and-a-half month run.
    Young Crime was helping unload the trunk and he was ready to kick-it. They got everything out of the trunk and into the house. Crime commented:
    "Big G, why don't we call-it-a-night right now...? We can bring some hoes over and chill. We got some orange-kush, we got plenty of drank already... let's go get some **hoes, Big G!**"
Gambino looked at Young Crime questioningly then said:
    "You got kush... you got drank... Where yo heat at lil-nigga...?"
Crime looked at Gambino confused.
    "What?" said Crime.
Gambino fired back aggressively:

"Where yo 'heat' at nigga... in case some muthafuckas try-ta get at us... what-the-fuck you gone use to get-em up-off-us?!"

Trying not to sound too defensive, Young Crime responded:

"Big G, you know I ain't got no heat."

"My **case** and **point** lil nigga." said Gambino, still glaring at Crime. Less aggressively, Gambino continued:

"That's exactly why we need to check-out this house. We about-ta get into this street shit **heavy**, so we **all** need to be strapped up, you feel me?"

Young Crime nodded and Gambino continued:

"Just have somma-dat kush rolled up when we get back... and don't chief until we get back. I need you to be on point here at the spot. The Mosberg is in the closet."

Gambino looked at the rest of his crew then said:

"Y'all take ah piss, shit, or whatever y'all need to do and let's get ready to roll-out."

The rest of the crew got up and got ready to head to the next hit.

Flashback To May 14th, 1984

Detective Schlesta drove out to South County Saint Louis, to Officer Harris' parent's house. He pulled into the driveway of the two and a-half-story, reddish-brown brick house. Detective Schlesta was blameworthy for the reason behind his unfortunate visit to the Harris residence... and the guilt on his face would be hard to conceal. Jerry sat in the car for a while until he felt he was able to face Mr. & Mrs. Harris...the doorbell never rung...

The door of the house opened. Mrs. Harris had noticed the car sitting in the driveway and informed her husband of it. Sensing that it was a police officer, Mr. Harris walked out to the car, curious as to why the officer was just sitting there. Jerry's eyes were fixed on Dennis' personal items... his wallet, his badge-fold, his black .38 snub-nose with the rubber grip...

Jerry hadn't noticed Mr. Harris approach the vehicle. Dennis' father tapped on the window lightly... Jerry gathered himself quickly then opened the car door.

"Mr. Harris... I uuh... I was just about to come to the door... I

uuh... I was just trying to get myself together here", said Jerry.
The guilt was no longer on his face, grief now pervaded over him.
Seeing Dennis' father made it difficult for Jerry to keep the guilt and
grief suppressed. Mr. Harris noticed the clear bag of items on the
passenger seat. Jerry exited the car and tried to continue:

"Mr. Harris... I..."

Mr. Harris stopped Jerry and began speaking solemnly:

"You don't have to say anything Jerry... My Son had a tough job...
The streets are **mean….** and they'll take **whoever they can**... He and I
both knew what could happen... this is the main reason why his
Mother didn't want-um to become a police-man... afraid that this
very day might come... just tell me one thing... tell me you got the
son-of-a-bitch who did it?"

Jerry dropped his head in shame for a brief moment and quickly
brought it back up, dismissing the truth that was in his mind. He made
no comment but nodded his head, gesturing "yes." He reached into
the car and grabbed the clear bag then said:

"Mr. Harris... here are some of his things."

Mr. Harris spent a long moment holding and looking at the items...
the gun had a menacing presence about it... something bad, thought
Mr. Harris... The feeling was mutually felt by Jerry, for he knew
exactly why the presence of the gun was menacing... Mr. Harris was
an ardent gun collector and full of zeal in his fascination with guns,
but **this** gun... he felt had a bad story behind it... Never-the-less, he
took his son's belongings.

"Thank you for coming out here Jerry... Dennis always spoke
highly of you." said Mr. Harris, clutching his son's things.

"I'm really gonna miss him." said Jerry, looking Mr. Harris in the
eyes sympathetically for a short moment. Then he continued:

"Please give Mrs. Harris my condolences."

"I will." said Mr. Harris.

The two hugged and shook hands then Jerry got back in the car and
went his way... Mr. Harris stood outside for a-while, watching as the
car drove away. He went back inside the house to give his wife the
unfortunate news, which she already suspected. Mr. Harris put his
son's things in a small case and tucked them away, deep in the back
of a closet in his son's old room.

Back To The Present Time May 1988

Gambino made a phone call before they left the Maffitt street stash-house:

"Hello?" said a young female voice through the receiver. Gambino responded:

"Whatz-up Amber... you still up out there?"

"Yeah.... I've been waiting for you to call... My brother left some money for you... He said when you called, to remind you, not to forget about him", said Amber.

She was laying on her bed in her bra and panties. Gambino looked at the small bag of goodies he had then responded:

"Yeah, I got him taken care of."

"And what about me?" said Amber, putting her hand in her panties, letting her fingers slide through the amber hairs on her young pussy. She continued in her young girly voice:

"Are you gonna take care of me too?"

She was feeling the naughtiness that the night brings and wanted him to hurry and get there. Gambino responded:

"Amber, I got ma home-boy with me... I don't wanna have him sittin out there while we doin our thang... plus, I can't stay too long. And you know if I get-off in that hot-ass-pussy, I'ma have to sleep in it."

Amber's pussy was getting hotter and wetter just thinking about Gambino's, big brown dick inside of her little pink pussy. Still rubbing on herself, she responded:

"Aarons coming back with some girls... him and his friend, so it's cool... your home-boy won't be alone... he can chill with them. Then... you can come upstairs and fuck my pussy, any.....way you want."

Gambino was grinning wide listening to Amber. She made herself sound sultry and seductive, trying to persuade him to come fuck her. Gambino responded:

"Oooo, you naughty girl... I don't think I can refuse that offer... I'ma be out there in about forty minutes, alright?"

Amber smiled and said seductively:

"This hot wet pussy will be waiting Baby." Then she hung up the phone.

Gambino smiled big and hung up his phone as well. He went back into the living room, sexually simulated (in the mind), ready to fuck-the-shit out of his little white girl. He readied his crew.

"Let's roll-out fellas. Flame, I need you to ride with me... we headed out by Aarons house. Ghost, you can drive Crayzo and KG out to the house. Remember... all we lookin for is guns... don't spend time lookin fah nothin else... get that shit and head straight over to Aarons house, alright?"

The small crew of Gangstas nodded yes.

"What that fool 'doin out there tonight?" asked KG, referring to Aaron.

"His sister said he about to have some girls come through... They probably about to have a-lil-fun." said Gambino, holding up the little bag of ecstasy pills and weed.

After hearing that, Young Crime had a disappointing expression on his face. Gambino glanced at him then said:

"You gone learn lil G... business first, hoes later... let's roll y'all."

The crew loaded up and were on their way, leaving the stash-house in the care of, Young Crime and the Mosberg shotgun...

The two cars headed east on Union Blvd to interstate 70. At the light, they made a right onto the access ramp to I-70. They drove on I-70, passing the downtown Saint Louis skyline until they came to the beginning of I-55. They took I-55 to the Meramac Bottoms exit. From there, they went right at the exit and drove down a little, making another right into Breaking Ridge Estates...

The house was dark... no cars were in the driveway. KG got out and checked the garage window. Only one car was in the garage. Things appeared to be just as Gambino said they would be. Crayzo got out of the car next then they both took a different side of the house, walking around to check for an alarm system. From what they saw, there was none. They entered the house through the patio-door and set their wristwatches for ten minutes, although they wouldn't be there that long.

KG hit the stairs and entered a room that appeared to be an office sitting room. A lavish bookshelf lined the wall with **hundreds** of books... A chaise-lounge sat therapeutically in the room. And a huge, light-pine desk sat over by a large window. Every piece of furniture complemented the light colored carpet... KG's light shined on a curio-cabinet, almost the same color of the desk and it **immediately** caught his attention... He stepped over to take a closer look. The light glared on the glass but when he was close enough, he seen he found what they'd come for. The glass and wood curio-cabinet was locked. KG took out his tools from his lock-pick-set then made easy work of the cabinet lock...

Crayzo was about five minutes into his search, downstairs in a room. He'd come across some valuable items already but no guns. He left the items as they were and continued to look for guns. Crayzo made his way over to the closet of the room and pulled out each container, each box. One-by-one, quickly as possible, examining the contents then placing them back as they were... Still, no guns though. He reached up to the top shelf and begin taking those containers down. As he was reaching for one of the containers, a small black case caught his eye. He pulled it down and when he opened the case, he said:

"Jackpot" quietly to himself.

The police badge that was in the case, brought some alarm to him. He quickly it shook-off and didn't wanna search the rest of the house. Still, he took the gun from the case to admire it then put the case back where it was minus the gun. He searched one last container hoping to find more guns, but there were none. He quickly found his partner-in-crime upstairs, loading the gun collection and boxes of ammunition. KG wanted to comment on the cache of weapons but he contained his excitement until they were in the car. They had to be quiet to listen for anything that could be a potential threat.

Ghost drove around to Aaron's house then pulled the car over next to Gambino's car. KG hopped out-of-the car and quickly loaded the two bags into the trunk of Gambino's car. He locked it then hopped back in the car with Ghost and Crayzo. The trio was now ready to head back to the stash-house on Maffitt Street. They were all clear and KG could now express his excitement.

"**Man**! We got like **fifteen guns nigga**! **Some exclusive shit, you hear me**!"

Crayzo wanted to express his excitement as well, but the police badge had put somewhat of a frightening memory in his mind. He knew that they could never get caught with those guns, because if they did...

they would more than likely receive the maximum sentence for stealing from a cop... Ghost headed back towards I-55 to get on the freeway. Everything had gone smooth like always.

12:25am: The crew was back on Maffitt Street, except for Gambino and Flame. The house was illuminated the same as it was when they left. The trio came in through the front door.

"Crime G! Where you at lil nigga?"

KG called out for his young comrade as he walked inside the house. They heard the low-thud-of-bass coming from the basement and KG went to check on Crime. Ghost and Crayzo sat in the living-room. There was a loveseat against the far wall and a sofa on the window wall. Crayzo took the loveseat and Ghost took the sofa. A feeble coffee table sat in between the two. An entertainment center was on the back wall. It held a 27-inch Zenith color TV and two different gaming systems. There was a **cache** of video games stacked neatly on the entertainment center as well.

On the coffee table, there was a breakfast-style serving-tray. Crayzo and Ghost could see, that Crime had rolled about twelve joints and placed them on the weed tray.

"Fire somma-dat shit up Ghost." said Crayzo.

He was asking Ghost to light one of the marijuana joints, but Ghost was reluctant.

"What about what Gambino said...? He said to wait for him."

Ghost was one of Gambinos' white homeboys and Ghost was grateful to have Gambino as a friend. He never wanted to do **anything** that might cause a conflict in their friendship. He was loyal to Gambino. Ghost was also a newly blessed-in member to the crew and Crayzo didn't like him that much. Crayzo felt that Ghost was a coward and had no backbone. Crayzo didn't think Ghost could hold his own when it came to this gangsta shit... some real-live get-down in-the-street-shit.

Crayzo grabbed the lighter off the table, snatched one of the joints from the tray and fired it up... He took a generous puff from the potent pot cigarette, let the smoke out of his mouth then inhaled the smoke again through his nostrils... Crayzo held the smoke for a few seconds then let it out, purposely blowing the smoke in Ghost's direction... He hit the joint again and began talking, sounding as if he were trying to conserve his breath as he spoke:

"Ghost... you ah cool white boy..." Crayzo took another puff from the joint then continued, calm and cool:

"You seem like you **real** down fo-the-cause-and-shit... You know why I fired this shit up?" Crayzo held the joint up.

Ghost responded:

"Cause you wanna smoke I guess?"

Crayzo responded aggressively:

"**That's right nigga...**! Cause **I** wanna **smoke**... This ain't ma **shit...!** This ain't **Gambinos** shit... this shit ain't **no** bodies individually... Ain't no **big** I's and **little** you's in our circle... this **all** our shit... and when I'm done with ma muthafuckin job and wanna **smoke,** I'm gone **smoke!**"

Crayzo took another hit of the weed, calmed himself a-bit then continued:

"Gambino asked Crime to wait until **we** got back... **we** back ain't we?"

"Yeah, **we** back", said Ghost.

Crayzo continued:

"Don't you wanna smoke nigga?"

"Yeah, I wanna smoke... but"

Crayzo became more annoyed with Ghost then expressed his annoyance.

"**But nothin nigga...! That's** what I don't **like** about yo-ass... you act **too** muthafuckin **scary...** I don't like scary muthafuckas around me..."

Just as Crayzo was about to tell Ghost what he **really** thought of him, KG walked in:

"**Daaamn...** that shit smell **good-as-ah-muthafucka!**"

Crayzo passed the joint to KG... KG hit the joint then continued:

"Gambino called Crime... he said, him and Flame gone stay out at Aarons house until tomorrow morning so don't wait up fo-em."

KG took another puff on the kush-joint then Crayzo looked at Ghost and asked him:

"You still wanna wait?"

Ghost glared at Crayzo for a few seconds, reached for the tray then grabbed one of the joints and a lighter. He looked at Crayzo and held the joint up as if he were making a toast. Then he lit the joint. Ghost loved to smoke weed. The relief and satisfaction he felt after taking a hit of the kush-joint, showed in his body language and on his face. He took another short hit, tossed the lighter on the table then leaned back on the sofa. Crayzo smiled cleverly at Ghost, took another joint from the tray, held it up then said:

"To our shit." then fired-up the potent Mary-Jane-Joint.

CHAPTER 15: Aaron's House

The house had a finished basement. Aaron designated it as his own space almost four years ago when he became a freshman in high school. He was a senior now and very popular at his school. Aaron decided to decorate one of the rooms in the basement to his liking. He painted the walls in his room 'smoke-gray', the ceiling was royal blue with silver glitter flakes and glow-in-the-dark stars on it... On the walls he had velvety fuchsia and neon colored posters that glowed whenever he turned on his black-light. Bob Marley holding a marijuana-blunt was his favorite. Second, was the huge neon green marijuana-leaf on a velvety black background. Then, there were the posters of wizards, and dragons and enchanting women. All of which glowed bright in their bizarre colors under the black-light... When a person walked into Aaron's room, they were walking into a psychedelic world.

His stereo system was equipped with green and red LED lights. He had a string of blue Christmas lights, lined around the bottom of his bed. You couldn't see the actual lights but when he turned the lights on... the bottom of the bed glowed blue. Some would say Aaron was an eccentric person. He liked listening to recordings of 'Sounds of Nature' while he smoked on some kind-buds. When he studied, he listened to smooth-jazz instrumentals.

One day, when he was at school. His mother went down to his room just being curious, as most mothers are. She turned on the black-light and walked across the black and gray marble style carpet.

Mrs. Chandler stood in the middle of her son's room, looking around, inhaling the remnant aroma of reefa. She walked over to Aaron's stereo system, pressed the power button then the play button... The sounds of waves crashing against the surf and seagulls singing siren songs, sounded through the speakers... Mrs. Chandler sat down in Aaron's royal blue swivel recliner... she actually took pleasure in the surroundings. She sat there, smiling at the irony-of-the-matter. She felt herself drifting into a truly, tranquil state-of-mind. The sounds of the surfs had relaxed her... the aromatic smell of cannabis had become an anesthetic... Mrs. Chandler's eyes closed and she dozed off...

About thirty minutes later, the tape stopped in the tape deck, making a loud click in the quiet room and she came to. She got up out-of the recliner feeling soothed. Mrs. Chandler walked over to the door to exit her son's room then took another glance around. She glanced at his books... at his posters and the glow-in-the-dark stars... She inhaled the aroma once again and closed the door. As she ascended the stairs, she thought about her son and felt a sense of pride. Regardless of his cannabis smoking habit, Aaron was a great son. He was a good student as well, with a 'B average and an occasional 'A. Aaron kept his priorities in order. Mrs. Chandler never had to get-on him about anything... Aaron's female friends loved how laid-back he was, and as for his male friends, Aaron only had a hand full.

The Party Begins

Amber and Aaron's parents were always gone on business trips, so whenever they had the house to themselves, they would have small get-togethers... only a few friends, nothing outrageous though. That night, Aaron's good friend Zach brought a couple-of-girls over he was cool with... and Aaron picked-up two of his home-girls that were always down to kick-it with him. Aaron and his guest were in the entertainment area of the basement. It was equipped with a full bar and bars stools, a pool-table, a nice size lounge area, an old-school jukebox stocked with a variety of music. The lighting was just right for a bar setting... relaxing and not too bright.

"Gambino... Flame... I haven't formally introduced y'all to my home-girls", said Aaron, standing behind the bar playing bartender. He proudly introduced the young Ladies:

"That's Janet, and that's Janette... Girls. That's my big homie, Gambino and that's my homeboy, Flame."

"Nice to meet y'all." said Janet, and Janette waved friendly at Gambino and Flame.

Both girls were beautiful brunettes who could have passed for sisters, but they weren't. They were best-friends since elementary, now seniors at the same high school as Aaron... Next, Zach introduced the two young Ladies he brought, except to Aaron.

"Everybody, this is Heather and Kristen."

The young Ladies exchanged pleasantries with everyone. Both had their own striking looks... Heather was a gorgeous redhead with a few speckles of freckles on her face, looking like a mature Shirley Temple. Kristen was a beautiful blond with deep green eyes... eyes that Flame were **instantly** drawn to... Zach met Kristen and Heather at a nightclub on 'The Landing' in Saint Louis about two months ago. They both knew Aaron already. He was with Zach at the club the night Zach met the two gorgeous girls. They would get together every-now-and-then but this was Heather and Kristen's first time out at Aaron's house. They were from the South-City area of Saint Louis. Aaron and Zach were the only friends they had, who lived in upper class areas, so they were impressed with the South-County house.

The music was playing and the vibe was 'young and sexy'. Aaron placed eight shot glasses on the counter of the bar then said:

"This is how we do it at my spot."

Showing off his bartending skills, Aaron grabbed a bottle of Vodka, flipping it with one hand, letting it spin on his palm... Aaron stopped the spinning bottle in the upright position, and like a gunfighter changing a quick loading cylinder on a revolver... he pulled the cap off and pushed a spout in. Aaron poured full shots into each shot-glass then sat the bottle down.

"Alright... everybody grab-a-shot and **slam** that shit!" said Aaron. They downed the premium vodka and slammed their glasses on the bar counter then Aaron poured a second round. The small get-together was now on its way.

Aaron had already taken one of the ecstasy pills that Gambino brought him... it was starting to kick-in and he was feeling good.

"Whatz-up Gambino? Rack-that-shit and let's get-a-game goin." said Aaron. He stepped from behind the bar and over to the pool-table area. Aaron chose his pool-stick. Gambino shook his head then responded:

"You **know** I'm not no competition... you not about to embarrass **ma-ass**... you and Flame get-that-shit-crackin... Flame the **man** on the pool-table... go-a-head Flame. Do-yo-thang G."

"I'ma **whoop** Flame's ass!" said Aaron confidently.

"Alright... we'll see." said Gambino.

Flame stood up from the bar then stepped over to the pool-table area and selected a pool-stick.

Gambino stood up then said:

"I'ma go holla at Amber real quick."

"Alright, big homie... you gone miss this ass-whoopin I'm about-ta give Flame", said Aaron.

Gambino smiled then headed upstairs.

"Nice meeting y'all Ladies." he said to all the girls. They all responded the same and Gambino went upstairs...

Aaron smiled, shaking his head slowly, watching Gambino leave... He knew Gambino and Amber liked each other. And he knew Gambino didn't plan on coming back downstairs anytime soon.

"Flame G... Rack-that-shit-homie... let's get-this-shit-crackin." Flame racked the balls and Aaron continued:

"Ladies, y'all wanna play partners?"

Kristen was the first to respond:

"Yeah, we'll play... I'll be Flame's partner", she said, smiling at Flame.

Kristen saw the way Flame looked at her when they first saw each other. She knew he liked what he saw. Kristen was attracted to Flame's look just the same. Flame was 5'10" with a slim frame. He had ear piercing, penetrating gray eyes and blond hair. He had tattoo sleeves on both his arms. On his neck, he had flames all the way around it with two pitchforks crossing each other on the right side of his neck. Kristen was feeling him... Even though she was Zach and Aaron's friend, they were just and only that... friends. Plus Zach had his eyes on Heather but Heather didn't quite know it yet. Zach was the reserved type.

Aaron, Janet and Janette were amorously devoted to their relationship. The intimate love amongst the three had developed over the years they'd known each other. The beautiful brunettes didn't mind sharing Aaron, as long as he didn't mind being shared. Their relationship was an 'exclusive poly-monogamous' one and it was working well for the threesome.

"Come on Janette... let's put some **balls** in some **holes**" said Janet, emphasizing the balls and holes parts.
Janet got up first then Janette and both girls walked over towards the pool-table. Aaron watched as they strolled over to him, both with lusty, licentious looks in their eyes. Aaron could tell that their ecstasy pills had kicked-in too, and now that they **had**... the girls had no problem showing their sexuality... Normally they were conservative but at Aaron's house, they could ostentatiously be who they were and do what they feel... Janette grabbed a pool-stick, looked mischievously at Janet while sliding the pool-stick in and out of her hands then said:

"Ooooo... I think we're gonna need some lubrication."
Aaron was enjoying his home-girls as he always did.

"Get-y'all freaky asses over here." said Aaron.
He stood in the middle of both girls with an arm around Janet and an arm around Janette. He squeezed Janette tight into his body and kissed her hard and wild... their tongues twisted-and-twirled like two tornados dancing with each other in an open field. He ended the wet & wild kiss with Janette then engaged in the twisting of tongues with Janet as well. However, Janet incorporated her sucking skills into their kissing frenzy.

The scene of the three kissing was sexually stimulating to everyone in the room... The sounds coming from the wet & wild kissing only increased the intensity of everyone's sexual arousal. Flame paused from racking the balls. He felt his dick growing in his pants. He tried, inconspicuously to hide it, but Kristen was all over him with her eyes. She took notice of it, stepped over to Flame looking him **straight** in his eyes, face to face with him. Then she turned around and placed her body against his. He could now feel the soft cushioning of Kristen's ass against his hard dick. She was wearing pants made-of some-type-of spandex-jean material and she could feel everything Flame was trying to hide. Kristen had choice up on him and he had done nothing... except give her a look that said, "I want you."

Gambino was always talking about macking and now, for that reason a-lone. Flame, felt as though he were now coming into his "mack-hood." He put his arm around Kristen's waist and she nestled her ass, snug against him, letting his bulge press deeper into her, cushy-ass... Flame welcomed her bold move. She looked back at him, smiling then asked:

"You like that?"

He responded with a benign grin which Kristen thought was **so** sexy... She answered for him:

"Yeaaah... you like it."

Kristen bounced her ass on Flame once to push herself forward. She took hold of the ball Flame was holding then took-over racking for him. She also made a suggestion:

"Let's make this a little more interesting... if you miss a shot, you have to, **take-a-shot**... or... you can take-off a piece of clothing."

Aaron responded to Kristen's challenge, talking shit in a friendly competitive way:

"Y'all might-as-well get ready fa-this **ass** whoopin... and get ready to-be naked or **drunk-as-a-muthafucka**! Come on Babies."

Aaron smacked Janette and Janet on the ass simultaneously... Zach and Heather were still at the bar sitting next to each other, finding humor in watching their friends. They both were rolling joints of the weed Gambino brought them.

"Flame ... here you go man." said Zach.

Flame's bulge had calmed down and he was able-to walk over to Zach and get the joint without embarrassing his self, or showing-off, however you wanna look at it... Flame fired the joint up and took a big pull from it, putting the potent smoke of the orange-kush in his lungs then in the air. Flame passed it back to Zach and Zach took a generous hit from the joint as well. Everyone downstairs except for Flame G, took an ecstasy pill. It is a rule in the Growth & Development Nation that: 'no member is allowed to use illicit-drugs...' with the exception of marijuana, only because it was a natural stimulant and not man made. But even still... that exception was not to be abused.

The ecstasy pill enhanced the mood everyone was in. The mood that Aaron and his lusty Ladies set with their, 'Three's Company' like performance. Their 'vibe' felt **extra** good... The threesome had captured everyone's imagination of what the night could and more than likely would bring... good sex... The temperature was about eighty degrees in the basement and Zach was burning up. It was his first time smoking 'orange-kush' and it had definitely done something to him... that along with the x-pill and his bottled up feelings for Heather. He had to get some air. He got up from the barstool and when he stood, he became dizzy and wobbled a-bit.

"You alright Zach?" asked Heather ("concerningly").

"Yeah... I just need some air... I'm cool though."

Zach began to step away from the bar and before he could take another step, Heather grabbed his hand...

"I think I better go with you Zach... just to make sure you're okay."

Still light-headed and a little dizzy, Zach smiled feebly at Heather and gazed into her eyes for a couple of seconds. She put her arm around his waist and he put his arm across her shoulders to stable his self. Then the two left the entertainment area and went into Aaron's room... He flicked on the black-light and everything started to glow, even them. Zach stepped over to the basement window in Aaron's room, opened it and stood there for a moment, breathing in the fresh night air. Heather stepped over to the window:

"You okay now?" she said, rubbing on his back.

With an unsure expression on his face and his brow frowning, he responded:

"I... I don't know... I think something is wrong with my heart."

"Let me feel it" said Heather, putting her hand on Zach's chest.

"**Zach**... your heart is beating like a drum! What's wrong?"

An alarming expression was on Heather's face. She continued.

"Is it the ecstasy pill...? Maybe you need some orange juice!"

Her hand was still on his chest and Zach put his hand on top of hers then said softly:

"I think I love you Heather."

After hearing his words, Heather was now the one needing some air. The cool breeze coming in from the basement window was welcoming to her nostrils. She found herself inhaling deeply, taking in the crisp mix of nitrogen and oxygen. Heather was flattered and blushing. Zach's words had finally registered in her mind and she didn't know how to respond. She **really** liked Zach... she thought he was a really nice guy and she enjoyed being around him but... she was a little more than apprehensive about dating a black guy... She didn't wanna be looked at by her peers in that, bias, judgmental way she knew they would look at her, with the exception of Kristen... What would her parents think...? The **same** parents who had taught her that: "Niggers are nothing but trouble! They're the **main** reason behind all the crime in the country and you need to **stay** away from **all** Niggers!"

Zach had proven her parents ideology wrong. He had been a perfect gentleman from the very first time they met... much more of a gentleman than any of the white guys she knew. Zach was always respectable and never tried to pressure her into having sex with him, unlike the white guys she had been with or around. Heather felt that Zach was **by far** the best male friend she ever had. She didn't want her prejudice friends or parents to come between her friendship with Zach. That's why Zach had never been to Heather's or Kristen's house... Heather and Kristen were the rebels in their families, but only in ("clandestinity"). Heather gathered herself then responded to Zach:

"Zach... I aah... I don't know what to say."
They kept eye contact with each other and Zach took hold of Heathers hands then said smoothly with his deep soft-spoken voice:

"You don't have to say anything... just let me say this... I like being your friend, but I would **love** to be more...."
Heather's gaze was affectionate and she squeezed Zach's hands as he spoke. Zach continued:

"I **love** being around you, you're beautiful and laid-back... not **too** wild."
They both smiled, thinking of how **bold** Kristen could be at times.

"I just think we'd be good together... Heather, I'm crazy about you girl." said Zach.
Heather responded:

"Zach... no one has ever said anything like that to me before... I'm really at a loss for words."

"Come here" said Zach then Heather stepped into his arms,

feeling them wrap around her waist. Zach continued:

"I told you... you don't have to say anything... if you feel something for me... just show it."

The moment had come for Zach... He was finally about to find-out if Heather had any feelings for him or not, passionate feelings. He lowered his head slowly down towards Heather's face. His lips touched hers softly then he pulled back. Heather's head was slightly tilted back and her eyes were closed. He did the same thing again... if she turned away, her feelings weren't mutual... but if she kissed him back... then she probably had mutually romantic feelings for him. Once again, he lowered his head down slowly towards her face to kiss her... As he did, he felt her arms wrap around his neck... She did feel something for him and she was showing him that she did... They kissed with the passion of two lovers, who had been **long awaiting** to be reunited with each other. The temperature in the basement was hot, but the temperature upstairs was even hotter...

CHAPTER 16: Explicit Text Be Advised

Amber and Gambino were in her room on her bed. All Amber's clothes were off and she was laying on top of the covers. Gambino had taken off everything except his jeans and boxers. The bedside lamp was still on. They wanted to see each other's body as they made-out. He admired her petite frame, while rubbing on her tits, smoothly letting his hands glide across her breast, squeezing her nipples hard. He lowered his head and began kissing her stomach while still massaging her breast.

He worked his way down to her private area and began kissing her labia-majora, letting his tongue slip inside a little, circling the inside of her pussy. It was driving Amber wild and Gambino loved the way she squirmed. She sprawled out with her legs open wide, giving him full access to her vestibule then, clamped her muscle tight when his tongue touched her most sensitive spots... sprawling and squirming, clamping-up then releasing...

"Oooo Baby that feels sooo good." said Amber in a low erotic voice, rubbing her hands wildly over Gambino's head.

"You like the way I lick on that pretty little pussy?" he said while his lips kissed the inside of her pussy.

"Yes Baby... Yeaaah... lick that pussy good Baby... **suck** that wet pussy **good** Baby." said Amber.

Gambino was really into it and so was Amber. He started to suck on her clitoris softly.

"**Ooooo, yesss** Baby...."

Her body was having-a-fit, convulsing and already near its climactic point. He felt her pelvis thrusting upward into his mouth. Gambino put an arm under each of her thighs and scooped her lower body off the bed, flinging her legs over his shoulders and holding her thighs firmly as her lower body rested on him. Amber's naked ass was on Gambino's bare chest. The wetness from her pussy and his mouth, made her ass so moist, that it slid across his bare chest with ease as she squirmed... His hold of her was firm and her pussy had no chance of getting away from the tongue-lashing. She continued to squirm from the pleasure she was feeling, and Gambino's hunger for her hot sweet wet vagina intensified.

He vigorously sucked on clitoris, circling his tongue around and around on her clit while ferociously, plunging his tongue deep inside of her tight pussy, He sucked the inside of pussy, thrusting his tongue in and out in and out pass her pussy-lips, fast then slowing down to lick the inside of her pussy again. Amber took a firm hold of Gambino's head then said:

"**Ooooo, Baaby... Oooo shit.....** suck my pussy, **suck** my pussy, **suck** that **wet, juicy** pussy." said Amber wildly, unable to control herself.

Her legs stiffened and her thighs tightened around Gambino's neck. Amber began to shake in his grasp and her pussy began to pump out thick white cum. He gently put Amber's bottom back down on the bed and kissed her pussy lips softly as she enjoyed her climax...

THE MORNING AFTER:

May 12th, 1988

Back at the Maffitt street stash-house:

The car pulled into the backyard driveway. Flame and Gambino exited the car.

"**Man**.... ole-girl was off-the-**chain** last-night!" said Flame.

"Which one?" asked Gambino.

"**Man**.... the blond with the emerald eyes!"

Flame was ecstatic about meeting and making-out with the Beautiful, Blond Bombshell. He continued:

"Man... she walked right over to me and put that **ass** on me... like she was my girl already...! We played 'strap-pool' right... yo boy Aaron acted **a-fool** with his two hoes...! but ole-girl **Kristen**... that's me all day, all the way, you feel me?"

Gambino clearly could see Flame was excited about Kristen. She was several steps up from the girls Flame was use to dating, which were dope-head-hoes who would fuck you as long as you had the drugs they craved... meth was the main drug of choice for most of the girls Flame knew. A lot of them stopped caring about their appearance. However, from what Flame and Gambino seen in Kristen... they could see that she was a different type of girl... Her and Heather liked to party but they weren't big drinkers or drug users. Every-now-and-then they would pop an ecstasy-pill and have a few drinks, but only in good company.

The girls had seen **too** many of their friends become addicts of cocaine, meth and even alcohol... becoming **so** strung-out, that they'd do immoral things, debasing themselves to the cost of their drugs... which in most cases, was a-little-of-nothing.

Gambino responded to Flame:

"Yeah... I feel you G... but did you fuck her?"

They were at the back of the car now, about to open the trunk and take the bags inside the house. Some of the fizz in Flame had fizzled. He responded:

"Naah man... I didn't... But I **could** have!"

The light lit-up in Flame's eyes again then he said:

"We got-a-chance to talk and get to know each other a-lil-bit. Man... it was some cool shit... you know how **long** it's been since I actually **sat down** and **talked** to a-chick like that? That shit felt good G... I held her and we talked about **all kinda**-shit... we kissed a-lil-bit ,and it was cool, you know."

Gambino teased Flame:

"Awww, you-ole, lovey-dovey ass-nigga... you on some, I wanna love-a-bitch befo I fuck, type-shit."

Flame shot back:

"Aww nigga... what-was-**yo-ass** upstairs doin? eatin pussy and makin love. Tellin hoes you love-um-an-shit."

"Naaw nigga... I was up-there **beatin** her asshole up! **That's** what I was doin!" said Gambino boastfully, with a smirk on his face.

Gambino opened the trunk, grabbed one of the bags, looked at Flame then playfully said:

"**Get** the bag nigga... Mr. Lova-Lova lookin-ass."

And jokingly, Flame responded:

"You **need** ta-wash that booty-juice off-yo-ass... that shit funky. I was wonderin what I was 'smellin in the car."

"**Get** the bag muthafucka... wit-cho-**love**-at-first-sight lookin ass."

The two joked and laughed and Flame grabbed the bag. Gambino shut the trunk and they walked up the pathway to the backdoor of the house.

CHAPTER 17: Very Good Dope-Boy

Young VG, a thorough lil-nigga with dreads, who had been schooled by the best, on the street game... and he was still being taught on how to represent the GD Nation the **proper** way, the **prosperous** way... and prosperous doesn't always mean financially... That morning, VG decided to get up early to see what the set was looking like and to his surprise... The set was 'poppin. It was unusual for the 12th of the month, and on a Thursday.

He had been on the set since seven that morning and it was now 9am and so far, he made seven hundred dollars. He stood on the corner of Emma and Mimika to peep the scenery then walked towards the other end of Emma. A car came up the street from the West Florissant end of Mimika then turned cautiously onto Emma. The car drove passed VG and parked in the middle of the block. As VG neared the car, a man got out. It was Byron. A light-skinned-older nigga who VG knew from around the neighborhood that bought dope from VG on a regular.

Byron was also a good runner. A runner would go-out and find customers then bring their money back to whoever he was running for, or whoever was on the set at the time. He would earn his little commission off the sell, which was paid in crack-cocaine. If he brought a fifty-dollar-sell, he would get ten dollars worth of crack-cocaine. His commission increased as the number of dollars spent increased. Normally, Byron would break-off a-small-piece of the 'actual buyer's' piece of crack before he took it to them. He'd add that to his commission. Byron approached VG.

"Whatz-**good** wit-It, **VG**!"

Byron was high already and VG could tell from how loud Byron was. VG had a baritone voice, very deep. He responded:

"Whatz good crazy-ass Byron?"

"VG, man**,** I got-ah **C-note ma nigga**!"

Byron pulled out the one hundred dollar bill, the "C-note." He was happy to be dealing with VG and not one of the other young cats from the set. VG respected muthafuckas... even crack-heads. As-long-as they respected him. The other cats didn't give-a-fuck. "Just gimme-ma-muthafuckin money and get-the-fuck-on", is how they felt... Byron continued:

"VG, **hook me up** ma nigga... let me get seven dubs." Byron was anxious.

"Byron, **calm** yo high-ass **down** nigga... you know I'm gone hook you up... who is that in the car?" VG asked curiously, being cautious.

"**All**... 'dat's-ma white-potna, Bobby from Saint Ann."

"**Saint Ann**!" VG exclaimed.

"Yeah, yeah... he cool, he cool." said Byron.

VG looked at Byron and Byron looked at VG.

"Walk wit-me Byron." said VG.

They walked away from the car back towards Mimika. VG pulled out his sack of crack-rocks inconspicuously, took out seven fat twenty-dollar crack-rocks then tucked his sack away.

"Where that C-note?" asked VG.

Incognito like, Byron handed VG the one hundred-dollar-bill and VG gave Byron the crack:

"Here you go Byron", said VG, handing Byron the drugs.

Byron opened his hand and VG dropped the little stones into Byron's palm. Byron immediately took two stones out of the small pile, pulled out his cigarette pack, stuffed the crack inside of it then put his pack of smoke back in his pocket. He kept the rest of it in his hand.

"Ma nigga, **ma nigga...**! I'm **glad** you-was-out-here-man... right on, **right on VG...**! I **might** be back with another C-note... you-gone-be-out-here?" asked Byron.

"I don't know Byron... I might be... just come back through and if you see me out here, holla at me."

"All-ight, all-ight... in-a-minute VG."

"All-ight Byron." said VG then turned to walk away.

Byron called VG:

"VG!" VG turned to face Byron then Byron continued:

"You should add ah D to yo name ma nigga... it's gone stand fah, VERY GOOD DOPE!" said Byron, smiling big, showing the wide space in his mouth from his four front teeth being missing.

VG smiled, shaking his head in humor then turned, continuing about his way. Byron got in the car with his so-called "**potna**" Bobby, and they drove off in the opposite direction of VG.

As young VG walked back down the street, a funny feeling came over him. He felt as if he was being watched... and he probably was. People in the neighborhood were always peeking-out-of their windows and looking-out-of their doors to see what was going on. On a nice day like it was that morning... it wasn't strange for people to be out on their porch, smoking a weed-blunt or a cigarette, or just enjoying the fresh air. The neighbors were cool with the dope-dealers in the neighborhood... The people remained cool, as long as there wasn't any bullshit and drama kick-in-off, from dope being sold in their area... Another reason why they were so cool with it was; the neighborhood basically, was ran by members of the GD Nation. Members lived throughout the neighborhood and they made **sure,** that there were no problems... but if there **was** a problem... they'd take care of it... their way, without the police getting involved.

We Take Care of Ours

The Saint Louis Coordinator, Ron-Ron had established a day called "Help The Hood Day." Once a month, members would gather to clean up the neighborhood and cut grass where ever it was needed. Each area where there was a 'GD deck' or set... the members in those areas would participate in "Help The Hood Day." They also would set funds aside for children in need of school clothes and school supplies. They would do other things to show their love for their hoods, on special-occasions and certain holidays...

The Gangsta Disciples brought order to the hood when there was none... Even though society looked upon them as "ruthless ruffians" and in some cases, they were... but the people in the hood liked what the GD Nation was doing... and they respected how they were doing it. The people in those neighborhoods didn't respect the police... They wanted the police to stay **out-of** their neighborhoods... and all for good reasons.

Ron-Ron lived by the Growth & Development Concept... When Larry Hoover, the Chairman of the GD Nation, saw how destructive our environments were, due to our **own** actions and behavior and not the actual geographical-environment itself... He incorporated the Growth & Development Concept into the GD Nation... He wants us to change, for the better... He wants us to **stop** our destructive behavior and build **solid** foundations on **righteous** values... He wants us to become **positive productive** men, **prospering** and establishing ourselves in society as, 'Brothers-of-Success...!'

He wants us to be Bosses of our **own** businesses and corporations so that **we** can provide jobs for our people and not have to be so dependent on others... Larry Hoover has inspired me to continue striving towards the betterment of myself... the 'Success of Self', S.O.S. Success in every aspect of the word...

The Growth & Development concept is truly beneficial to those who apply it, and Ron-Ron wanted **his** application of it, to show in all that he did. He made sure that a portion of the money coming from the drugs sells in the hood... were put **right** back into the hood and not wasted on inessentials... Most drug dealers and so-called organized-gangs would bleed-the-block until it was dry and dilapidated. **Never** once, thinking about replenishing it... but not Ron-Ron and his GD brothers... they believed in building-the-block-up. With the help of like-minded members of the GD Nation, they invested in rundown houses, rehabbed them then put them on the section-8 government-housing program. The houses were rented to family and friends. The more family and friends they had in their neighborhoods, the more they could operate the way they needed to.

The whole point is... that under Ron-Ron's watch, the GD members were doing more good in the hood then bad. And just for the record... there are **plenty** of GD members who are just as wise and just as productive as Ron-Ron, who are teaching and leading in the same, if not, better example.

Back to the Dope-Boy:

VG thought for a moment: 'I got about eight hundred on me... I should head-on-in... Yeah. I'ma head-on-in.' He started on his way to the house. A car, turning off-of Laura Avenue, onto Mimika, headed in his direction. VG recognized the car and who it was as it passed him by... it was Pat. She caught a glimpse of VG as she drove pass him then pulled into a driveway to turn her car around. Pat drove back towards VG then slowed the car to a stop, next to the sidewalk where VG was standing. When VG got in, Pat began talking:

"**Baby**... I'm **glad** to see **you**!" she said, still very frustrated from what just happened not too long ago.

"Bend the block Pat", said VG.

He wanted her to drive away from the set so they could talk and not have to worry about anybody 'jumping-down' on them while they sat in the car. Pat pulled off and continued speaking. She spoke fast, expressing her anger as she told VG about what just happened to her.

"**VG**, you know them **punk-ass-muthafuckas**-down-on GoodFellow and Laura, '**ganked me**!'"

VG shook his head in disappointment. He was a little pissed-off at Pat because he told her once before, not to deal with them dudes over there. He continued:

"Pat... I thought you wasn't **fuckin** with them niggas no-mo?"

"I **wasn't** VG...! That **bitch** Tracie was-with-me talking about, she **know**-amuthafucka over there and he was gone hook us up... that bitch **shooo** got-me-**hooked-up-alright**! The bitch **gave** the nigga the **money** befo we even **seen-da-crack**!"

VG laughed then responded, more lighthearted now.

"Pat, I **told** yo-ass, don't **fuck** wit-them niggas on GoodFellow... you never know when they gone be on some bullshit... what he give y'all?"

"**Some bullshit...!** I don't know **what-the-fuck**-this-**is...**! But I know it ain't crack-cocaine, I know **that...**!"

VG laughed some more at Pat's expense.

"Ha, Ha, Haaa...!"

She slapped VG's arm playfully then said:

"**VG**, that shit ain't **funny**! I was about-ta **beat** that bitch ass fah-that shit...! I put the bitch out-ma-car! Shit I'm **mad**-as-**hell** about **ma** money!"

VG tried to contain his self.

"All-ight, all-ight... let me stop laughin." he got his self together then continued:

"So I guess you want some-shit on credit huh?"

Pat gave VG an offended look then said:

"Naaw-naaw, no I don't... I **pays** fa-ma-shit."

Pat had calmed down and her voice was back to normal. She continued:

"VG, I just need you to hook-me-up fah-what I got."

He peered at her...

"All-ight... What-chu-workin-wit?"

Pat responded:

"I got sixty dollars, VG."

He knew Pat was looking for a little sympathy, and he would show her some... though not without reproving her first.

"Pat, you got ma pager number, right?"

"**Yeah**, I got it."

"So why-da-fuck you didn't use it?" said VG, scorning Pat a little so she wouldn't make the same mistake again.

"**VG**... come **on now Baby**... I **know** I fucked-up but **trust** me... that shit won't **ever** happen again! I promise I'm gone page you whenever I need somethin."

Pat looked at VG with puppy-dog-eyes and smiled. She was almost twenty years older than VG, he was eighteen and she was thirty-five.

Regardless of her crack-cocaine habit, she was still a very good-looking woman. As she looked at VG with her big brown eyes, he took in the sight of her and a sudden yearning flooded over him. It was a sexual yearning.

Pat had driven to a 'Schnucks' grocery store down on West-Florissant and parked on the store lot. The lot was full-of cars already and it was a good spot for them to sit and conduct business. VG reached over and patted Pat on her thigh then said:

"You lucky I like you Pat, because I normally wouldn't do this."

He reached into his crotch and pulled out the little plastic sack of crack-cocaine. VG glanced at Pat. He could clearly see that she was yearning for what he was holding. She watched the plastic sack, eagerly waiting to see what he would give her. VG stopped what he was doing then looked over at Pat. A question was burning his brain so he asked her:

"Pat... you ever fuck-a-nigga fah-this-shit?" said VG, holding-up the plastic sack of crack.

Pat was taken aback by the question. It was so, out-of-the-blue... VG had never asked her anything like that before... Although, it wasn't uncommon for a woman to trade sexual acts for crack-cocaine. She didn't know whether to take it as a compliment, be offended by it, or take it as an ordinary question... She kept her voice relaxed and cool then responded:

"Naaw Baby... I pay-ta-play, I don't play-ta-pay... you know what I'm sayin Baby?"

VG smiled a-bit, liking the clever answer she had given him.

"Yeah... I know what-you sayin Pat."

He continued with what he was doing. VG had about two hundred dollars worth of crack-cocaine left in his sack... He took out six large stones; one hundred and twenty dollars worth of crack-cocaine then held his hand out...

"Here you go Pat."

She held her hand out and he dropped the six crack-cocaine stones in her palm. Her eyes widened at the sight of what he had given her. She reached over and hugged him tight.

"Thank you, **thank** you VG. **Thank** you Baby... You just made ma **week** VG..."

He hugged her just as tight, feeling her upper and lower back. She felt good and she smelt good too, thought VG. Her body was soft and warm and he didn't wanna let her go... He wanted to take the hug further. As she hugged him, she put her lips to the side of his face and said softly:

"Thank you Baby" then she kissed him on the cheek and continued speaking:

"Don't stop huggin me VG... the po-po's ridin by... let-um go-pass first", she said.

VG was glad to hold her longer... He actually took the opportunity to kiss her on her cheek and inhale the sweet scent of her body. She smelt **really** good. Pat took good care of herself, despite the fact she had a crack habit.

The cruiser drove pass slowly but the officer wasn't paying them any attention. He pulled up to the front of the store and parked, responding to a shoplifting call.

"Alright, we good." said Pat, letting go of VG and he released her as well.

"You want this money", said Pat, securing her drugs first then reaching into her pants pocket to retrieve the three twenty-dollar-bills.

As she slid her hand into her pants pocket, her jeans tightened... and as she pulled her hand out, her jeans pulled upward into her crotch. VG noticed the imprint between her legs and his body instantly got hot. The impulsive urge he felt, made him reach-over and grab Pat's pussy... He rubbed on it like a man in-need of **immediate** sexual attention then said:

"Naaw Pat... I think I want some-of-this."

Pat was **shocked**! She sat still, hand halfway out-of her pants-pocket, stuck, watching VG's hand rub on her pussy. She relaxed then gently put her hand on top of VG's. She took hold of his hand and smoothly moved it back to his side of the seat then said:

"VG, Baby... you wouldn't know what to do wit-this-old-pussy."

He responded:

"**Old**... Shiddd, you don't look old to **me**... you got-ah nice face, ah nice body... every time I see you, I be feelin more and more curious... I like what I see and I wanna know what's-up-it."

Pat's caramel colored face showed her flattery. Her skin turned reddish brown... She contained her urge to tell VG: "Alright young nigga... you want some-of-this pussy? Ok... I'm gone take you home with me and **fuck** yo young-ass until yo **dick-is-sore**!" Pat laughed at the thought then continued:

"VG, that's sweet Baby... you-got-me-over-here blushin-an-shit... You wanna go back to the set?"

Pat handed VG the sixty dollars, nonchalantly dismissing the lusty little moment they just had. She felt the lust on her part as well... After VG had done what he did, she too was wanting some sexual attention. If he were a-little-older, she would've taken him up on his offer.

VG thought about what he wanted to do for a few seconds then responded:

"Yeaaah... I guess I can get this last-bit-of-dope-off... yeah, take me back-to-the-set." he said dejectedly.

During the drive back, he hadn't said a word since they left the store parking lot.

Back on Mimika, VG got out of the car and Pat told him:

"I'm gone page you if I need you VG, okay Baby?"

"All-ight." said VG, unenthusiastically then walked away.

Pat knew he was probably a little discouraged. She had dismissed his advance but didn't wanna be the cause of his discouragement too. She called his name:

"VG!"

He turned around and stepped towards her car.

"Whats-up Pat?" he said.

She continued:

"When I page you... I hope you be ready to put-in-some-work!" She smiling seductively at VG. She could discern from the modest smile he now wore, that he comprehended what she was saying then she drove off... She restored His confidence. He smiled, relishing in the thought, which was, having sex with Pat, a very much more mature woman.

Pat thought about VG as she drove down Mimika to West-Florissant, headed to her house: "that young nigga is so good to me... every time I come through to get somethin, he take care of me. **Ooooo,** and the way he grabbed ma **pussy**... **shit** it felt good!"

The recollection of getting her private grabbed and rubbed-on by Young VG, sent tingles to her pussy. She wiggled her thighs in an attempt to stop it but the tingling wouldn't stop. VG had aroused her sexual-senses with his bold move. She liked the way he touched her... very **manly** like with authority. She squeezed her thighs together in another attempt to stop the tingling, but that attempt too, went unsuccessful.

"**Oooo shittt!**" she exclaimed, squeezing and opening her thighs. She came to a stoplight near West-Florissant and Union... she sat at the light and thought contemplatively about VG. Pat considered it then she decided:

"Fuck this... I'm goin-na-**get that** young nigga." she said to herself, now wanting to satisfy her sexual craving.

The light turned green and she continued through it, pulling onto a liquor-store parking-lot that was on the right, at the corner of West-Florissant and Union. She turned around and headed back to pick-up her young-tender. She felt a-little-foolish at first, but the feeling faded fast as she thought about young VG, banging into her pussy hard in the missionary position... she wanted to see his young face while he fucked her... she wanted to touch his strong young body... Pat was now the anxious one.

She made the left onto Mimika and drove up the street, passing a couple of adjoining streets before she began looking for her young-tender. She made it back to where she dropped VG off at, but there was no sign of him. She drove to the next adjoining street then glanced down it... something grabbed her attention. A white cargo van sat in the middle of the block, close to the sidewalk but it didn't appear to be parked. Pat frowned curiously. She could see three men tousling and **instantly**, she knew it was probably some muthafuckas trying to **rob** VG.

A couple of cars were passing by the street she needed to turn down, so she had to wait. The cars passed and Pat turned onto the street as-quickly-as she could. By the time she turned completely onto the street, all three men disappeared from her sight, into the side of the van. The side-door of the van closed and the van drove off, hastily pass Pat's car then turned off the street. She caught a glimpse of the driver, took a mental note of the license-plate-number and the-make-of-the-van. It was a middle-aged white-male with dark hair. XMO-621 was the plate number. A white-ford-cargo-van was the make. She still wasn't sure if it was VG that she saw tousling with the men, however. She was starting to worry about him.

Pat drove to the middle of the block where the scuffle had taken place... She noticed an elderly black woman coming from the side-of-the house, almost as if she'd been hiding. The elderly woman had went to empty her trashcan in the bin in the alley. As she made her way back to the front of her house, by-way-of the side-of-the-house-walkway, she caught the whole scuffle, unseen by the men.

Pat's senses told her to stop, so she did... She parked the car and got out... The elderly woman stopped in her step, being cautious of Pat's approach.

"Excuse me Ma'am... I'm trying to find ma friend. His name is VG. I think he might be in some trouble... do you know him?" asked Pat, with a worried looked on her face.

The elderly woman knew who VG was, and she had witnessed everything that just happened to him. She felt no threat from Pat so she responded honestly, continuing to walk to the front of her yard.

"Yeah... I know him... he-done-got-his-self **snatched-up** by two white-men... they **threw-um-in-a-van** and **took off**... He tried to fight-em-off. But one-of-em, **hit** VG with sometihn and all the fight went-outta him **just** like that."

The elderly woman snapped her fingers at the end of her statement.

She sat her trashcan down on the patch of grass near the curb. It was the trashcan she kept outside for people to put their trash in, instead of them throwing it on the ground. A few other neighbors on the block had trashcans in front of their houses as well. They were trying to encouraged children as well adults, to keep their neighborhood clean.

Pat responded to what the elderly woman just said:

"**Well, we should call the police...!**" she said frantically.

The elderly woman looked at Pat and **huffed** at the suggestion then said:

"**Police**... childdd, I've been-around-fa **seventy-six-years** and I know police when I see-em... in, and outta uniform and them white men, was the police... you can call-em if you want to... but it probably ain't-gone-do-no-good... what you **need** to do, is let VG's **people** know what done happened to-um."

Pat looked at the elderly woman with curiosity then said questioningly:

"His people...?"

The elderly woman responded:

"Yeah, **his** people... they more likely to know what-to-do-about-it than the police..."

Pat was non-receptive of the woman's suggestion and said:

"Ma'am... I **think** we should to call the police...!"

The elderly woman glared at Pat for a-few seconds, seemingly, to examine her.

"What's-yo-name-child?" she said.

Pat frowned, feeling frustrated because they were wasting precious time... and she was already upset for not taking VG home with her from the start. Her thoughts were racing and she was in a daze. The elderly woman's glare at Pat became more intense and she asked again:

"Child... I asked you, what-yo-name-was..."

Pat shook out of her daze then responded:

"Pat... ma name is Pat, short for Patricia... Patricia Stewart."

The elderly woman extended her hand then said:

"Nice to meet you Patricia... I'm Ruth Kimble."

They shook hands gently. Pat's **entire focus** had changed. Not even five minutes ago... The only thing that was on her mind was getting high and fucking. And now... the only thing that was on her mind was finding VG.

To her surprise, her craving for crack-cocaine was gone completely. She was astonished at the amazing and seemingly **instant** deliverance from her mild addiction. It was a moment-of-clarity for Pat... She understood that regardless of what society and those bullshit ass clinical research studies said... if a person **really** wanted to leave crack-cocaine alone... they could. It's about putting what's important in front of you, and putting what's not important, behind you... All it took for her to come to this candid conclusion... was for someone to genuinely show her they cared about her, regardless of her imperfections. She had an 'equilibrant-epiphany', or "balancing manifestation." She truly felt she was back to her stable-state-of-mind, pre-addiction.

Ms. Kimble continued:

"Come-on-in Child."

Pat followed Ms. Kimble into the house, passing the living-room and into Ms. Kimble's cozy little den.

"Gone and have a-seat Patricia. I'll be right back."

Ms. Kimble excused herself and Pat took a seat. She saw the phone sitting atop a little side-table next to an old comfortable looking recliner.

"Ms. Kimble!" Pat called out, with her voice slightly elevated.

"Yes Patricia!" answered Ms. Kimble.

"Should I call the police now?!" asked Pat.

Ms. Kimble was headed to her room to get her personal address/ phone number book. She stopped in her step then responded:

"Gone and call-em if you feel that's what you need to do. But like I said, it ain't gone do much good!"

Ms. Kimble continued to her room. Pat got up and stepped over to the little table. She picked-up the receiver and paused... Pat wondered why Ms. Kimble felt so adamant about the police not being able to do anything. She began dialing the number, bewildered by her sudden aversion for wanting to do so... She pressed the buttons slowly, 9-1-... and the reluctance continued to flood her. Pat put the receiver down on its cradle... She was at a conflict with her own 'social-sense' and with Ms. Kimble's 'lack of faith' in the police. Her social sense told her: that when a person witnessed a crime, they should call the police, especially if the crime happens to them or someone they knew. But Ms. Kimble's convictions, in regards to the police... were stronger than Pats social sense.

"**Damn-it**!" said Pat, just as Ms. Kimble entered the room.

"You alright Patricia?"

Pat looked a little confused, but she told Ms. Kimble she was alright.

"Yes Ms. Kimble. I'm okay. I'm just frustrated with the situation, that's all."

Ms. Kimble walked over to the cushy-recliner and sat down, exhaling, glad to be relieving her weary legs.

"**Swhooo**." she sounded.

She reached for her glasses that were on the little side-table, put them on then began flipping through the pages of her address /phone book. Ms. Kimble spoke to Pat, in regards to Pat's previous comment while flipping the pages.

"You know Patricia... when we go to do 'somethin... then a voice in our head tells us, '**Naaw**, don't do that! Just **hold**-up a-minute...'

That ain't nothin but the Spirit of God, tryina-get-us to-be patient. He got somethin **already** planned... He just need us to have an understanding of what we have to do, so we don't go **messin** thangs up... Most of the time, we ain't gotta do too much at all... here it is." she said.

Ms. Kimble had found the phone number she was looking for. She looked up from her phone book then continued:

"We gotta listen **close** to that Spirit so we don't mess-thangs-up that God already got worked out... we **all** got common-sense... but alotta us still need to get-in-tone with our '**God**-Sense'."

Ms. Kimble lifted the phone off the small table and placed it in her lap. She peered over at Pat then continued:

"God stopped you from 'callin the police..."

Pat looked at Ms. Kimble mysteriously, not understanding where Ms. Kimble was trying to go with this. "What did **God** have to do with **anything** at this point?" thought Pat. "And why would God wanna help a, crack-cocaine dealing, gang-banging, street nigga?"

Ms. Kimble began dialing the phone number.

Real Gangstas Do Real Thangs

The telephone rang out at the two-story, brick-house in Cool Valley, a district of Saint Louis County.

Ron-Ron got up early to watch Fox 2 news but he was now watching CNN... he like to keep-up with what was going-on in his city and the political world. A mysterious string-of-murders and missing people had plagued the urban communities... No GD member or their families were affected by the murders and missing people... not until now...

Ron-Ron answered the phone.

"Hello?"

"Good morning Ronny."

He instantly knew who it was. Only one person called him, 'Ronny' and that was Ms. Kimble. Ron-Ron smiled and responded:

"Good mornin G-Momma Kimble." that was her official title.

Ms. Kimble and Ron-Ron met each other at the very first "Help The Hood Day." She was outside admiring what the old and young men were doing... young boys were helping as well. When she saw them picking-up trash, cutting grass and cleaning-up the neighborhood... she noticed Ron-Ron seemed to be the one in charge of the project. As the crew made its way towards her house, she approached Ron-Ron with an idea:

"It would be nice if there were a-few trashcans out here so the kids could throw they trash in... instead of on the ground."
She looked down the street then up the street, and then back at Ron-Ron and said:
"Ooh, I'd say... one just at the beginning of the street, one at the end, and one **right** here in the middle."
At that time, they were standing in front of Ms. Kimble's house. He smiled at her and understood, she wasn't just suggesting that a trashcan be put in front of her house... she was asking.
Ron-Ron was a manner-able, respectful, intelligent young man. She could sense that about him. He introduced his self:
"Ma'am. My name is Ron-Ron... I'm the coordinator for the Growth & Development Nation here in Saint Louis."
Ms. Kimble glared at him then said:
"The **what**?"
Ron-Ron smiled then repeated his self politely:
"The Growth & Development Nation."
Ms. Kimble gave him that 'curious-eye' and extended her hand. Ron-Ron shook her hand gently then Ms. Kimble introduced herself:
"I'm Ruth Kimble... **born** and **raised** on the north-side of Chicago... but I been in Saint Louis for twenty years now."
There it was... if Ms. Kimble was from the North-side of Chicago... then she knew **exactly** what Ron-Ron represented. He sensed her knowledge of the streets was keener than what she led on to be.
Ron-Ron's light skin blushed a-bit... Then with a serious tone-of-voice and an expression of gratitude in her eyes, Ms. Kimble continued:
"I like what I see in you young man... you keep 'doin what you 'doin and being the righteous man you've grown-to-be."
Ron-Ron smiled modestly and responded:

"Thank you Ms. Kimble. I'ma keep doin ma best."
Ms. Kimble nodded then walked back to her house and went inside... The very next morning when she got up to check the mail... she saw a brand new black Rubber-Maid trashcan in front of her house. She stepped out on her porch and took-a-look down the street... there was a trashcan at that end... she looked in the other direction. And there was a trashcan at that end of the street as well. Ms. Kimble smiled indulging in the fresh morning air for a moment then went through her mail... There was a plain envelope with her name on it. She went inside the house, sat in her favorite chair then opened the envelope. The note read:

*Ms. Kimble... Thank you for seeing in me, what I hope everyone will see in me, mainly... my Growth & Development brothers, so they can follow the example that I'm doing my best to lead by. We **all** are trying to live by the righteous concept that we stand on, but for whatever reasons... it's easier for some than it is for others. I just wanted you to know... that both of your neighbors on each end of your block, agreed to have a trashcan in front of their house. Thanks for the suggestion. I hope it helps... I also want you to know... that if you ever need help with anything, please feel free to call me... And if there's ever a problem in the neighborhood, let me know about it and I'll have our guys get on it, ASAP...We like to take care of our own problems...*

Sincerely, Ron-Ron

House: 588-6774
Pager: 393-1680

That was three years ago. Since then, the two have built a genuine grandmother and grandson relationship. Ron-Ron would go by Ms. Kimble's house just to converse, soaking-up some of her worldly and spiritual wisdom... He loved how she would open her Bible and give him scriptures to remember for his own spiritual growth. His favorite scripture was *Galatians* chapter 6, verse 1-7... He felt it pertained to the very core of the Growth & Development concept. We have to help our brothers, young & old.

Galatians chapter 6 verse 1 to 7: Brothern, if a man be over taken in a fault, ye which are spiritual, restore such an one in the spirit of meekness; considering thyself, lest thou also be tempted... Bear ye one anothers burdens and so fulfill the law of God... For if a man think his self to be something when he is nothing, he deceiveth himself... But let every man prove his own work and then shall he have rejoicing in himself alone and not in another... For every man shall bear his own burden... Let he that is taught in the word communicate unto him that teacheth in all good things... Be not deceived; God is not mocked: for whatever a man soweth, that shall he also reap.

Back to Ms. Kimble's phone call to Ron-Ron:

"Ronny, I got some bad news Baby... I think you should get-on-over here so I can tell you what happen."
Ron-Ron's smile turned into a frown instantly... He knew it **had** to be something serious if Ms. Kimble was asking him to come over **just** to tell him about it. He responded:
"G-Momma Kimble, give me about, fifteen minutes and I'll be there."
"Alright Baby... I'll see you when you get here", said Ms. Kimble.
Ron-Ron hung-up the phone, dashed up to his room and put on his navy blue pocket-tee-shirt and his black and blue Nike-Airs. He already had-on some black sweatpants. He went back downstairs to the kitchen where the small 13-inch color TV sat on the counter, still showing the news. He grabbed his glass of orange juice that was half-full then downed it. He sat the glass in the sink, picked-up his keys off the kitchen counter then left out-of-the house through the patio-door.

The sun was bright in the backyard... and the navy-blue paint with metallic flakes that was on his Buick Regal T-Type, gleamed and glistened as Ron-Ron walked towards it. He pressed the button on the alarm remote: '**Chirp, chirp**'! Then he got inside.

The smell of purple-kush-weed and new car scent hovered in the air... Whenever Ron-Ron cleaned his car, he would spray the new car scent on the carpet then fire-up some of his finest Mary Jane and chill in his car for a minute, 'bumpin his music at the self-services-car-wash. He would hit the joint a-few times just to get his buzz right then rollout. The smells together were aromatic and from what his lady-friends say... 'The smell is somewhat soothing and arousing'.

Ron-Ron cranked the engine and the motor growled, rattling the dual-exhaust-pipes a-bit. He let the engine run for a-few minutes then ran back inside the house to make a phone call. He dialed Chicago's phone-number... Chicago was Ron-Ron's second in command or, 'Coordinator Assistant' is the proper title. Chicago was also an Enforcer.
He answered the phone:
  "Hello?"
  "Chi! what-up G." said Ron-Ron.
  "What-up-wit-it Family."
  "Chi, I need you to meet over G-Momma Kimble's house... She say she got some bad news and we need to hear-it-in-person."
  "I'm-on-ma-way-right-now Family." said Chicago.
  "All-ight. Plenty much love G." said Ron-Ron.
  "Never too much." said Chicago and they both hung-up their phone.
'Plenty much love' and 'never too much', were a Gangsta Disciples way of saying; thank you, you're welcome; it's used also as a 'parting' and it also meant just what it said... 'plenty much love and never too much'... Ron-Ron dashed back out-of-the house, hopped in his cool-wip then turned on the radio. *Stevie Wonder's* hit song *"Very Superstitious"*, thumped softly out of the speakers... Ron-Ron was now ready to go. He pulled out of his driveway, in route to Ms. Kimble's house...

CHAPTER 18: If A Die Bury Me Ah G.

"Aaaaa! what-the-**fuck**... **Aaaaa**!" yelled VG, struggling trying to get loose from the chair he was tied to. He jerked his head back shaking his body hard in another attempt to free his self.

"Aaah, shit", he said, grimacing from the pain.

The back of his head was still hurting from the black-jack-blow he received during the scuffle. It was the blow that had knocked him unconscious. The pain surged through his head and the dizziness came back. He relaxed for a moment, trying to let the pain mellow out.

"Man, what-the-fuck **is** this." he said quietly to his self as he took in his surroundings.

The men had taken VG to an old warehouse somewhere off-of North Broadway Ave... The warehouse was unoccupied and the street was abandon. The smell of the warehouse was pungent and the air was dank. VG coughed and spit, tasting the damp thick stench of the air. Bird shit, literally covered the floor and though VG couldn't see them, he heard the coos-of-pigeons that sat-up-high in the rafters of the warehouse. He wasn't afraid. He was **mad**-as-**hell** at his self for getting **snatched-up** by two white boys. During the scuffle he wished he had his pistol... he would have deaden both-of-em. VG was a true G, though still young and learning.

He tried to free his self once more but to no avail, the ropes wouldn't loosen.

"Damn..." he said quietly...

He wanted to yell but his head would hurt too much and yelling would probably do no good... VG decided to just sit there... patiently a-waiting his fate... no more yelling; no more struggling, "I'll just sit here and see what comes next" he thought. VG sat there, thinking about all of the movies he'd seen where muthafuckas end-up in the **same** predicament he was in now. Feeling like he was in a scene straight-out-of-a-movie, he laughed at the situation. He settled down a-bit and took notice of his surroundings again. There were no windows on the ground floor, at least not from his point-of-view. But up-top, the light shined in from the morning sun, though he still couldn't see any windows.

Beep Beeep, Beep Beeep, Beep Beeep.

His pager went off and he instantly thought of Pat and what she said to him before she drove off. He wondered if it was her paging him. He tried to wiggle his right hand free but it was bond tight by the rope.

"Fuck..." he said quietly in frustration then...

He heard something behind him... It was the sound of iron wheels rolling slowly and grinding on their track. The sound vibrated the concrete floor under him. It let him know that he was somewhere by the train-tracks.

As the sound of the heavy iron locomotive faded and the vibrating stopped... a huge sliding door began to open right in front of VG. The sound and sight of the giant sliding door opening, reminded him of a mid-evil-movie when the gates-of-a-castle were being opened or drawn... the heavy wood and stone, dragging and creaking as it moved into place.

The sound echoed throughout the empty warehouse... VG's gaze was intense. He watched, anxiously waiting to see who or what would emerge from the darkness that lied beyond the huge doorway. The beat of his heart increased and a small bit of anxiety set in. VG gathered his self:

"Stay cool nigga, stay cool." he whispered to himself then took a deep breath, trying not to choke-on the-stink-of-the-air.

The huge sliding-door came to a stop. VG didn't know what was about to come out-of-the darkness. The sound of someone walking, replaced the creaking, dragging sounds of the heavy door... As the sound of footsteps grew closer, the outline of a man's figure became clearer. VG could see that it was an older white man... late forties, maybe early fifties... At first, VG thought it might-of-been one of the men who attacked him, but it wasn't... They were younger looking. The man was now right in front of VG... He peered down at VG and VG frowned at the man, angrily.

"It stinks in here doesn't it?" said the man, taking a-pack-of-Marborel Lights from his shirt pocket. VG didn't respond.

The man continued:

"You smoke kid?"

Still VG gave the man no response. The man put one of the cigarettes in his mouth and lit it.

"You sure you don't want one?"

VG slowly turned his head in another direction and the man continued:

"Yeaaah... you're probably doing right by not taking one... these things will kill you."

He took a long pull from the Marborel Light and blew the smoke up towards the rafters. He continued:

"You know what else will kill you... those big ass rats over there." The man lifted his arm and motioned in the direction of a dark corner of the warehouse. He took another pull from the cigarette then flicked it into the dark corner. The cigarette hit like a small missile and the corner **erupted** into **loud** shrieks and squeaks, sending the humongous rats into a scatter. The man walked over to the dark corner and flicked his Zippo. VG looked around on the floor frantically, trying to see if any rats had scattered over his way, none had. He peered over to where the man was and the bright flame revealed him standing near something. The man lowered the Zippo a little, and it became visible to VG what the man was standing near... The sight was gruesome.

What VG saw, was enough to scare anyone into a frightened panic, but he held fast to his fearlessness. The body of someone was being devoured by the rats! The face was unrecognizable... The image sent chills through VG's body and he shuddered from the chills... he kept calm though. The flame went out and the man walked over from the dark corner and stood in front of VG again.

"It looks like those rats are **hungry**... the meat on that guy is damn-near gone!" said the man with a modest fascination of the rats' ravenous voracity... he was literally relishing in the moment.

VG finally spoke:

"Maaan, why am I here? What-the-fuck-you-want wit-me?"

The man looked at VG, astonished by VG's calm, cool demeanor then said sarcastically:

"**Damn**! You're not even the **slightest** bit afraid are you...? Your voice is smoooth as-a-piece-of-glass."

VG had taken mental notes from the movies: 'the best way to get-out-of shit like this or at least, stay alive longer... was to have no fear, pretend to be afraid, stay cool and slightly copy the demeanor of the psychopathic muthafucka that held you captive".

VG responded:

"What-do-you-think...? **You** think I'm scared...? You think this shit is supposed to scare me? ah-dark, **stankin**-ass warehouse, rats eatin on bodies an-shit... me tied to this-**fuckin** chair... **Yeah** I'm afraid!"
VG let out a small dose of the anger he was feeling, as he ended his answer... His captor could hear the anger in his voice, but the one thing his captor **didn't** hear... was fear.
The man responded:
"You're not afraid **ma man...**! You're pissed-off...! I know afraid when I see it."
The man grinned and laughed then he continued:
"You're **really** mad-as-hell, huh?"
VG responded:
"Look man... I'm just doin ma best to stay calm... I wanna get-outta-this-shit... if I can that is."
The man glared at VG. He admired the fearlessness and the respect VG displayed. It showed the man VG understood, just who was in control of the situation... And it showed him VG was willing to cooperate...
The man eyed VG for a moment, trying to feel-him-out. He couldn't tell if VG was being a-crafty-little-fucker, or... just trying to play it smart so he could get his self out of the predicament he was in... Either way, Detective Jerry Schlesta was still in control... Jerry continued:
"I like you kid... you got nerves of steel and you know-how-to-think... you're smart... I like that, kid."
Jerry walked over to VG and stepped behind the chair. He grabbed VG's shoulders and gave them a-little shake then stepped back in front of VG:
"You know how many **dumb** fuckers have sat right there in that **same** spot you're in, who thought they were tough... who thought **they** were the ones running-shit and didn't make-it-outta-here...?"
VG shook his head no, playing the little, "ego-power-trip" game with Jerry.
Jerry continued:
"They ended-up like that piece of **shit** over there."
Jerry gestured towards the dark corner then continued:
"The **smart**-guys... the guys who cooperate... **they're** the ones who make-it-outta-here... You seem like you're willing to cooperate,

so-I'm-gonna-cut-the-chase... The reason you're here, ma-man... is because it's been brought to my attention... that out-of-the **whole city**... you're area is the **only** area with the **best** shit in town... and I'm kind-of-curious, as-to-how that-is... it's supposed to be a-drought... most cats are-out-there selling peanuts and wax! But **you** ma-man."

Jerry reached into his shirt-pocket and pulled-out a small vile with blue liquid in it and a dissolving piece of crack-cocaine then continued:

"You have some eighty-five-percent pure-**shit**! How is that...?"

Jerry shook the little vile and held it up for VG to see it. VG responded in a contemptuous tone:

"So **that's** what this about? Who got the best **dope**? Wooow... Never-in-a-million-years would I've thought I'd be-in-ah situation like this because I got some good dope."

He cracked a grin in disbelief, chuckled a little and shook his head then continued:

"What... you with some type of **drug task** force or some-shit?"

VG wondered: "how did this dude get-a-hold of **ma** dope?" The only logical thing he could think of was, "that muthafucka Byron and his so-called potna, **Bobby,** from Saint Ann."

VG's mind recalled the very words Byron had spoken when he came to spend the one-hundred-dollars. Jerry responded to VG's comment:

"You don't need to worry about who I am kid... but just to satisfy your curiosity, no... I'm not with any special drug task force... now... how about answering **my** question... How is it that you're area is the only area with the-best-shit-in-town and the rest-of-the-city is dry and selling bullshit?"

VG didn't wanna answer the question, but that would probably lead to a sure death. He thought quickly then said:

"Shiddd, I don't know... I guess ma connect-is-a-little better than everybody else."

VG saw the mischievous smile on Jerry's face and knew what question was coming next.

Beep Beeep, Beep Beeep, Beep Beeep...

VG's pager went off again and Jerry stepped over to him then said:

"You wanna check that?"

VG gave Jerry a crazy look, for his hands were still tied.

"**Ooh,** I'm sorry... you're **all** tied up."

Jerry tried to joke and smiled at his own humor. He reached for one of the ropes that bound VG's hand.

"Here... I'll untie that left arm for you... Now I'm trusting you won't try anything stupid, right?"

Jerry glared at VG for acknowledgment.

"Naw man... I'm not gone try nothin stupid." said VG.

"Good... like I said. I like you kid... I would hate-to-have-to-leave-you here as the rats next meal... but I **will** if you **fuck**-with-me, **you understand...**?" said Jerry, commandingly, glaring at VG.

VG nodded yes, indicating that he understood. VG wanted to deaden Jerry...

Jerry untied VG's left arm then stepped back.

"There you go kid."

VG reached for his pager, quickly checking the first page received, expecting to see Pat's code and her phone number. It was a number from his neighborhood but he didn't know whose it was. The second page was an important code:

74-3-181514-412-1-1. He deciphered the code and it basically said: G.D. Coordinator, Ron. Understand, aid and assistance. The message let VG know, that his Gangsta Disciple brothers were already on-top-of-the-situation. He wanted to smile but he resisted the urge to do so. He held it back, not wanting his captor to become suspicious of anything. VG put on a stern face then said:

"I don't know **who** the fuck this is?"

"Probably one-of-your customers trying to get-a-hold of some of that good-shit-you-got" said Jerry.

VG could smile now.

"Yeah, you probably right." said VG and both of them smiled.

Jerry recognized that VG's smile was genuinely confident. Jerry figured it was because VG knew he had the best cocaine on the streets, and being a "young thug from the hood", Jerry thought VG took pride in that... but that wasn't it... that was that white-mans bullshit way of thinking... VG took pride in what he was part of and what he represented. VG was confident that he was gonna come out-of-the situation alive... and the muthafuckas who had **anything** to do with it...! They were in for a **rude** fucking awakening... You can't just, **go around snatching** people up...! **especially** not a member of the GD Nation! No **sirrr**! Extreme consequence and repercussions would be dealt-out to the perpetrators of **any** unlawful acts against the GD Nation... and Young VG **was** the GD Nation.

VG was the next generation of Gangsta Disciples, coming-up, under the righteous guidance of elder Brothers who lived by the Growth & Development concept. He was learning how to become the **essence** of Growth & Development, utilizing the educational system, economical resources and communities-ties to grow financially. Developing mind, body and souls, all to grow and develop into the men we were made to be... not the men that corruption turned us into.

Back at G-Momma Kimble's house:

Ron-Ron, Pat and Ms. Kimble were all in the cozy den waiting and hoping for VG to call them back. Ron-Ron was getting impatient. He got up then said:

"G-Momma Kimble, I can't wait around here like this. I know he might not call back if he in trouble. I gotta put my guys on alert and get some teams out there in the streets to look fah VG."

Pat didn't know **what-in-the-world** Ron-Ron was talking about! "Put his **guys** on alert? Get some **teams** out in the streets? Who-the-fuck-was-he?" she thought... To Pat, he looked like a regular nigga from the hood, just with more manners.

Ron-Ron continued:

"Ms. Pat, what's that license-plate-number again?"

Pat shook out of her thoughts then answered Ron-Ron.

"Yeah, it's ah, XMO-621, a white Ford cargo van."

Ron-Ron wrote the info down on a small piece of paper... Ms. Kimble had already given Ron-Ron the details of what happened.

Ron-Ron continued:

"Alright... I'ma have somebody check-out the plate-number and see who the van belongs to. Hopefully that'll give us a start."

Leaving the den, Ms. Kimble and Pat followed behind Ron-Ron. Chicago was standing on the porch in somewhat of a guards position. Ms. Kimble knew Chicago was out on the porch but Pat didn't. As they exited the house to the porch, Pat was startled by Chicago's presence.

His tall frame stood in the shaded part or the porch with the shade hiding his dark skin and his chiseled stone facial features.

"Chi, we need to go holla at Big Sis a.s.a.p. and put every deck captain on-alert. G-Momma Kimble, thank you fah-callin-me."
Ron-Ron gave her a big hug and a kiss on the cheek and so did Chi.

"That's what I'm here fo Baby... y'all be careful out there."

"We will G-Momma." said Chi.

"Thank you too Ms. Pat." said Ron-Ron.

"You welcome." said Pat, still curious of just **who** Ron-Ron was.
Chicago and Ron-Ron stepped off the porch and left. Chicago's black Monte Carlo SS and Ron-Ron's blue Buick Regal T-Type left the block growling down the street. They were on their way downtown to see Big Sis. The big block engines opened up when they hit the freeway.

The Shell building was buzzing when they arrived... buzzing with business class professionals, lawyers of all sorts, building-personnel and per-pending bystanders who were looking for answers to their unsolved problems... Chicago and Ron-Ron signed-in at the security desk then walked to the east elevator, got on and headed-up to the eighth floor.

Ding! The elevator bell sounded and the doors opened. A young pretty receptionist greeted them:

"Good morning gentlemen. How can I help you?" said Tina, eying them both.

Chicago was casually dressed. He wore a pair of, immaculate all white, Nike Air Force Ones, navy blue Dickie pants that were totally wrinkle free. And a long-sleeved all white Nike cotton-shirt. It fitted perfectly over his muscular torso. Tina had never seen either of them until today, and she liked what she saw.

Ron-Ron stood at 6' 1", had a light skin-complexion, a clean shaved head and a muscular physique... he reminded Tina of an Egyptian Pharaoh. Chicago stood at 6' 2", had a dark skin-complexion and had a very muscular build as well. He reminded Tina of a warrior from an African tribe in Zambia... Both men were clean in their appearance and they both wore grave looks on their face... indicative of the seriousness of their visit.
Chicago answered Tina:

"Yes, we need to see Ms. Lewis... it's very urgent."

Tina snapped back into her receptionist-mode, trying-to-not let the attractiveness of the men captivate her too much.

"And who might I tell her is here to see her?" said Tina, in her most pleasant voice.

"Ron Turner and Lenn Dukes." said Chicago.

Tina quickly pressed the button on the, inter-office-communications-system.

Evelyn pressed the button on her phone to answer Tina's buzz:

"Yes Tina?"

"Ms. Lewis. There are two gentlemen here to see you, a, Mr. Ron Turner and Mr. Lenn Dukes... they say it's urgent."

Tina listened to Evelyn's response through the headset:

"I'll be up front in a moment Tina."

"Okay Ms. Lewis."

Tina then pressed the button on the phone.

"She'll be up front in-a-moment gentlemen... You can have a seat over there if you'd like."

Tina pointed to the waiting area.

"Thank you." said Ron-Ron.

"Thank you" said Chicago then they strolled over to the waiting area to have a seat.

Chicago commented quietly about the receptionist:

"G. Lil-momma **nice** over there, right...?"

He was admiring Tina's beauty... her beautiful brown-skin and her baby-doll face.

"Yeah.... She nice." said Ron-Ron, not really focused on anything else except finding Young VG.

Evelyn's office-door opened and two women came out, still conversing while they walked down the short hallway towards the reception area.

"Ms. Lewis. I really appreciate you for what you're doing for Porshaé." said Keisha.

Evelyn gave Keisha's arm a little caress then responded:

"Ms. Pulliam... I know there're bad cops out there and its part of my duty, as an advocate of the law, to fight against that, in **any** way I can... **So many** of our Black Men have been falsely accused and sent to prison... or have even been **killed** by crooked police-man...

Pg.267

somebody has to fight for our men when they can't fight for themselves."

Keisha responded:

"I just wish there were more lawyers like you, who cared about finding the truth."

It was Keisha's first time being in Evelyn's office and for some reason, it made Keisha admire Evelyn more after seeing her office... Evelyn was a beautiful African American woman with her own law office and she was passionate about making a difference in the legal system.

Ron-Ron and Chicago could hear the women conversing as they rounded the corner stepping into the reception area. Ron-Ron was a-little distant as far as Chicago's interest in Tina, but when he saw Evelyn and Keisha standing in front of him, everything in his mind stopped... He couldn't even hear sound. The sight of Keisha bedazzled him and his focus was completely on her. The women finished their conversation and gave each other hugs and bided each other farewell.

"Okay Ms. Lewis. I'll see you later. Take care."

"You too Ms. Pulliam. And don't worry... we're gonna find that gun."

Keisha nodded at Evelyn then the doors opened on the elevator and the so very beautiful, Keisha KeKe Pulliam, waved goodbye to everyone then disappeared into the elevator...

"Ron-Ron..? Ron-Ron..?"

Chicago called out to him but Ron-Ron was still gazing at the closing doors of the elevator. Evelyn walked over to them.

"It looks like somebody is a-little spellbound", said Evelyn playfully while smiling at Ron-Ron.

It was not until he heard her voice, did he turn to face them. Chicago added his comment:

"Yeah G... Lil-momma had you in ah **trance**."

Ron-Ron put his hands on his head then responded quietly:

"Man.... I don't know **what**-hit-me...? Its like, ma head got cloudy, all the sound stopped... everythang was gone except-fah-ole - girl... That ain't **ever** happened befo..."

Ron-Ron shook his head as if he were trying to clear the cobwebs out.

Chicago responded:

"Yeah, well... shake-it-off, G... we gotta holla at Big Sis about this situation."

Chi stood up and patted his GD brother on the back.

"Come on fellas... we can talk in the conference-room." said Evelyn then Ron-Ron stood and him and Chicago followed her into the conference-room...

The conference-room was tastefully decorated. A large ebony conference-table, shaped almost like an oval, sat in the middle of the room. A heavy lacquer covered the table allowing it to emit an impeccable shine. Eight burgundy high-back leather-swivel armchairs, sat spaciously around the table. They complemented the dark grayish-purple carpet.

Embedded in the wall, was an eighty-gallon-aquarium, sparse with exotic fish. The aquarium could be admired from the outside of the room or the inside. The lighting was recessed with dimmer switches to control the illumination in the room. The walls were painted 'clair-de-lune' a color chosen by Evelyn because of its soothing qualities... it also complemented the rest of the décor.

Against the middle wall, there was a large armoire matching the conference-table. It housed a 32-inch color TV and a VCR to watch things that needed to be viewed such as: videos of evidence and the news. The room had other amenities but I won't get into those... you get my point. Evelyn had style and taste and her entire law office was the evidence of that. The three of them sat at the beginning end of the conference table. Evelyn at the head, Ron-Ron to right of her and Chicago to her left...

"Big Sis, here's the situation." said Ron-Ron, going into the details of the incident that took place in front of Ms. Kimble's house... While he gave Evelyn the details, Chi excused his self from the table and stepped over to the large picture window.

The beautiful burgundy drapes were drawn-back. Chicago looked outside at the downtown scene. The day was gorgeous he thought; making the concrete and brick downtown scene appear pleasant and soft, regardless of its, hard insidious reputation. A long credenza matching the armoire and table, lined the window wall. Atop it sat a set of drinking glasses and a matching water pitcher, all of which were turned upside down on a clothed tray. At the end of the credenza where Chicago was, there sat a phone. He picked-up the receiver and began making the phone calls to the deck captains to inform them of the situation. They all were now on the lookout for the white cargo-van.

By the time Chi was done making the phone calls, Ron-Ron had finished talking to Evelyn. She was ready to check the license-plate-number to see who the van belonged to.

"Give me about an hour and I'll have something for y'all. But let me know what y'all plan on doing to get VG back. I wanna make sure it isn't something that's gonna cause more problems."

Ron-Ron glared at Evelyn and Chicago stepped over after hearing what Evelyn said then he commented:

"Big Sis... you already **know** how we move... we gone handle this without causin **no** problems, at least not-fah-us... just find out who that van belongs to and we got it from there."

Chicago was highly confident in himself and the GD Nation's capability to contain and handle a conflict. Evelyn glared at them both then said:

"I'll page y'all when I find-out something. Y'all be careful out there, alright...."

Evelyn stood up and Ron-Ron stood as well. She gave both of them a tight hug and they all exited the conference-room.

"I'm about to get-on-top-of-this **right** now. I know time is crucial", said Evelyn, holding-up the piece of paper with the license-plate-number on it. Then she darted-off to her office.

"See you later Big Sis." said Ron-Ron.

Evelyn threw up a hand and continued to walk forward while waving backwards.

Chicago and Ron-Ron stepped passed the receptionist over to the elevator then Ron-Ron pressed the arrow-down button. They hadn't been to Evelyn's office since she hired the new receptionist, until now, and Chi was showing his interest in Tina. While Ron-Ron waited for the elevator, Chi stepped over to Tina's receptionist station and nonchalantly in a polite manner, sparked-up a conversation with her, trying not to sound too desirous. Ron-Ron shook his head and snickered a little at Chicago's, 'persistence in pursuing the pussy' regardless of the present situation. The elevators doors opened. Chi, was caught-up in the conversation with Tina:

"Yeah, I like the zoo... I like the monkeys the most. They so **cute**." said Tina.

"I like the **gorillas**!" said Chi.

"Why-do-you-like the gorillas?" asked Tina.

"Because they remind me of **me**!" said Chicago.

"Ha Ha Ha Haa!" Tina erupted in laughter at Chi's answer, though she tried to hold it back as much as she could.

"Ooh, so you're a gorilla huh?" asked Tina.

"**Chi**... come on G... we got business to take care of." said Ron-Ron, halfway irritated, holding the elevator door.

Chi turned to Ron-Ron then said:

"Alright G, here I come." then he turned back towards Tina.

"It was nice meeting you Tina."

She smiled at him then responded, keeping her eye contact:

"It was nice meeting you too, Lenn."

Chi extended his hand and Tina took hold of it. He shook her hand gently then let go and stepped into the elevator. Before the elevator-doors closed, Chi said:

"I'm gone call you to find out when you want me to take you to the zoo."

Tina put up a pretty hand and waved goodbye and the doors closed. Ron-Ron was a little upset, in disbelief at Chicago's, pursuit of the pussy.

"**Fa-real** G! Tryina fuck-with Big Sis's **receptionist!**"

Ron-Ron shook his head. Chicago responded:

"Chill-out Fam... I'm feelin lil-Momma **waaay** pass ah-fuck-thang... She might be-the-one... and how you gone talk G... yo-ass was **hypnotized** by one of Big Sis client's... you shoulda got-at-her if you was 'feelin-her like that... G, I'm **done** fuckin-wit hood-hoes who ain't got shit goin-fah-they-self...! Lil-momma up there... she nice and I wanna see what she about."

Ron-Ron could see that this wasn't one of Chi's regular, "I'm tryina see what that pussy is like" moments. Chicago was really feeling Tina...

Ron-Ron responded:

"Yeah, she **is** nice... But the other shorty was nice too", said Ron-Ron, referring to Keisha in the latter part of his statement.

Ron-Ron continued:

"I probably shoulda got-at-her."

"No doubt G." said Chicago, agreeing with Ron-Ron.

Chi was right thought Ron-Ron. It was time to stop fucking with girls who only looked good and were **always** down for '**whatever**'... He had a purpose in life and he should be around women who had a purpose in life as well. He had a sudden 'intuitive-realization' of reality, which stemmed from what Chicago had said. The status he held in the GD Nation was an important one. He wanted to make a positive change in **his** society and he should be associating his self with women who **also** want to make a positive change in **their** society... not being with and around "hood-hoes who have no vision..."

A scripture popped into his mind that Ms. Kimble had given him: **Genesis,** *chapter 2, verse 18. "And the Lord God said: that it is not good that man should be alone; I will make him a helpmeet for him."*

It basically said: that the woman was made to help a man, in **his** righteous endeavors. Ron-Ron's endeavor was to help uplift a fallen nation of Black Brothers and to keep the ones who hadn't fallen, **from** falling. From what he seen in Keisha, in the brief moment he had seen her... He sensed that she had a cause that corresponded with his own. She could be the perfect helpmeet for him... He understood what Chicago was saying.

Ding!

The elevator reached the lobby and the doors opened. Chicago promptly got off but Ron-Ron was slow to do so. He was still ruminating on his thoughts. As they walked out of the Shell building to their cars... a few lines from a piece of GD literature, called:

"The Preface", popped-into his mind:

"It is necessary that we go through change... we are either living or dying and to stand still is to die. Our leadership has decided that we

shall live and flourish into something great."

That part was so significant to him because it spoke of evolution... Evolution of man... from what man once was, to what man is today. Not so much the physical aspect, but the mental aspect. The evolution of the mind has given man the dexterity to live a much healthier, stronger and longer life... all under better conditions. Ron-Ron looked at the two cars parked next to each other as him and Chicago approached them. He viewed them differently now... Just yesterday, he looked at both cars parked side-by-side and thought it was cool-as-a-muthafucka for him and his closest GD brother to be rolling-so-clean. Now... he felt they were nothing but targets for negative attention, and in-a-way, he was right...

Ron-Ron asked his self two questions in his mind: "What do people think when they see me driving this car...? Does it really matter what they think...?" The answer to the second question surfaced immediately in his mind: "Yeah... it does matter what they think... especially if I want people to take me seriously in my endeavors."

"Where-we-headed, G?" asked Chi, leaning against his Monte Carlo SS. Ron-Ron hit the button on the alarm-remote, opened his car-door then said:

"Big brother Jack Pot's car lot."

"Jack Pot's **car lot**?" said Chicago, questioningly then continued: "Why we goin there...?"

"You'll see", said Ron-Ron.

Jack-Pot was the nick name of Paul Norfleet. He was a member of the GD Nation though no longer 'active'. After Jack-Pot turned 35 he retired from the GD Nation and opened a car-lot. Although, he still would aid and assist his Disciple brothers with certain things... He won't get involve with anything that could jeopardize his success.

Ron-Ron got in his car and cranked the engine... He was gonna miss the growl of his Buick Regal. He glanced over at Chi, pressed the gas and smiled. Chi didn't know what Ron-Ron was up to, but he followed suit, hopping in his Monte Carlo SS, cranking the engine, letting his motor growl too... They pulled-off heading towards 'Jack-

Pot's car-lot'.

Back inside of the Shell building

Evelyn had already made a phone-call to one of her friends who worked at the DMV. Evelyn hadn't told Monica the urgency of the situation, but she was hoping Monica could get to it sooner than later. Who knows how much time VG had if he wasn't already dead. Monica wrote down the license-plate-number and told Evelyn that she would get-to-it when things slowed down a little. That morning, the DMV near Martin Luther King Boulevard, on Kings-Highway, was packed with customers.

The low monophonic tone on Evelyn's office-phone, sounded off. Tina had put a call through and Evelyn answered it.
"Evelyn Lewis speaking."
The robust voice of Monica, sounded through the receiver.
"Evelyn... It's Monica."
"Monica! I didn't expect to hear from you until later on."
"Yeah..... I know girl. But I figured I better get-it-done now and get it out the way... I know time is of the essence when it comes to y'all lawyers." said Monica with a little laughter in her comment.
Evelyn was grateful. She responded:
"Monica, thank you **so** much girl... I **did** need that info asap, but I didn't wanna rush you or anything."
"Evelyn, you know you ma-girl... whenever I can help you, I'm glad to... It's nice having one of the best lawyers in the city, as a friend."
Evelyn valued her friendship with Monica, and she showed it by spending time with her whenever she had a free moment. And free moments were rare when it came to Evelyn's time. Monica continued:
"Okay... here's what I got for you."
Evelyn grabbed an ink-pen and a note tablet, preparing to take down the information. Monica continued:
"The license-plate is registered to a, Jerry, Kane, Schlesta, and the address on the registration is, 3511 Bridget Ln. Saint Ann Missouri."

Evelyn's pen stopped. She couldn't believe what she had just heard. Evelyn thought: "Could this be **true**? Could this **really** be the **same** Jerry Kane Schlesta who was involved in Porshae's case?"

"Monica are you **sure**?" asked Evelyn with a strong hint of doubt in her voice.

Monica responded:

"I'm one hundred percent sure Evelyn... I entered the license-plate-number into our data-base-system and that's what popped up... XMO-621, right?" asked Monica, seeking Evelyn's confirmation that it was the right license-plate-number.

"Yeah, that's it", said Evelyn, glaring at the piece of paper Ron-Ron had given her. Monica had to ask:

"Evelyn, why-do-you sound so surprised girl?"

Evelyn wanted to explain but she couldn't. She gave Monica the best answer she could give, without lying to her friend:

"The name has been mentioned in-another-case that I'm working on and it's really surprising, that's all."

Monica knew Evelyn couldn't speak about the cases she worked on, so she accepted the answer and was satisfied with that.

"Evelyn, I gotta get back to work girl... it's a mad house in here right now. I hope that info helps you out."

"Alright Monica... thank you **so** much once again girl. I owe you **big** time."

"Ain't no thang Evelyn. Like I said, I'm glad I could help out... I'll talk to you later Evelyn."

"Talk to you later Monica." said Evelyn then hung-up the phone.

Evelyn was still in disbelief... Keisha was **just** in her office, telling her about the situation in its entirety... the ordeal her Uncle Clyde had gone through, and the ordeal she and Porshaé had gone through as well... Evelyn's thoughts were tangled.

"Is this some, 'divine plan of God', bringing things to light after four years? And **eighteen** years in Clyde's case. How am I supposed to put things together to bring forth the justice that is rightfully deserved?" thought Evelyn... Ron-Ron and Chicago had brought her the clue and now she wondered: "should I divulge this info to them, considering that it's a police-officer's information?" She didn't want them to get into serious trouble from trying to handle the situation 'their way'. And she didn't want them getting hurt either. She pushed her chair away from her desk and quietly asked the question to herself:

"Why would this guy use his **own van** to kidnap someone?"

The answer quickly popped-into her mind: "Because he's a cop and he figures he can get away with anything... He's been getting away with shit for almost **twenty-years**." Evelyn thought about all the mysterious murders and missing people that had been on the news. The coinciding coincidence, created a chilling, calculative cogitation in her mind. "This could **really** be the guy responsible for Lord **knows** how many murders!" thought Evelyn.

"Shit", she said quietly as the thought traveled through her mind. She rubbed her temples trying to relax her laboring mind.

"Okay Evelyn... what's next?" she asked herself.

This guy had to be stopped, if in fact, he was the one behind these crimes. But what Evelyn didn't know was... was that Jerry Schlesta wasn't alone... there was an entire **force** of corrupt officers involved with Jerry... although, he was the 'main mind behind the malice'. Evelyn weighed her options, speaking quietly to herself, trying to formulate a plan.

"The main objective now, is to find VG... and this Jerry guy seems to have **everything** to do with that... let me go ahead and call Lenn and Ron-Ron."

Just as she was about to pick-up the phone-receiver, the red light flashed on her phone. She pressed the button:

"Yes Tina?"

"Ms. Lewis. Your Uncle Greg is on line two."

"Thank you Tina."

Evelyn pressed the line-two button and began speaking:

"Uncle Greg! Hey, I was just about to make a phone call. What's-up?"

"Well Evy... I got some good news and some not so good news."

"Well, if none of it is bad, go on and tell me", said Evelyn.

Then Greg continued:

"I talked with Daniel yesterday evening... I showed him the bullet and told him the whole story behind it... He said he remembered the case. He told the detective handling it, not to do an investigation and to close the case. He said he felt they had their guy and that was that."

Evelyn was appalled at her eldest uncle's, injudiciousness.

She responded:

"Uncle Daniel actually **did that**? I can't **believe** he would **do** something like that...! He's supposed to be **fighting** crime, not trying to keep it from being discovered! Oooo, I can't **believe him**..."
Evelyn was **clearly** livid.

"Evy, calm down Baby... don't be so upset with your Uncle Daniel. He was just doing what he thought was best for the Department... He said he's willing to help us."
Evelyn was fuming. If her Uncle Daniel had let his detectives do their job, they wouldn't be going through this right now, possibly. The crooked-cops would've been punished and people's lives could have been saved. She was **furious** at her Uncle Daniel, knowing he had the authority to do something about it and he didn't... suddenly. Evelyn remembered what she told Keisha at their initial meeting in the studio... about "how it was a good thing that no investigation was done."
Greg continued:

"Your uncle is a good Police-Chief, Evy... and like I said, he felt he was doing what was best for his Department. Why you so upset?"
Greg sensed that there was more to Evelyn's anger then what she was letting on. Evelyn let out a long sigh then said:

"Uncle Greg... I'll explain it to you later, but I have to make a phone-call, it's really important."

"Hold on Evy. I still haven't given you the good news yet... Daniel told me where Detective Schlesta took Officer Harris' personal belongings... **including** the gun... He took it out to Officer Harris' parent's house."
Evelyn's eyes lit-up with excitement and she stood up then said:

"That's **great** Uncle Greg! You think they still have it?"

"I don't know, but I have their address and I was on my way out to their house to find out. It's in the Meramac Bottoms. I was calling to see if you wanted to ride out there with me."

"Uncle Greg, I would like to but... I **really** need to take care of this other situation like **right** now."

"Alright then... you go-a-head and handle yo business... I'll see you when I get back."

"Okay Uncle Greg. Talk to you later."

"Talk to you later Evy."

Evelyn pressed the button on her office-phone and celebrated moderately.

"**YES**!" she shouted and threw her fists in the air, happy to hear the news about the gun.

Evelyn knew right then and there, that her earlier thought was correct... It **was** the 'plan of God' bringing things together. She felt **so** thankful and **so** grateful to God, that she knelt down, put her arms on her office-chair and laced her fingers together. She closed her eyes and began praying to God, quietly, behind her desk:

"Father God... I know I don't pray that often, but it doesn't mean that I'm not thankful for all the things that you've done for me because I am thankful... it doesn't mean that I don't love you Father God, because I do love you... This morning has been **quite** a revealing morning."

Evelyn smiled and let out a short laugh, still a little surprised about the "morning-manifestations and revelations."

She continued:

"Father God... I'm praying to you this morning because I'm having trouble deciding what to do next, in regards to this other situation. You have allowed **so much** to come to light and I don't wanna make **any** wrong decisions that could mess up the progress of things."

Evelyn paused for a long moment to meditate on her words... then she continued:

"So Father God, I ask you... to **please** guide me in the right direction... help me make the right decisions so that justice will be brought for the people who have been afflicted by police-corruption... the people who have **lost** their **lives** to police-corruption... and the families who have suffered from the lost of their loved ones... Father God, I also pray... that once justice has been served, it will give peace to the Spirits of those who have been victimized... keep all of us safe who are in pursuit of the truth and justice... this I ask of you Father God... awoman."

Evelyn meditated for a moment longer before she got up. While she was kneeling, a cool came over her... not a chilling cool, but a soothing cool. Her body became very relaxed to the point where she felt she might fall asleep... The cool ascended and Evelyn rose from her kneeling position shortly after. The words in her mind were loud and clear: "Help VG. Help VG", is all she could hear, as if someone was standing next to her saying the words aloud.

Her first mind was right. She would call Ron-Ron and Chicago. Evelyn dialed Ron-Ron's pager number and after the beep, she entered her office-phone-number then entered her code at the end of the number...

CHAPTER 19: To Be Loyal Or Not To Be

Back at the old warehouse, Jerry had retied VG's arm then left him to think about what he ask him to do. VG reviewed the conversation in his mind:

"Kid, I'm not gonna play games with you... if you lead me to that connect of yours, you can go free, unharmed... All I want-to-do is get-in-on-the good stuff... is that too much to ask for?"

VG knew he couldn't trust this guy, but he wanted to get out of the situation alive. He responded:

"So if I lead you to ma connect, what happens to them?"

"Well ma-man... that's all up to your **connect**... either they can do business with me or not."

"And if not?" VG asked.

"Well... let's just hope there is no, 'if not'.... but if there **is**... I'll go my way... you and your people can go your way... although, your connect might have some problems... they might end-up **right** there where you are."

Jerry was sitting in a chair that he had sat in front of VG. He stood-up from that chair, stepped over to VG, patted him on the shoulder then said:

"Think about it kid... you don't have too many options, or time... I'll be back." Then Jerry walked away, back into the dark abyss beyond the huge sliding door, where he emerged from.

Jerry returned not too long after and sat down in the raggedy old chair again.

"So... what's it gonna be kid...? You gonna help yourself outta this or what?"

VG had weighed his options while Jerry was gone, and he really didn't have any... not any that would save his life. He could say no then more than likely die... or, he could give up his connect... which would be the hardest thing he'd ever have to do in his life... for two reasons. One: his connect was a high-ranking Gangsta Disciple member... And two: his connect was also like a big brother to him, and that brother... was Gansta-Bam.

G.A.N.S.T.A. B.A.M. was an acronym... it stood for: Growing-up A Nigga, Subject To Assassination, By Any Means. Gansta-Bam was from *Flint Michigan*, and the story behind how he ended-up in Saint Louis, in an interesting one, but for the sake of continuity, we'll save that for another time. No one really knew where Gansta-Bam was from or what his real name was. He had lived all over the United States and the name he was using, had been duplicated so many times, that even the police couldn't determine who the real one was... But Gansta-Bam had all the official-papers to prove he was who he said he was. The name was clean though, as far as, not having any wanted warrants or outstanding tickets, however... it **did** have a couple of convictions on it to blend with the character of the person using it, just to make-it-appear legit, because Gansta Bam was a street nigga. The id and background fit him fine.

He held a position in the GD Nation that no one knew about, except for the Chairman and the Board of Directors. It was a position that only the diplomatic, honorable and prudent members of the GD Nation could uphold, and for Gansta-Bam, those were just a few of his qualities.

G.O.I. was the position he held. He had rank far before he got to Saint Louis, yet all the members he came across, knew nothing of it... except for one young man, VG. Everyone thought Gansta-Bam, was just a thorough member of the GD Nation, and he was. And that's all he wanted them to think, in-order to fulfill his duties as G.O.I.

The duties of a, "Governor of Investigations" were extremely important to the Disciple Nation. The G.O.I. had to investigate specific cities of the Disciple Nation, observing them; seeing whether they were operating accordingly under the new Growth & Development concept and if they weren't... He would try to get them on the right track as best he could... making suggestions and quoting laws and policies that govern the Disciple Nation... he'd try to influence proper functioning and operating. If the GD members chose to continue moving bogus... then the G.O.I. would give his report to the Board of Directors and move-on without anyone knowing. Then that specific city or area would be 'marked for violations'. The G.O.I. would have **no** knowledge of what the sanction would be. Nor would he know, when or who would execute the sanction... A G.O.I could spend years in one city alone.

From his years of traveling the States and its border-countries, Bam developed a great level of diplomacy... That diplomacy, helped him in establishing associations and oftentimes, friendships with influential and sometimes 'infamous' people... He had political connections, military ties, business connections, street ties, and not your average street ties... but street ties running deep underground to Mexican Cartels... and believe-it-or-not... the Jewish Mafia as well. He was definitely a man with 'street-resources'.

Small in his statue, standing only, 5-feet 6-inches tall, weighing a-buck-fifty, his status in its entirety, was gigantic... He humbly, portrayed-to-be, equal-to or less-than, those who were around him. Gansta-Bam took-a-liking to young VG, because he seen a-lot-of-his younger self, in VG... hence VG knowing about Bam's G.O.I. rank. Bam had showed VG the love that a father would show a son... There was **no way** VG wanted to compromise that... but he knew there was no way out-of-his predicament... except-for-one.

"Come on kid... what's it gonna be?" said Jerry.
VG disconnected from his thoughts, answering dejectedly:
"Yeah... I'ma holla at ma connect fah-you."
Jerry smiled, clapped his hands once and popped up from the old chair.
"**Good** answer ma-man! **Now**... let's get this show on-a-roll."
He untied VG's left arm from the chair, stepped back then pulled his pistol from his holster. Jerry didn't point the gun at VG though... he only held it to show VG he had it, and it would be best, not to try anything foolish.
"Alright kid... go-on and untie yourself."

VG thought as he untied his self from the chair: "I don't know **what's** about to happen, but I **gotta** think of another-way outta this shit."
He finished untying the ropes.

"Alright... let's go kid."
Jerry motioned for VG to walk forward pass the huge sliding door into the dark. VG got up, wanting to tell Jerry to stop calling him "kid" but he thought against it, and walked into the darkness.

Back at the Shell building:

The phone rang at the receptionist desk in Evelyn's law office. Tina answered it promptly:

"Good morning. Law Office of Evelyn Lewis, how can I help you?"
Chicago was already in-love with the girl. The sophistication she possessed, the sweetness in her voice, the sereneness.

"Girl, you know you-got-a sexy voice", said Chicago.

"**Who** is this? And how can I help you **sir**?" Tina fired back.

"It's **Lenn**... we just met about 20 minutes ago... you-done fah-got-about-me already?"
Tina smiled in relief then responded:

"**Boy**, I almost hung-up-on-you... and **no,** I haven't forgotten about you, Mr. Chicago... so did you call up here to harass me? You know I work for one of the best lawyers in town, right... don't make me have to heir her." said Tina jokingly while smiling on her end of the phone-line.
Chi knew she was only joking-around. He responded:

"Naah, I'm not callin to harass you, but you got jokes huh?"
He smiled, enjoying the vibe he was receiving from her... it was a positive sign that she was just as interested in him, as he was in her.

"Who said I was joking?" said Tina.
Chicago tilted his head and his jaw dropped a little.

"**Oooo**, it's like **dat!**"
He heard Tina let out a cute little laugh and he smiled wide.

"Lenn, I'm just playing."

"I know", said Chi smoothly.
Tina found herself wanting to converse more with Chicago but she was at work.

"Lenn, let me put you through to Evelyn before you get me in trouble", she said, still in a playfully pleasant voice.

"Alright" said Chi, smiling big at the fact, Tina was feeling him.

The soft tone sounded on Evelyn's office-phone. She picked the receiver up this time:

"Evelyn Lewis speaking"

"Big Sis, it's Lenn... you paged us?"

"Lenn...! I need to talk to you and Ron-Ron like, **right** now! Can y'all get back over here?"

"Yeah, we not too far away. We at Jack-Pot's Car-Lot" said Chi.

Evelyn's face frowned a little and she responded questioningly:

"What? Jack-Pot's Car-Lot...? Why-are-y'all at a car-lot?"

Chi shrugged his shoulders to himself then responded:

"Big Sis... I just followed Ron-Ron over here, but I don't know what he got on his mind... he talking with Jack-Pot right now. I think he wanna get somethin low-key to-ride-in."

Evelyn wondered why the sudden urge to switch cars had come over Ron-Ron. 'It must have something to do with what happened to VG.' she thought... but that wasn't it... it was the moment-of-clarity he had that brought on the urge.

Evelyn responded:

"Well... I need y'all to get over **right** now. I think I know who has VG and VG might not have much time considering who it is."

Chi sensed the urgency in Evelyn's voice.

"Big Sis, we on our way." he said then hung-up the phone in Jack-Pot's office.

He hurried out to the lot and over to where Jack-Pot and Ron-Ron were standing... they were next to a, "low-key" car.

"G, we gotta go back to see Big Sis, **pronto**... she said she thinks she knows who got VG."

Ron-Ron turned to Jack-Pot then said:

"Jack-Pot, right-on fah-showin me this ride. I'ma get back with you soon on that, all-ight?"

"Okay Lil-Bro. Go ahead and handle y'all business. Get-with-me later... let me know what's goin-on with VG."

"All-ight Big Bro. Plenty much love... we out", said Ron-Ron.

"Never too much, G." said Jack-Pot.

"Later Family", said Chi then him and Ron-Ron left, on their way back to Evelyn's office.

Chicago was solely thinking about: "**who**-in-the-fuck could have VG? And **why**-in-the-fuck would they kidnap him?" Ron-Ron was ready to get into some real-live gangsta-shit with **whoever** it was. He had no mercy for someone who brought harm to members of his Family. He was already formulating what he was gonna do to the person or person involved. The Buick Regal T-Type and the Monte Carlo SS **zoomed** down Manchester towards Kings-Highway, back towards the downtown area. There was definitely a different demeanor about them.

Evelyn had to see what this, Jerry Schlesta looked liked, so she called back down to the DMV:

"Department of Motor Vehicles. Crystal Jacobs speaking, how can I help you?"

"Hello Crystal... This is Evelyn Lewis."

"**Ooh hey** Evelyn!" said Crystal with a cheerful voice.
She continued:

"What can I do for you?"

"Crystal, I really need to speak to, Monica James... it's **very** urgent."

"Okay Evelyn. I'll get her for you. Hold on for a moment."
Crystal whisked-off to get Monica. Monica was giving a customer, a vision test when Crystal approached.

"Monica. Evelyn is on-hold in the office. She said it's urgent."
Monica knew already what Evelyn wanted, she anticipated Evelyn's second call. Monica pointed to a photo-identification-sheet and vehicle-registration-history for, Jerry Schlesta.

"Crystal, can you fax those to Evelyn for me."
Crystal took the papers, went back into the office then picked-up the phone.

"Evelyn?"

"Yes, I'm here", said Evelyn.

"Monica is giving a vision test right now, but she asked me to fax some papers to you. What's your fax number?"
Evelyn was confused, so she asked:

"Umm, Crystal... can you tell me what the papers are please?"

"Yeah, sure... it's a photo-identification-sheet and a registration history for, Jerry Schlesta."

Evelyn was surprised at Monica's anticipation

"My fax-number is: 314-521-1001."

"Okay, the papers are on the way now."

"Thank you Crystal. And please tell Monica, thanks again for me okay?"

"Will do... take care Evelyn."

"You too Crystal." said Evelyn then hung-up the phone.

Evelyn waited by the fax-machine, anxious and uncertain of whether the info would come through. The fax-machine sounded:

Beeeep....

Indicating there was a fax coming through then the machine started printing the information. The registration history came through first then, the photo-identification-sheet, the one she **really** wanted to see... It came out slow, revealing little by little, the face of the man 'possibly' responsible for multiple murders. The fax-transmission ended with another beep, though not as long as the first one. Evelyn pulled the papers from the tray and studied the face.

Jerry looked like a nice guy, thought Evelyn. He reminded her of, Robert Déniro. Evelyn looked closer at the photo, peering at the eyes on the page. She could now see the coldness Jerry possessed. She stepped over to her desk and sat the papers down then sat herself down in her chair. She wasn't so much concerned with the vehicle-registration history but something told her to look at it anyway... Evelyn picked-up the sheet, taking a look at all the cars Jerry had registered. One stood-out the most... Keisha had **just** described it, that **same** morning in her story, **just** as her Uncle Clyde had described it to her... A 1968 orange Dodge Charger... "This **had** to be the guy?" thought Evelyn. She leaned back in her chair, letting all the **new** news sink-in. After a short moment, Evelyn got-up and went into the conference-room. She turned on the TV and the Fox 2 News, Anchorman Elliot Davis, was in mid sentence:

"Chief Daniel Isom, of the Saint Louis Metro Police Department, is under fire by **outraged** citizens. Those citizens have alleged **countless** acts of police brutality by his officers. Citizens mostly in the African American neighborhoods of Saint Louis, have gathered together to approach the mayor with their grievance, and **demand** that something be done about the so-called, "Crime Prevention Tactics". They say... their complaints have gone unresolved with-in the police department... A woman expresses her anger at a local town meeting near the Walnut Park District..."

The picture went from the Anchorman to a small town-hall then to the inside, where a woman was standing behind a podium. The heavyset Black woman was clearly livid. The evidence of that was on her facial expression and then the sound kicked-in:

"I'M TIRED OF OUR SONS, WHO ARE, A & B STUDENTS, BEING HARASSED LIKED THEY SOME KIND OF CRIMINALS IN THE STREETS!" the woman shouted.

"I'M TIRED OF OUR YOUNG BLACK MEN, WHO ARE TRYING TO DO GOOD IN LIFE, BEING FALSELY CHARGED WITH DRUG POSSESSION AND **ALL-TYPES**-OF OTHER CRIMES THEY HAVEN'T COMMITTED! MY SON...!"

The woman paused and lowered her voice a little then she continued:

"**My Son**... was **beaten** by the police and charged with resisting arrest... all because he couldn't tell **them**, where to find **crack**... **My son** is not a **drug dealer!**"

The woman was now showing another emotion... tears were in her eyes.

She continued:

"My Son is part of the **teen** ministry program at **Church**! He's not some, **street-thug** or some **drug dealer**! Now he has a record for something he **didn't even do!**"

The woman's feeling of anger, rose again and so did her voice.

She continued:

"SOMETHING HAS TO BE DONE! WE HAVE TO STAND UP AND **FIGHT** FOR OUR CHILDREN'S SAFTEY AND THEIR WELL BEING!"

The town-hall audience erupted into shouts and applauses then the picture went back to the Anchorman and he began:

"If you would like to, express your concerns or report any acts of police brutality. Please call, The Internal Affairs Hotline at, 1-800-267-8868."

The number showed up on the TV screen and the Anchorman

continued:

"Chief Isom, has yet to make a comment... In-other-news"

Evelyn turned the TV off before the next segment could show. She was upset... the Black woman's anger and indignation, added to Evelyn's own anger and feelings of injustice. "The woman was right... something definitely had to be done... we have to stand up to corrupt police-officers and **fight**... and who better to fight than my little Gangsta brothers." thought Evelyn. It was time to get-down-to-business. The fire was definitely burning inside of Evelyn. She left the conference-room and went to her assistant, Yolanda's office.

"Yolanda... I need you to comprise a file of **all** the complaints made against policemen for police-brutality, in the past four years. I want "comprehensiveness" Yolanda, so take your time with it... it's the start-of-a **long** mission."

Yolanda wrote down her assignment then said:

"I got it Evelyn. 'Comprehensive...' I'll get right on it."

"Thank you Yolanda."

"You're welcome", said Yolanda.

Then Evelyn went-up-front to the reception area.

Ding!

The elevator reached the eighth floor and the doors opened. Chicago and Ron-Ron stepped out of the elevator and Evelyn was right there to meet them. There was no small talk... she directed them straight to her office. Chi smiled and waved at Tina.

"Have-a-seat-fellas." said Evelyn then she stepped behind her desk and took her seat.

She pushed the registration history over to Ron-Ron. He took hold of it and examined it closely.

"Jerry Schlesta." he said quietly, seeing the white cargo van was registered to that name.

He passed the paper to Chicago... As Chicago took-a-look at the registration history, Evelyn pushed the second page over to Ron-Ron. He studied the face then asked:

"So who-is-he?" he said with a slight frown on his face then passed the photo to Chi.

Evelyn clasped her hands together then waited until Chicago was done studying the image. He looked up from the photo at Evelyn then she proceeded to answer Ron-Ron's question:

"That... is Detective Lieutenant Jerry Schlesta."

Both Chi and Ron-Ron glared at Evelyn then simultaneously said:

"**Detective!**"

"Yeah fellas... we're dealing with **real** bad cops here. The Detective... is more than likely responsible for unsolved murders dating back, far as 1970... He thinks he's untouchable."

Chicago was curious but not in disbelief, so he asked Evelyn:

"Big Sis... How you find out about all this so quick?"

She was hesitant to say, but she thought about it briefly and figured, "what-the-hell... we're all on the same team here." then responded:

"Y'all remember the lady that was here this morning?"

Evelyn looked at the two of them for conformation, peering a-bit longer at Ron-Ron, for he was the one who was spelled-bound by Keisha. They both nodded yes then Evelyn continued:

"Well... she and a friend went through an ordeal involving the **same** detective, and back-in 1970... So did her uncle... hell-of-a coincidence right?"

"Yeah, it is." said Chi.

Ron-Ron felt a little concern for Keisha and asked:

"Was he targeting her?"

Evelyn tilted her head slightly to her shoulder then said:

"I don't think so. I **just** officially started on her friend's case yesterday."

Evelyn stood and continued:

"Something needs to be done about this **today**." she said, slapping her hand down on the paper-photo of Jerry's face.

Chi and Ron-Ron smiled at each other. They were moderately-amused by Evelyn's frail display of fury.

"Big Sis... I don't think I've ever seen you mad like **this**." said Chi with a smile on his face.

He continued:

"From what I'm seeing and hearing... it looks to me, like you ready to **get**-into-some-Gangsta-shit..."

Evelyn's anger broke loose from the hold she was trying to keep on it.

"**YOU GOT-DAMN RIGHT I AM!**" she said, slamming her hand down on Jerry's face again as if she were crushing a large bug.

That's what she wanted to do... crush Jerry... him and **all** the other bad cops like him. Chi and Ron-Ron got up from their chairs, slapped hands and shook them.

"That's what **I'm** talkin bout." said Chi, calm and cool.

"Damn-right... I'm ready-ta-serve some crooked-ass-cop like bacon fah-breakfast, you-feel-me-G." said Ron-Ron just as cool, slapping hands with Chicago again.

Chi, knew Ron-Ron was ready-to jump right-into-action... it wasn't often they had to get into that 'Gangsta shit'... muthafuckas knew-not-to-fuck-with the Gangsta Disciple Nation.

Chicago was a soldier by nature it seemed. But situations like this didn't really excite him as much as they did Ron-Ron. Chi, would convert into his, 'quiet soldier' mentality and begin mapping out a strategy. Several things passed through Chicago's mind on how to handle the situation, but he wasn't gonna act on anything not solid. They would have to sit down and come-up-with an infallible plan... after all... they were about to go-up-against men who were trained to do battle. These were not just street-niggas with guns... They were trained Officers... trained to kill.

"So how we gone get this fool and get VG back?" asked Ron-Ron peering at Evelyn.

"Fellas... I'm gonna be completely honest with y'all... when I said I was ready to get into some gangsta shit... that's what I meant."
Evelyn's demeanor was serious and her tone of voice was sinister. Calm and composed, she sat down and continued:

"I don't know **how** we're gonna get VG back... but we have to use what we have... I got the info for y'all." she motioned to the papers.

"Y'all got the streets... however y'all have to handle it, handle it." Evelyn's position was stern and her mind was made up. Chicago and Ron-Ron were ready to do what they were known for doing best... taking care of Gangsta Disciple business.

"Big Sis, we gone get outta here so we can get our guys together and try to find VG." said Chicago.
Evelyn grabbed the two DMV sheets and tore the top part off that had the 'sent from and received' info on it then gave them to Chi.

"Here, take these... Fellas, y'all **please** be careful out there, and call me and let me know what's going on, alright?"

Evelyn had a concerned motherly look on her face.

"We will Big Sis, but don't worry yo-self about us... we got this." said Ron-Ron, nonchalantly.

Evelyn stepped from behind her desk and gave both of them a hug then Chi and Ron-Ron exited the office.

They got to the reception area, Ron-Ron pressed the button for the elevator and neither of them said a word. The doors opened almost instantly and the two of them stepped inside. Tina was a little surprised that Chicago hadn't said anything to her, so before the elevators-doors could close, Tina asked:

"Is everything alright Lenn?"

Chicago was in his 'soldier-mode' and he honestly had no focus on Tina until she said something. He stepped out of the elevator and responded:

"I'm sorry fah-not-speakin Tina... I'm in-ma-zone. But yeah, I'm cool... we just have to find our little brother before something happens to him... can I call you later though?"

Tina peered into Chi's eyes and could see... his focus **was** somewhere else.

"Yeah, I would like that", said Tina.

She wrote her number down, really quick then handed it to Chi.

"I'm gone call you later Tina." he said with a half-smile then stepped back into the elevator.

The doors closed and Chicago and Ron-Ron were gone. Tina wondered what was going on and she wanted to ask Evelyn but decided against it. A couple of minutes went by and the elevator bell sounded again:

Ding!

Tina ready herself to greet another client. The doors opened and to her surprise... it was Chi. He stepped off the elevator and Ron-Ron held the door. Chicago instantly made eye contact with Tina then walked over to her. He saw her eyes light-up and he held her gaze as he approached her. He extended his arm out to her, offering his hand and Tina took hold of it. Chi held her hand firmly in his then said:

"When I'm done takin care of what I gotta take care of... I'm gone take you to see them cute little monkeys you like."

He smiled, but this time, more lovingly at her then, he kissed her hand softly, let it go then stepped backwards into the elevator, and once again, he was gone. Tina was in a state of awe and admiration. Chicago had just made her feel really good with his act of spontaneity, though she still worried that something might happen and he wouldn't call. She shook that thought from her mind and tried to remain positive. After remembering the way his eyes looked when he said what he had said, she felt a slight hint-of-assurance that he would return. Tina really liked Chicago. And she was looking forward to getting to know him better.

After leaving the Shell building, Chicago and Ron-Ron drove over to the 'Royal Palace' on Natural-Bridge Blvd. It was a club like lounge and they knew the owner really well. They spent a-lot-of money at the Royal Palace. The owner would let them gather there when they needed to meet. They had other spots where they congregated but the Royal Palace was the closest from where they were coming from. At the Royal palace: Chicago was on the phone connecting with all the deck captains.

"Head-over to the 'Royal Palace', bring two soldiers... everybody be unit-up." Chi told them.
'Unit-up' meant: 'everyone have a gun on them.'
Ron-Ron was also on the phone with the GDN Regional-Overseer, Yomy Norwood. Ron-Ron was letting him know about the situation. It was Ron-Ron's duty to report the situation to the next upper link in the chain-of-command.
"Y'all gone be able to handle this thang without no problems right?" asked Yomy.
"Yeah G... we gettin the plan together now. Things shouldn't be too complicated. We got the info on this dude already. Once we find him, hopefully we find VG too."
"Alright G, keep me posted." said Yomy.
"Fa-sho... plenty much love Family." said Ron-Ron.
"Never too much G." said Yomy then hung-up the phone.
Yomy wanted to get involved but his position as the Regional-Overseer said: 'he wasn't to get involved in any street conflicts, for his position was too valuable to the Disciple Nation to jeopardize.' He looked at the phone then said:
"**Damn!**"
And with a powerful hand, he knocked the phone off the table. He

didn't want his GD brothers to battle with the police and him not be a-part of it, for his aversion towards crooked-cops, ran deeper than the average.

The cars started pulling onto the lot of the Royal Palace. Deck captains from all-over the city, got out of their cars with two soldiers in company, each with a 'unit' tucked snuggly in the small of their back or in their waistband. They knew why they were there, for Chicago had put them on alert earlier. It was now time to devise a plan then execute it.

The twelve deck captains sat in the center of the lounge, at small round cocktail-tables, all of them facing Ron-Ron. The twenty-four soldiers stood facing the perimeters of the lounge, at an arm's-length, creating a semi circle around the deck captains and Ron-Ron. Chicago stood by the door.

The owner, Mr.Jones, give them thirty minutes. The lounge served lunch so customers would be arriving soon. He put a sign on the door that said, 'Will be open in 30 minutes.' The kitchen staff were already in the back, tending to their duties.

Ron-Ron began to speak:

"Alright fellas... we know why we here... one-of-our lil-brothers is in trouble. This is the man who has VG. For what reason, we don't know."

Ron-Ron held-up the photo of Jerry. He handed the photo to one of the deck captains then continued:

"I want y'all to take a look at that picture, soldiers too... remember that face... don't forget it. Him and two other white dudes jumped-out on VG and attacked him. They threw VG in-a white cargo van and took-off. One of our G-Mommas informed me about it this morning after it happened... Like I said... I don't know what-the-fuck fo, or what these muthafuckas want, but we gotta do our best to find VG. The license-plate-number on the van is, XMO-621. The napkin on the table got the description of the van and the plate-number on it... Fellas, I want y'all to know... we not dealin with no regular white boys... these dudes are cops, **bad-**cops. But that shit don't even matter... we-gone-get-at-they-ass like we would any other enemy, but we gotta be cautious... y'all feel me? I don't want **nobody** gettin caught-up, alright?"

They all nodded and Ron-Ron continued:

"We know our city better than **anybody** so what I need y'all to do, is get-out in-them-streets and look-fah-that-van... We gone start on the outskirts and work our way into the city. If y'all spot this muthafucka, I want y'all to call me, **pronto**... stay low-key and don't do no dumb shit that might get you caught-up, all-ight."

They all nodded again and Ron-Ron continued:

"That's it fellas. Let's roll out."

They all said, "GD !" simultaneously and the meeting was adjourned. Chicago unlocked the door and took the sign down. They filed out of the lounge, to their cars. Chi and Ron-Ron let the owner know they were done and they got ready to head-out also.

"Fellas, y'all be safe out there." said Mr. Jones.

"We will Mr. Jones", said Ron-Ron, shaking the older gentleman's hand. Mr. Jones felt something in Ron-Ron's hand as he shook-it. He knew what it was. Ron-Ron had given Mr. Jones a small 'token of appreciation'. Mr. Jones tightened his grip and as their hands slid out of the handshake, Mr. Jones took hold of the folded one-hundred-dollar-bill.

"Thank you young blood... you-know how-ta keep the-game-good... y'all stay one hundred young G's and be smooth out there."

Chicago looked at Mr. Jones respectfully, shook his hand then said:

"We will Mr. Jones."

Then Chicago and Ron-Ron headed-out.

CHAPTER 20: Really Wanna Be With Her

Gansta Bam had an apartment near the south side, on Jefferson and Lafayette. Five reddish-brown, two and a-half-story brick apartment buildings sat joining each other. Each building housed four apartments. Gansta Bam was on the second floor, and out of the four, his was the only one with a balcony. He had just returned from Houston Texas, him and one of his closest partners, Adrian, nicked named "Ole Boy." They went down to Houston to pick-up fifty-pounds of some good commercial marijuana and two kilos of cocaine. They made-it-in around 8pm yesterday evening. All the drugs had been secured in their safe houses, one on Alcott Avenue in the Walnut Park area, and in another house over on Labadie Avenue off-of Union Blvd.

Bam was up that morning relaxing on the balcony, sitting in a white plastic outside-chair, smoking on a blunt of the commercial marijuana from Houston. He was on his house phone talking to a beautiful young woman by the name of Chanel Ormé. Bam met Chanel in Pittsburgh Pennsylvania, at the Greyhound bus station. He was on his way back to Saint Louis from visiting his Mom and Chanel was headed to Denver Colorado. They ended-up sitting next to each other on the Greyhound bus, all the way from Pittsburgh to Saint Louis, where Bam got off, and Chanel continued on to Denver.

Back to Chanel and Bam's phone call:

Bam had been on the phone with Chanel, for a little over an hour now. His pager went off for the fourth time. He had already checked it twice and saw an unfamiliar number, and he didn't call unfamiliar numbers back, not unless there was a code behind it to let him know who was paging. He checked the pager again and saw the same number, without a code. And once again, he paid it no mind. He was enjoying his conversation with Chanel and she was enjoying the conversation with him.

Her smooth soft voice was soothing to him... He had never heard a woman with a voice like hers. After coming back from an out-of-town-drug-run, he was always a little edgy and nervous... her voice helped at alleviating that nervousness.

"So... you've been to Houston to see your family, you've been to Pennsylvania to see your Mom.... When are you comin to see me?" asked Chanel.

"I don't know Boo... I just got back last-night. I gotta-lot-of work to do... Why don't you come out here to Saint Louis. I'll buy you a plane-ticket, round-trip of course."

"Awww..... You would do that?"

"**Damn**-right I will... I'm feelin you Chanel. And I wanna get to know you better."

Chanel was smiling on the other end of the phone-line.

She responded:

"Sooo, are you gonna be too busy to have time for me if I come see you?"

"Not at all Boo... ma job is flexible... as long as I'm here in town, I can get ma work done, and I will **definitely** have time for you Beautiful."

Chanel smiled again. Bam was wooing her. He did indeed, like the vibe he got from her and he felt they were compatible too.

Gansta Bam continued:

"Chanel... I liked how I felt when we were together comin from Pittsburgh. It felt so natural and **so good** being next to you... I felt comfortable with you... I want that type of feeling around me **all** the time... You the first woman that I've met who makes me feel that comfortable, right-off-the-bat-like-that... I could really get use to having you around."

Chanel responded:

"Awww, that's so sweet.... You just saying **all** the right stuff. You got me over here smiling big... I felt-the-same-way-too-though... I really felt good sitting next to you and that don't normally happen when I first meet somebody. It takes me awhile to get comfortable... but with **you**... it was like, **instantly**... like I already knew you or something, you know?"

Bam got excited when he heard her say that, and he responded:

"**Yeah**! That's **exactly** how I felt! like I knew you already!"

"That's a really good thing you know." said Chanel.

"Yeah, it is... I'm happy I met you Chanel."

"I'm happy I met you too Bam", said Chanel.

Gansta Bam smiled, feeling the love already...

Beep Beeep, Beep Beeep, Beep Beeep!

His pager went off for the fifth time. Bam got a little irritated and wanted to go ahead and call whoever-the-fuck-it-was that was paging him like crazy. He threw his pager into the apartment through the balcony-door and it landed on the big blue denim sofa. After about ten more minutes on the phone with Chanel, Bam concluded their conversation, feeling he should check out his pager:

"Baby, I'm about to get ma day started. You want me to call later?"

Chanel smacked her lips together then said:

"What-kinda question is that? Of course I want you to call me later. I would be upset if you didn't... Call me at about eight... by then, I'll have the kids feed and in the bed and then we can **really** talk."

Bam laughed a little then said:

"Oooo..... it sounds like you tryina get freaky on the phone?"

Chanel laughed, smiling on the other end then said:

"I don't know... maybe I **might**..." with a smile still on her face.

Bam loved her laugh.

"Ooo-wee..... You got me, not even wantin to get off the phone now!"

Chanel laughed again then said:

"Baby, go-on and take care of your business and I'll be waiting on your call at eight. Don't forget, I'm an hour behind you so it'll be nine your time."

"Alright Boo... I want forget... I'll talk to you later." said Bam.

He heard Chanel kiss him through the phone.

"Uummm Maah."

Then he gave her a kiss back, through the phone:

"Uumm Mah."

"Oooo, juicy..." said Chanel. Bam smiled.

"Alright Boo, I'll talk to you later." said Bam.

"Okay Baby... Talk to you later." said Chanel then she hung-up her phone.

CHAPTER 21: Fuck With Ours We Gone Fuck With You

B am got up from his comfortable position then walked into his apartment. He picked-up his pager from-off the sofa and checked it. This time, it was a number he recognized and there was a code behind it... It was Gambino. He pressed the button on the cordless phone and dialed the number.

The phone rang at the Maffitt street stash-house and Gambino answered:

"Hello?"

"What-up Family." said Gansta-Bam.

Gambino was happy to hear from Bam and glad that he called back so quick. Gambino responded:

"Gansta **Muthafuckin** Bam! What's crackin G! Where you been? I've been tryina get-at-you fo-ah couple of days now?"

"Shiddd..... I just got back from outta-town, so the early bird get the worm, you feel me."

Bam was referring to the products available to make that 'street-money'. Bam could move ten pounds of weed in one day. And his partner, Ole-Boy, usually could sell half-a-kilo of cocaine in a day... so what they had brought back from Houston, would be gone in about four-to-five days at the most... so if a person missed out... they were shit-out-of luck until Bam and Ole-Boy made their next trip, hence the term: "The early bird gets the worm." Bam liked using the term to indicate to his people, he had what they were looking for.

Gambino responded:

"Yeah, I feel you G. That's why I been paging you Bro... I'm tryina be that early bird gettin the worm, ya-dig?"

"Yeah... So what's good Family?" said Bam.

Gambino responded:

"I was hoping you could come by the spot and holla at me about some business."

"Yeah, I can do that... give-me-about thirty-four minutes and I'll be there."

"Alright G... see you in-a lil-bit."

When Bam first got to Saint Louis, he learned his way around the city pretty good using the public-transportation-system. Bam got his self together, checked the bus-schedule and headed-out. He favored taking the Bi-State buses and riding the Metro-Link. He felt safer using public-transportation, especially when moving dope around the city... and he could get where ever he needed to go, fairly quick considering his means of transportation.

The bus came down Jefferson, heading north into the downtown area. Bam set his pager on vibrate then boarded the bus, and was on his way. Once the bus was downtown at the transfer-station, he boarded the 'Saint Louis Avenue' bus-line. The bus left the transfer-station, got in route and rode down Saint Louis Avenue, all the way to Belt Avenue where Bam got-off. He walked half-a-block on Belt then made a right on Maffitt and he was now on the block where Gambino was. Bam went to the back of 5525 Maffitt, walked up the steps of the back porch and knocked on the door. The curtain moved in the little window, the locks on the door began to unlock then the heavy wooden door opened.

"**What-up ma-dude!**" said Gambino, showing his enthusiasm for Bam's presence.

"Let me unlock these bars G."
Gambino grabbed the keys off the kitchen counter and unlocked the security-door. Soon as Bam stepped in the house his pager went off again. He grabbed it:

"Man! **Who**-the-fuck **is this!** They been **blowin** ma-shit-up!" said Bam.

"What side of town they callin from?" asked Gambino.
Bam looked at Gambino then responded:

"G, you know I ain't from Saint Louis. I can't tell where a-nigga callin from just by lookin at the number... I ain't that good yet."

"Let-me-check-it-out G." said Gambino and Bam handed him the pager.
Gambino took a look at the number then said:

"This looks like it's somewhere over by North Broadway."
"North Broadway?" said Bam questioningly.

About twenty minutes earlier:

Chicago and Ron-Ron were still on the Royal Palace parking-lot talking and contemplating:

"G, we need everybody on this." said Chicago.
He was leaning on his car and so was Ron-Ron. Chi continued:

"I know you might not think so but that nigga Gambino could be useful right now."

Ron-Ron was upset with what Chicago was suggesting. He glared at Chicago then responded:

"Chi, are you **for-real**! Not too long ago you wanted-ta-**wack** that nigga! I **gave** the nigga a-pass already and now you want him to **help us**?"

Chi responded with visible emotion.

"Ron-Ron... I'm not feelin like that no-mo G...! VG's **life** is-on-the-line and that's **all** I'm thinking about right now... for some reason, that nigga Gambino just **popped**-in-ma-mind when you was talkin to the brothers about the situation... G, we should at **least** go by there and put the nigga on look-out-detail... the more eyes the better, right?"

Ron-Ron was thinking about it. He thought about what Gambino had done... it was bad, but not so bad to the point there was no room for forgiveness. Gambino had fucked one of Ron-Ron's main chicks and had been fucking her on a regular... all the while, looking Ron-Ron in his face, fellow-shipping as brothers.

The girl didn't even matter, she wasn't the issue... it was his own **cousin's** disloyalty... Ron-Ron was still upset about that... Ron-Ron and Gambino grow-up together and they were like brothers. He was done thinking about it and voiced his opinion:

"Man.... **fuck** that nigga! We don't need him fah-shit! Let's roll and try-ta find this van."

Ron-Ron was about to step away to get in his car and Chi stopped him, reaching-out to grab Ron-Ron's shoulder firmly.

"Ron-Ron!" said Chi, letting his hand fall free from Ron-Ron's shoulder.

Ron-Ron turned around then Chi continued:

"I know you still mad-as-ah muthafucka at that nigga fah what he did... but **I'm** askin you... as yo brother **and** yo assistant... put yo anger to the **side** fah-right-now... fah VG's sake... G, I just got this feelin that we should go holla at the nigga... it's like, God **tellin** me to go holla at that nigga."

Ron-Ron laughed, and in a ridiculing tone of voice and a mock look on his face, said:

"So now you havin premonitions from God, right?" then he let out a mocked laugh.

He stepped over to his car and Chi responded:

"Ron-Ron!" Chicago shouted then continued:

"So you just gone **laugh** at me G...? What, ma input and opinions don't mean shit...? Is that what you sayin...? I'm yo **assistant,** G! That means: I'm supposed to **assist** you in handlin shit... not just, sit-back and take muthafuckin orders! I'm just-as-much the governin coordinator as you are, so don't get that shit twisted G... don't do that shit G... Don't disregard ma-shit... especially when it comes to God and ma input."

Chi calmed down. Ron-Ron knew Chi was right. They both had practically equal authority and they **were** supposed to work **with** each other, not **for** each other...

"You really wanna go holla at that nigga huh?" asked Ron-Ron with his pride still in the way.

Chi responded:

"Yeah G... I wanna follow ma first mind... that God-Sense, you know." said Chi, smiling at Ron-Ron.

Ron-Ron couldn't help but smile back at his GD brother.

"God-Sense huh?" said Ron-Ron, remembering Ms. Kimble speak of the same thing, one time or another.

"Yeah G... we all got it, but some of us just don't use it... or we let other-shit get-in-the-way of it, like **Pride**. You know every time you do somethin and it don't go the way you wanted it to, you say: "**Damn**... I should've went with ma first mind." That's, that God-Sense... yo first mind... I would hate it if I don't follow ma mind and somethin fucked up happens to VG that we could've prevented."

Ron-Ron had his hand on his chin, mentally assimilating what Chi was saying, and it all made sense.

He responded:

"All-ight G... let's go holla at-the-nigga."

Chicago glared at Ron-Ron then said:

"Next time, don't make me have to go through all this **bullshit** with yo-ass."

Ron-Ron smiled and extended his hand and said:

"All-ight Family... that's ma-fault." they shook hands the Gangsta way and the two, Boss-Gangsta got in their cars and drove down Natural-Bridge towards Union Boulevard, headed to Gambino's spot.

Back on Maffitt:

Bam was wondering who was paging him.

"Gambino, you got yo burn-out-phone?" asked Bam.

"Yeah, I got it G."

Bam followed Gambino to the living-room. Flame and Crime were battling-it-out on one of the gaming-systems. Flame saw Bam step in just after Gambino and with moderate enthusiasm, he hopped-up to greet Bam:

"Gansta **Muthafuckin**-Bam! What-up Big Bro!"

Flame gave Bam a hug. Bam was smiling, seeing how almost **all** the G's called him "Gansta Muthafuckin Bam."

Bam responded:

"What-up Flame."

Bam was always glad to see Flame. Flame stayed in good-spirit seemingly **all** the time and Bam appreciated having people with good-spirits around. Young Crime didn't know Bam, but he'd heard a lot about him. Gambino introduced them:

"Bam G, this is Young-Crime-G... He a-solid-little-brother... we just blessed him in not too long ago but he been down with me for awhile now. I told the lil-nigga he had to stay in school and graduate first or get his GED before he could be part of the Disciple Nation... **This lil-nigga...**! Went and got his GED **two** weeks later. He-on-point... he got dedication, determination and passion fah-the-Nation."

Bam extended his hand then said:

"What-up Lil-Bro." They shook hands and Bam continued:

"Stay on that righteous-path Lil-Bro. Learn yo Growth & Development literature... apply it to yo-life everyday so you can know **fah-sho** you movin forward, properly, you feel me Lil-Bro?"

Crime-G nodded and Bam continued:

"I'm always ready to aid and assist ma lil-brothers who wanna go from being a brother-of-the-Struggle to a brother-of-Success."

Crime-G wanted to show-off a little bit and the time was perfect. He recited the number eleven law of the GD concepts:

"Aid and Assistance. The eleventh law of the Sixteen-Concepts.

Aid and assist my fellow brothers in all righteous endeavors... GD."
Bam smiled at Young Crime-G, happy to see he was learning the literature.
Bam looked at Gambino then said:

"I see you gettin him right, G."
Bam looked at Young Crime again then said:

"16-13-12 Lil-G."
Crime gave Bam the proper response in code:

"14-20-13 Big-Bro." and he smiled.

"That's what I like to see... keep-up the good work Lil-G."

"All-ight, all-ight." said Young Crime, happy and feeling good about his self.
He made a good first-impression on Gansta-Bam... someone who Gambino, Flame, KG, Crayzo, and Ghost, respected highly.

Gambino grabbed his Motorola-burn-out-phone. He was about to hand it to Bam, but there was a knock at the back-door. Everyone paused, looking at Gambino... The only person Gambino expected to come-by was Bam, so the knock on the back-door was a startling surprise, considering what they were involved in.

Flame grabbed the pistol-grip-Mosberg-pump-shotgun then headed to the back-door. Gambino walked cautiously behind him. Flame stepped closer to the door and with the barrel of the Mosberg, he moved the curtain back from the small window... From a distant, Gambino peered out of the window to see who it was.

"Put the gun down G." said Gambino after seeing who it was.
Flame lowered the shotgun and stayed close while Gambino opened the door. Chicago and Ron-Ron were standing on the porch with stoic faces, unmoved by the sight of the Mosberg barrel.

Gambino was a little apprehensive and confused by their visit, though he still opened the door all the way and greeted his former GD brothers questionably:

"Chi... Ron-Ron... what-up G...?"
Chicago and Ron-Ron could see the nervousness on Gambino's face and hear it in his voice. Chicago began speaking:

"What-up Gambino... we got-a-situation... we need to holla at you 'Bra."
While Chicago and Ron-Ron stepped inside, Flame went back to the living-room to let Gansta-Bam know everything was cool. Knowing

there were two other Gangsta Disciples in the house, Bam didn't hesitate to see who they were and what the situation was Flame had mentioned. Chi, Gambino and Ron-Ron were all sitting at a rectangular wooden dinning-table, in the dinning-room adjacent to the kitchen, When Bam stepped into the area, instantly Gambino thought about the burn-out-phone which was still in his hand then said:

"Ma-fault-G... here you go." and handed Bam the burn-out-phone. Chi and Ron-Ron's stoic expression disappeared at the sight of Gansta-Bam. They all knew each other, though Bam was the closet to VG, so they were definitely surprised to see him there at **that** particular point in time. Ron-Ron and Chi stood up and both greeted Bam with GD handshakes and Gangsta hugs then right after that, Ron-Ron got straight to the situation at hand.

Back at the warehouse:

Jerry had taken VG to another part of the building. It was a room that once served as an office. Jerry was looking at VG disappointingly. He let out a long sigh:

"Haaah....." then moved the telephone away from VG and continued:

"Well kid... it looks like your Connect doesn't wanna be **connected** with right now... and I can't sit here all day and wait for him to call."

Jerry pulled the pack of Marborel-Lights from his shirt pocket, took one out and lit-it. He sat in a chair behind an old dusty metal desk, puffing-on his cigarette. VG sat quietly on the other side, glancing at the gun that sat atop the desk, close to Jerry. The Detective continued:

"Ma-man... it looks like you can't help me... so now... I need to figure-out what to do with you."

VG had paged Gansta-Bam afew times, but wasn't leaving his code at the end of the number. VG **knew** Bam wouldn't call back... he was only trying to buy himself sometime to think of something else. But there was nothing else and he had run out of time.

VG responded:

"You can let me go if I can't help you."

Jerry peered at VG suspiciously then said:

"You're right kid. I **can** let you go... But I have something else in mind."

Jerry's voice and demeanor had been calm and cool up until this point... He became **so** sinister, that when he spoke, his words alone seemed to hit VG in the face.

Jerry continued:

"I'm gonna **tie** you back up to that **fucking** chair out there... in that **rat** infested **shit-hole**! And then... I'm gonna leave."

His demeanor became calm and cool again, as he spoke the last three words of his sentence. VG was fuming inside and wanted to grab the gun off the desk and shoot Jerry in his fucking face. Jerry noticed VG's anger growing and picked the gun up, eliminating the temptation from VG's presence. VG was in a lose-lose situation... He had no way of letting Gansta-Bam know what he was about to bring his way. And if he didn't make the proper phone-call, he would more than likely die.

VG put his head down and closed his eyes. He whispered quietly, words that he had **never** spoken before, up until that moment. His spirit had taken over and pushed the words out of his mouth:

"Father God, please help me outta this... **please** Father God..."

Jerry's ears were deaf to VG's words. VG's spirit had spoken the words **so** quietly, that only the Father God could hear and God received the call instantly... VG had besought Gods Divine help, though God's plan had been put into motion over four years ago... and Gods plan... was infallible.

As VG lifted his head and opened his eyes, he saw Jerry was about to unplug the phone-cord from the phone-outlet in the wall. Jerry's hand was on the plastic-release-lever and then... the phone rang... The loud Bell-phone startled Jerry **so** much, that he almost pulled the trigger on his Beretta-nine-millimeter-pistol. He smiled and laughed a-bit then said:

"**Shit**! That might be your connect kid... you wanna answer that?"

VG frown at Jerry then said:

"What-the-fuck am-I-supposed-to-say?"

The phone rang again.

"Come on kid..... I thought you were smart... we already **talked** about this."

The phone rang a third time. Jerry pushed the phone over to VG and VG lifted the receiver on the third and a-half ring.

"Hello?"

"Yeah, somebody called a pager?" asked Gansta-Bam.

"This VG, Big-Bra."

Bam had **just** been filled in on the situation about VG, so when he heard the abnormalness in VG's voice, he knew VG was definitely in trouble. VG had no idea that Ron-Ron and Chicago were with Bam.

"Lil-Bra, is it CTT?" asked Bam.

"Yeah Big-Bra, it's cool."

'CTT' only met: cool to talk.

Bam continued:

"Folks done-already-put-me-on-point about-what-happened, so, do-what-you-need-to-do ta-get-up-outta-that-shit... play the game and stay cool you hear me?"

"Yeah, I hear you Big-Bra."

Jerry glared at VG and mouthed the words quietly:

"What is he saying?"

"Hold-on Big-Bra."

VG lowered the phone-receiver and answered Jerry:

"He said he just got back in-town, that's why it took him so long to call back."

Bam knew VG was being forced to contact him, "but why" he thought. The police had no clue of his little drug operation. Bam's thoughts raced. He tried to think of if he had slipped up somewhere, but he hadn't... this was sheer-bad-chance and that's all. Bam asked VG:

"What them muthafucks want Lil-Bra?"

VG responded:

"This dude say he just wanna get in on some of the good shit... He say he wanna do business with you... them his exact words."

Bam's anger was growing and he was mad-as-hell... "These muthafuckas **kidnap** ma lil-brother... **then!** Have the muthafuckin **audacity,** to ask to do **business** with me! These muthafuckas outta they rabbit-ass-mind..." thought Bam, but he played along.

"Lil-Bra, let me holla at the dude."

"He wanna talk to you." said VG, handing the phone-receiver to Jerry... Jerry took hold of the receiver:

"**Hey**! **Ma-Man**! You had us worried for a-minute there... we didn't think you'd call... How's business?" said Jerry with enough enthusiasm that one would've thought he was on the phone with a long-time friend he hadn't spoken to in a while. Bam responded semi-cordially:

"Business could always be better, but right now, it is what it is."

"Aaah, a man of modesty and appreciation I see." said Jerry.

Bam was wise in an all-around type of way, but he had never been in a situation like this... He knew he had to be tactful as possible dealing with this guy, in-order to produce a positive outcome.

Ron-Ron had given Bam a full detail of, **who** it was that kidnapped VG, just as Evelyn had done for him and Chi, so Bam had an advantage and he was ready. Jerry had no clue that Gansta-Bam knew about him or of what he had done to VG, and Bam wanted to keep it that way... Jerry was a detective so he was fairly good at reading in-between the lines to detect authenticity or bullshit. And like wise, Gansta-Bam was a Governor of Investigations, so in a sense, they were equally matched, wit-fully speaking.

Jerry was right about Bam being modest and appreciative. That's how Gansta-Bam kept his self humble. Bam's initial evaluation of Jerry was accurate as well, although Bam didn't reveal it to Jerry, what he thought of him. He contained it for his own cognizance... Bam sensed that Jerry was crafty, cunning and confident. Three characteristics that seemed natural to Jerry...

Bam responded to Jerry's comment:

"I'm also a man interested in knowin, how did you and ma-lil brother meet and who-it-is I'm talkin too?"

"A cautionary man as well... I can respect that." said Jerry.

"That's the best way to be in a business like this." said Bam.

"You're absolutely right ma-man. I couldn't agree with you more."

Jerry felt comfortable talking, now that he had analyzed Bam's tone of voice and his words. He was convinced that Bam suspected nothing out-of-the-ordinary, so Jerry thought.

Jerry continued:

"Let-me-get-right-to-the-point-here-ma-man... and cool-off that burning curiosity of yours. My name is Jerry, and I'm just-a-guy looking for some good product because I'm tired of the bullshit that's out here... And how I met your lil-brother? Well... a client and friend of mine bought some **really-good-shit** one day, and I wanted to know where he got it from. I had some-of-my-people get-in-touch with the kid, we setup a little meeting of sorts, and now... here we are."

Jerry was telling the truth, just in a round-about-type-of-way that was befitting and fashionable for him.

Bam responded:

"So, ma lil-brother just **agreed** to introduce you to me and he don't even **know** you? I'm gone have to talk to him about that."

"Well..... hold-on ma-man."

Jerry heard the disappointment in Bam's voice and Jerry continued:

"Don't be **too** mad at the kid... I was very persuasive... he really couldn't say no." said Jerry, chuckling a-bit at the humor behind his comment then he continued:

"Look... let's just skip the formalities and talk business."

Jerry was trying to get Bam's mind off of how he came to know VG... Bam picked-up on it quick. It was the first sign of deceit on Jerry's part. Bam played along though and responded:

"Okay... how much business you wanna talk about?"

"That all depends on you ma-man... how much business do you have?"

The question was **ridiculous** thought Bam, and he laughed a little, enough to cause Jerry to frown on the other end of the phone.

Bam responded:

"You don't ever hear of a customer goin into McDonald's, asking the cashier, how many burgers can you make?"

Jerry Chuckled a little at Bam's witty ability to express insights amusingly. Then he responded:

"You're right ma-man. I've never heard of that one before, and I get your point."

What Jerry wanted to know was, how much cocaine did Bam have on-hand... so he put a modest number out there just to hear what Bam would say, and also, **how** he would say it... with confidence or with uncertainty.

Jerry continued:

"Let-me-be-straight-up-with-you-ma-man... I need two-whole-days of work from you."

Bam laughed again, and Jerry asked him:

"Did I say something funny?"

"Naah, naah...I just thought you was about to say somethin else."

Jerry caught on...

"Ooh, no. I'm a business man too and know how to talk the business, you know what I'm saying ma-man?"

They were referring to how people spoke about drugs over the phone-lines.

Jerry continued:

"So, can you help me on those two days?"

Bam responded without hesitation **and** with certainty:

"Yeah, I can do that... as long as you can afford ma rates."

Jerry felt sure now, that Bam could really deliver...

Over the many years of dealing with drugs from working in the narcotics division, Jerry and **quite** a-few other officers acquired a taste for the "bogga-suger", but their 'nose-candy' habits were very well hidden. That was until the recent cocaine shortage in Saint Louis. Things started to unravel for some of the officers... their tempers were flaring, their actions were becoming irregular and reckless... people really started to take notice of them, especially in the Black communities...

Jerry was getting excited. The thought of having two kilos of premium cocaine, had him feeling a little anxious and his ability to remain cool and patient was wearing thin. Young VG could actually see the slight change in Jerry's demeanor... it kind-of reminded VG of the symptoms a crack-head had, when they needed a fix... real jittery, moving fast... Jerry wanted the cocaine right now. He asked Bam:

"So what's it gonna cost me and how soon can we meet?"

Bam hit Jerry with some of Jerry's own words:

"Well ma-man... that all depends... How soon can you get fifty-six yards of field ready?"

Jerry quickly calculated that Bam wanted twenty-eight-thousand per kilo then he responded:

"I can have it here where I am in thirty minutes... when can you be ready?"

Bam could smell the bullshit, though there **was** some realness in Jerry's voice saying: "I really have the money and wanna do business."

"I'm actually ready right now." said Bam.

Jerry was taken aback. VG watched Jerry's eyes widen and a greedy-grin grew across Jerry's face. He wasn't expecting for Bam to respond the way he did... it made him all the more eager... Bam could tell from the brief moment of silence, he had put Jerry in check on the chessboard of bullshit they were playing on, and Jerry was carefully thinking of his next move. Bam was in control of the tempo and flow of things and he wanted to move quickly as possible. Bam broke the silence:

"You wanna let me know where y'all are and I can be on my way to you. I'm out here in, Washington Missouri, so it's-gone-take-me-about, 40 minutes. That'll give you time to get that paperwork together."

Jerry's face frowned as he recollected what VG told him at the beginning of the phone-call... that Bam had just got back in town. Jerry responded:

"I thought you were already in town?"

"I am... **ma** town where I am is, Washington Missouri. It's not far from Saint Louis, and like I said... it'll give you time to get that paperwork in-order."

Bam was lying, and actually buying his self time to put things together. But Jerry believed him and that's all that mattered. Jerry conducted one more 'test-of-truth' just to make sure Bam wasn't bullshitting him.

"Say ma-man... I got another fifty-six to put with that, so can we make it four days?"

Bam chuckled a little then responded:

"Woooh, slow down a little Jerry... I like aggressive business, but I gotta get to know you first... let's see how these first two days go and then we can go from there... if they go good, trust me... I can have more days open on the calendar for you."

Jerry's thought's raced: "this guy sounds like he has an abundant supply of the shit... maybe I **should** do some real business with him...

Pg.309

it could definitely be beneficial."

Jerry's initial plan was: 'to take a large portion of the cocaine for himself, arrest both, Gansta-Bam and VG on possession and attempted sells, and then pressure Bam into giving-up his source'. But he was now reconsidering.
Jerry responded:

"Alright ma-man... we can take things slow... if you don't mind me asking you though... what do I call you?"
Bam thought VG had already divulged his name to Jerry.
He responded:

"Ma lil-brother didn't tell you who I was already?"

"Nope... he didn't mention your name... he only told me he didn't think you would do business with me."

"I normally **wouldn't**... but I trust ma lil-brothers judgment. I know he would've told me if he thought you was bad business people, if you know what I mean."
What Bam meant by his statement was: the police. Jerry caught on and laughed a-bit. It was a different laugh from any that Bam had heard from Jerry so far. It was a mocking laugh.
Jerry responded:

"No, not me ma-man... No bad business people here."
Bam knew Jerry was lying... Jerry **was** the fucking police. Bam smiled genuinely at the thought passing through his mind: "this muthafucka don't even know what's about to hit-um."
Bam responded:

"Good, good... no bad business people... they call me Bam."
Jerry felt a good vibe coming from Bam and he didn't feel the need to be on guard so much.

"Alright then, Bam... I'm gonna get that paperwork together and we can meet over-off-of North-Broadway. There's a Mobil gas-station right before the West-Florissant exit if you're coming from I-70 headed west... When you get there, you can call this same number back... we're just right around the corner and down the street from there."

"Yeah, I know where it is... over by the Hostess Bread Company right?"

"Yeah, that's it." said Jerry.

"Okay then... I'll see you in about forty minutes... let-me-talk-to-ma lil-brother."

"No problem Bam ma-man, here he is."

Jerry handed the phone to VG. VG could see that Jerry was happy about the conversation he just had. VG took hold of the receiver:

"Hello."

"Hey lil-bra... you cool in there?"

"Yeah, I'm cool big-bro."

"Good... you already know how I get down, so just stay cool... You gone be smokin on some Acapulco-Gold and chillin-wit-ah beautiful-chic in-a-minute, you hear me?"

VG smiled and let out a quiet laugh then said:

"Yeah big-bro, I hear you."

"I'ma see you in-a-lil-bit, lil-bra." said Bam.

"All-ight."

VG handed Jerry the receiver. Jerry was curious of the smile VG had on his face.

"You look pretty happy there kid... what-he-say?" asked Jerry as he hung-up the phone.

VG answered, still smiling slightly:

"He said, when he get done doing busy with you, we gone smoke on some of that, Acapulco-Gold and chill wit some beautiful girls."

"Aaaah, to celebrate good business, right?" asked Jerry.

"Yeah, right." said VG with a slightly mischievous smile on his face, but Jerry had no clue.

He was too caught-up in the blissful thought of having two kilos of premium cocaine. Jerry's behavior grew hasty... He walked over to the door, opened it and left-out-of-the old office, closing the door behind him... Not three seconds later... he came back in:

"Hey kid... unplug that phone and hand it to me will-ya."

VG did so. Jerry stood in the doorway for a few seconds as VG walked back to the chair to sit down. Jerry's conscience had sprung-up and he felt obligated to address it:

"Hey kid... I'll be back in about twenty minutes... you hungry, you want something to drink?"

VG could see a tiny glimmer of compassion in Jerry's eyes... but that shit don't matter now, thought VG... Big-brother-Bam is on his way, and **he** not gone give-a-shit about this muthafucka having compassion... all Bam would care about, was punishing and making

Pg.311

an example out-of-the muthafuckas who violated and crossed that line when they kidnapped ah young brother of the Gangsta Disciple Nation.

VG answered:

"Naah... I'm cool."

"Okay... suit yourself kid." said Jerry then closed the door...

The old office had no windows so it was lit-up only by a single light-bulb-fixture. VG stepped over to the door and attempted to turn the knob but it was locked, the door didn't bulge. He didn't worry though... He was untied, unharmed and feeling confident he would be out of there soon. He sat back down in the chair. VG hadn't paid it any attention before, but as he sat down, he felt the sack of crack-cocaine shift inside of his underwear, and his money was still in his pocket. VG pulled out his money and counted it, trying to pass time, waiting on the unknown near future.

Jerry left Officer Vincent and a rookie cop name, Ken Kinshinger, to keep watch of the building... he told them things were cool but to stay alert. Jerry drove downtown to the Metro-Police station's parking-lot. Jerry's personal car was on the lot; he was driving a department car. The gray Crown Victorian pulled up to the gate and the security guard, knowing who Jerry was already, opened the gate for him. Jerry gave the lot security guard a friendly wave and pulled passed the guard shack. He headed towards his car which was one row down and to the right, about ten cars down. He put the Crown Victorian in park right behind his car, got out then popped the trunk of the black Ford Grand Marquis.

He moved some things around until he was able to get to what he was there for. Jerry had a stash of cash and he felt the best place for it was the trunk off his car. He pulled out three stacks, each worth twenty thousand dollars. Jerry tucked the brown satchel, back into its cubby-hole, secured the cash on his person then closed the trunk. He got inside the Crown Victorian and drove back around to the gate. After it was clear to go, Jerry gave the security guard another friendly wave, exited the police parking-lot then headed back to the old warehouse.

Back at the Maffitt street Stash-house:

Gansta-Bam was acting as, "General at Arms" assembling a plan of attack. He asked Chicago to call all the deck captains and have them meet at 'O'fallon-Park'. Chi and Gambino went into the front room to make the phone-calls. The park was on West-Florissant avenue, close to Broadway and the Mobil gas-station. Bam asked Ron-Ron:

"G, y'all got any units with y'all?"

"We only got two, G. Chi got one and I got one." he said disappointingly, wishing he had another gun in the car for Bam to use."

"Good, that's cool... Gambino!" Bam called-out for Gambino and Gambino came back into the dinning-room.

Bam continued:

"G, y'all got any units here in the house?"

"Yeah... they downstairs in the basement."

Gambino went to the basement-door and walked down the stairs. He returned with two bags, not even knowing exactly what they contain because he hadn't looked inside of them yet. Gambino sat the bags on top of the table and unzipped them... Gansta-Bam and Ron-Ron looked inside, astonished at what they saw. Gambino commenced to pulling the weapons out of the bag, placing them on the table.

"**Damn G**! You got some top-of-the-line **heat** right here!" said Bam, admiring the firearms.

Gambino unzipped the other bag, moved some things out-of-the way trying to see what was in it, and there it was... his eyes were glued to it... the black-snub-nose-38 with the black-rubber-grip, gleaming wickedly up from the bottom of the small black carrying bag.

He picked-up the gun gently and released the cylinder, seeing that only one chamber was empty then he closed the cylinder back in place. Bam and Ron-Ron saw how much Gambino was mesmerized "by the gun." Gambino snapped out of the trance, still half under the spell of the gun. He looked over at Bam then said:

"I'ma hold-on to this one."

Bam began loading up a, Colt-45-1911 Special-Combat-Government-Model, black and nickel-cadmium. Ron-Ron followed suit, taking a box of ammo from the bag to match the gun he was about to load. It was a Ruger-P89 semi-automatic, all black. Bam loaded the bullets using his trusty-gray-bandanna, and Ron-Ron was using a black tee-shirt. After Gansta-Bam finished stacking the rounds into the Colt .45's magazine or 'clip'. He sat it down on the table then went in the front room where Chicago, Flame, and Crime-G were.

"Let me use that when you get done, G."
Bam was referring to Gambino's burnout-phone. Chicago nodded then wrapped up his phone call.

"Yeah G, we need y'all in the area in-case-some-shit-pop-off."

"Okay Chi... We'll be at the park, Family." said the voice on the other end of the phone-line.

"Right-on... plenty-much-love G." said Chi.

"Never too much Family." said the voice on the other end of the phone.
Chicago pressed the call end button on the Motorola phone then took it to Bam when he was done.

Bam dialed the phone-number. He was calling his close friend and partner in business, "Ole Boy."
'Ole Boy' answered the phone in a low 'altoish' southern-draw:

"Hello?"

"What-up 'Ole Boy'... this Bam..."

"Hey, hey... What-up Beezee." That's what 'Ole Boy' called Bam sometimes, "B.Z."
Bam responded:

"Say 'bra... can you meet me over on Maffitt... I'm right-off-of Belt. I got ah customer who needs two yards done?"
Bam was basically asking 'Ole Boy' to bring him two kilos... That was the way they communicated over the phone about drugs...
'Ole Boy' wanted to make sure he understood what Bam was talking about so he asked him:

"Is it two small yards or two big yards?"
'Two small yards' meant: two pounds of marijuana. And 'two big yards' meant: two kilos of cocaine.
Bam answered:

"Two **big** yards 'bra."

'Ole Boy' had a lawns service business. It was just **one** of the ways him and Bam, used to transport their cocaine and marijuana around.

'Ole Boy' was surprised at Bam's request for the simple fact: Bam was the one who normally sold the marijuana and 'Ole Boy' was the one who normally sold the cocaine. 'Ole Boy' responded:

"Two **big yards**!"

"Yeah 'bra... two big yards."

'Ole Boy' was happy about that. The quicker they sold their product, the better. 'Ole Boy' trusted Bam. Bam knew how to handle business on all levels of the dope game so 'Ole Boy' wasn't worried about anything going wrong. But in this case... it was **Bam** who was a-little worried. He was trying to stay optimistic though, and he had to do whatever it took to get his little GD brother back safely.

"I'm over by you right now, so give-me-about ten-minutes and I'll be there... What's the address?" asked 'Ole Boy'.

"5525... I'ma be standin outside." said Bam.

"All-ight... I'll be there in a-minute."

'Ole Boy' was on Labadie Avenue, at his big sister's house. Sometimes he would keep the cocaine and weed there for convenience... About ten or fifteen-minutes after Bam had spoken to 'Ole Boy'... an old burgundy Ford F-150, with a trailer on the hitch carrying lawn equipment, turned onto Maffitt off-of-Belt Avenue. Bam stepped off the porch, from under the shade of the porch-roof and into the front yard. 'Ole Boy' pulled in front of the house and Bam stepped pass the gate over to the pickup-truck. Bam leaned on the passenger side-door, said a few words to 'Ole Boy' then 'Ole Boy' reached down by the seat and picked-up an old toolbox. He said a few words to Bam then handed Bam the toolbox. If anyone **was** watching... all they would've seen and thought was: that's just his homeboy, lending him some tools to fix something. Bam stepped away from the old Ford and 'Ole Boy' drove off. Bam took the toolbox inside the house then got back to planning:

"Okay fellas... we got about fifteen minutes before I gotta call this dude back." said Bam, walking back into the dinning-room.

Bam hadn't told anyone what he was planning, and no one knew what him and Jerry talked about on the phone... They only inferred from what they heard... Bam would inform them of the plan once he had it all-mapped-out. But everyone was still curious as to what was going on, especially Gambino, so he asked:

"G, what-the-fuck this dude want with VG?"

Bam stopped what he was doing and everyone looked at him, waiting for him to respond.

He responded:

"Apparently, VG sold some of the cocaine he got from me, to somebody this dude fuck with... it got back to this dude that it was some-of-the best shit In town... so this dude, Jerry... this crooked cop muthafucka... wanted to know where it came from... so... they snatched VG up to find out."

"So this cop **kidnapped** VG to find out his **dope** connect! What-the-fuck kind-of-shit-is-that?" said Gambino in disbelief.

"Yeah... same thing I was wondering." said Bam then he paused. He picked-up the .45 clip, pushed it into the Colt 1911 then he continued:

"He wants two kilos."

"**Two kilos**!" exclaimed Ron-Ron.

Bam responded:

"Yep... that's what he said he wanted... two bricks of cocaine."

"But he won't get the chance to walk away with them two kilos" thought Gansta-Bam.

"**Man**..... where-the-fuck we gone get **two** keys-of-coke from, in fifteen minutes." asked Chicago with clear and evident skepticism.

Bam pulled the slide back on the Colt 45, loading a round into the chamber then put the safety on. The sound was soothing to Bam, .45's were his favorite gun. He looked at Chi and said:

"Chi, we have two keys right here bro." Bam tapped on the toolbox gently with the tip of the .45 then he continued:

"Now let's go get our lil-brother back and take-**care** of these muthafuckas..."

Bam had something more up his sleeve but he wasn't letting it be known just yet... he couldn't for the simple fact... he wasn't quite sure his self, of how things were gonna play-out.

Going over the plan, he continued:

"Gambino, I need somethin low-key to drive. Flame, I want you to ride with me over there. This dude wants me to call him when I get to the Mobil gas-station on Broadway... he gone give me the directions from there. Gambino, I need you to follow us over there... you gone have the two kilos in the car with you. Chi, Ron-Ron... y'all follow us too but I need **all** y'all to play-it-cool, like y'all just regular customers at the gas-station... this dude is a cop so I know he probably gone have somebody watchin to see if anybody is with me... so play it cool alright."

They all nodded, and Bam continued:

"Ron-Ron, when you see me go into gas-station, I want you to come in and holla-at-me, discreetly though... I'ma let you know where we headed. I want you and Chi to keep goin though and get the Gangsta together and cover the street and cover the exits of the building or house... **where ever** we at, I want it covered. Gambino, you wait outside the building or house me and Flame go into, so Chi and Ron-Ron will know where to send the soldiers. Take yo burnout-phone too, and when me and Flame see that things are cool... Flame is gonna call you, to bring in the two keys."

Bam looked at Flame then continued:

"Flame, when you call Gambino... let him know how many dudes we seen comin in... if it's two say; what-up B, bring them two books in... if it's five, say; what-up E, bring them two books in... you got it G?"

Flame responded:

"Yeah big-bro, I got it."

Bam continued:

Bam looked at Ron-Ron and Chi then said:

"Y'all let the soldiers know... if we not outta there in **ten**-minutes after Gambino go-in... y'all come-in and get us G. Y'all **rush** that muthafucka... Now when we got VG, and we **all** walk out in-the-clear... we gone **raid** they ass and drop everyone of them crooked muthafuckas!"

Bam was winging it. How things would **really** turnout, only time would tell. He took a deep breath, exhaled then said:

"Alright fellas... I don't know how this shit is gone play-out, but one thang I do know is this... I don't want this crooked muthafucka **or** his goons walkin away from it, all-ight?"

Bam looked around at everybody and they all nodded in silence. They were charged up and ready for action.

"Which car you got fah-me, Gambino?" asked Bam.

"You can take the Ford Taruus, G."

"**Alright...!** It's almost that time... Y'all stay-on-point and be careful out there... Check y'all units and let's get ready to-do-this-shit." said Bam.

CHAPTER 22: Shorty Wanna Be Ah Thug

Young Crime was listening to the game plan and hadn't heard his name get mentioned in it... He came in then asked:

"What y'all want me to do Big-G.?"

Gambino answered him:

"Lil-bro, I need you to hold the spot down until we get back."

Young-Crime's facial-expression showed his disappointment from the answer Gambino had given him. He was about to walk back into the living-room. Bam looked at Gambino as to ask his approval. Gambino shrugged his shoulders and tilted his head as to say, "Go-ahead."

Bam called young Crime:

"Lil-G!"

Crime turned around and Bam continued:

"What-you-wanna-do Lil-G?"

Young-Crime didn't hesitate with an answer, and he answered with fury:

"I wanna **shoot** one of them crooked ass **cops**! They beat ma lil-brother up, fah-**nothin**! That nigga was on his way to-ah teen program at **church**, Big Bro...!" said Crime with a little sadness in his voice along with the anger.

Bam responded:

"Gambino, you know if Lil-G got the stomach fah-that-shit?"

"He probably does. I won't doubt it." said Gambino.

Gansta-Bams demeanor grew more serious and he glared at Young-Crime then said:

"Check-this-out-Lil-G... we don't do this shit to get strips... We do this shit to keep the GD Nation members, **safe** from the opposition. **No** muthafucka is gone know about what we do today except us... This shit is real Lil-G... This ain't no movie shit or some, **wanna**-be Gangata shit! Niggas could **die** today if shit don't get handle the right way."

Bam reduced his glare on Crime and let his words sit on Crimes mind. Bam picked up the toolbox and handed it to Gambino. There was a long break in conversation then Crime spoke:

"I still wanna help Big Bro..."

Everyone peered at Bam as he peered at Young-Crime again. Bam's glare was intense for just a second then it softened... He searched the eyes of the young GD brother to see how his inter-being looked. Bam saw no fear... no uncertainty... no relenting. All the things he **thought** he would see, after saying what he said to Crime. Bam's stern glare turned into a quirky little smile and he said:

"Gambino... open that toolbox and take them two kilos out." he did so.

There was a dark green backpack in the front room, Bam noticed it earlier and it looked empty.

"Gambino, is that backpack in the living-room, empty?" asked Bam.

"Yeah, it is. Lil-G, can you grab that backpack?" said Gambino. Crime went to get the backpack.

Bam could see a small smile form on Crimes face as he left the dinning-room to retrieve the backpack, and he hurried back with it. The two kilos were sitting on the table, still wrapped in the shinny light-brown tape. Bam continued:

"Take this bandanna and wipe those packages off real good then put-em in the backpack."

Young-Crime did as Gansta-Bam asked him to do and Bam continued:

"Gambino, let Lil-G get that unit you got if you don't mind."

Gambino really didn't wanna give-it-up, but he did so. He understood why Bam asked him to give the unit, or gun, to Crime... it was smaller and safer than all the other guns they had. Bam continued:

"Wipe the unit off good too... and **don't** squeeze the trigger Lil-G, not yet anyway."

There were a few chuckles of laughter at the comment. Young-Crime wiped the gun off completely then Bam grabbed the photo of Jerry. He took a few steps back towards the kitchen, holding the photo up like a target. Then with anger on his face and indignation in his voice, Bam continued:

"You see this muthafucka Lil-G?" Crime nodded yes.

"**This** is the muthafucka responsible fah-niggas like you and me comin-up-missin and dead! Lil-G, **this** is the muthafucka responsible fah-yo lil-brother gettin his **ass** kicked...!"

Bam's anger was clearly visible, and young Crimes anger was festering. Bam continued:

"I **hate** muthafuckas like this! And when you **hate** something, you supposed to **kill** that shit! This **bitch-ass** cop!" said Bam poking at Jerry's photo-face then Bam continued:

"This pussy who hides behind a fuckin **badge...!** Do you **hate** this muthafucka Lil-G?"

Bam was glaring intensely at Crime again. Crime nodded yes. Bam calmed his self then said:

"Point the unit at this piece-of-shit."

Young-Crime did so. Bam continued:

"That's where I wanna shoot this bitch, in his muthafuckin **face!**"

Gansta-Bam lowered the photo and stepped back over to the table. He took one of the kilos of cocaine out-of-the backpack. He pulled back a piece of tape from each end of the package. Then he placed the photo of Jerry on top of it, smoothing the tape back down over the edges of the paper-photo. He wiped the package down with the bandanna and put it back in the backpack using the bandanna.

"Put that unit in the backpack Lil-G and let me holla at you."

Crime did so then followed Gansta-Bam into the living-room. No one knew why Bam wanted to talk to Crime, but after a few moments they both returned.

"Gambino, Lil-G gone ride with you. I want him to bring the backpack in... so when Flame calls you, send him in, alight?"

"Alright G." said Gambino.

They all left-out-of the backdoor and Gansta Bam, Flame, Ron-Ron and Chi, walked to the front of the house where their cars were parked. Gambino and Young-Crime got into the car that was parked in the back driveway....

The multi-lane Mobil gas-station was right off the freeway and it was busy. Cars were zooming in and out-of-the-lot. Customers were buying gas and others were there to buy something out of the large mini-mart. There were a few payphones at the end of the mini-mart and Bam pulled into a parking space right in front of the phones. The small convoy pulled up discreetly at separate gas-pumps, except for Ron-Ron. He pulled into a parking space, sat in his car, keeping a covert watch on Bam while Bam made the phone-call to Jerry... Chicago got out of his car and walked into the gas-station to pay for gas and so did Gambino...

CHAPTER 23: The Phone-call

The phone rang. Jerry made it back just in time to plug it back into the phone-outlet. He answered the phone, already knowing who it was:

"**Bam! Ma Man!** Are you there yet?"

Bam responded:

"Yeah, I'm at the Mobil gas-station."

"Good, good... you're not far from us. Do you see the old building across the street from the gas-station... it's to your right if you're facing the gas-station?"

Bam glanced across the street and saw the building Jerry was talking about then he responded:

"Yeah, I see it."

Jerry continued:

"Get on that street, drive to the first stop sign and make a right... go pass the first street then make a left on the second street called Holly. Go to the end of the street and park... you'll see two of my guys outside... they'll show you in... You got all that?"

"Right at the stop-sign, left on Holly to the end of the street, got it," said Bam.

"Okay ma-man... I'll see you in a-minute." said Jerry then hung up the phone.

Bam headed towards the mini-mart-doors and Ron-Ron followed suit. While in the mini-mart, Bam went over to the beer coolers where Ron-Ron met up with him. Bam discreetly gave Ron-Ron the directions to where Jerry wanted them to meet. Ron-Ron reached into the cooler and grabbed a six-pack of Budweiser just as Bam had done. They both walked to the check-out counter as if they didn't even know each other. Bam returned to the car where Flame was waiting.

"You ready G?" Bam asked Flame as he shut the door.

"Yeah big-bro. I'm **ready**." said Flame, high spirited as usually.

"What's up with the beers G?" asked Flame.

Bam look at Flame with a grin on his face then said:

"Those are ma tools, G."

Flame peered at Bam sideways then said questioningly:

"Yo **tools**?"

Bam continued to grin, cranked the engine then pulled the car, out of the parking space. Bam knew Gambino was about to follow him so as he drove pass, he put his hand out of the window, letting it hang down on the side of the door so Gambino and Young Crime could see it. Bam made a subtle hand signal indicating to Gambino that he wanted them to hold-up, so they stayed put, watching as Bam and Flame drove off the lot.

"What-the-fuck is he doing!" said Chicago with a-bit of frustration. Wondering why Gambino wasn't following Bam as planned.

Ron-Ron walked over to Chi and saw the agitation on his face then said:

"I think this Jerry-cat, got somebody watchin us."

Then Gambino came over next. Chicago was still agitated even after hearing Ron-Ron's words, and he immediately said:

"Gambino, why y'all not followin-em?"

Gambino answered:

"He waved us off... He signaled for us to fall-back so we did."

Gambino's words alleviated the agitation in Chicago. Then Chi looked around and said:

"So what-the-fuck we supposed ta-do now...? We can't just sit here... This nigga got two kilos in the car... we got units on us..."

Chi glanced around again then looked at Ron-Ron... Ron-Ron spoke:

"Allight fellas... check-dis-out, change of plans... We know where they goin already, and Chi is right... we don't need to be out here like this with all this shit on us. Let's head over to the park, 'post-up' with the rest of the Gangstas until Flame call's... after he call's... it's back to the original game plan, but until then... we gotta stay cool. Big brother Bam knows what he doin, so let's mob-out Family."

They all got into their cars. The Buick Regal engine started and the Monte Carlo engine started and they both growled sequentially... Gambino got inside his Oldsmobile Cutlass and cranked his engine as well, but there was no growling. However though... his Cutlass **was** super clean... The trio of cars filed out of the gas-station lot and headed to O'fallon Park, just across the freeway.

Officer Vincent and Officer Kinshinger were standing just outside the door of the building when Gansta-Bam and Flame pulled up. They parked at the end of the street as Jerry had instructed them to. Bam gave Flame some last minute advice before they went in:

"Flame... I want you to be yo usual self G. I don't want these fools to suspect **nothing,** you feel me?"

Flame looked dubiously at Bam and responded:

"Big-bro... I'm gone try... but it's gone be kinda hard tryina be cool when shit **ain't** cool."

Self-assured, Bam responded:

"G... everythang **is** cool... I got this under control, you gotta trust me all-ight... I need you to be yo-self G.

Bam was telling the truth. He knew he would be dealing with a white man, and since Flame was white... Bam felt that having Flame there, would lessen the tension, if there was any. That's why Bam wanted Flame to come with him and no-one else. Flame looked at Bam and saw the confidence in his eyes. It gave Flame his own sense-of-assurance that things would turn out good...

"Allight... be-ma-self, be-ma-self..." said Flame quietly, psyching his self up.

He made a funny noise, almost horse like and then shook his head wildly. Bam stared at Flame, humored by the 'get loose' exercise Flame was doing. Flame finished then Bam said:

"You ready now?" while staring at Flame.

Flame let out a big breath then answered:

"Yeah G... I'm ready."

Bam grabbed the plastic bag containing the six-pack, got out of the car and Flame followed. They walked over to the awaiting duo and Bam noticed... the eldest guy was a little antsy, like he was inching for something to happen so he could have a reason to shoot a-nigga. Thankfully, Flame was with him. Bam could see their bravado. He wanted to defuse the tension as soon as possible. He greeted the men cordially:

"How y'all fellas doin. I'm Bam." he said extending his hand.

Both men looked at each other, questioning whether they should shake hands with Bam. Their answer was evident and they left Bam's hand hanging. Bam lowered his hand and continued sarcastically:

"**Alright** then... this is ma good friend Flame."

"What's up fellas, how y'all doing?" said Flame.

He was being his self... he smiled, extending his hand as Bam had done, half expecting a different result and half receiving it. Ken, the younger officer shook Flame's hand. After they shook hands, Flame glanced at Bam then said jokingly:

"See, Bam... It's a-white thang... you gotta get with-it G." and he smiled.

Bam looked at Flame and wanted to laugh because the shit was funny he thought. Flame was playing the part, no, excuse that. He was being his self. The younger officer chuckled then looked at James... James didn't smile or grin, but he was thinking: "Jerry said everything was cool, but I wasn't expecting things to be **this** cool...! Does this guy have a **six-pack?**" The eldest officer spoke stoically:

"You guys can follow him..." said Officer James motioning to Ken.

Bam had accomplished the first part of his task: creating a friendly state of affairs. The rookie cop opened the heavy metal door and entered first. Bam and Flame entered next and Officer James Vincent followed, though first, checking the outside once more to see if anyone was lurking around. He saw no one then stepped inside and secured the door behind him.

As they walked into the warehouse Bam and Flame saw the white cargo van parked near the bay-doors. James tapped on the door of the office then opened it. Jerry was sitting at the desk and VG was still sitting across from him. When Jerry saw the two new faces he immediately waved them in and assuming Bam was the black guy. Jerry got out of his chair and gave him an energetic and lively greeting.

"**Bam! Ma-man!** I'm glad you could make it on such-a-short-notice." said Jerry, as if he had invited Bam to a weekend barbeque.

Jerry continued:

"James, can you go get a couple of chairs for our guest here."
James left then Bam responded:

"Yeah, I'm glad I could make it too... I would hate to miss an opportunity to do some good business. Thanks to ma lil-bro."
Bam touched VG's shoulder un-expectantly and VG jumped a little at Bam's touch. Bam knew VG's nerves would be a-bit sensitive because of the situation he had been placed in. He was expecting VG to be a-little jumpy.

"You alright lil-bro?" asked Bam, shaking VG's shoulder a-bit then Jerry hurried to respond for VG:

"**Yeah**..... The kid is alright... I asked him if he wanted something to eat or drink but he said he was cool."
Bam looked at VG and VG answered for his self:

"Yeah big-bro, I'm good... I'm thinkin about that beautiful chic and that Acapulco Gold." said VG with a sly grin on his face.
VG was no long worried. Big brother Bam was there and now he could relax... Bam grin back at his little GD brother then looked over to Jerry.

"Well... I brought you guys some beer... I figured we could have at least one while we take care of this business."
Bam lifted the plastic bag containing the six-pack, took a bottle out then gave it to VG. VG was elated! Up until that point, he wasn't certain of whether he would see his family and friends again, let-a-lone, drink his favorite beer. VG took hold of the dark brown glass bottle then said with great appreciation and moderate excitement in his voice:

"Right-**on** big-bro! You must have been readin ma mind cause I **shoo** wanted one of **these**!"
VG twisted the cap off and took a generous swig of the tasty brew.

"Aaaah." said VG after the swig.
His thirst was quenched... He smacked his lips a little and smiled appreciatively at Bam.
Gansta-Bam took two more beers from bag, handed one to Flame and kept the other for his self then sat the bag down on Jerry's dusted desk. There were three beers left. The second part of Bam's task would be revealed as soon as James and Ken returned... The two officers made it back to the office, each carrying a chair. They sat the

chairs down, one next to Bam and one next to Flame. Flame took his chair then sat down, Bam remained standing.

"Thanks fellas." said Bam, adjusting the chair, positioning it where he wanted it.

Then he continued:

"It looks like there's enough beer for everybody. You fellas are welcome to have one if that's cool?"

Bam looked from James and Ken, back to Jerry to see if it was cool. Jerry glared at Bam briefly then said:

"All..... What-the-hell, go ahead fellas."

Bam picked the bag up, took one more bottle out and sat it in front of Jerry. Then he gave the bag containing the last two beers, to Ken and James... Jerry's interest in Bam was started to increase: 'this guy is too comfortable... or is he just trying to feel-me-out so he **can** be comfortable?' thought Jerry.

"Bam, ma-man... so what-do-you-say we get down to business?"

Jerry twisted the cap off the bottle of Budweiser, smelt the mist that rose from the nose of the tasty suds, he took a sip discerning that the beer was okay to drink. Jerry took another sip peering over at Ken and James then lifted his bottle. Officer James and Officer Kinshinger opened their bottles of beer and headed out of the door.

Bam's second task was accomplished: he had come to the conclusion that there were only two men backing Jerry up. Now Flame kind-of got the idea of why Bam bought the beers and said, they were his "tools."

Bam responded to Jerry's comment:

"Jerry... I just wanted to get comfortable first... you know, kinda get-a-feel of the place, see what type of vibe I pick up before we do any business, you feel me?"

Jerry smiled at Bam then said:

"Right..... A man of 'cautionality'... once again, I gotta respect that."

Jerry took another swig then continued:

"So... what kind of vibe are you getting so far?"

Bam glared at Jerry for a short moment, acting as if he were trying to read Jerry. Then he responded with modest assurance:

"So far... it's cool, but you could make it even cooler by showin me that paperwork." said Bam, smiling and patting the top of the desk as he made the comment.

Jerry asked:

"So where are the two days I asked for?"

Bam responded:

"Jerry... I got you covered... one of my guys drove-em down for me and he's not too far away. I just have to call him, let-um know where we are, and that everything is cool and he'll be here in a matter of minutes."

Jerry didn't want to prolong the situation. He was ready to get his cocaine.

"Alright then... let's get to it!" said Jerry, pulling open a drawer of the desk.

He took the money out of the drawer then slapped the sixty thousand dollars down on the desk, boastfully motioning to the money then said:

"There you go ma-man." and he glared at Bam, as to say: "now where's yours?" Jerry continued:

"I hope your part of the deal is just as good as that money."

Jerry grinned smugly, leaned back in his chair, inter-locked his fingers then placed his hands on his stomach. Bam picked the money up and thumbed through it.

"All hundreds... it should be easy for you to count." said Jerry, smiling at Bam.

Bam gave VG a stack.

"Count that fah-me lil-bro." and they both started counting the money.

Bam quickly counted his stack and began counting the other stack. He counted two-hundred, one-hundred-dollar-bills, in each stacks. He asked VG while banding the money back into stacks:

"How much you count lil-bro?"

"Twenty-thousand." said VG.

Bam looked at Jerry, pointed to the stacks then asked him:

"So what is this...? you payin me extra for the trip and short notice or something? It's four-thousand-dollars over..."

Jerry glanced down at the money knowing exactly how much was there then looked at Bam and said:

"I'll tell you what ma-man... put three-grand towards my next order... two keys at twenty-five-a-key... that will be forty-seven-thousand I'll owe you. Give the kid a-grand for his troubles."

Jerry was doing more testing and analyzing. He looked at VG, winked his eye then looked back at Bam and continued:

"Now how about making that phone-call?"

Jerry pushed the phone towards Bam then Bam responded:

"Yeah, it looks like we all good here... but on that other three grand... just keep that and we'll see what we can work-out... Flame, go-ahead and make that phone-call." said Bam then slid the phone over Flame's way...

Flame got up, stepped over to the desk, picked up the receiver then dialed the number to Gambino's phone...

CHAPTER 24: Finna Get Hurt, Murked

Gambino and the rest of the Gangstas were waiting anxiously for the call from Flame and Bam. Gambino's Motorola burnout-phone rang and he answered it on the first ring.

"Hello?"

"What-up C... we ready fah you to bring them two books in."

Flame gave Gambino the directions to their location.

"Alright G. we'll be there in-a-minute." said Gambino.

"Alright... in-a-minute." said Flame then hung-up the phone.

Gambino informed Chicago and Ron-Ron of what Flame said:

"They ready, and it's only three dudes in the place."

Chicago peered at Gambino and asked:

"That's it! Only three muthafuckas?" Chi was dubious about the number of men Jerry had with him.

"That's what Flame said on the phone." said Gambino.

Chicago went over and spoke to the deck captains:

"Fellas, it ain't nothin but three dudes who got VG, so we gone minimize the mob... Tear-Drop, I want you and yo guys to come with us... the rest of y'all can head back to y'all deck if you want to, or y'all can 'post-up' here until we resolve this situation."

All of the Disciples choose to stay. Chicago finished what he had to say then Ron-Ron spoke:

"Alright Family, let's mob-out then."

Ron-Ron led the way, Gambino followed in the middle, Chi's Monte Carlo was behind the Cutlass, and Tear-Drop and his guys were at the end of their small convoy, in the 85 Cutlass Supreme...

Trigga-G and Sniper-G were both outstanding members with an undisclosed number of 'righteous kills' for the GD Nation... Ron-Ron crossed Holly Street and parked just passed the entrance of Holly. He watched as Gambino and Crime turn onto Holly Street. Chi and Tear-Drop parked on the other side, opposite of Ron-Ron. Ron-Ron walked over to where Chi and Tear-Drop were parked, to speak to them.

He wanted to make sure they understood the plan.

Gambino got to the end of the street and turned the car around to face in the direction he had just come from. He put the car in park and cocked the H&K .40 caliber... Him and Crime, sat in the car for a short moment, looking at the building then Gambino call the number on his burnout phone.

Jerry answered the phone:

"Hello?"

"Yeah. I'm out front, fah Bam." said Gambino.

"Alright, good!" said Jerry.

He was excited that things were rolling right along. He called for James and Ken to escort Flame upfront to bring Bam's guy inside. The trio walked upfront.

"It's dark as-a-**muthafucka** in here! I feel like a vampire... if I step outside I might **burst** into flames." said Flame, being his self, funny and joking as usual.

Officer Vincent went unfazed by Flame's comments and said nothing, nor did his facial expression change. He kept his same, seemingly natural, stoic look. However, Officer Kinshinger was amused by Flame's jester characteristics.

There were no windows on the front of the building, except for those of the bay-doors. It allowed only a minimum amount of light to shine in. James stepped over to the door and opened it. He looked directly at Gambino and Crime then called Flame over to the door.

"Is that your people?" asked James.

"Yeah, that's them." said Flame then waved for Crime to come in.

"Alright lil-bro... they ready fah-you... stay focused on whatever you supposed to do, alright." said Gambino.

Young Crime looked at Gambino with a serious and focused expression on his face then responded:

"Allight big-bra... I got it."

Young Crime grabbed the backpack, opened the car door, got out then walked over to the door where Flame was. Crime and Flame disappeared into the building and the door closed.

The walk through the warehouse seemed longer to Flame than it did the first time... things felt different to him. He put his hand on Crime's shoulder and Crime flinched, startled by Flame's touch... Flame understood right then, where the uneasy feeling was coming from. He continued holding Crime's shoulder and he spoke to him as they walked through the warehouse:

"Every-thang is cool Lil-G... we gone make this deal, get this money and be out, allight."

Flame gave Crime a little shake, trying to loosen him up. Young Crime was only sixteen years young. And now that he was actually **in** the situation... his young nerves were a lot more on edge than when he only **spoke** about being involved in it. However, Flame's words and Crime's familiarity with Flame, helped to eased Crime's nervousness a little.

"Y'all gotta excuse him... this is his first time doin shit like this... he ah virgin." said Flame, jokingly.

Crime **snatched** his shoulder away from Flame then responded definitively:

"I ain't no virgin!"

More-fire was now in Crime's body.

"He does look a little young." said Officer James.

That little comment added more fuel to Crime's fire.

"Here we are." said Ken then motioned for them to go inside of the office.

James and Ken headed back upfront after Jerry gave them a nod. Jerry had the first view of Young Crime and greeted the new face robustly:

"**Aaaah**... our little delivery boy finally made it!"

That comment... more fuel to Crime's fire. Crime stood at the doorway staring at Jerry. It was the face he pointed the snubnose-38 at. Crime was stuck in the spot he stood in. Jerry continued:

"Come in Kid! Come in... No one is gonna bite you." said Jerry, smiling and laughing.

He was overly excited now that the cocaine had arrived. His happiness was clearly evident in his tone of voice and demeanor. But Crime loathed all the, 'little delivery boy and kid' comments that Jerry had made. Bam saw the disdain building-up in his little GD brother, so he hurried to intervene, before Jerry picked-up on it too. He stood and walked over to Crime then said:

"What's up lil-bro? You alright?"

Bam extended his hand to shake Crime's, trying to take Crime's focus off of Jerry. Crime's focus was now on Gansta-Bam. He could see that Bam's eyes were saying, "Stay cool lil-bro, just stay cool." Crime responded:

"Yeah, yeah big-bro, I'm good... just ready to take care of this business."

Bam grinned and Jerry grinned as well... but they were grinning for two separate reasons. Bam turned to Jerry then said:

"Jerry, ma-man...! You about to have some-of-the best coke in the mid west... Let me get that backpack lil-bro."

Crime handed the backpack to Bam then stepped back. Jerry was grinning practically from ear-to-ear. Bam took one of the packages out then sat it on the desk across from the money, which was still in three neat stacks. Bam nonchalantly handed the backpack to Crime. Jerry examined the package, loving the way it felt; the solidness of it... that was a good sign.

Jerry sat the package down on the desk then pulled a small pocket-knife from his side pocket. He pressed a button on the knife and it unfolded. He chose a random spot on the package then stuck the knife into it. Jerry made a, u-like-shape the size of a half dollar coin then pulled the wrapping back, exposing the cocaine, **instantly** liking what he saw.

The white powder was glimmering and sparkling. It had a pearly appearance, emitting the different colors of a pearl. Jerry dug the knife into the brick of cocaine and scooped about a quarter-of-a-gram onto the knife. He put the tip of the knife to his tongue, tasted the powder. Then he put the knife to his nose and snorted the rest. His eyes closed tight then opened wide and repeated the process once more. The cocaine was stronger than he expected it to be and his face contorted from the potency... It was by far, the best cocaine he had ever come across.

After a brief moment, the cocaine's powerful hold on Jerry's contorted face, released.

"**Shittt..! Damn** that's some good stuff!"

Bam was grinning big, knowing Jerry would love the product. Bam commented:

"I knew you would like it... normally I charge thirty-grand a-key. But since this is our first deal... I figured I'd give you a-lil-discount."

"**Shit**! Even at thirty-grand this stuff is still worth it!"

Jerry paused... then continued:

"Bam ma-man... you just don't know how happy I am that we're doing business."

Now... it was vividly clear to Bam, of what type of cop he was dealing with; one with a cocaine habit that would do whatever it took to feed it. The worse kind of cop; a dope head with a badge and a gun...

Bam responded:

"Yeah, that shit will make **any** dope-head happy."

Bam's remark flew right over Jerry's head. Bam continued:

"Lil-G... give ma-man, that other brick."

Crime stepped over to Jerry, who was still seated behind the desk. Bam glanced at Flame and smiled slyly. Flame already knew what time it was... Crime pulled the other kilo of cocaine from the backpack, sat it on the desk then took a couple of steps back. Jerry pickup the package and glared hard at the piece of paper that was attached to it. His smile faded instantly and was replaced with a questioning frown. His glare remained intense as he stared at the paper-image. Jerry was in disbelief of what he saw. And seemingly, for the first time in Jerry's crooked, corrupted cop career... he was at a lost at what to do. He didn't know **what** to think or **what** to say...

Thinking he was untouchable, Jerry had gotten too comfortable. He hadn't even checked Bam and Flame for weapons before letting them in, and that was his normal protocol ... Jerry had slipped up and he was stuck. His nine-millimeter-Beretta was secured in its holster. Not wanting to be too hasty, he decided against trying to pull it. James and Ken were still up front keeping an eye out. After ten-minutes, two GD soldiers took covert routes toward the building.

Jerry figured the best thing for him to do, was be calm and find out, just what-in-the-hell was going on. He held the package up once again, glancing at it then looked at Bam. With a slight hint of disappointment in his voice, he said:

"Bam... ma-man... What-the-fuck is this about." tossing the package down on the desk.

Bam got serious. No more playing 'Mr. Nice Business Guy'... Gansta-Bam had finally emerged on the scene.

"Flame. You think you can take care of them goons?"

"Yeah big-bro, I got it." said Flame then left-out-of the office. Jerry was about to move or get up, but before he could do **anything**. Gansta-Bam pulled-out the Colt-45 that had been concealed up until that point... Looking at Jerry with a "Gangsta's Glare" Bam said:

"Don't... fuckin... move..."

Jerry put his hands up and sat back in his chair. Bam stood up from his seat then asked VG:

"VG... put that money on you lil-bro."

VG picked-up the stacks of money, stuffing one stack in each of his front pockets and one stack in his back pocket. Bam was about to continue then...

Boom, Boom, Boom! Gunfire sounded...

Flame had walked up to the front of the warehouse, calm and casually, like everything was all cool. With his gun already cocked and aimed, he got James and Ken's attention.

"Y'all wanna try some-of-this shit?" said Flame.

James was thinking: "some of the coke" but Ken asked the question:

"Some-of-what?"

Then, as Ken and James turned around, Flame continued speaking while opening fire on the two men:

"Some-of-this **hot shit fah-dat-ass**!" he said, while squeezing-off three rounds.

Flame was having fun now. It was like a video game and it was the main reason they called him, "Flame"... he **loved** to blaze (shoot) shit... Two rounds hit James square in the chest and Ken **just** escaped the third round, jumping out of Flame's sights as the bullet left the chamber. James was hurt bad. Two rounds from the Luger P89, hit his bulletproof vest **so hard**... James felt he had been hit in the chest with a sledge hammer... his upper ribs may have been broken and his chest was searing with pain and he could barely move...

Ken ducked-off into a darker part of warehouse and there was no way for Flame to see him, not without risking being shot. Gambino heard the shots and immediately got out of the car with caution, gripping the H&K-40-caliber-pistol. The rest of the entourage heard the faint sound of gunfire, but when Ron-Ron saw Gambino getting out of the car with his gun drawn, he knew something was going down. They all were out of their cars now and Chicago and Tear-Drop wanted to rush down to the building but Ron-Ron told them to hold-up. They watched as Gambino cautiously approach the door of the building. Trigga and Sniper were already covering other exits of the building; each took a separate flank-of-building, making sure that no one got away if they decided to flee the scene. Gambino got to the door and tried to turn the knob, but the door didn't budge.

"Fuck this." said Gambino.

Then he stepped back, lifted the gun then pumped two 40-cal rounds into the doorknob and latch area. After Ron-Ron saw that, he rushed down the street to the building... The powerful force of the 40-caliber, weakened the lock and latch then... Gambino's six-foot-four inch, two-hundred-and-fifty-pound-frame, breached it. He lifted his huge leg and kicked the door open with the force of a police battering-ram. The heavy metal door swung open slowly, making an eerie noise as it did. Ron-Ron made it down the street to see the door swing open.

After hearing the second set of shots... Trigga and Sniper hurried to the front of the building. The four of them were now standing cautiously at the entrance. The light, poured inside and they saw Flame standing there with his gun, as if he were playing 'Duck-Hunt' on the Nintendo game... Gambino stepped in shaking his head at Flame's crazy-ass. Gambino also saw the wounded man on the ground, breathing hard and gasping. Gambino felt sorry for the poor son-of-bitch, but he kept moving forward. Flame signaled to Gambino that the other guy was in another part of the building, by holding-up one finger then pointing to their right.

The rest of the Gangstas filed in. Trigga-G was the last in but he stayed close to the door. They all saw the wounded man on the ground. Ron-Ron, Sniper, and Gambino were passed him... they all assumed Flame had injured him enough to incapacitate him. Trigga-G observed the man reaching for something. Trigga walked over to James and without any warning to anyone...

POW!

Trigga-G squeezed one round into James' head without any hesitation...

Trigga-G was a natural killer it seemed. He had the word "**KILLA**", tattooed on his back, in huge Old-English style letters. James' body jerked one last time, but after that... it would never move on its own again.

Gambino, Ron-Ron, Sniper and Flame, all peered over at Trigga-G as he stepped passed the dead-man. They could see the darkness in Trigg's eyes, which made for a distinct contrast because of his light skin. To say that 'Trigga-G embodied the spirit of a Grim-Reaper' would probably be an understatement. The look in his eyes was menacing... like he had just eaten a man's soul and was hungry for more. The other Gangstas looked at Trigga-G, probably all thinking the same thought: 'I'm glad that nigga on our side.'

Gambino tightened his jaw, trying not to look weak, being the biggest in the bunch. Trigg stood guard over by the door while the other Gangstas Disciples moved passed the bay area, seeking to find the other crooked kid-napper cop...

Ken shook uncontrollably, trying to pull his self to a calmer state. He was in a dark part of the building, next to an old stack of wooden pallets, hardly able to see anything with his weapon drawn... Ken knew James was dead. He wanted to raise-up and start shooting anything that move, but he would compromise the advantage he had... which was the darkness and the cover of the wooded pallets. Ken thought: "an all-out gunfight is the only chance I have of making-it-outta-here alive." Then another thought popped into his mind... Ken thought it wiser to stay put... Maybe someone had heard the shots and called the police and help would come soon, Ken was hoping...

He was embarrassed at the thought, for he was the police. He figured Jerry was dead too... Ken put his head down then did the only thing he felt he could do, to get his self out of the situation alive... he prayed quietly to God.

CHAPTER 25: The Big Payback

After the gunfire ceased. Bam answered Jerry's question:
"What's this about...? You should already know **Jerry**... I'm surprised you even asked that **stupid**-ass question... this is about **karma** muthafucka... The total effects of your **own** actions and your **own** misconduct during the phases of your existence, **now** determining your destiny."

Jerry peered at Bam, curiously searching his eyes, wondering what all Bam knew about him. Bam could see Jerry's wonder. Bam continued:

"Yeah, that's right Jerry ma-man... **All** the low down and crooked shit you been 'doin, is coming back to bite-you-in the-ass... Lil-G, can you stand over there next to VG."

Young-Crime went and stood by VG then Bam continued:

"You see them two young men right there."

Bam pointed the .45 at Jerry, prompting him to look at the young African American Brothers. Jerry peered over at them reluctantly then Bam continued:

"Both of them got big brothers out there who've been teaching them the **right** way to live instead-of the wrong way. Yeaaah, I know they might sell drugs but **them** young men right **there**... have **never**... took someone's life... **especially** not over no drugs... they've been 'schooled' by big brothers like me, to know that... if you have-to-**kill-a-muthafucka behind this shit...**! "

Bam nudged the package of cocaine with the .45 and continued:

"Then it ain't worth havin at all... ain't that right lil-bro?"

"That's right big-bro." said VG.

Then Bam continued:

"You honky-muthafuckas have been using this shit for **centuries!**"

Bam nudged the package again.

"But when it get put in the **black's** hands... you crooked muthafuckas wanna start makin **laws**-against-the-shit... puttin together **extreme** sentencing-guide-lines, tryina target **us** because of how **we** sell the shit!"

Bam paused and stared at Jerry for a few seconds then continued:

"Jerry ma-man, you lucked up today... I'm not gone kill you... that shit would be too easy fah-me... I'm gone leave it up to you to decide whether you live or die."

Bam walked over to Jerry and stood behind him. He put the barrel of the .45 to the back of Jerry's head, reached down to Jerry's side, un-snapped Jerry's holster. Then he took the nine-millimeter Beretta, off Jerry's person. Bam continued:

"You see Jerry... I'm **really** hoping these young men **and** you as well... learn a-valuable-lessons here today."

While Bam was speaking... he sleekly tucked his .45-1911 in the small of his back then, quiet and smoothly, ejected the 'round' from the chamber of Jerry's nine-millimeter-Beretta. Bam put the 'round' or (bullet) in his pocket...

Normally: "if a 'round' were ejected from a pistol while the clip was in, another 'round' would pop-up into the chamber, however. If a person does it **slow** enough, while holding the next 'round' down, through the chamber... the chamber will be empty once the 'slide' slides back in place..." It's easy if a person knows what they're doing, and Bam knew what he was doing; (Junior Marines, training when he was younger, and his father Master-Drill-Sergeant Lay). Don't sleep on Gansta-Bam.

Bam was careful and quiet, using the gray bandanna to assure his prints didn't end-up on the Beretta... He pulled the .45 from the small of his back then walked to the front of the desk... Holding the Berretta with the bandanna, Bam continued from where he left off; 'explaining the lessons he hoped VG, Young-Crime and Jerry would learn:

"Never pull a gun, unless you **absolutely** need to use it... to protect yourself or somebody else. And if a man **lives** 'by the gun'... then that man will probably **die** 'By The Gun'.

Bam continued:

"But if a man chooses to change his ways and live by a better concept that respects life. Then **maybe**, just **maybe**... God might give-um another chance at his **own** life."

Bam stared Jerry directly in the eyes, leaned forward then sat the Beretta safety-side-down, on the open package of cocaine. He had put the safety on before he walked around to the front of the desk. Now, pointing the .45 at Jerry, Bam stepped back from the desk then quoted a scripture out of the *Bible*:

Galatians *Chapter six, verse seven: 'Be not deceived; God is not mocked: for what so ever a man soweth, that shall he also reap'.*

Bam let the hammer down on the Colt-45 lowering it to his side. He was uncertain of what would happen from this point, though his minds intuition told him, 'that Jerry was too-far-gone to be offered a second chance.' But it was something he had to do. He had to respect the life that God gifted a person with... and at the same time, he was also exercising his faith in God and the Spirit of God in himself.

In this case, Bam would only use his gun, **if** he knew his life was in absolute danger of being taken. In a Godly-Spiritual way, Bam was hoping Jerry would make the right decision... but only God can straighten a man's mind from being crooked and corrupted. Moreover, if God wanted a person's mind to remain corrupted and lost... then that's how it would remain... The words of a righteous-man, speaking to a crooked-man... would only fall on deaf ears if God's intentions were not to save the man being spoken to... What choice would Jerry make, Bam wondered... Bam looked over at Young-Crime then said:

"Lil-G... put that brick in the backpack."

Jerry erupted and Crime stopped in his step.

"**HOLD-UP!   HOLD-UP**...!   NOW   JUST-A-GOTDAMN-MINUTE HERE!" said Jerry, slamming an open hand down on the package of cocaine.

Jerry's voice lowered but he was still outraged and expressing his anger. He continued:

"You can't just, **come** in here, **kill** my men and take what I've already **paid** you for!"

Bam was irritated at Jerry's concern for the cocaine, as supposed to his own life... Gansta-Bam lifted the Colt-45 and pointed it directly at Jerry's face. In an angry tone of voice that conveyed his irritation, Bam said:

"You lucky I don't take **yo life** muthafucka..! And besides..."
Bam calmed his self then continued:

"I'm not taking nothin from you that you haven't already taken from ma-people. I know **who's** behind all the fucked-up shit the police been doin fah-**years** in the Black-Communities... the muthafucka sittin **right** in front of me... I know all about you Jerry... **Detective** Jerry Kane Schlesta..."

Jerry was shocked when he heard Bam speak his entire name. No one had said his full name since his father last spoke it before he passed. The words sent chills through-out Jerry's body. Bam turned the .45 sideways... he wanted to squeeze, just **one** 'round' into Jerry's face. It would've made him feel really good at that point, but he couldn't... he had to give Jerry that chance at deciding his own fate. "Calm down Bam, calm down." Bam told his self mentally. He lowered the .45 and continued:

"And in regards to yo men... when soldiers step-on the battlefield sometime they don't come off... not unless they get carried off."
Jerry was raging... His eyes were burning like hot coals. He had finally been out-witted and it was killing him inside.
Bam continued calm and smooth:

"It's up to the General to make sure his soldiers are fightin-for-ah righteous-cause. If not... they all might die in vain... So **General**... you better make sure you train yo soldiers to fight for the right shit like they were sworn to do... because if you don't, and if they don't... y'all gone **always** lose..."
Bam was smiling smugly and Jerry was becoming more infuriated. The color of Jerry's face displayed the boiling inside of him. He was tired of Bam's 'philosophical' and 'spiritual **bullshit'**. Bam continued:

"Let's go lil-bro."
VG headed out of the door first and Bam remain standing in front of Jerry. Bam instructed Crime again:

"Lil-G... grab that package, put it in the backpack and let's get outta here."
Bam actually turned, taking a few steps towards the door, trusting his faith in God, letting destiny take its course. He heard a loud 'thud' then a 'growling' of Jerry's voice. When Young-Crime went to grab the package... Jerry pushed him hard to the floor and Crime landed flat on his back. Crime was to the left of Jerry... He had been holding the

backpack in front of him, so when he landed on the floor, the backpack laid on his stomach as he fell. To Young-Crime, it felt like things were happening in slow motion, without sound. Jerry lips were moving... mouthing some words but Crime couldn't hear them... The words that Jerry had so viciously growled at Bam were:

"You lousy fucking **gang-banging MONKEY! FUCK YOU!**"

Crime saw Jerry reach for the Beretta on the desk and at the same time, Bam was turning around to face Jerry... Bam didn't raise his gun. Crime saw Jerry lift the Beretta, point it at Bam's face and pull the trigger. Crime froze... He thought Bam was definitely about to die... When Jerry pulled the trigger and the gun didn't go off... Young-Crime snapped out of the frozen state he was in, his fire was burning full-force now. He felt the weight of the snub-nose-38 on the lower part of his chest. The gun had slid from the bottom of the backpack to the top, during his fall. Crime took hold of the gun and at the same time... Jerry took the safety off the Beretta, frantically cocking the gun back to load a 'round' into the chamber. Things were still moving in slow motion for Crime. He saw the 'slide' of the Beretta move back slow and before the 'slide' could get back to its firing-position...

POW, POW, POW, POW!

Lying on the floor with his arms extended slightly upward, Young-Crime fired the gun. The first bullet traveled upward through the left side of Jerry's face and out through the top right side of his head. Jerry was dead instantly. But Crime continued pulling the trigger until he saw Jerry fell.

VG quickly stepped back into the office after the shots stopped. The loud shots left Bam's ears ringing... Bam peered down at Jerry and the blood began to pool-out on the floor from the hole in Jerry's head...

Up until that point, Young-Crime had no connection to Keisha and Porshaé or Detective Schlesta and Officer Harris. Nor did he have any knowledge of the incident that took place four years ago involving the four of them... but the Universe had knowledge of it, and God... **is** the Universe...

*As the Earth rotates slowly on its axis, which is held by the Universe... the Universe, slowly and strategically, puts together **all** the* *right circumstances and all the right stars, to act-out the roles in its script of "Life."... the roles in which the stars agreed to play, because of the choices and decisions they made...*

"Lil-G...! Lil-G!"

Bam called out to Crime 'seemingly' for a while. Young-Crime was having an out-of-body experience. He could see the entire room from an over-head-view, as if he were floating. He could see VG standing over by the door; he could see Jerry's body lying lifeless on the floor. He stared at the body for a long moment and said to his self:

"I **killed** somebody... is I'm dead too?"

He was still floating. His out-of-body-self, peered over at his physical-self, and he saw Gansta-Bam kneeling down by his physical-self. Crime was laid out on the floor. He couldn't hear what Bam was saying though. Bam took the gun out of Crime's hand then sat it on the desk, continuing to call Crime, trying to wake him up.

"Lil-G, wake up! Wake up 'lil-bra! 'Lil -bra!"

Crime felt his self falling slowly back towards the ground and Bam's voice became audible. At first it was muted, but now it was only muffled.

"**Lil-G! WAKE UP 'lil-bro!**" said Bam one last time with his voice at an elevated shout.

Bam was about to pick Crime up so they could get out of there, but just then, Crime's eyes opened slowly. He regained his mental-faculties and focused in on Bam. He could see the grave concern on Bam's face as his head sat in Bam's hand. What Bam saw when he made eye connect with Young-Crime... was the most innocent child like look that he had ever saw. It brought a tear to Bam's eye but he didn't let the tear fall... The innocence in Lil-G, made Bam understand why he **had** to do more to guide, groom and give to his little brothers the essentials of man-hood... essentials that will help them live their life better as "men".

Bam tilted his head back, drawing the tear back into his eye-duck then in a slightly slurred voice, Young-Crime said:

"Is I'm dead?"

Bam couldn't help but breakout into a hefty laugh. He was glad the little dude was alright. He answered Crime:

"Naaah Lil-G... you ain't dead bro."

Crime sat-up with a little assistance from Bam. Bam grabbed the backpack and handed it to VG then said:

"Lil-bro, can you put that money and that 'brick', in there fah-me? Tear that picture-off too, and leave it on the desk."
VG did so... He was also about to grab the open package of cocaine but Bam stopped him:

"Lil-bro, leave the open package here. Leave the gun too... Here you go, use this"
Bam handed VG the gray bandanna.

"Wipe it off good bro... wipe off **everythang** we **touched** in this muthafucka and let's get-the-fuck outta here."

VG hoped into action, wiping down the phone, parts of the desk, the chairs, the doorknob he touched. He grabbed the bottles of Budweiser that they had drunk from and he put them in the backpack **with** the twist-off caps included. VG did one more thing before he finished his clean-up-job... He took the sack of crack-rocks from his crotch and dumped it out on Jerry's body then put the plastic bag in his pocket to dispose of it later.

Dirty cops would always sprinkle crack at the scene of a crime after murdering a black man in cold blood... making it look like a 'drug deal gone bad'. VG found it highly amusing now that rabbit had the gun... and the rabbit had taken his shot. Bam looked over at what VG had done then said:

"You off the-chain fah-that shit Lil-Bro."
Bam was smiling at his little GD brother. He continued:

"Lil-bro, make sure you find that plastic-bag and those other bottles before we leave the building... ma prints on that shit."
Bam was helping Crime keep stable and he asked Crime:

"You alright Lil-G?"

"Yeah, I'm cool... what happened to me?"

"I guess you blacked-out and fainted, Lil-G... but good-lookin-out on takin dude down", said Bam as they left out of the office, headed up front.

Flame heard the gunshots and left the dark-side of the warehouse, heading back around to the office to check it out.

"Big-bro! y'all all-ight?" asked Flame with earnest concern, seeing that Bam was helping Young Crime out of the office.

"Yeah, we good G... Let's get-the-fuck outta here..."

As they walked to the front, they peered over at James' body. It was sprawled out on the floor. Trigga-G was still keeping guard by the door. Flame saw Bam's curiosity and commented:

"I hit-um twice in the vest and Trigga-G finished him off... Sniper, Ron-Ron and Gambino, tryina find the other dude right now. He 'dip-off over there somewhere." said Flame, pointing to the dark-side of the warehouse.

Bam was about to walk over towards the darkness and the young rookie cop emerged from the dark, with Gambino holding the H&K-40-caliber to his back, and Sniper-G and Ron-Ron coming in right after them.

"He gave his self up G.", said Gambino.

Ken had surrendered his self to Gambino, feeling that it was his best bet to stay alive. Ken had chosen wisely... They sat him down on a small stack of old pallets that were by the van and the bay doors. Bam walked over and looked at the man, contemplating on what they should do with him.

Ron-Ron asked everyone except for Gambino, VG and Crime, to step outside.

"Don't let this muthafucka outta yo sight G." said Bam to Gambino.

The five of them were in front of the building, listening to what Ron-Ron was saying:

"Family, I appreciate y'all fah-helpin us get this shit under control. We about to leave as soon as we take care of this loose end... Trigga and Sniper, y'all can head back up there with Tear-Drop and Chicago... let-em know we all good down here and we got everythang under-control."

Ron-Ron gave Trigga-G and Sniper-G Gangstas hugs then Sniper responded:

"Alright Family... we glad everythang turned out good... We'll see y'all in-ah-minute Family."

Then Sniper and Trigga made their way up the street towards Chicago and Tear-Drop.

CHAPTER 26: Is Your Faith In God Real

Flame, Gansta-Bam, and Ron-Ron went back inside of the warehouse. Bam walked right over to Ken, keeping his eyes on him then stood directly in front of Ken. Ken was sitting quietly on the wooden pallets, looking up at Bam... Bam hadn't really taken notice of it before, but Ken was young, probably the same age as Flame; early twenties maybe.

Bam began speaking:

"I want you to know somethin before we decide on what to do with you... we know who yo-boss-man was back there in that office... He was-ah... crooked-ass Metro-Police, who snorted cocaine... who murdered innocent people... who brought-**all kinds**-of terror to the black neighborhoods... Detective Jerry Kane Schlesta... Well-he-ain't **none**-of-that no-more... now... he's just another dead-man..."

Bam glared hard at the young man. His voice was serious but not sinister. He continued to speak:

"Lil-bro, come over here for-a-minute."

VG walked over to where Bam was. Bam put his arm around VG's shoulders then asked him:

"Is this one of the dudes who attacked you?"

"Yeah... that's him big-bro", said VG.

Bam glared at Ken hard again.

"What's yo name man?" Bam asked Ken.

Ken's voice was a little shaky when he answered:

"Ken... Ken Kinshinger."

Bam continued:

"Ken, huh...? Lil-bro... What-do-you think we should do wit-ole Ken here?"

VG 'mean-mugged' the man and answered viciously, maintaining his normal cool level voice then said:

"We should do-dat-muthafucka like they did me. Tie-um up to dat muthafuckin chair out there in dat **stankin-ass** warehouse and leave-um fah-the rats to eat. That's what they was gone do to me if I didn't call you big-bro."

Bam was a little shocked and his facial-expression displayed his surprise at what VG just said.

Bam responded:

"**Damn** Ken! Y'all was gone let the **rats** eat ma lil-brother?!"

Ken's voice elevated when he began trying to defend his self of the allegation.

"**Hold-on man**...! I had **no** knowledge of leaving **anyone** out there for rats to eat! I **just** got assigned to Detective Schlesta's division, **two** weeks ago...! He told me that he wanted me to be a-part of his special drug task unit. He said they were an aggressive drug unit and they used aggressive tactics. I joined the unit this week and this was my **first** assignment with him, **I swear!**"

"So how did y'all find out about ma lil-brother?"

Bam wanted to find out anything and everything he could, to make sure he was safe to continue with his small drug operation. Ken's voice was a little calmer now that Bam was listening to him. It was a good sign for Ken.

Ken answered:

"An informant that Jerry knew brought him some drugs. The Detective and the informant went into the office back there then came back up front not long after. Schlesta said he tested it then he asked the informant where he got the drugs from. The informant told him and after that... The Detective asked me and Officer Vincent to go pick the guy up and do whatever it takes to get him here, he said. That's when we went and picked-up that guy."

Ken motioned to VG. Bam was being very attentive. He asked Ken:

"What was the informant's name?"

Ken recalled the informant introducing his self before him and Jerry went into the old office...

"Bobby Mckinzie... yeah that's it." said Ken.

VG looked at Bam then said:

"**Yeah**..... Big-bro! That's the muthafucka **Byron** drunk-ass brought over to the set!"

Bam would remember that name.

"So you mean to tell me... that you didn't know nothin about the crooked shit the muthafucka was doin?"

Ken put his hands up then answered:

"**Man**... I **promise** to **God**. I didn't know **anything** about any crooked shit, and nor was I trying to be a part of it... I **swear**! My Fiancée and me, God knows I love her **so** much... We **just** moved here from Davenport Iowa!"

Bam peered over at VG and VG commented, but this time, he was expressing more anger.

"**Man, fuck-that-shit** big-'bra! They put me out there with dead bodies and rats-an-shit! We got two dead cops already, one mo ain't gone hurt... **this** muthafucka need ta go **too**! Give-me-da unit let **me** put his muthafuckin face to the back of his head."

VG was livid. Ken responded pleadingly:

"**Man I swear**! **I don't know anything about any dead bodies**!"

Ken tried to stay calm. He lowered his voice then continued:

"I stayed up front when Officer Vincent and Schlesta took him back there. He said he would interrogate him when he came-to."

For some reason, Bam wanted to believe Ken but he wanted some type of verification and still... even if he got the verification, what would he do with Ken afterwards? Ken knew they had just murdered two police-officers... He was definitely a threat if they let him live... Bam thought then remembered what Ron-Ron told him about Big-Sister Evelyn wanting to help, however she could. Bam stepped over to where Ron-Ron was standing and spoke.

Then Bam asked Gambino:

"Where yo burnout-phone G?"

"It's in the car." said Gambino.

"G... show Ron-Ron where it is so he can make a phone-call."

Ken wondered who they would call. Gambino and Ron-Ron stepped outside of the building and went to the car to call Evelyn... Young-Crime, VG, Flame and Gansta-Bam, waited inside of the old warehouse, keeping a watch on their prisoner... Bam put the .45 away, stepped closer to Ken then spoke:

"Ken... I know right now it looks like we the bad guys here, but we not. If we were, I would've just shot yo-ass and left... The **only** reason we came here today, was to get our lil-brother back, after **y'all** kid-napped him... In the process of doin that... we found out the person **behind** the whole thang, was a **real** corrupt crooked piece-of-shit! Ken, we got people everywhere... That's how we found out about ole Jerry so quick... All we wanna do is... live our lives peacefully, make a little money to take care of our families and build-up our communities."

Bam's voice was calm. He continued:

"I'm gone tell you Ken... God **gave** that piece-of-shit back there in that office a chance to walk away from this. But he chose to pickup his gun... then... he died by the gun... Now it's unfortunate yo comrade over there didn't have that same chance, but that's how shit goes sometimes... but he probably would've chosen his gun too... You should be thankin God fah givin you the right mind to surrender, cause yo-ass would be dead right now too."

Bam's voice was still calm but he was glaring intensely at Ken. Bam continued:

"Are you a-spiritual man Ken?"

Ken peered up at Gansta-Bam, humbly looking him in the eyes then he answered:

"Yes... I am."

Bam could see the water in Ken's eyes.

Bam continued:

"Those tears in yo eyes... that ain't nothin but God's Spirit touchin you. He lettin you know that He showed yo-ass some mercy today. He kept yo-ass from gettin **shot**...! He also kept you from gettin **too** involved with some **reaaal bad** men."

Bam motioned over to the body on the floor and towards the old office then continued:

"I know it might not seem that way to you Ken, but God works in ways that a-lot-of-us don't and **won't** ever understand."

To others, it may have sounded like a bunch of bullshit coming out of Bam's mouth, but nevertheless, to everyone in the room, hearing what Bam was saying... it was the truth... It was the reality God had allowed to unfold. Quoting a scripture from the *Bible,* Bam continued:

Proverbs *Chapter 3, verses 5 & 6: 'Trust in the Lord thy God with all thy heart and lean not unto thy own understanding... in all ways acknowledge God and let Him direct thy path.*

Ken **did** feel that God had intervened. Moreover, he felt it in his heart and mind, that Bam would have some compassion and let him go.

Bam continued:

"So Ken... you about to get marry huh?"

Ken nodded yes and Bam continued:

"You gotta a picture of yo Fiancée?"

"Yeah, it's in my wallet."

"Can I see it, if you don't mind?" ask Bam.

Ken just wanted to get-the-hell out-of there so he could get home to his Fiancée. He pulled his wallet from his back pocket, unfolded it and handed it to Bam. Ron-Ron and Gambino came back in, just as Bam was about to look at the picture of Ken's Fiancée. He walked over to them and Ron-Ron began telling Bam what Evelyn said:

"Big-Sis called her people and they verified what dude said... he just got here two weeks ago G."

Bam looked over at Ken, who was looking over at them.

Evelyn had called her uncle Daniel, Chief of the Metropolitan Police. He asked her why she wanted to know about Ken Kinshinger and Evelyn told him, 'she was working on a case and needed to eliminate Ken from having any involvement with it **or**... put him right in the middle of it. It was a faint truth but still the truth. Daniel didn't ask any more questions. He told Evelyn what she needed to know. He also told her:

"Your uncle Greg called and told me about his trip out to the Harris residence. When he made it out there, Mr. & Mrs. Harris had not too long made it back home and discovered there was a burglary. Several things were missing... including what you and Greg were hoping to find... Officer Harris' old gun... When Greg made it out there the police were still dusting for prints."

"Why didn't he call to let me know this?" Evelyn asked Daniel disappointingly.

"He didn't wanna upset you... he said he would tell you later but I figured since you called, I might-as-well tell you now."

Evelyn wanted to **scream**! However, she stayed cool, got off the phone with her uncle then called Ron-Ron back to relay the info...

Bam nodded at Ron-Ron then stepped back over to an afraid and anxious Ken K... Bam looked at the wallet size photo of Ken's Fiancée.

She was very attractive, and to Bam's surprise, she was of African descent. Her and Ken left Davenport, coming to Saint Louis trying to escape the prejudice... figuring Saint Louis to be a more diverse city, which it was. Nevertheless, Ken ran **right** into the burning-core of prejudice when he met Jerry and joined the special unit. Bam also glanced at Ken's id then he continued:

"She's a nice lookin woman Ken... what's her name?"

"Her name is, Katrina", said Ken, smiling subtly.

"I know she would hate to lose you", said Bam, implying what could be a near reality for Ken.

"Yeah... that would crush her." said Ken dejectedly.

Bam wiped the wallet off thoroughly with another handy gray bandanna then tossed the wallet back to Ken. There was a long pause in the conversation. Bam's mind was contemplating. He looked around at everyone then finally spoke:

"Who's got his gun?"

Gambino pulled it from his waistband and brought it over to Bam.

"Y'all go outside... I'ma be out in-a-minute. Lil-bro, put that backpack in the truck of the car me and Flame drove." said Bam, tossing VG the car-keys.

"All-ight." said VG nodding.

The group of Gangsta Disciples moved out of the warehouse slowly, wondering what Bam was about do. Flame was the last one at the door. He looked over at Bam... Without taking his eyes off Ken, Bam said to Flame:

"Close the door G."

Flame closed the door as he left out... Bam continued glaring down at Ken. He was still contemplating on whether he should go through with what he was thinking. The idea seemed fine in his mind. But the reality of it was this: it would put him **and** the rest of the Gangstas in grave danger if it didn't turn-out the way he hoped it would. Bam began speaking again:

"Ma brothers out there"

Bam motioned towards the outside then continued:

"They do the best they can to keep order in the neighborhoods they live in... they do-a-better job than **y'all** do... if some shit go-down in our neighborhoods, the people gone call us before they call y'all... You know why that is, Ken?"

Ken shook his head no then Bam continued:

"They don't **trust** the police, Ken... That's **you**...! They **know** us... and they know we don't tolerate that **bullshit** in our hoods and we gone handle whatever need to be handle, **quick**... Me and ma brothers **are** the streets. You and yo boys just ride around in-em, **playing** cops... we take care of ours, but **yo** brothers... **yo** police brothers... the people cannot **stand** them muthafuckas... all the brutality, all the false arrest... all the crooked-shit they do to ma people, the hardships they put-em through... in **their own neighborhoods**, where they're supposed to feel **safe**... Ken, I'ma tell you like this... unless you can give me a-**good-enough-**reason, other than yo light-skinned ass Fiancée, as to why I shouldn't believe you gone turnout like yo crooked brothers... then I'm gone put a bullet in yo head, then walk the fuck outta here."

Bam's words were exact and to the point, and his voice was calm. Ken **knew** Bam wasn't fucking around. He defended his character.

"Hey man... I'm **nothing** like those other officers who do that type of shit... I **respect** the law, I swore to uphold it and I **will**... Whether it's a criminal **or** a cop, I **will** enforce it. I don't believe in racism... me and my fiancée, left Davenport trying to get **away** from that shit...! I respect the black-race like I respect my own, if not **more...**! Trust me man... I'm not gonna be influenced by corruption **or** racism. I love my girl **too** much and I care about the well-being of others... that's why I chose to **serve** on the police-force, so I could help people... I understand what your people have been through and are **still** going through." said Ken compassionately.

Ken glared intensely at Bam, hoping Bam would see the honesty in his eyes and the sincerity in his answer, and it was a great answer... However, Bam was trying hard to go against his God-Sense... he really wanted to shoot Ken and eliminate the risk of being arrested for murder and all-sorts-of other charges... but His spirit wouldn't let him go against it...

Bam snapped in regards to Ken's comment...

"**Muthafucka!** You'll **never** understand what me and ma people been through..! You don't know our muthafuckin mind-set! You don't know **shit** about the **threats** we feel **every fuckin day** when we step out the doors of our houses..! You white muthafuckas with them badges, act like its ah-license-ta-hunt **niggas**! Ma people **always** on

survival mode muthafucka! **Do you know what that feels like..?"**
Bam calmed down then said:

"You know what... I don't even know why-the-fuck I'm still talkin."

Then he cocked the gun back and pointed it at Ken. Ken **immediately** threw up his hands and tried to plead with Bam one last time.

"HOLD-UP MAN! **PLEASE...! Didn't you say**... that God was showing me mercy today by not allowing me to get shot!? Well I **did** thank God for that! I **prayed** back there in that warehouse and asked God to help me get out of this alive...! **That's** why I gave myself up...! I could've tried shooting it out with you guys but I was trusting in God to help me! **I put** my fucking gun **down** because I wanna **live! What-do-I-have to do man? PLEASE, just tell me!"**

Ken was almost at a cry and that's what Bam had been waiting to see and hear. Bam wanted to know if Ken **really** had faith in God and now... he saw that he did. He could now go through with what he had contemplated on earlier.

Bam lowered the gun, which was Ken's then said:

"Put yo fuckin hands down Ken... I'm not gonna kill you... I just really wanted you to understand who saved yo-ass today and hear you acknowledge it authentically... and to answer yo question... I don't want you to do nothin... what God wants you to do, should be your question... and all God wants you to do... is live righteously under **His** laws... not these 'man-made-laws..'. A lot of these laws were made to fit some-ones 'personal agenda', not to lookout for the common-people's well-being. The only people the government really care about, are the super-rich muthafuckas that you and me **never** see or probably never even heard of."

Bam paused for a moment then continued:

"Ken... what I'm tryina say is... just do what you know is right in yo **mind** man... It's the first thing that develops when we're being formed in the womb, and there's a reason for that. God is installing His mind, in ours... so that we 'develop the right way'... physically and mentally... Just listen to that inter-voice... follow yo God-Sense and I promise you... it won't ever steer you wrong."

Bam took out his trusty bandanna, wiped the gun down thoroughly and extended it out towards Ken, handle first. Ken's thoughts raced... he didn't know if, by accepting the gun, Bam would take it as, him

choosing the gun... or... if Bam was just giving him his weapon back, trying to show that he was sincere about not killing him. Bam motioned the gun towards Ken once more and Ken took hold of it slowly. The Colt-45 was still tucked in Bam's waistband. Ken now had sole possession of his weapon again. Bam took a few steps back, watching Ken, knowing what he was thinking.

Ken looked over at Officer Vincent's dead body and lifted his gun, aiming it at Bam... While Ken held Bam in his sights, he thought about the feeling he had when he joined Jerry's unit. Ken felt something was amiss almost immediately after... maybe this was something he had to go through in-order to understand **why** he was feeling the way he was towards Jerry and his "Special Unit". Moreover, to better understand the brutal reality about the men he worked with... Maybe it was God's way of calling him to a bigger cause... a cause that consisted of handling problems... problems caused by the "problem solvers". Policing the police so-to-speak.

However, despite the fact there were two dead police-officer in the building, and the guy seemingly responsible for it, was standing right in front of him with his hands slightly raised... Ken didn't feel right about aiming the gun at Bam, so he lowered his weapon. It was that God-Sense telling him to do so.

Bam lowered his hands and he looked at Ken, wondering 'where does it go from here?' Ken finally spoke:

"So, how am I supposed to explain all of this?"

Bam smiled admirably at Ken, for Ken had just told Bam (though not directly) that he wouldn't turn them in... Bam held eye connect with Ken then gave him some advice... the **same** advice that Gods words had given him over seventeen years ago... the **same** advice that Bam himself was trying hard to live by, each day of his life... Bam said:

"In all ways, acknowledge God and let God direct your path."

Ken actually smiled at Bam then said:

"Yeah... **Proverbs**... *chapter 3, verse 5 & 6*. I'll never forget."

Ken could see the elated emotions that radiated from Bam's eyes...

Bam's Spirit felt refreshed and relieved. Bam commented:

"I'm thankful that things turn out the way God intended them to."

He gave Ken one last look of solemn-appreciation and admiration that said, 'You're a young man with honor and integrity and I hope you remain that way."

Ken nodded, almost as if he had heard Bam speak the words aloud. Ken glared back at Bam solemnly, and his look said, 'Thank you... Thank you Brother for seeing my faith in God and showing God's mercy... Take care."

Then, Gansta Bam turned towards the door and walked out of the building, closing the door behind him...

*Writer's thoughts: There is this funny thing about fate that a lot of us do not quite understand... Most of us think that it's already predetermined, but it is not. Destiny and fate both stem from the decisions we make in life. That left or right turn that we take... The slow or fast pace at which we choose to move throughout our life's course. That wrong or right thing that we do or did to make someone feel sad or good... Destiny and fate, are so misunderstood... **Galatians** chapter six verse seven are Gods words so do take heed... Think before you act, to make sure... that you are sowing good seed.*

Epilogue

❝This is Elliot Davis, reporting **live** for Fox 2 News. We have breaking news this afternoon. **Two** police-officers from the Metro Police Department's Narcotics Division were **shot** and **killed** this afternoon in an abandon warehouse near North-Broadway's industrial-district. Apparently, there were **three** undercover officers acting as drug-dealers, about to conduct a drug bust and the bust went **fatally** wrong... Here standing with me is, Chief Daniel Isom of the Metro Police Department.

Chief, can you give us **any** details as to **what** went wrong here today? And can you give our viewers **any** information that might be useful in helping apprehend the people behind this?"

"Elliot, right now we've just started undergoing our investigation into this tragic incident, so there's not much to disclose at this point.

A third officer who survived this ordeal, **is** being debriefed by our top homicide detective as we speak... He's also been trying to work with our sketch-artist to come up with composites of the suspects."

"So there's **more** than one suspect?"

"Yes... there **is** more than one suspect Elliot."

"When will the sketches be released?"

"Well Elliot, like I said... the officer has been trying to work with the sketch-artist... it's very dark inside the building and in some areas, visibility is almost non-existent... but he's doing the best he can at this point. But as soon as we put together something, they'll be released."

"Chief Isom, one last question if you don't mind and I will let you get back to your investigation?"

"Sure Elliot."

"How did you determine this was a drug-bust gone wrong?"

"We determined that from the information our officer involved gave us. And we also found a substantial amount of drugs inside the building."

"Chief Isom, thank you for your time Sir. You have my **deepest** regards for this tragedy."

"Thank you Elliot."

"Chief, would you like to add anything?"

"Yes. I'm asking that if **anyone**... heard or noticed **anything** pertaining to what took place here... to please contact our Metro Homicide Division at, 314-444-5620."

"Thank you Chief... I'm **so** sorry about this."

"Thank you again Elliot."

"I'm Elliot Davis... reporting **live** for Fox 2 News..."

A few hours later:

Evelyn had not long made it back to her office from her last court appointment for the day. She was tired and ready to close-out her workday... then her office phone rang. She debated on whether she wanted to answer it, but with all that was going on, she decided she (Best-to) answer it. ☺

"Evelyn Lewis speaking."

"**Evy!** Its Uncle Greg!"

Her uncle was excitement, like someone he was close to, had just won the lottery. He continued:

"I'm glad you still there!"

"Well, I was on my way out." said Evelyn.

"Evy... I got some news for you."

"Uncle Greg... Uncle Daniel already told me that the Harris residence was burglarized and the gun was stolen... **there** goes our big-break, right." said Evelyn dispiritedly.

Greg was smiling on the other end of the line, still excited about the news he had for his niece, knowing it would bring her back to life, 'figuratively-speaking.'

"Evy, I know I should've called to tell you about that earlier but that's not why I'm calling you now... Did you see the news this afternoon?!"

"No, I've been in court all afternoon... why, what's up?"

"Evy, somethin happened this afternoon... two policemen were shot and **killed** today in some kind-of, 'drug-bust gone wrong'... Your uncle Daniel was on the news, live... I saw where they were at and went down there to talk to him... you know, just to see what-in-the hell happened... Evy... when I got down there, Daniel pulled me to the side, away from everything... He looked like he was confused about something, staring at me with this curious look then asked me:

"Greg... what type of case is Evelyn **really** working on...? Why does she have you looking fah-this, **gun**? What-the-fuck-is-goin-on Greg...? I got **two** dead officers and a-rookie cop that doesn't know **shit**...! And it appears that one of the officers was shot with the gun **you** and Evelyn are **lookin for**!"

"Evelyn, I was in shock! I asked Daniel was he sure it was the same gun. He said:

"Yeah I'm sure! It was Officer Harris' personal gun... Four years ago, Detective Schlesta brought Dennis' things straight to me after he left that recording studio. He thought I should be the one to take Dennis' things out to his parents... But after that shit sat on ma desk damn near the whole day... I told Schlesta, he was closest to Dennis and he should take Dennis' things to his parents. I looked at that damn gun for-ah long time... I remember the serial numbers like my own... it's the **same damn gun**."

"Evy, I asked him, 'who were the two officers killed?' and guess who they are?"

Evelyn's heart felt like it stopped beating and it seemed as if she stopped breathing as well. Greg continued:

"Officer James Vincent and Detective Jerry Schlesta."

The two officers had met their fate... they had finally reaped what they sowed.

Evelyn was stuck where she stood, unable to move. She had a good idea of who was behind the two police-officers being killed. She instantly thought of Chicago and Ron-Ron and wondered what took place. She knew they would probably never speak to her about it though... it was their 'G-code' not to... No one involved would speak of it. She continued to wonder, asking herself mentally: "how did the **gun** end-up there?" There were **so** many questions that she would probably never have the answers to... As a lawyer, Evelyn would always try to piece things together, but **this** puzzle... was waaay too intricate for her to try to complete on simple assumption. She was lost. She shook out of her confusion for the moment and finished her conversation with her Uncle Greg. Greg continued:

"Daniel told me to bring the bullet down first thing tomorrow so the ballistic team can examine it."

"Uncle Greg, that's **great** news!" said Evelyn.

She was excited. She wanted to call everyone who had anything to do with the case; Keisha, Porshaé if she could, but he was still in prison; Mr. Cochran out in Los Angeles... She sat her purse and her expandable-leather-briefcase down on her desk then continued:

"So all we have to do is wait on the ballistics report and we'll have some new evidence to present to the appellate-courts... **God** this is **great! Thank** you God!" Evelyn exclaimed...

As she expressed her joy, Greg smiled big on the other end of the phone-line. He was happy that things had **somehow** come together for the best... The only thing Evelyn had to do now to get Porshaé out of prison, or at least get his charges amended: was work her magic in the appellate-courts, and that would be a bike-ride in the park now with the new evidence. Nevertheless, knowing how Evelyn operated, she would go a few steps farther than just using the ballistics evidence...

Evelyn would interview the two people she had been wanting to interview since she first looked at the photos in Porshae's case file: the two coroners, Jonelle and Ted. She could get their professional opinions on the figuration of the hand that was photographed. She could ask them, from their experience: 'what could have caused the hand to position itself that way?' Evelyn could now start putting her ducks in a row, compiling what she could **assuring** that it would be enough... and it would be...

The ballistics report came back, proving the bullet had **indeed** come from Officer Harris' gun and at the **least** two years prior to finding it. That was also determined by the chronological testing on the bullet. It was actually the only evidence needed to get Porshaé back in court. But the professional statements from the coroners, the report that they did on the body that was never sub-mitted into evidence, not until Evelyn submitted it into Porshae's appeal evidence... It all acted as tools to substantiate Porshae's claim of self-defense. That report showed, Officer Harris **was** wearing some type of ski-mask or facial-covering. Jonelle and Ted found fibers in the facial-hairs **and** on the head of Officer Harris which indicated it.
When the appellate-court Judges heard the new evidence, it was clear to them that the crime scene had been disturbed by one of the officers initially arriving to the scene. Now... coincidentally, those officers were dead. Evelyn wanted the courts to overturn the sentence and clear Porshaé of all charges, but that was wishful thinking. They only amended the murder to manslaughter as she thought they would, and amended the sentence, to five years. The court ordered **and** scheduled Porshaé for immediate release, with the one year remaining to be discharged, after four months of supervision was completed.
There was a lot out there in the free world waiting on Porshaé and he was ready to embrace it. His Mom, Sabrina and his Daughter Porsha... *M.I.G., Make It Good entertainment*, the branch part of the business Clyde helped build for Porshaé... And last but by far not the least... The woman he had protected on that unfortunate day of the shooting... The woman who had come to see him practically **every** week for four years... The woman who had accepted his phone calls whenever he wanted to talk, so he could keep his mind-off the madness and misery of the penitentiary. The beautiful and dedicated

Keisha, KeKe Pulliam... still a virgin and still wanting Porshaé to be her first... I mean, he did save her life, she thought... so can you blame her...?

This is the end to one chapter of my life but there are more to come. Thank you all for taking the time to read my very first book.

BY THE GUN

Sincerely, Derrick D. Williams
A.K.A.
GANSTA BAM

About The Author

Out of the 36 years I've been on this earth... 22 of those years have been spent experiencing the highs and lows of the street life. Born and raised in Flint Michigan, I quickly adapted to the life of a drug dealer. I traveled to different states around the country in pursuit of better drug prices and more clientele. In Saint Louis Missouri, I was arrested for trafficking and distribution of a large amount of marijuana.

While serving my time in the Missouri Department of Corrections, I did a lot of self-improving. During that self-improving process, after spending almost a decade in prison, I realized that hustling in the streets was not worth spending more of my precious time in prison. I came to the understanding that I had to do something different when I returned to the free world. While in prison I wrote music and poetry the entire time, though during the last 8 months of my sentence, I began writing my first book "By The Gun" based on a true story.

I was released from the Missouri Department of Corrections on April 12th, 2012 and paroled to Oakland California with my Mom, who has been a huge support of my new found interest in book and movie-scritp writing. I am currently living in Oakland and working on turning my first book "By The Gun" into a movie-script and my second book "Black & Blue Bay".

Thank you all for supporting a Man on a mission to change his life, as well as others, for the better...

Made in the USA
Middletown, DE
27 October 2022

13603117R00205